An Armada Three-in-One

*Three Great
Hardy Boys Stories*

Armada

Hardy Boys® Mystery Stories in Armada

* *For contractual reasons, Armada has been obliged to publish from No. 57 onwards before publishing Nos. 43–56. These missing numbers will be published as soon as possible.*

The Hardy Boys® in

63 The Stone Idol
64 The Vanishing Idol
65 The Outlaw's Silver

Franklin W. Dixon
Illustrated by Leslie Morrill

Armada

This Armada *Hardy Boys*® *Three-in-One* was
first published in the U.K. in Armada in 1987
by William Collins Sons & Co. Ltd
8 Grafton Street, London W1X 3LA

Armada is an imprint of the Children's Division,
part of the Collins Publishing Group

Published pursuant to agreement with
Simon & Schuster Inc.

Printed in Great Britain by
William Collins Sons & Co. Ltd, Glasgow

The Hardy Boys® in

The Stone Idol

Franklin W. Dixon
Illustrated by Leslie Morrill

The Stone Idol was
first published in the U.K. in a single volume
in hardback in 1982 by Angus & Robertson (U.K.) Ltd,
and in Armada in 1982

Contents

1 A Mysterious Advertisement

"Joe, listen to this!" said Frank Hardy, who was standing at the window holding a newspaper.

His brother was relaxing on the bed with a sports magazine. "What is it?" he asked, looking up. "Yesterday's baseball game at Yankee Stadium?"

"Maybe a game," Frank replied, "but it sure isn't baseball. It's an ad in the *Times*: 'Wanted: A sleuth to investigate a strange mystery.'"

Joe got off the bed and joined Frank at the window. They studied the ad together.

The Hardy boys had just solved an embezzlement case for a New York bank and were in their hotel room trying to decide whether to stay in the city for a few more days or to return home.

"What do you make of this ad?" Frank asked.

Joe shrugged. "Why don't you call up and see what it's about? School vacation isn't over for a month yet, so we have plenty of time to solve another mystery."

Eighteen-year-old Frank pushed a strand of dark hair from his forehead and grinned. "Good idea." He dialed the number while his blond brother, who was a year younger, held his ear close to the receiver so they both could hear.

"South American Antiquities," a woman answered. "May I help you?"

"I'm calling in reference to your ad in the *Times*," Frank said.

"You want to speak to Mr. Kimberley," she replied. "I'll ring him for you."

A man's voice came on a moment later. "This is Kim Kimberley. My secretary tells me you're calling about our ad. You must be a detective."

"That's right, sir. My brother and I are amateur detectives."

"Any credentials?" Kimberley barked.

Frank described the bank embezzlement case they had just solved.

The antique dealer sounded impressed. "I saw the newspaper accounts. They say you boys cracked the case all by yourselves. You're the kind of

detectives I need. Do you want to come to my office for an interview?"

Frank looked inquiringly at Joe, who nodded eagerly. Joe was the impulsive Hardy boy. He liked to plunge into any kind of mystery, while Frank was more likely to figure out a game plan first.

"Well, are you interested?" Kimberley asked impatiently.

"Yes, we are," Frank assured him. "We'll be right over."

"Empire State Building, seventy-fifth floor," the man said and hung up.

The Hardys left their hotel and flagged down a passing taxi. Soon they were riding through the rush of Manhattan traffic amid a din of honking horns and squealing brakes. Crowds of pedestrians crossed at the corners as the lights changed.

"A bit more lively than Bayport," Joe quipped.

Bayport was their hometown, where their father had moved the family after spending years as a New York City detective. Now Mr. Hardy was a famous private investigator who had trained his sons to follow in his footsteps.

The taxi deposited them on the sidewalk in front of the Empire State Building. At the seventy-fifth floor, they found South American Antiquities. In the waiting room, they spoke to the secretary. Smiling, she ushered them into Kimberley's office.

The antique dealer was a short, wiry man with red hair and a red beard. He kept flexing his fingers in a nervous manner.

He's worried about something, Joe thought.

Kimberley motioned for the Hardys to sit in front of his desk.

"I'm a partner in South American Antiquities, a business dealing in art objects from South America and its islands," he explained. "We sell artifacts from such places as the Andes Mountains and Easter Island."

"What's your problem, Mr. Kimberley?" Frank inquired.

"It concerns an idol from Easter Island," Kimberley revealed.

"Wow!" Joe exclaimed. "You mean one of those big stone heads?"

Kimberley smiled. "I'm not talking about the huge stone heads. This is a small figure of one of the ancient gods of the island. It was bought at the branch of South American Antiquities in Santiago, Chile."

"Easter Island belongs to Chile, doesn't it?" Frank asked.

"That's right. We maintain the Santiago office to handle pieces from Easter Island as well as from Chile itself."

"Who obtained the idol?" Joe asked.

"I did," Kimberley declared. "I was in our Santiago office when a Scandinavian collector came in and offered it for sale. I saw it was authentic, so I bought it. Later I showed it to my partner, Charles Bertrand. He agreed that I should take it to New York and sell it to a museum. Easter Island artifacts are much in demand, so it would fetch a good price."

"How did the idol get out of Easter Island?" Joe wanted to know.

"That's a good question," Kimberley said. "I see you boys are aware that the ownership of art objects is often in dispute."

"We've investigated cases for museums and private collectors," Frank admitted.

Kimberley nodded and made a pyramid of his fingers. "So you want to know if South American Antiquities has title to the Easter Island piece. Well, it's all open and aboveboard. The Scandinavian collector gave me this document."

He reached into his desk drawer, removed a paper, and pushed it across the top. It was a copy of an official certificate stating that the idol had been legitimately purchased on Easter Island. Only the name of the buyer was blocked out.

"We can't tell who the Scandinavian collector is," Frank noted.

"He wants to remain anonymous," Kimberley

14

stated. "I have the original with his signature in my safe. I can produce it should it ever be needed. At this point, I prefer to respect his right to privacy."

"So the purchase was legitimate and you brought the idol to New York," Joe said. "Where's the mystery?"

"But I didn't bring it to New York!" Kimberley spoke up.

"Why not?"

"Well, I put it in my handbag in Santiago. I took the bag to the airport and brought it with me to New York. At customs, I opened the bag for inspection."

"And then?" Joe prompted him.

"The idol was not there! It had been stolen!"

2 A Strange Message

"Someone must have sneaked the idol out of your bag on the trip," Joe suggested.

Kimberley shook his head. "Impossible! I had the bag with me from the hotel to the Santiago airport, where I took it aboard the plane and kept it between my feet during the flight. No one could have opened it!"

"Maybe someone switched bags on you," Frank said. "Someone might have taken yours and left a dummy while you were buying your ticket at the airline counter."

Kimberley shook his head again. "I carried a number of small artifacts in the bag. The others were there when I opened it in New York. Only the Easter Island piece was missing."

"Then it must have been stolen in Santiago," Frank concluded.

"That's what I think!" Kimberley boomed.

"Do you suspect anyone?"

"Not really."

"Did anyone else know you had the idol in your bag?"

"Charles Bertrand, my partner. But he can't be the thief."

Frank shrugged. "Mr. Kimberley, if Bertrand is the only other person who knew about the idol, he's a suspect. Would he have any motive for stealing it?"

Kimberley hesitated. "Well, if I were out of the way, Bertrand could take over the company," he said finally.

"But how would the theft of the sculpture get you out of the way?" Joe asked.

"Because I have to account for it. You see, whenever we take a piece from the office, we sign a release for it. I signed one for the Easter Island idol. I'm responsible for it, and I have no idea where it is. I could be accused of stealing it myself!"

"Tell us what happened in Santiago," Joe suggested.

Kimberley squinted as if to gather his thoughts. "I took the piece from our office in my handbag. Bertrand came to my hotel that evening and we discussed the price we might place on it in New York. The bag was in the room, zippered and locked."

"Did you leave the hotel room at any time?" Frank inquired.

"Only once. I had to go down to the jeweler's in the lobby to pick up my wristwatch. I was having it repaired."

"Did Bertrand stay behind?"

"Yes. But I don't know whether he was in the room all the time."

"If he had left, even for a few moments, someone else might have sneaked in."

"I'd like to think so," Kimberley insisted. "I don't like to throw suspicion on my partner."

"The handbag was locked," Joe commented. "Whoever opened it must have had a key. Could Bertrand have made a duplicate of your key?"

"It's possible," Kimberley confessed. "I've often left my key ring lying on the desk in our Santiago office. Anyway, it didn't occur to me to unlock the bag and check the contents at the time. I carried it all the way to New York without realizing that the idol was missing."

Joe looked puzzled. "Since it was stolen in Santiago, why don't you ask the Santiago police to find it?"

18

"I can't!" Kimberley protested. "I'd be the prime suspect. After all, I had the idol in my possession, and now I can't produce it!"

"So you want us to go to Santiago and investigate?" Frank asked.

Kimberley nodded. "I need someone smart enough to find the idol without any undue publicity. That's why I placed the ad in the *Times*. You boys were the first to call me."

"What does the idol look like?" Joe inquired.

Kimberley took a photograph from his desk drawer and handed it to him.

Frank looked over Joe's shoulder and saw a stone head with eyes like circles, a broad nose, and an open mouth. A fierce scowl distorted the features. The most noticeable thing, however, were the ears, with the lobes hanging down almost on a level with the chin.

"The Easter Islanders did that deliberately," Kimberley commented, pointing to the ears with his finger. "You can see the lobes are pierced. People hung weights on them so they would become enlarged. Of course, the practice has stopped in modern times. But long ears have always been a feature of Easter Island art."

"How big is this sculpture?" Frank wanted to know.

"About six inches high," Kimberley informed him.

"Then it's not heavy. You wouldn't have felt the loss of its weight in your bag."

"No," Kimberley agreed. "I never noticed that the bag was lighter, not with all those other stone artifacts in it. Well now, let's get down to the bottom line. You boys are obviously top-notch detectives. I'd like you to take the case. What do you say?"

The Hardys explained that they would have to talk to their father first.

"Fenton Hardy?" Kimberley queried. "Yes, I saw he was mentioned in the newspaper reports about the embezzlement case you just solved."

"If we take your case," Frank said, "we need a little more to go on besides what you've told us so far—some clue or starting point. We can't just go to Santiago and hope we'll be lucky."

"I have something," Kimberley said slowly. "A strange message I received. Here it is." Again he reached into his desk drawer and drew out a piece of paper, which he handed to the boys.

The message was composed of words cut from a newspaper and pasted on a South American Antiquities letterhead bearing the Santiago address. It read:

WHEN THE MOUNTAINS ARE COVERED WITH
MIST, AND THE FULL MOON IS OVER THE PEAK,
THE IDOL IS SAFE IN THE CAVE.

Frank and Joe looked baffled.

"Mr. Kimberley, where did you get this?" Frank
asked.

"And what does it mean?" Joe wanted to know.

"It came in the mail from Santiago," the antique
dealer told them. "And I have no idea what it
means. But since it mentions an idol, I think it must
refer to the Easter Island god figure."

"It's on note paper from your Santiago office," Joe
pointed out.

"True. But lots of people have access to that."

"The message must be a clue," Joe stated.
"Maybe it came from somebody who knows where
the idol is but doesn't want his identity revealed."

"It might be one of our Santiago employees,"
Kimberley said.

"Well, whoever wrote this is telling us to investigate the Santiago office," Frank declared. "That's
where we'll begin if we take the case."

"When can you let me know?" Kimberley asked
in a tense voice.

"After we talk to our father," Frank replied.
"We'll phone you this afternoon."

When the Hardy boys returned to their hotel, Frank called long distance to Bayport.

Aunt Gertrude, who was their father's sister, answered. "Why aren't you home yet?" she demanded in a tart voice.

"Well, we might have another case, Aunty," Frank said. He knew that although Aunt Gertrude was often critical of her nephews, she was basically proud of their accomplishments.

"Hmph!" Miss Hardy snorted. "Don't you ever give up? Can't you stay home for a change like other boys? Seems to me that if you're not in danger, you're not happy."

"Don't worry, Aunt Gertrude, this case isn't dangerous," Frank said and quickly explained what had happened. "And now may I talk to Dad, please?" he added when he was finished.

"Just a moment."

Fenton Hardy took the phone. "I found out how you solved the mystery," he began. "An old friend of mine in the New York Police Department called me about it."

"It was easy," Frank said modestly.

Fenton Hardy chuckled. "That's not what my friend reported. He considers your performance a remarkable example of detective work. What are you going to do now?"

"More detective work—maybe," Frank announced. "If you think we should take the case."

"What does it involve?"

Frank described their conversation with Kim Kimberley and his request for their services.

Fenton Hardy thought for a moment, then said, "Go ahead. It should be interesting."

Frank detected a slight hesitation in his father's voice. "You sound as if you're not all that happy with the idea."

"Well, I've just taken a new assignment, and I might need your help. It concerns the theft of government materiel from several naval bases. The navy has no idea who the thieves are, and hired me to find out."

"Shall we come home, then?"

"No, not yet. You see, I'll have to tour the naval bases where the thefts have occurred. If I do need you, it won't be until after the tour is over and I've checked out several clues."

His father paused a moment, then went on, "Tell you what. Go to Santiago for the time being, and stay at the Inca Arms Hotel. I'll get in touch with you there if necessary."

After Fenton Hardy had hung up, Joe rang Kimberley's office and told him that they would be able to work on his case, but might have to take time off to help their father.

The antique dealer hesitated for a moment, then

said, "Okay, why don't you come back here and we'll talk about it."

"We'll be right over, sir."

Joe hung up and the boys taxied to the Empire State Building for the second time that day. The secretary showed them into Kimberley's office, and he motioned for them to sit down.

"I'm hoping you'll find the idol before your father needs you," the antique dealer said. "If not, I'm in trouble. But I decided to give you the job anyway because I feel that boys your age will be less conspicuous. You realize, of course, that you can't walk into our Santiago office and tell my partner I hired you to investigate him and his staff."

"We understand, sir," Frank said. "What kind of cover do you have in mind for us?"

"I thought you could be high-school students with a special project in Incan history. You contacted me and I referred you to Santiago, because our staff there can help you study the artifacts we have. You have a research grant from your school to cover your expenses."

"That sounds like a plausible plan," Joe conceded.

Kimberley nodded. "Now here's where you go when you get into town. Our office is on Avenida Bernardo O'Higgins, or as we would say in English, Bernard O'Higgins Avenue."

He handed the boys a card bearing the printed legend of South American Antiquities, with the address and phone number underneath. "And take the strange message and the photograph of the idol with you, too."

Joe took the two items while Frank pocketed the business card.

Kimberley sighed. "I don't like to deceive my partner, and I'm sure he has nothing to do with the theft. But someone in our office must—our staff were the only people who were in on the transaction and knew what hotel I was staying in."

Frank nodded.

"My secretary will give you your expense money on your way out. Call me as soon as you have any news."

"We will, Mr. Kimberley," Joe promised.

"Oh, there's one other thing you should know about."

"Yes?"

"Depending on how you look at it, you might be in danger from the idol's *aku-aku*!"

3 Aku-Aku

Frank and Joe stared at Kimberley in surprise.

"What's an *aku-aku?*" Joe asked.

"An uncanny spirit. The people of Easter Island believe that *aku-akus* watch over them and all their possessions, especially those objects connected with the old religion. If the people obey their traditions, the spirits protect them. But if they step out of line, the *aku-akus* haunt them and bring bad luck."

"The old whammy," Frank said with a grin. "When an *aku-aku* puts a spell on you, you've had it."

"Sounds somewhat like voodoo," Joe commented.

"Right," Kimberley said. "Thor Heyerdahl wrote

a book called *Aku-Aku* about his experiences on Easter Island. He found the people convinced of the power of the spirits. They say anyone who disturbs an idol of the gods is in for trouble. Looks like it came true for me. I've had nothing but headaches since I bought that piece."

"Why are you telling us this?" Frank queried.

"Because you may run into the idol's *aku-aku* before your investigation is over. I don't want to frighten you off the case, but I feel I should warn you."

"We won't be frightened off," Frank promised.

Kimberley nodded. "Good. I've heard you boys aren't afraid of danger. That's why I'm depending on you to find the idol and have whoever stole it from me arrested. When can you leave?"

"On the next available flight," Frank declared.

"That's fine. Solve the mystery as quickly as you can. I'll be waiting to hear from you."

The boys returned to their hotel and discovered that the next plane from New York to Santiago was scheduled for the following afternoon. They spent the night in the hotel. After breakfast the next day, they went to a bookshop to buy a book on Incan art and did some sightseeing. Then they took a taxi to Kennedy Airport. Soon they were airborne, winging their way south along the eastern shore of the United States.

The boys took turns studying the book they had bought.

"We'll have to beef up on the subject," Frank said. "Otherwise Bertrand will never believe our cover."

After dinner was served, both Hardys fell sound asleep and did not wake up until breakfast the next morning. Meanwhile, they had reached South America; the massive peaks of the Andes could be seen below.

After they landed near Santiago, the brothers took a taxi to the Inca Arms Hotel. Large crowds were thronging the streets. Most people wore ordinary dress, but here and there the flash of brightly colored robes showed that Indians from the mountains were visiting the city.

The taxi turned into a broad thoroughfare with a street sign reading "Avenida Bernardo O'Higgins."

"This street's wider than Fifth Avenue in New York!" Joe said, surprised.

A drive of about a mile took them to the Inca Arms Hotel. It was near the building in which South American Antiquities was located. The boys could see the long range of the Andes from the window of their hotel room.

After they had stowed their things away and freshened up, Frank used his high-school Spanish to phone South American Antiquities. He continued struggling with the language when he got an answer on the other end. The man he was speaking to chuckled.

"You can speak English," he said in a jovial voice. "I'm Charles Bertrand from Saint Louis. My receptionist's on vacation, but perhaps I can help you."

"Oh, hello, Mr. Bertrand," Frank said, and introduced himself. "You're the person I wanted. My brother Joe and I are students working on a special project on Incan art. Mr. Kimberley said you might let us study the artifacts you have."

"Kim called me about it," Bertrand said. "I'll be glad to help you. Come on over to my office and we'll talk."

Frank thanked him and hung up. "Bertrand wants to see us, Joe."

"I hope we can check out his office while we're there," Joe said tensely.

The Hardys strolled over to South American Antiquities, which was in a building of ornate Spanish design. They mounted a flight of stairs and saw the name on a door at the end of a corridor.

They walked over and entered the outer office. It was empty. Joe banged the bell on the receptionist's desk with his palm, and a metallic peal sounded from the inner office.

A few second later, the door opened and Charles Bertrand appeared. He was a stout man with a twinkle in his eye. He wore a tiepin decorated with an Incan motif, a vicuña delicately chiseled in gold.

Smiling, he shook hands with the Hardys.

"I'm always glad to meet someone from the States," he declared. "Especially people who are as interested in the Incas as I am. I trust Mr. Kimberley explained what we do here at South American Antiquities."

"Yes, he did," Frank replied.

Bertrand led the Hardys into his office. A number of shelves held pieces of sculpture dating from the Indian cultures that existed in South America before the voyage of Columbus. Behind Bertrand's desk hung a photograph of Machu Picchu, the city hidden in the Andes to which the Incas retreated after the Spanish conquest.

Near the desk sat a tall, dark man with black, piercing eyes.

"Boys," Bertrand said, "meet Julio Santana. He's our chauffeur. By the way, you can speak English to him. He learned the language from American missionaries on Easter Island."

"Easter Island?" Frank's eyebrows shot up.

Santana smiled. "That's where I was born. But I left quite some time ago to work as an oil driller in Punta Arenas down in Tierra del Fuego. Then I came to Santiago and got the job with South American Antiquities."

"We're very interested in Easter Island artifacts," Joe spoke up.

Santana scowled. "Are you selling any?"

"Oh, no! We're students working during our vacation studying Incan art."

Santana smiled and seemed to relax. "You had me worried for a moment. You see, plenty of artifacts have been stolen from my island lately. Many pieces are being sold illegally on the international market."

"I heard about that," Frank said.

Bertrand fingered his vicuña tiepin. "We have no Easter Island pieces here at the moment. But we do have Incan sculptures for you boys to examine."

The conversation continued, and it was agreed that the Hardys would come back to the office on the following day to begin their studies.

Then Bertrand accompanied them through the outer office, which was still empty. This time Frank and Joe were able to survey it more thoroughly than when they entered. They both noticed a photograph on the wall. It showed a section of the Andes covered with mist while a full moon gleamed over the tallest peak.

Opening the door of the reception area, Bertrand ushered the Hardys into the hall. "My secretary will be back in a few days," he said. "She can help you when I'm not here. See you tomorrow!"

With that, he closed the door. The Hardys heard his footsteps as he crossed the waiting room, then the door to the inner office slammed shut.

"Joe!" Frank exclaimed in an undertone. "Did you notice? That photo on the wall fits the message Kimberley gave us!"

"It sure does, Frank!" Joe took the paper out of his pocket and read: " 'When the mountains are covered with mist, and the full moon is over the peak—' "

He broke off with a puzzled look. "That fits all right, but what about the rest? 'The idol's safe in the cave'?"

"Maybe there's a secret compartment behind the picture!" Frank guessed. "That could be the cave in the message. Let's go back in and look. We might not get another chance once the receptionist comes back."

Joe nodded. "Let's hope Bertrand and Santana stay in the inner office long enough for us to check behind the photo!"

Gingerly, the boys opened the door again and slipped into the reception area. They made their way across the room to the photograph of the Andes hanging on the wall.

All the while, they could hear the voices of Bertrand and Santana inside. The two men were talking about making a company car available to a wealthy buyer who would soon arrive in Santiago.

Frank carefully lifted the photograph up far enough to release the wire from its hook. As the wire came clear, the hook snapped upward like a control switch.

Silently a secret panel slid to one side, revealing a small compartment in the wall. The Hardys peered in curiously.

A small stone sculpture with round eyes, a flat nose, and open mouth was staring out at them!

Frank lifted the figure from its hiding place, while Joe pulled the picture Kimberley had given him out of his pocket. The idol and the picture matched perfectly!

Suddenly the door to the inner office swung open and Bertrand and the chauffeur stood framed in the doorway. They stared at the boys in disbelief.

"W-what are you doing there?" Bertrand cried out. "And where'd you get that statuette? My partner took it to New York with him a while ago!"

"He didn't," Frank said. "We found it in this secret compartment!"

"Found it! It seems to me you were about to steal it!" Bertrand thundered. "You have no business snooping around in my office. Good thing we caught you red-handed!"

"I'd say *you're* the one who was caught," Frank replied evenly.

"What do you mean by that?"

"We're turning this over to the Santiago police. Mr. Kim—"

He was interrupted by Julio Santana. "Oh, no, you're not!" the chauffeur snarled and lunged at the boy, snatching the idol from his hand. Reeling from the force of the blow, Frank crashed into Joe and the two fell to the floor.

In a flash, the Easter Islander ran out into the corridor and disappeared!

4 A Thief Escapes

Scrambling to his feet, Frank rushed after Santana with Joe close behind. By the time the Hardys reached the corridor, the chauffeur was already at the stairs. He glared furiously at them over his shoulder, then hurried down to the ground floor. The boys followed, taking the steps three at a time.

Santana rushed through the revolving door and ran up the street. Just then an elderly woman stepped into the door, turning it slowly. Frank and Joe had to wait until she was through before sprinting after the fugitive. However, once in the street, they closed in on the Easter Islander again. Frank was only a few feet away from him when Santana suddenly leaped off the sidewalk. He maneuvered through the traffic as cars jolted to a

halt to avoid hitting him and drivers shouted angrily. Then he wrenched open the door of a taxi and jumped in. The next instant the taxi sped off!

The Hardys looked for another cab, but none was in sight. "We've lost him!" Frank cried disappointedly, as he watched the car vanish up Bernard O'Higgins Avenue.

Joe nodded in disgust. "What do we do now?"

"Stop blocking traffic, Joe!"

Frank had become aware that the blaring horns were aimed at them. One driver leaned out of his window and shook his fist.

Grinning apologetically, the Hardys hastened to the sidewalk and made their way back to South American Antiquities. Bertrand was running up the street, looking wildly for Santana and the boys. When he saw them walking toward him, he stared in surprise.

"You came back?" he panted.

"Of course," Frank replied. "Unfortunately, Santana escaped."

"I thought you three were in with each other," Bertrand declared. "After all, you took the idol out of the wall compartment—"

"Why don't we go to your office?" Frank suggested. "We'll explain everything to you then."

The businessman nodded. "We'll have to call the police," he said, his voice shaking.

"Perhaps not," Frank said. "Maybe you'd like to give us the job of finding Santana."

"Are you kidding? I wouldn't ask a couple of school kids to catch a thief!"

"Mr. Bertrand," Joe said, "we're detectives. Mr. Kimberley hired us to find the Easter Island idol, which he had packed in his bag to bring to New York. When he arrived, it was missing. He felt someone in your Santiago office must have stolen it and suggested that we investigate while pretending to be students interested in Incan art."

Bertrand stared at him, his mouth open. They had arrived at the office, went inside, and the antique dealer sat down heavily behind his desk.

"Now let me digest this for a moment," he said. "You're right. Kim did take the sculpture and signed a release for it. But then, what was it doing in that compartment outside?"

"That's what we'll have to find out," Joe said.

"But how did you know it was there?"

"We didn't," Frank replied. "Mr. Kimberley received a strange message." He pulled the note out of his pocket and handed it to Bertrand. "When we saw the photo in the reception room," he continued, "we decided to look underneath. And there was the secret compartment with the idol in it!"

"I don't understand why Santana snatched it and ran off," Bertrand declared. "He constantly delivers things for us—many of them more valuable than the stone figurine—and he never once stole anything!"

"We'll have to find the answer to that question," Joe said. "Mr. Kimberley did not want the police involved in the case because he feared a scandal. If it's all right with you, we'll try to catch Santana for you."

"Oh, it's all right with me," Bertrand said. "You're probably correct in saying the less publicity we have, the better."

"A thief on the run has to hide somewhere," Frank spoke up. "Have you any idea where Santana might go?"

"Well, he has relatives in an Indian village in the Andes. He could go there."

"Where is it?"

"On a slope of the high peak directly to the east of Santiago."

"Then that's where we'll start," Frank said. "But there are a few things we have to know. For instance, what about that secret compartment?"

"It was there when I rented the office," Bertrand replied. "However, I've never used it as a hiding place."

"Who else knew about it?"

"Kim did, and I suppose some of our employees. There are twelve, including Santana, and of course visitors come and go."

"So, many people had access to the stationery on which the note was printed," Joe suggested.

Bertrand nodded.

"When did you last see the idol, except for just now?"

"The day before Kim left for New York. It was right here in this office. Kim put it in his bag when he went to the hotel. I saw him later in his room. The bag was there and locked, and I figured the idol was in it."

"He told us you watched the handbag while he went to collect his wristwatch," Frank stated. "Did you stay in the room all the time?"

"I went down the hall for ice," Bertrand replied.

"Were you gone long enough for someone to sneak into the room and steal the idol?"

"It's possible. Most of the ice was gone and I had to wait for the machine to make more."

"That's when the thief must have entered!" Joe declared. "Santana could have overheard you talk about the idol earlier, and he probably knew about the secret compartment. He could also have a duplicate key that would unlock the handbag."

"Santana's from Easter Island," Frank observed. "Maybe that's why he wanted the sculpture. He could have shadowed you and Mr. Kimberley to the hotel, climbed up the fire escape, and watched through the window. When you left the room to get ice, he could have entered, unlocked the bag, taken the idol, and escaped."

"Then he hid the idol in the secret compartment in your office until it was safe for him to dispose of it," Joe continued his brother's line of thought. "That's why he hit the ceiling when he saw we had found it. So, he grabbed it and ran off."

"It's just a theory," Frank pointed out. "We'll see if it holds up when we interrogate Santana. But we have to find him first."

"I think you should get right on to it," Bertrand advised.

"We will," Frank said.

The Hardys left South American Antiquities, rented a car, and drove through Santiago. Joe was at the wheel and Frank held a map of the Andes spread out across his knees. Gradually the city gave way to the suburbs, and then they were rolling through the country toward the Andes, the great mountain chain of South America.

Joe broke the silence. "This is a weird case, Frank. We came down here to investigate Bertrand for Kimberley. Now we're investigating Santana for Bertrand."

"It's a switch, all right. And there's no doubt

about Santana's guilt. We all saw him take the statuette."

They went on, mulling over the problem. Soon the pavement beneath their wheels was replaced by a rough dirt road that made the car bounce up and down over large boulders and into deep potholes.

"This ride's giving me a crick in the neck!" Joe complained as he wrenched the wheel to avoid running into a gulch on the right.

"And I just banged my knee on the dashboard," Frank lamented with a grimace, rubbing the injured spot.

When they entered the foothills of the Andes, the road led steeply upward. The air became thinner and colder, and they found breathing difficult.

"If we get any higher, we'll need oxygen masks," Frank joked.

But the road soon flattened out and they were able to catch their breath as they got used to the altitude. They drove along narrow ledges bounded by rocky mountain walls on one side and precipitous cliffs falling away for hundreds of feet on the other.

Suddenly, as they rounded a hairpin turn, they saw another car hurtling directly at them! The road was too narrow for the two vehicles to pass. If they tried, one would go over the cliff!

Frantically, Joe slammed on the brakes. The other driver did the same. Tires screeched on the stone surface of the road, and they came to a jolting stop with their front bumpers nearly touching. A man got out of the other car and walked up to the boys. He was obviously an Indian and shouted something in what the Hardys took to be his native language. Frank shrugged and held his hands up to indicate that they did not understand.

Gesturing in sign language, the Indian let them know that he was going to back up and that they should follow him. Frank nodded, smiling gratefully.

Joe trailed the man's car until they reached a place where the road widened sufficiently to let them pass. They waved their thanks to the Indian, who waved back.

"That was a close shave!" Frank exclaimed. "Good driving, Joe! You stopped just in time or the car would have turned into a pile of junk!"

"Give our friend half the credit, Frank. If he hadn't hit the brakes, he'd have plowed right into us, no matter what I did."

They continued on their route until they saw stones bouncing from a slope above them.

"Watch it, Joe!" Frank warned. "It looks like a landslide's coming our way!"

Joe stopped. More stones hit the road and careened over the side of the cliff into the valley below.

43

Then a clatter of hooves became audible, and a herd of small, woolly animals with long necks came bounding down the slope.

"Vicuñas!" Frank exclaimed. "There's our landslide!"

The animals, which resembled small llamas, leaped nimbly onto the road and continued over the side of the cliff. Finding footholds on what appeared to be a sheer wall, they zigzagged down the slope and began browsing on the bushes at its base.

Joe resumed the drive. They entered a valley where they saw tents pitched near a trench. A dozen men were digging, and a station wagon parked nearby bore the legend INCA EXPEDITION U.S.A.

"Let's ask them if they know where the village is," Joe suggested and pulled up to the station wagon.

The leader of the expedition came forward. "You look like Americans," he said.

"We are," Frank confirmed. "Frank and Joe Hardy from Bayport."

"My name's Professor Yates. I'm in charge of this expedition. What are you boys doing this far back in the Andes?"

"We're looking for a nearby Indian village on the slope of the tall mountain," Joe informed him. "Can you tell us where it is?"

"Straight ahead, about five miles. Some of the men from the village are working here on our dig. We're excavating one of the main Incan sites in this region, searching for articles of a civilization that flourished centuries ago."

"Sounds fascinating," Joe said. "Have you found any?"

"Oh yes, lots of stuff. What about you fellows? Are you visiting someone in the village?"

Frank nodded. "A man named Julio Santana."

"Julio? What a coincidence. You don't have to go any further."

"Why not?" Joe asked.

"He's right here in our camp!"

5 Mistaken Identity

Frank and Joe stared at each other in amazement. What luck to catch up to Julio Santana so quickly!

"He must have come directly here after he escaped from us," Joe thought. Aloud he said, "Can we see him, Professor Yates?"

"No problem. Come on."

Yates led the way over to the spot where the excavation was taking place. A mound of earth rose beside the trench where the men were working. Figurines, shards of broken pottery, and other archeological discoveries were laid out on a table next to it.

A young woman sat at a table writing in a

notebook. Yates introduced her to the Hardys as Gloria Nemitz from Milwaukee.

"I'm listing all the stuff we dig up," she said. "Each piece gets a number and a description."

"Gloria, where's Julio Santana?" Yates asked.

"He left camp a little while ago. He said he'd be back later on."

"Why don't you wait here till he returns?" Yates invited.

"We'd like to, Professor," said Frank. "We could use a rest."

"You can have chow with us in the meantime."

Joe patted his stomach and grinned. "That's even better!"

Yates introduced the Hardys to the rest of the crew on the dig. Then loaves of bread and cans of food were brought from the store tent, and all sat down on the ground and pitched in.

Gloria Nemitz was next to the Hardys. "Are you friends of Julio's?" she inquired.

"We met him," Joe said evasively, "in Santiago."

"That figures," she said. "He spends a lot of time in Santiago."

Then they began to chat about the Incan Empire that extended through the Andes before the coming of the Spanish Conquistadors. After the meal was over, the Hardys helped clean up. Santana still had not arrived.

"You boys look strong enough to help with the dig," Yates declared. "Want to give us a hand while you're waiting?"

"We'd be glad to," Frank and Joe agreed enthusiastically.

Yates chuckled. "Good. Let's see what you find." He handed Joe a pickax and Frank a spade, and showed them where to work. Joe began cutting a furrow along a line indicated by a cord stretched between two posts. Frank got down in the trench and turned over the earth carefully so as not to break anything he might strike. Other members of the dig worked beside them, lifting the earth out of the trench and adding it to the mound.

After some labor with the pickax, Joe felt his implement strike stone. He scratched away the earth with his hands and uncovered a series of stones in a straight line. Beneath them he came to a second series.

"Professor, this looks like a flight of stairs," the boy called out.

"I thought the steps might be there," Yates commented after surveying Joe's discovery. "That's why I had the cord tied as a guideline. My men can now start excavating the rest of the stairs."

Meanwhile, Frank had been cautiously digging in the trench and uncovered a pot. Using his fingers, he carefully brushed the earth away, removed the

48

container, and held it up. The sunlight gleamed on the representation of an animal with a pointed snout, heavy leather plates around the body, and a long tail.

"I found a pot with an armadillo on it!" Frank exclaimed.

"That's a real treasure," said Yates enthusiastically. "All we had dug up so far were shards, or bits and pieces of pottery. Now we have an intact container. It's an example of armadillo ware from Central America. Shows trade was carried on between Central America and Chile in ancient times. Well, you boys have done enough. Have a rest until Julio gets here."

"There he is!" Gloria called out. She pointed to a pickup truck rolling into the camp. It stopped near the Hardys' car. The boys ran forward and waited expectantly as the driver got out. However, they gaped in surprise when they saw he was a portly man with blond hair and blue eyes!

"Julio, the Hardy boys are here to see you," Yates said. "They've been waiting for you."

"Why is that?"

Frank gulped. "Mr. Santana, we thought you were somebody else. We're looking for a man with the same name. He's from Easter Island and is dark-complexioned with dark hair."

Santana grinned. "I am from Santiago. I deliver

49

provisions to this camp." He pointed to boxes of food stacked in the back of the pickup.

"You don't know the other Julio Santana, by any chance?" Joe queried.

"No, I do not."

Yates had been listening to the conversation. "A case of mistaken identity, eh?" he said. "That's too bad. And there's no use asking the Indians on the dig about your Julio Santana. They're very close-mouthed with strangers."

"Then we'll have to go on to the village," Frank said. His voice showed his disappointment.

"Well, it's not far," Gloria pointed out sympathetically.

The Hardys said good-bye to their hosts and drove on toward the Indian village. People were tramping along the road, and Frank, now at the wheel, had to slow down frequently to avoid running into one of them.

They were dressed in their native clothing. The men wore rough boots, heavy shirts and trousers, broad-brimmed hats, and ponchos over their shoulders. The women had on colorful skirts, shawls, and aprons. Many of them wore hats with high crowns resembling derbies.

Most people gave the Hardys sullen stares. Some deliberately stayed in the middle of the road and forced Frank to drive around them.

"What's eating them?" he wondered. "What do they have against us?"

Joe shrugged. "Maybe they don't like strangers. Professor Yates said something to that effect, remember?"

At last the Hardys came to the village. They saw a number of wooden houses, but the main square was surrounded by rows of two-story buildings of modern, prefabricated design that looked like military barracks.

"They must have been put up by the Chilean army," Joe guessed.

Just then a tall, muscular Indian stepped in front of their car, held up his hand with a scowl, and made Frank stop. He shouted something to the people in the square, and they began to gather around the boys.

"I don't think we're going to get much cooperation out of them," Joe said apprehensively.

"Looks like a freeze-out for us," Frank agreed. "I don't like it one bit."

The crowd was large and hostile. Some of the men started to push the Hardys' car, which rocked back and forth.

Frank rolled down his window and tried to explain in Spanish why he and Joe were there. But threatening cries drowned out his words, and the Indians rocked the car more violently.

"They're going to turn us over!" Joe cried.

The Hardys braced themselves against the dashboard, while the natives violently tilted the vehicle up on two wheels.

Suddenly an older man pushed through the crowd and shouted something at the Indians. The men let go and stepped aside, as the car fell back on its four wheels with a crash.

"Who are you?" the man demanded.

"Frank and Joe Hardy from Bayport in the United States," Frank replied, glad that the man had spoken English.

The Indian nodded. "I thought you were Americans. I learned your language when I worked for an archeological expedition. My name is Ata Copac. I am the village leader."

"Why are your people so hostile to us?" Joe asked.

Copac smiled. "They thought you were tax collectors from Santiago." He turned and spoke to the villagers in their native language. Their sullen stares turned into pleasant smiles, and a number came up and shook hands with Frank and Joe. Then the men drifted away from the car, leaving the Hardys alone with Ata Copac.

"Why are you here?" the village leader inquired. "Are you tourists?"

"No. We're looking for a man named Julio Santana," Joe explained.

"From Easter Island," Frank put in. "We were told he might be in this village because he has relatives here."

"I know Julio Santana," Ata Copac said. "But he is not here. His village is on the opposite slope of the mountain."

"How do we get there?" Frank inquired.

"Over the mountain pass."

"Then we'd better be on our way. It's getting dark."

Ata Copac shook his head. "You cannot drive. The path is too steep. You will have to go on foot. And you will not find your way in the darkness. I suggest you stay here for the night and set out in the morning. You can sleep in an empty hut."

The Hardys gratefully accepted the invitation. Ata Copac got in the car with them and showed Frank where to drive. The hut was a one-story building with a table, a couple of chairs, and several canvas cots. Blankets were piled on the cots.

"I think you will be comfortable here," the village leader declared. "Tonight we celebrate one of our holidays. Perhaps you will join us?"

"We sure will!" The boys grinned.

When they stepped outside, night had fallen and

torches shone in a field just behind the hut. The villagers were piling up logs in the middle of the field. When they finished, they lit the kindling and an enormous bonfire roared up through the logs.

Women began to roast meat over the fire, and the rest of the feast came from jars of corn, peas, and potatoes. The natives filed past, plate in hand, to get their share of the food.

"Chet should be here," Frank said to Joe. He was referring to their best friend, Chet Morton, who liked eating better than anything in the world.

Frank chuckled. "You're right. Chet could devour all this food by himself."

Ata Copac and the Hardys sat down at one end of a long table set up in the field and pitched into their dinner with gusto.

Afterward, the Indians performed on drums and wind instruments. Frank and Joe found the music strange at first, but after a while began to appreciate the rhythmic beat.

"We could play these numbers at high school graduation," Frank said jokingly.

"And we could cut a disc for our stereo," Joe quipped, "except that we don't have a sound stage. I'd like to have a go at those drums!"

"So would I. They're as good as the ones we have at school."

Frank and Joe were in the band at Bayport High.

They usually played guitars, but they recently doubled on the drums.

Ata Copac put his arms around the Hardys' shoulders. "Oh, please give us a demonstration!"

Then he translated for the villagers. Many voices called out to the boys.

"They want you to play for them," Ata Copac interpreted.

"Okay, let's go, Joe," Frank said. "We can't say no to our public. What'll we start with?"

"The Bayport Rag," Joe suggested.

Taking over a couple of drums from the grinning Indians, the Hardys went into their familiar routine. They began with a low rhythm, and then increased the sound until their drumming echoed over the village. The audience clapped and shouted. They swayed in time to the rhythm, and applauded loudly at the end.

The celebration finished shortly afterward. The boys returned to their hut, slipped under the blankets on their cots, and went to sleep.

A noise outside wakened Joe in the middle of the night. He stepped to the window and looked out. In the moonlight, he could see a man at their car, twisting the cap off the gas tank!

Joe rushed to the door and swung it open. The man heard him and looked up.

He was Julio Santana!

6 *Disguised as Natives*

Santana darted away from the car, and Joe ran after him. The chase led between rows of barracks-like houses, behind the main store of the village, and across the square.

The young detective strained his eyes in the moonlight to keep Santana in sight. But he was hampered by running in his bare feet. By the time he reached the opposite side of the square, the Easter Islander had vanished into the night.

Joe came to a halt, wincing at the sharp pebbles underfoot. Realizing that any further pursuit was hopeless, he turned and went back to the hut where Frank and he were spending the night. After making sure that no gas had been siphoned from the car's tank, he woke Frank up and told him what happened. The boys decided to take turns standing watch for the rest of the night, in case Santana came back. However, all was quiet until eight o'clock in the morning, when they decided to get dressed.

"Santana must have been watching from the mountain to see if anybody was after him," Frank said as he pulled on his jeans. "He recognized us and tried to put our car out of commission by emptying the gas tank."

"And I'm sure he must be at the other village now," Joe added. "We've got to check him out."

The boys made a breakfast of some army rations they found in the hut. They were just finishing when a knock sounded on the door and Ata Copac entered.

"I have come to give you directions," he said. "You follow the road over the pass, turn right along a cliff, and you will come to a bridge over a deep gorge. Cross the bridge and you will see the village on the other side of the canyon."

"Thank you," Frank said. "And something else has just occurred to me. It would be better if we had a disguise."

"Why is that?"

The Hardys explained about Santana and his theft of the Easter Island idol.

"He might stir up the villagers against us if we

57

look like outsiders," Frank said, "Or we might be mistaken for tax collectors again."

Ata Copac nodded. "I understand, and I will help you. If Santana is a thief, I wish him to be caught. If you find him with the idol, I will ask his village leader to have him arrested. Now, come with me."

Leading the way to his house, he produced Indian clothing, a wooden washtub, and a bushel basket full of blackberries. The Hardys crushed the blackberries in the water until it became a dark color; then they rinsed their hands and faces to hide their light complexions. Joe also drenched his hair to make it look black.

Next the boys donned rough shirts, trousers, and boots. They slipped ponchos over their heads and pulled broad-brimmed hats down over their foreheads to mask the light color of their eyes.

Joe grinned. "Think we'll pass for Indians, Frank?"

"As long as we keep our hats on. Let's see if these getups work."

Keeping their eyes fixed on the ground, the Hardys walked through the square, mingling with the natives who were dressed just as they were. No one seemed to notice the two Americans.

"Looks as if we can get away with it," Frank muttered. "They can't tell the difference."

"Have your Spanish ready, Frank, in case some-body talks to us," Joe advised.

The Hardys said good-bye to Ata Copac and thanked him for his help. Then they walked along the road beyond the village leading to the mountain pass. Whenever they met an Indian, they hurried by quickly in order to avoid any questions. They followed a narrow, rocky trail up to the pass, where they could see snow-covered mountain peaks in the distance. One huge outcropping towered over their heads.

"That's the cliff Ata Copac mentioned," said Joe, pointing to the right.

He led the way onto a narrow ledge running along the top of the cliff. Frank was directly behind him, and they edged forward carefully.

Suddenly Joe stepped on a boulder that gave way under his foot. Shaken loose, it hurtled down onto the jagged rocks below. Joe clutched wildly at the air in an effort to regain his balance. However, he failed, and with a frantic scream, toppled off the cliff!

Frank lunged forward and reached for Joe's poncho. For a moment, the younger Hardy boy was suspended in the air with nothing between him and the rocks at the bottom of the cliff. Then Frank got a firm grip on the poncho and pulled his brother back to the safety of the ledge.

Joe blew his breath out in a great gasp. "Wow! That was too close for comfort!"

"It sure was, Joe! Don't step on any more boulders. You almost scared me to death!"

Moving cautiously along the cliff, they reached the other side. From there, a short walk brought them to the deep gorge Ata Copac had mentioned. The bridge crossing was made of narrow branches tied with heavy ropes to trees on both sides of the canyon. Two more ropes were strung about three feet above the first pair, and fastened to them at three-foot intervals, providing the handrails.

The makeshift bridge swayed in the wind as the Hardys approached it. They looked down and saw a small stream meandering at the bottom of the gorge.

"You have to be an acrobat to cross over that thing," Frank muttered. "It's a death-defying stunt!"

"I just hope the guy who anchored it to the tree knew how to tie a good sailor's knot," Joe added apprehensively.

Placing a foot on the first branch, and steadying himself by holding onto the handrails, Joe started across. Frank followed. The bridge rocked from side to side as they moved, and the ropes strained at their moorings. The branches creaked under the weight of the two boys.

It was slow going, and their hearts were pounding by the time they reached the opposite side. With relief they jumped onto solid earth.

The Indian village they were looking for lay right in front of them. The people and the buildings resembled the ones they had just left. It was market day, and stalls were set up in the village square. Vendors were selling food, clothing, utensils, and farming implements. A pen held a small flock of vicuñas being offered for sale.

"Joe, let's pretend to be Indians from the mountains, in town for market day," Frank advised. "And keep an eye open for Santana."

Joe nodded tensely. Holding their heads low, the Hardys walked into the throng in the village square. Stall owners called out to them, offering their wares. Shaking their heads to indicate they were not interested, the boys moved on. After a few minutes, they began to feel secure in their disguises.

Suddenly Frank tugged on Joe's poncho and nodded toward a booth where small stone sculptures and other artwork were being offered. A man with his back to them was arranging the exhibit on a table behind the counter.

"Let's take a look at what he's got for sale," Frank said.

Joe shrugged. "You don't expect to find the Easter

Island idol there, do you? Santana knows its worth. He'd never sell it to a guy like that. He wouldn't make any money on it."

"I know. But maybe the vendor can give us a clue as to where one might sell a valuable sculpture."

Casually the boys strolled over to the stall and looked at the pieces on the table. The man turned around with a smile, which froze on his face as he recognized them.

Frank and Joe gaped. He was none other than Julio Santana!

"The Hardys!" Santana exclaimed. "Welcome to our village. Would you like to buy one of my artifacts?"

"Where's the Easter Island idol you stole from South American Antiquities?" Joe demanded.

"Here it is!" Santana replied. He turned and took a small sculpture from the table. With an icy stare, he thrust it into Joe's hand.

The boys examined it. "This is an imitation Incan piece!" Frank declared.

Santana paid no attention. Instead, he screamed in Spanish: "Thieves! Thieves!"

A number of Indians whirled around and stared at the Hardys.

"Thieves! Thieves!" Santana kept yelling. Quickly a crowd began to gather, making threatening gestures at the young detectives.

"Let's get out of here!" Frank hissed.

Joe dropped the sculpture and the boys took to their heels, pushing people aside as they ran past the stall.

When they reached the open area leading to the bridge, a mob of Indians was behind them in headlong pursuit. In Spanish, they shouted threats of how the thieves would be punished once they were caught.

Frank dashed onto the bridge, followed by Joe. Desperately they tried to run over it fast, but the dipping of the branches under their feet and the swaying of the ropes held them up. They were about three-quarters of the way across when Santana arrived at the canyon. He took hold of one of the handrails.

"Grab the other one!" he shouted to a man beside him. "Now, do as I do!"

He moved the rope back and forth, and his companion followed suit. Together, the two men caused the bridge to sway dangerously from side to side.

Frank and Joe clung to the rails as the motion became more violent. High up in the air they fell to the right, then swung clear around to the left. The mountain spun before their eyes, and with each swing, they hovered over the gorge for a split second.

At last the bridge was flung too high for a return swing. It turned upside down and collapsed.

Frank and Joe were thrown off into the deep gorge below!

7 Downhill Danger

As the Hardys flew through the air, their fingers closed around one of the handrails. Gripping the rope tightly, they braked their fall and hung suspended over the gorge. Their Indian hats fell off and drifted down into the stream.

Frank was unable to turn his head. "Joe, are you there?" he called out anxiously.

"Right behind you!" Joe panted.

"Move ahead hand over hand," Frank yelled as he began to pull himself along the rope. Joe did the same.

"They're getting away!" Santana shouted. "They're getting away, and we can't follow them with the bridge turned upside down!"

Frank and Joe reached the opposite side of the canyon and pulled themselves up onto solid ground. They collapsed on the soft earth to catch their breath. Meanwhile, the bridge began to swing again. Staring across the gorge, they saw that Santana and a group of natives were trying to turn it right side up.

"Let's get out of here!" Joe exclaimed. "They'll be coming across in a minute!"

The boys rushed into the underbrush and concealed themselves beneath some tall bushes. They were still too exhausted from their ordeal to run very far. Peering through the branches, they could see the bridge hurtling back and forth in a wide arc. Finally it reached its peak and fell down into its original position.

Santana and his companions ran over it as fast as they could and began to scout through the underbrush for the Hardys.

"We can't stay here!" Frank said in a hoarse whisper.

"We don't have to!" Joe whispered back. He pointed to a spot where a cave extended into the mountainside.

Hitting the ground, the Hardys crawled into the cave and pulled small bushes and twigs over the entrance. Then they lay flat, gasping for breath and waiting to see what would happen.

Their pursuers had split up and were running in all directions. Suddenly Frank and Joe heard Santana's voice. "They got away!" the chauffeur complained in English.

"Perhaps you were foolish to come here," another man said.

"It was an obvious choice. I wanted to stay with you until we could go on."

"It was too dangerous," his companion declared.

Frank and Joe could hear his footsteps as he came closer to the cave. Then they saw the outline of his figure through the brush. He stretched out his hand and the Hardys froze in terror.

Had he discovered their hideout?

But the man only plucked a few berries from a bush, popped them into his mouth, then said, "What will you do now, Julio?"

"I will return to Santiago with the idol and hide out at Ernesto's until you are ready. The Hardys will search the village and the mountains for me and they will never suspect I went back to the city."

"Good," the other man agreed. "I will find you at Ernesto's when the time comes."

Both men walked off. Frank and Joe remained in their hiding place for a long time. Then they finally emerged cautiously, hoping that all the Indians had returned to the village after their futile search.

"Now what?" Joe asked.

"Let's go back to our car and drive to Santiago," Frank advised.

"Too bad we can't follow Santana," Joe said. "But I'm sure he's left already. I wonder where he plans to go with the other fellow."

Frank shrugged. "I have no idea."

The boys followed the return route along the ledge and through the mountain pass. They hurried to the Indian village without encountering any hostile natives, and quickly made their way to Ata Copac's house, where they told him what happened.

"I am sorry you did not catch the thief," the village leader said.

Frank nodded. "Well, at least we know he's headed back to Santiago," he said. The boys thanked Ata Copac for his help and washed off the dark dye they had used to disguise themselves. Then they exchanged their Indian garments for their regular clothes, said good-bye to their host, and drove off with Joe at the wheel.

As they reached the steepest segment of the mountain road, he stepped on the brakes to slow their speed. Nothing happened. The car careened crazily forward!

"The brakes don't work!" Joe shouted.

"And we're going too fast to jump out!" Frank judged. "Keep steering, Joe!"

Gripping the wheel, the boy struggled to stay on course. Rocky walls threatened the Hardys on one side, plunging cliffs on the other! Joe veered around curves at top speed, dodging boulders and potholes, while the speedometer of their car went up and up!

As he rounded one corner, Joe saw another car racing directly toward them. Realizing there was no room for both, he made a split-second decision. Wrenching the wheel to one side, he steered off the road and the other car whizzed past.

The Hardys bounced into an open area and slowed down as the wheels became entangled in grass and bushes. Joe swung around in a circle, and his vehicle gradually came to a stop.

Bruised and shaken, the young detectives stared at one another. Joe mopped his forehead with a handkerchief.

"That was a close call," he said in a trembling voice.

Frank nodded. "I want to look at those brakes. I bet—"

Just then a familiar voice called out, "Are you boys all right?"

Gloria Nemitz came running up, followed by Professor Yates. Without realizing it, the Hardys had reached the area of the American archeological dig.

"I saw you drive off the road," Gloria continued. "It looked like you were in trouble."

"We were," Joe admitted, as he and Frank climbed out of the car. "Our brakes didn't work."

"You can get them repaired here," Yates declared. "We service all our own vehicles."

"Thanks. That's great, Professor," Frank said. "But first I want to find out what went wrong."

He crawled under the car and inspected the machinery. Then he emerged with a grim face. "The connecting rod is nearly filed through," he reported. "It snapped when Joe stepped on the brakes at the top of the hill!"

"Somebody tried to kill us!" Joe exclaimed.

"But who would want to do that?" Gloria questioned.

"Julio Santana, the man from Easter Island," Frank replied, and described their adventures since their visit to the dig, and the reason they had come to Chile.

"I'm sorry to hear you have such a dangerous assignment," Yates said. "Why don't you walk over to our supply tent? We've got spare connecting rods."

The boys accepted his offer and repaired their car.

"Why don't you stay for some food?" Gloria invited when they were finished.

71

Frank shook his head. "Thanks, but we can't. We have to go back to Santiago as fast as possible."

"We don't want to let Santana's trail grow cold," Joe added.

Soon afterward, the Hardys were on the road again. They reached Santiago, turned their car in at the renting office, and walked to South American Antiquities. Bertrand was in his office inspecting some Incan artifacts.

"Did you catch Santana?" he asked eagerly.

"We caught up with him," Frank replied. "But he got away again."

Bertrand stared at them in disappointment when they explained what happened.

"Well, that leaves me no choice," the antique dealer said finally. "I'll have to call the police."

"Mr. Kimberley didn't want that," Joe objected. "Why don't you give us another chance to look for Santana in Santiago?"

Bertrand was doubtful. "I'll let you know tomorrow morning," he said with a sigh. "It's late now, and I want to go home." Wearily, he escorted the Hardys to the door.

The boys discussed the case in their hotel room that night. "All we have to go on is a name—Ernesto," Joe said.

Frank nodded. "We might be better off asking the police for help, as Bertrand suggested," he said.

"Kimberley didn't want the authorities involved, but that was because he signed the release for the idol and would have been the prime suspect. Now we know he didn't take it. And the police might have some idea who Ernesto is, or even have a record of Santana!"

"You're right," Joe admitted. "Let's—"

Just then the telephone rang. Frank answered, and his face broke into a smile. "Hi, Dad," he said. "What's happening?"

"You tell me first," Fenton Hardy replied, and the young detective explained their adventures in the Easter Island idol case.

"You did fine work," his father commended him. "But as far as Santana is concerned, I'm afraid you'll have to let the police handle him."

"We were thinking of asking the authorities for help," Frank admitted. "But we want to keep searching for him, too. We have the Ernesto clue."

"I know," his father said. "But I'd like you to put the case on the back burner and help me for a while."

"Why, Dad? Do you need us?"

"I do. I'd like you to leave Santiago as soon as possible."

"Where are we going?"

"The Antarctic!"

8 A New Plan

Frank and Joe stared at one another. They could hear their father chuckling over the phone.

"I thought that would interest you," the detective said. "I can't tell you any details at this point. Just catch a flight to Punta Arenas. It's in Tierra del Fuego at the southern tip of South America. Belongs to Chile. There's a plane out of Santiago tomorrow. I've already made reservations for you."

"What do we do after we land?" Frank wanted to know.

"You'll find out when you get there. An advisor will meet you at the information booth. I have to go now. Bye." With that, Fenton Hardy hung up.

"Dad's really being mysterious," Frank observed. "I wonder where he is."

"Probably in Washington," Joe said. "Anyway, we won't be going back to New York for a while. What do you say we call Kimberley?"

"Good idea. He must be wondering if we've found the idol. But it's too late now. Let's do it in the morning."

After breakfast the following day, Joe phoned South American Antiquities in New York.

"What have you found out?" Kimberley demanded. "Any progress to report?"

"That strange message you gave us was a clue," Joe responded. "It showed us where to look for the idol—in a secret compartment."

"Oh?"

"Behind a photo of the Andes in the outer office of your Santiago branch. A small panel slid back when we lifted the photo off the wall. The peg worked as an automatic control."

"I've seen that compartment!" Kimberley thundered. "It was there when we rented the office."

"I know," Joe said. "Mr. Bertrand told us most of the staff were aware of its existence."

"But what about the idol. Was it there?"

"It sure was. We were about to take it out when your chauffeur ran up to us and grabbed it."

"Julio? Are you talking about Julio Santana?"

"Yes, sir."

There was silence on the other end of the line.

Finally Kimberley spoke again. "I can't imagine that Julio is a thief. Do you know if—if he was the one who put the idol there in the first place?"

"No. But he *could* have done it," Joe said. "Mr. Bertrand left to get ice when you were picking up your watch that night in the Santiago hotel. Santana could have sneaked into the room and removed the sculpture from your case with a duplicate key."

"That must be it, then," Kimberley said. "Where's Santana now, in jail?"

"No," Joe replied and reported what had happened in the mountain village.

Kimberley grunted. "You let him escape? What kind of detectives are you? I'm going to ask my partner to call the police!"

"We wanted to suggest the same thing, sir," Frank said evenly. "Our father needs us to help him on his case and we have to interrupt our activities here temporarily."

"Temporarily!" Kimberley sneered. "By the time you come back, I hope Santana will have been caught!"

"So do we," Frank said politely.

After the conversation ended, Frank spoke with Bertrand and explained that he and Joe were leaving Santiago to help their father.

"We'll return as soon as we can to help find the idol if the police aren't successful," he promised.

"Okay," Bertrand said. "I'll call the chief and tell him the whole story."

The Hardys packed their things, checked out of the hotel, and left for the airport. Suddenly, Frank had an idea. "We're headed for Punta Arenas," he said. "That's where Santana once worked in the oil fields. Maybe he's planning to go back there, take his old job, and lie low until the heat's off and he can sell the idol!"

"He might even be on the same plane as we are," Joe added excitedly. "He and the other fellow!"

At the terminal, the brothers boarded their flight and took their seats. Holding magazines before their faces to conceal themselves, they pretended to read while furtively watching the passengers coming aboard. But they saw only strangers.

The plane took off on a flight that lasted several hours. Finally Punta Arenas came into view. The Hardys could see oil rigs spotted around the oil fields. Incandescent flames flared atop tall towers and showed where superfluous gas was being burned off. Trucks were carrying barrels of oil down toward the port where tankers waited at anchor for their cargo.

The plane landed at the airport outside the city, and the Hardys filed out with the other passengers.

"I wonder who the advisor is who's meeting us here," Frank commented.

"Since we don't know, he'd better recognize *us*," Joe chuckled.

They entered the terminal, collected their suitcases, and walked to the information booth, waiting expectantly for their contact to arrive.

Suddenly they heard a familiar voice behind them. "Hi, boys!"

Whirling around, they saw Fenton Hardy!

"Dad, you're the advisor we're supposed to meet!" Joe exclaimed.

"What are you doing here?" Frank inquired. "We thought you were in Washington."

"It's a long story. I'll tell you during our flight to Antarctica. We'll be boarding a U.S. Navy plane in a few minutes. It's standing by on one of the runways. You see, the American and Chilean governments cooperate in the air transport from here to bases near the South Pole."

Joe mentioned that Santana had once worked in the Punta Arenas oil fields. "He might be headed this way again."

"No time for that right now," Fenton Hardy declared. "But I'll alert the authorities."

He went to a phone, talked briefly, and returned. "The company Santana worked for has his name in its inoperative files. The police will get in touch with the personnel department in case he tries to get his job back."

An American naval officer approached and said, "Mr. Hardy, we're ready for takeoff."

"Thank you." The detective led the way to the plane, which bore on its side the legend: U.S. NAVY ANTARCTIC EXPLORATION. The Hardys found themselves among naval personnel and scientists who specialized in research in the area.

"It's safe to talk now," Fenton Hardy said as the flight began. "You boys already know that I'm investigating the theft of government materiel from some of our naval bases. I found that a big ring has been operating, and identified the small-fry. They'll be arrested. But I'm up against a stone wall with regard to one gang member."

"The ringleader?" Frank asked.

Fenton Hardy nodded. "My investigation indicates that he's one of the crew at Byrd Base, our newest Antarctic installation. But I have no idea who he is."

"So the navy wants you to go down there and find out."

"Exactly. I've had to be hush-hush about the case because the ringleader may have spies at Punta Arenas. I don't want them to tip him off. There are one hundred men at Byrd Base, so it won't be easy to identify the culprit. My cover story is that I'm a scientist reporting on the laboratories they're using."

"And what about us?" Joe inquired.

"I have a special assignment for you. There's a small advance installation beyond Byrd Base. It's called Outpost I. The gang chief might be there, so I want you to investigate."

"We'll need a cover story, too," Frank pointed out. "We can't just go barging in and say we're the Hardys boys looking for a thief!"

"That's been taken care of," his father assured him. "Two students who won scholarships for Antarctic training have been withdrawn from Outpost I. Your cover story is that you're replacing them temporarily. You've got enough science from Bayport High to fit in without any trouble."

"Just think—investigating at the South Pole!" Joe exclaimed. "We've never done that before!"

Fenton Hardy smiled at his son's enthusiasm. Then he became serious again. "Just remember," he said, "we're going to one of the toughest spots on the globe. Besides being cold, it'll be extremely dangerous!"

9 *Penguin Attack*

Fenton Hardy took a map of the Antarctic and spread it out on his knees.

"You can see that the continent around the South Pole lies almost entirely within the Antarctic Circle," he said to Frank and Joe. "The main exception is the Antarctic Peninsula pushing in the direction of Tierra del Fuego. These two large indentations of the coastline are caused by the Weddell Sea below the Antarctic Peninsula and the Ross Sea on the opposite side of the continent."

"Is Byrd Base near Little America?" Frank asked.

"It's about two hundred miles up the coast, on the Ross Shelf, which connects the Ross Sea and the

Antarctic Continent. We'll be on the continent itself. No neighbors near Byrd Base. A lot of nations have installations in the Antarctic. But it's a big place."

"And it's peaceful," Joe commented. "We learned that when we were studying about the International Geophysical Year in school. All the nations agreed not to fight over claims in the Antarctic."

The three Hardys began discussing the heroic days of exploration in the area, especially the race to the South Pole between Roald Amundsen of Norway and Robert Scott of Great Britain.

"Amundsen reached the pole first," Frank said. "That was in 1911, before the days of radio communication, and Scott knew nothing about it until he and his men got to the South Pole and found Amundsen's flag flying over it."

"Then the members of the Scott expedition were lost in a desperate trek back from the pole," Joe added. "Later, their bodies were found by a rescue team. Scott's diary tells the story."

"And of course you know about Admiral Richard E. Byrd, who established Little America and pioneered the use of airplanes in the Antarctic," Mr. Hardy spoke up. "Byrd and another pilot, Bernt Balchen, were the first to fly over the South Pole."

"We could go on forever talking about Antarctic

exploration," Frank said. "But I think I'll catch a little shuteye."

"Good idea," Joe agreed. "I'm bushed myself from all this traveling." He leaned back in his seat and soon all were asleep.

When they woke up, they looked out the window at the cold gray billows of the Polar Sea. An icebreaker, which seemed like a toy ship far below, was slowly cutting a path through ice several feet thick.

The plane crossed the water and land appeared. Tall, windswept mountains came into view. From their foothills, a grim wasteland of ice and snow broken by glaciers extended into the distance.

"Looks pretty desolate out there," Frank said.

Just then, the pilot came down the aisle and stopped in front of the boys. "I'm Captain Roeloffs," he introduced himself. "I understand you boys are student scientists. Perhaps you'd like to come into the cockpit and see what the Antarctic is like from there."

"We sure would," Frank and Joe said at once.

"Follow me, then," the pilot said. He led the way up the aisle into the cockpit. The copilot grinned a greeting as the Hardys slipped into the two seats behind him. Roeloffs sat down in his chair. "We're on automatic pilot," he said, "and we'll stay that way until we reach the South Pole."

Frank was studying a map of the Antarctic. "If we fly to the pole, won't it be to the left of the Ross Ice Shelf? Won't we miss Byrd Base?"

"We're dropping supplies to the Amundsen-Scott Station at the pole," the pilot explained. "After that, we'll turn right to Byrd Base."

The plane thundered on over a bleak landscape, and the Hardys could see directly ahead to the Transantarctic Mountains, a long chain of rugged peaks extending from one side of the continent to the other. As they crossed the mountains, deep valleys and enormous glaciers came into view.

"Want to go backpacking down there?'" Frank kidded his brother.

"It would be too easy," Joe quipped. "I like the real outdoors, like the Bayport Woods!"

Some huts became visible, and men emerged running toward the plane and waving their arms.

"Boys," Roeloffs said as he switched off the automatic control and began to fly the craft himself, "we're now at the South Pole!"

"Looks just like the rest of the snow," Frank observed.

"We don't need a compass now," Joe commented. "From here, every direction is north."

The plane circled over the Amundsen–Scott Station. Crates of supplies went out the cargo door, plummeted toward the snow, and pulled up sharply as their parachutes opened. They drifted down to where the men from the huts were waiting to pick them up.

The copilot, who had been talking to the station by radio, said a farewell. Then the plane turned away from the pole and headed for the Ross Ice Shelf.

When they arrived, Roeloffs cut the power and the plane landed on a frozen runway at Byrd Base.

The passengers filed out in the direction of a two-story building with wings extending to the rear on either side. It was made of prefabricated boards attached to a steel frame. A helicopter equipped with skis stood near a number of Antarctic vehicles such as motor toboggans and Sno-Cats.

About twenty men were handling the vehicles, conducting weather experiments, or collecting samples of ice and snow. They wore heavy clothing and waved at the new arrivals, who hurried in out of the frigid cold. The commander of Byrd Base greeted them in the main room. He held a list of names in his hand.

"I'm Admiral Ian Langton," he announced. "If you'll gather around, I'll tell you what your assignments are."

"We'll stay out of this," Fenton Hardy said to his sons in an undertone. "We're on a secret mission, so we'll talk to the admiral later."

The other men received their instructions and left to settle in and get to work. When the last one had disappeared, the Bayport sleuth introduced himself and the boys.

"I'm glad to see you," Langton said. "Come to my office and we'll discuss your mission. All I know is that the navy's keeping it under wraps."

In the office, Fenton Hardy described his discovery of a gang of thieves operating at American naval bases. "Clues indicate that the ringleader is here at Byrd Base," he explained. "My assignment is to find out who he is. Frank and Joe will help with the investigation."

The admiral shook his head. "It's hard for me to believe the ringleader is one of my men. But of course we've only been here a short time. I don't know all of them yet. Anyway, I received orders from the navy to bring a couple of student scientists back from Outpost I. I suppose you can tell me why."

"The man we're looking for might be at Outpost I," Fenton Hardy replied. "Frank and Joe will replace the students. I will stay here at Byrd Base in the guise of a scientist assigned to see how the labs are working."

"Since you three are using science as a cover story," Langton said, "I'd better introduce you to my scientific advisor, Professor Sigmund Muller. Come with me."

The admiral led the way to an office where a desk was piled high with reports and documents. Muller sat in a chair behind the desk writing in a notebook. He had gray hair and wore steel-rimmed glasses. Langton introduced the Hardys, and he gave them a warm greeting. The admiral then explained the secret mission that had brought them to Byrd Base.

"Oh, no!" Muller exclaimed. "How could the ringleader of a gang of thieves be among us?"

"I only got on to him by a process of elimination," Fenton Hardy explained. "I found it hard to believe he would operate out of the Antarctic. But every other possibility failed, which means he must be stationed at Byrd Base or Outpost I."

"If that's the case, I'm glad you're here," said Muller in a hearty tone. "I'll pretend you're new members of my scientific team."

"Sigmund, why don't you show Frank and Joe around?" Langton suggested.

"I'll be glad to," Muller agreed as the admiral and Fenton Hardy returned to Langton's office. Muller took the boys into one wing of the building, which housed the science department of the base.

In the first laboratory, a number of long columns

of frozen earth were laid out on a table side by side. Several men were working on them.

"These are core samples from the crust of the Antarctic Continent," Muller explained. "They tell us about the age of the Antarctic. We know it's been here for many millions of years."

In other laboratories, scientists were carrying out experiments in physics and chemistry. An aquarium held fish from the Antarctic Sea. Storerooms oocupied the end of the wing. They were filled with scientific instruments, samples of earth and rock, and stuffed birds, seals, and fish.

Muller introduced Frank and Joe to the staff as they moved from one room to another. The Hardys kept their eyes open for clues, but saw nothing to indicate that a crook was hiding at Byrd Base.

Finally Muller pointed to piles of heavy clothing on the shelves of a storeroom. "Now you'd better get into these," he said. "We're going outside."

"I don't see any furs," Joe commented as they dressed.

Their host laughed. "People wore furs back in the days of Admiral Byrd. Today we have special clothing designed by navy experts. You'll find those parkas as warm as a sealskin coat, and much lighter and more comfortable."

Pulling the hoods of their jackets over their heads, the three emerged from the building. A cold wind blew in their faces and momentarily took their breath away.

A meteorologist atop a steel scaffolding was knocking ice off a weathervane to allow the instrument to move freely in the wind. Other workers were releasing a weather balloon, which drifted upward, blowing wildly to and fro.

"The balloon is filled with helium," the leader of the group explained. "It'll reach the upper atmosphere and tell us how the winds blow around the South Pole. The temperature sometimes hits one hundred below zero."

After some discussion of the eons during which the Antarctic turned from a warm area into a frigid wilderness, Muller conducted the Hardys on a walk through the snow down to the shore. They stopped at a point where a cliff dipped in rugged contours into water filled with ice floes.

On one side, the terrain rose and fell in a series of low hills. On the other side, it stretched out in a level plain where the Hardys could see moving black patches against the white background of the ice.

"Penguins!" Frank and Joe exclaimed in unison.

"Come on for a closer look," Muller invited.

The three walked down into the penguin rookery. It contained hundreds of the black and white Antarctic birds. Some were roosting on the ice, others waddled around in an upright position, still others dived into the water.

The waddling birds made the Hardys laugh. Joe pointed to a penguin about three feet tall advancing toward them. Its color pattern gave it the appearance of wearing a white shirt and black coat. It moved in a shuffling walk.

"That one's as funny as a clown at the circus," Joe commented. "I think I'll take a picture of it."

He pulled his miniature camera out of his pocket. Moving forward, he dropped to one knee and started to focus on the approaching bird.

Suddenly the penguin thrust its neck forward and opened its beak menacingly. It rushed forward with an angry cackle, and Joe began to retreat. Just then he slipped on the ice and lost his footing, falling right in the angry penguin's path!

10 The Sno-Cat

The penguin snapped at Joe with its beak and flailed at him with its stubby wings before he could finally scramble clear and retreat.

"Saved by the bell!" Frank laughed. "Want to go a few more rounds with the champ, Joe?"

The younger Hardy boy gingerly tested a sore spot on his nose where the penguin had nipped him. "No thanks!" he groaned. "I'm hanging up the gloves after this one. What got into that critter anyway, Professor?"

Muller chuckled. "They're usually tame, Joe. This one must be an exception."

"That penguin got up on the wrong side of the nest this morning," Frank quipped, "and he just didn't want to have his picture taken."

"Let's look at the Antarctic vehicles," Muller suggested.

The three walked over to the helicopter. The Hardys noted it was just like the choppers they had flown at Bayport airfield except for the skis.

"That's the way to travel down here," Frank said. "No mushing over the snow."

Muller nodded but cautioned, "If you boys ever go up, look out for the wind. You might get blown off course."

"We'll watch out," Joe promised. "Who wants to crash-land at the South Pole?"

"Anyway, we do most of our traveling in these vehicles," Muller continued. He pointed to the machines standing near the helicopter. "Motor toboggans and Sno-Cats."

The toboggans were long, narrow vehicles, open on all sides but protected from the Antarctic blast by a windshield mounted on the front. They were propelled by a motor connected to revolving chains with cleats on either side. The cleats biting into the ice diminished the danger that the chains would spin instead of moving the toboggan.

The Sno-Cats looked like trucks for hauling heavy cargo except that the four wheels were replaced by tractor treads.

"This is the workhorse of the Antarctic," Muller commented. "It has four-wheel drive—or I should say, four-tread drive. Each tread can be operated independently, enabling the driver to maneuver over rocky terrain, through deep snow, and past crevasses where one tread may be hanging over the edge. Well, now you've seen all our equipment. We might as well go in."

The pleasant aroma of cooking wafted from the galley as they entered, and the chef beat on a small, copper gong.

"Chow time!" he called out.

The scientists and naval personnel began streaming into the dining room where long wooden tables were laid with dishes and cutlery. The men sat on makeshift benches made of planks nailed to crossbars extending from the tables at each end.

The Hardys found themselves sitting next to a youth about their own age.

"I'm Bob Field," he introduced himself. "I'm a freshman with a scholarship in geology, so I'm spending a year at Byrd Base. Actually, I was at Outpost I, but they ordered me and another student to come back here."

Frank and Joe questioned him about his work at Outpost I.

"How long were you there?" Frank asked. "My brother Joe and I find it pretty bleak in this icy desert. I bet after a while it gets to you."

"It does," Bob admitted. "But the work's extremely interesting. I've been doing research on core samples. We're using the uranium method."

"We're familiar with that," Frank said. "All rocks contain uranium, which turns into lead at a very slow, steady pace."

"And the amount of uranium in relation to the amount of lead gives you a fix on the age of the sample," Joe added.

The three continued a lively discussion of Antarctic rocks. Then Frank asked Bob if he did anything else at the base.

"Part-time radioman," was the reply.

"What kind of messages do you send? High-level technical information?"

"No. Just routine stuff—reports to navy ships in the Ross Sea, weather warnings to other Antarctic bases, things like that."

"Could we watch you work sometime?"

"Oh, I'm sure it wouldn't interest you."

After the meal was over, the Hardys went to a corner of the lounge to discuss the situation.

"What did Bob mean by saying we wouldn't be interested in his radio messages?" Joe wondered. "He sounded to me like he was afraid we might discover something."

"Could be," Frank responded. "As a radioman, he would be in a position to communicate with gang

94

members on other bases. We'd better keep an eye on him."

"He could hardly be the ringleader, though," Joe said. "I would think it takes more than a college freshman to run a gang of thieves spread out all over the world."

Fenton Hardy joined them, and they reported to him their suspicion of Bob Field.

"I'll keep an eye on him," their father promised. "You boys will be pushing off for Outpost I tomorrow. Any delay would look suspicious. Report to Professor Muller in the morning."

"Dad, have you spotted any clues?" Joe asked.

Fenton Hardy shook his head. "Nothing yet. But I'll keep checking while you two are investigating at Outpost I. I don't want to go into it now because we shouldn't be seen with our heads together too much. The ringleader of the gang might figure out what we're up to."

He rose to his feet and walked off. Frank and Joe picked a couple of books from the library shelves and read until it was time to turn in with the rest of the men. They all slept in one room, where each had a locker at the foot of the bed and hooks on the wall to hang clothes.

Bob Field had a bed next to the Hardys. As he was hanging up his shirt, Joe noticed a piece of paper in the breast pocket. The sheet was fine enough for Joe to see the word "radiogram" in reverse on the other side.

"That could be a message Bob's sending for the ringleader!" the boy thought excitedly. "I'd better have a look at it."

Joe waited until Bob and the rest were sound asleep, then he silently slipped out of his bed. He retrieved a pencil flashlight from his jacket pocket, stealthily edged over to Bob's clothes, and eased the paper out of the breast pocket of the shirt. Slowly and carefully, to avoid making any noise, he opened the paper and played the beam of his flashlight on it.

The message was:

TO SUPPLY SHIP *BALCHEN*. REQUEST MORE CANNED PEAS. STORES RUNNING LOW. SIGNED IAN LANGTON, ADMIRAL, USN.

Grinning in the darkness, Joe pushed the paper back into Bob's shirt pocket. He doused his flashlight, returned to his bed, and fell asleep.

In the morning, he took the first opportunity to tell Frank about the night's episode.

"Great detective work!" Frank laughed. "You set out to expose a crook and ended up with an order for canned peas!"

Joe nodded sheepishly. "Well, let's see if anything is cooking in the admiral's quarters."

The boys left the dormitory and found their father with Langton.

"I don't have a break in the case yet," Fenton Hardy told them. "You two go to Outpost I. We can communicate by radio if anything develops."

"How do we get there?" Frank inquired.

"By Sno-Cat," Langton replied. "You'll be traveling by yourselves because the route's quite easy to follow. Now, report to Professor Muller. He'll explain the details."

Frank and Joe walked down the corridor to Muller's office. The scientific advisor was shuffling papers on his desk.

"Here's what you need to get to Outpost I safely," he said and pulled a map out of his desk drawer. "This will show you where Outpost I is located."

He took a pen and made a cross on the map. "Go directly toward the inland mountain with two peaks," Muller advised, "then you stop at the large glacier at the base of the mountain. Turn west, go twenty miles, and you'll see the outpost on a broad plain of ice and snow."

He handed the map to Frank. "It really isn't very far and it's easy to find."

"What's it like?" Joe queried.

"It's made up of two small, wooden buildings.

You'll see an American flag flying from a pole out front. I'll have our radioman send them a message to expect you. All that remains now is your transportation. Come on outside."

The Hardys' Sno-Cat was ready. Antarctic clothing for them had been stowed in a compartment opposite the steering wheel, and the back of the vehicle was filled with crates of food. More provisions were lashed to a heavy sled tied to the rear of the Sno-Cat by a stout rope.

"These are supplies for the outpost," Muller explained. "You're to deliver them to Commander Noonan, who's in charge. Then you'll join the crew as student scientists and see if you can break the case you're on."

"We'd like to say good-bye to our father," Frank said.

"Sure," Muller said. "He's probably in the admiral's office. Go on inside. You can leave your things out here."

The boys put their overnight bags in the Sno-Cat and laid the map on the dashboard. Then they went to see the admiral and Mr. Hardy.

"Good luck, boys," the investigator said. "Make notes on everything that you find suspicious. I'll contact you later and we'll talk about it."

"Sure thing, Dad," Frank said and the boys shook hands with the two men. Then they went outside again and climbed into the Sno-Cat, waving to a few crew members who were watching them.

Frank started the motor. The treads of the vehicle began turning, and the rope grew taut in the rear as the heavy sled started to move.

"Here we go into the wilderness," Joe said with a wry grin. "Left out in the cold, so to speak."

"What I'd like to know," his brother said, squinting his eyes against the whiteness around him, "is—will we find what we're looking for?"

11 Lost in the Antarctic

The Sno-Cat clanked forward over the ice and the powdery snow. Occasionally, the treads ground over outcroppings of rock with a harsh, metallic sound. An hour passed.

"The motor's purring like a kitten," Frank observed.

"Good thing, Frank. If we stall, it's a long walk back to Byrd Base!"

Joe took a pair of binoculars from the glove compartment and focused on the terrain up ahead. "I see the mountain with the two peaks," he announced. Measuring the angle with his compass, he added, "Two degrees to the left, Frank, and you'll be on the beam."

"Okay."

Soon, they could see the mountain with their naked eyes. It rose like a solitary sentinel in the distance. There was no sign of life anywhere, no animals on the ground or birds in the sky.

"It's eerie out here," Joe commented as he gazed at the wilderness. A snowstorm was approaching.

"At least there's no parking problem," Frank joked.

The Sno-Cat rumbled forward through howling wind and falling snow. Hitting a slippery patch of ice, Frank had to use his four-wheel drive as first one tread and then another began to spin because it could not get a grip on the ice.

The Hardys crossed this slippery area and kept going until they reached the mountain. There Frank brought the Sno-Cat to a halt.

"Joe, do you see the glacier?" he asked.

Joe shook his head. "It must be on the other side. Let's see."

Starting the engine again, Frank drove around the base of the mountain. They strained their eyes to see if they could make out the glacier through the wind and snow.

Suddenly they felt the Sno-Cat moving sideways!

"We're *on* the glacier!" Frank shouted.

Desperately, he threw the vehicle into reverse. The moving river of ice caught it and spun it in a semicircle. They swung toward the end of the glacier where a tumbled mass of ice blocks threatened to crush them!

At the last moment, helped by the weight of the sled behind, the left rear tread caught on solid terrain. Frank quickly flipped the switch that fed all the power to that tread, and the Sno-Cat moved backward, pushing the sled as it went. Then the right rear tread gripped the ground. This permitted the vehicle to back all the way off the glacier.

Frank wiped perspiration from his brow. "Wow!" he gasped. "That's the first time I ever drove sideways!"

Joe chuckled, trying to overcome the fear he had felt only seconds before. "You just won your Sno-Cat driver's license."

"Anyway, we found the glacier, and are on the last leg of this trip."

"Right," Joe said. "Now go west for twenty miles."

He took a compass reading, and they clanked forward over hills and down into valleys. Checking his instruments, Frank counted off the miles.

"Twenty!" he said at last.

"We should reach Outpost I at any moment," Joe said, again resorting to the binoculars for a better view ahead. However, all he could see was endless ice and snow.

They rolled on and on, and the snow stopped falling. Now the terrain became more level.

After a while, Frank spoke up. "Maybe we bypassed the place. We could have missed it in the snowstorm. See if you can raise them on the radio, Joe. They can guide us in."

Joe took the receiver from the dashboard and flicked the "on" button. However, no sound came from the instrument! He banged it with the heel of his hand, but to no avail. Then he opened the back to check the batteries. The case was empty!

"No batteries!" Joe groaned. "How did that happen?" He quickly searched the cabin for spares, but there were none. "The guy who fixed the Sno-Cat for us must have forgotten them. What a mistake!"

"Let's look at the map Muller gave us," Frank suggested. "Maybe we made a mistake, too."

Joe picked up the map and unfolded it. Then he gasped. "The cross Muller made to indicate the outpost's location isn't there!" he cried out.

"What!" Frank stopped the Sno-Cat and stared at the map.

"Someone must have changed maps on us," Joe said. "While we were inside saying good-bye to Dad and Admiral Langton."

"Same guy who swiped the radio batteries," Frank added. "It figures."

"No, it doesn't," Joe insisted. "I remember Muller said to turn west at the glacier, and that's what we did!"

"Are you sure he didn't say east?"

"Yes—well—I thought he said west."

Frank pointed to a small hill to the right. "Let's climb up there and take our bearings. I'll maneuver as close as I can get."

He drove forward toward the hill. Suddenly, the snow gave way under the right front tread! He cut the engine instantly, but the Sno-Cat tilted up on end and the tread hung over empty air! The Hardys stared down into an icy crevasse hundreds of feet deep!

They shivered as they realized that any movement might cause the vehicle to lose its balance and topple over the edge, hurtling them to the bottom of the crevasse!

"We can't take a chance and climb out," Frank muttered. "I'll have to see if I can drive us out of this corner. Keep your fingers crossed, Joe!"

Carefully, he turned on the motor and put the vehicle into reverse. It teetered on the edge of the crevasse while the Hardys held their breath. Then the two treads still on firm snow took hold and rolled the Sno-Cat to a point where gravity took over and dragged the vehicle onto its third tread.

The fourth still hung over the crevasse, but Frank was now able to drive back and let it regain its normal position.

He mopped his forehead with a handkerchief. "We're driving an obstacle course!" he groaned. "This is very dangerous!"

"I know," Joe said grimly. "Well, we're close enough to walk to the top of the hill. Let's hope we can spot Outpost I from there."

He took the heavy Antarctic clothing from the compartment behind them. They donned thick leather boots, rough trousers, parkas, and fur gloves. Pulling goggles over their eyes, they emerged from the Sno-Cat into a high wind.

They roped themselves together. Using alpen-stocks—wooden staffs with metal tips—to help them keep their footing, they set out for the hill with Frank in the lead.

At every step, they tested the snow with their alpenstocks to make sure it was strong enough to support them. Skirting past the crevasse into which they had nearly fallen, they tramped along under a sky the dismal color of lead. The sun was barely discernible over their heads, and the only sound they could hear was the wind and their own footsteps.

Reaching the bottom of the hill, the Hardys

began to climb it step by step, sometimes over snow and ice, sometimes over the frozen earth and rock of the Antarctic. They gasped in the frigid air.

About halfway up, they came to a rocky ledge, where they stopped for a rest, discussing their predicament.

"Unless we took the wrong turn, Outpost I has to be in sight from the top of the hill!" Frank declared. "Even if we bypassed it in the storm, we can't have missed it by much."

"Right," Joe said. He made sure the rope connecting them was securely tied before they resumed their climb. It was a difficult ascent because they had to feel with their alpenstocks for places where they could get safe toeholds. The cold wind blowing in their faces made them lean into it in order to maintain their balance.

As they rounded a rocky wall, Frank stepped onto an icy cliff. At the same time, a violent gust made him stagger to one side. He slipped and skidded along the ice toward the side of the cliff, dragging Joe after him!

Then, finding nothing to break his momentum, he went right over the edge!

Suddenly Joe came to a bone-crunching halt as his boot soles slammed against an outcropping of rock protruding from the ice. The rope around his

waist tightened as it stopped Frank's fall down the face of the cliff!

"Frank, hang on!" Joe yelled.

"I've got my foot on a rock sticking out of the side," Frank called back. "I can climb up if you help me."

"Will do!"

Joe yanked on the rope with all his might. He played it in, hand over hand, so Frank could brace his feet against the side of the cliff and work his way back to the ledge. Then both sat down gasping for breath.

"It's good we're tied together, or I'd been at the bottom of the cliff," Frank muttered.

Joe peered over the edge. "Well, our alpenstocks are down there. I can see them lying in the snow."

"They'll stay there, Joe. I'm not about to go and get them!"

"Neither am I. Let's make tracks up the hill, okay?"

Getting to their feet, they again climbed toward the top. They moved more slowly and carefully than before because they no longer had their alpenstocks with which to feel for the safest path upward. Finally the slant of the hill became less steep, and they struggled to the summit.

Planting their feet firmly and bracing themselves against the wind, the Hardys surveyed the terrain all around them. They saw an expanse of ice and snow extending to the horizon in every direction except to the west, where a range of mountains cut the skyline in a series of tall peaks. No buildings, no flagpole, broke the uniformity of the white landscape.

The Hardys stared at one another in dismay as the meaning became clear to them.

"We're lost!" Joe exclaimed. "We might never find our way out of here!"

12 Two Suspects

Joe took the binoculars and looked around. He saw only ice, snow, and mountains. "What do we do now?" he wondered.

The wind was becoming stronger and colder, and the boys struggled to keep their feet on the hilltop. Shivering, they pulled their parka hoods across their faces for protection.

"Let's go back to the Sno-Cat," Frank said. "At least it's warm."

They made their way down the hill, which was easier than climbing up. Carefully they inched along the icy ledge where Frank had fallen, circled past the crevasse that threatened them, and got into the Sno-Cat, where they removed their Antarctic gear.

"There's no use continuing west," Joe pointed out. "We'd only end up in the mountains. Anyway, Outpost I isn't out there."

"We don't have enough gas to get back to Byrd Base," Frank observed. "And we sure don't want to get stranded. But if west isn't the right direction, then Muller must have said east."

"Right," Joe said. "Unless he sent us in the wrong direction deliberately, hoping our Sno-Cat would fall into the crevasse and we'd never be found!"

"He could have exchanged the map while we were talking to Dad and the admiral. This way there would be no proof," Frank added grimly.

Joe nodded. "And he might have snitched the batteries so we couldn't contact anyone."

Frank started the engine, and they drove back along the route they had taken. Spotting the mountain with the two peaks, they reached the glacier where the Sno-Cat had nearly been swept away. Twenty miles of travel beyond that point over the frozen terrain brought them within view of a tall flagpole flying the stars and stripes. Two small wooden buildings stood nearby, one bearing a sign reading: U.S. NAVY OUTPOST I.

"Boy, am I glad we made it!" Frank said, looking at the gas gauge. "We couldn't have gone much farther!"

Seven men were working with polar equipment

in front of the installation. One of them came up as Frank stopped the Sno-Cat and the Hardys got out.

"I'm Commander Noonan," he said. "Welcome to Outpost I. You must be the Hardy boys."

Frank and Joe shook hands with Noonan, but did not tell him that they almost had not made it.

"We'd like to radio Byrd Base and tell our father that we've arrived," Frank said instead.

"Sure thing," Noonan replied. "I'll have my radioman show you the equipment. He'll be here in a moment. Meanwhile, let me introduce you to my crew."

The men were scientists working on the geology and meteorology of the Antarctic.

"Stones and storms," Joe quipped.

"That's our subject." Noonan laughed. "We're big on weather reports."

An eighth man emerged from one of the buildings. He was short and thin. He glanced around uneasily as he walked up to the group.

"Al Ambrose, meet Frank and Joe Hardy." Noonan introduced them. "Al's our radioman."

Ambrose looked at the Hardys in astonishment. His eyes widened and his mouth fell open. However, with some effort he managed to regain his composure.

"He's worried about something," Joe thought. "And he's not glad to see us."

Noonan ordered Ambrose to show the Hardys to the living quarters of Outpost I. "Then take them to the radio shack. They want to send a message to Byrd Base."

"Impossible, sir," Ambrose replied quickly. "The radio's out. I'm trying to find the bug in the equipment."

"Well, let them know as soon as you have it fixed. Now, the three of you better go in."

The radioman conducted the Hardys into one of the buildings. "This is our living quarters," he informed them. "The other structure is for the technical work. I've got my radio shack over there."

A corridor led from the door to the rear of the building. Flanking the hallway at the front were a number of storerooms on either side. Then came the kitchen facing the dining room and living room, followed by an infirmary and a small gym complete with exercycle.

At the end of the corridor, the dormitory occupied most of the width of the building. Ten cots stood in two rows along the walls. The remaining space was taken up by the private room of the commander.

Ambrose pointed to the two cots nearest the doorway. "These are yours," he told the Hardys. "They belonged to the two students who went back to Byrd Base."

Frank thanked him, then asked in a friendly tone, "What do you think's wrong with your radio, Al?"

"Search me," the young man replied. "I'm trying to find out."

"Need any help? We've had a lot of experience in that field."

"That's all right. I'll handle it myself."

"He doesn't want us to see his equipment," Joe thought. Aloud he said, "Where do you come from in the States?"

"San Diego."

"There's a big naval base in San Diego."

"One of the biggest. Well, you guys are on your own now. I'm going to work on the radio. Tell you when I have it operational." With that, Al left whistling a tune off-key.

Frank looked at Joe. "I bet Muller tipped Ambrose off about the scheme to have us disappear! That's why Al was so surprised to see us. He was hoping we'd be at the bottom of that crevasse way off in the west near the mountains!"

"That means his radio was working earlier today," Joe continued his brother's thought. "I think he's only pretending it's on the blink. Let's sneak into the shack when he's not around and raise Byrd Base!"

"He might put the radio out of commission deliberately, Joe."

"I know. But it's worth a try."

The Hardys went outside to help unload the Sno-Cat and the sled. The crates and boxes were carried into the building and stacked in the storerooms.

By now it was getting dark, and the crew congregated in the living quarters. Ambrose, who doubled as a cook, was heading for the kitchen.

He stopped near the Hardys and said, "The vacuum tubes are gone and there are none in stock. We'll have to wait for Byrd Base to send technical supplies."

"Well, help should be on the way soon," Frank declared. "They probably know by now that our radio is out."

"Let's hope so," Ambrose mumbled and disappeared into the kitchen. While the radioman whipped up a spicy goulash, Frank made his way to the radio shack to check Al's story. He found the sender inoperable as Ambrose had told them, and quickly returned to the living room.

"It's out all right," he reported to Joe. "But I don't know whether it was done deliberately or not."

When the meal was ready, the men filed past a counter at the kitchen door, where Al, wielding a large ladle, filled their plates. Then they entered the dining room, which was just large enough to hold a round table and ten chairs.

Ambrose came in and sat between Frank and Joe.

"This is great goulash," Joe said as he downed a mouthful.

"A bit too hot for me," Frank muttered and took a long drink of water.

"The other guys like it hot," Ambrose explained.

After dinner, the three went into the dorm and talked for a while about the rigors of life in the Antarctic. Frank stretched and yawned. "I think I'll hit the hay," he declared. "I'm bushed."

"It's bedtime for us all," Ambrose stated. "We get up early here, and we need all the sleep we can get."

Frank crawled into his cot and fell sound asleep. One by one the others turned in. Joe noticed Ambrose snap out the overhead light just before he dozed off.

He was awakened in the middle of the night by a hand shaking him. A voice whispered into his ear, "Joe, this is Al Ambrose. Commander Noonan wants to see you. Frank's with him now and he says it's important. Put on your clothes and come along with me."

Instantly wide awake, Joe got off his cot and donned his clothes. Then he followed Al along the corridor, which was dimly lit by a small, yellowish bulb in the ceiling. Reaching the end of the hallway,

Ambrose unbolted the door and opened it. A blast of frigid arctic air rushed in.

Ambrose pointed out the door. "There are Frank and Commander Noonan," he said.

Joe advanced to the doorway and looked out. Suddenly something struck him on the head, and he was pushed out into the snow!

13 Rescued in Time

Joe hit the ground and lay there motionless for a second. Then he struggled to his feet. His head swimming, he pounded on the door, which had locked itself behind him.

"Open up! I can't get in!" he yelled as loud as he could. But the howling wind carried away the sound of his voice, and no one in the back of the building could hear his pounding.

The frigid cold bored through his light clothing and he shivered violently. He felt dizzy and blacked out momentarily, collapsing in the snow.

He came to when a hand slapped his face and a familiar voice shouted, "Joe! Come on, get up!"

The boy opened his eyes and saw his father standing over him!

"We're locked out," Joe muttered weakly.

"It doesn't matter," Fenton Hardy replied. "We'll spend the night in my Sno-Cat."

The Bayport sleuth helped his son across to the vehicle, pushed him in, and followed him into the cabin. The warmth soon brought Joe around. He stared in surprise when he saw his brother huddled in a corner with a blanket around him.

"Frank! How'd you get here?"

"Same as you," Frank responded. "I bet Ambrose told you Noonan wanted to see you, and then conked you on the head."

Joe nodded. "He figured he could get rid of both of us this way. In the morning, everyone would have thought we went outside and locked ourselves out by mistake."

"But Dad, what about you?" Frank inquired.

"I arrived just at the right time," Mr. Hardy replied. "I saw Frank being kicked out the door, so I brought him in here. Then Al pulled the same trick on you."

"What made you come to Outpost I?" Joe asked, while covering himself with a blanket his father handed him.

"Since I couldn't raise you on the radio, I decided to see whether you had arrived safely."

"We almost didn't," Frank said and reported what happened. "I think Muller sent us the wrong way deliberately!" he added.

"That only confirms my suspicion of him," Mr. Hardy said. "Here's what I found out. Muller wrote Admiral Langton a memo shortly after he arrived. Langton read it and put it in his desk. When he took it out the next morning, the writing had disappeared! He thought he must have made a mistake and put a blank sheet of paper in his desk. Since it was unimportant, he didn't pursue the matter."

"Muller wrote the note in disappearing ink," Frank concluded.

"Yes. The story interested me because a navy lab where Muller worked previously used pens containing disappearing ink for security reasons. But no one's authorized to take those pens anywhere else. Apparently Muller brought a few when he came here. I felt he might have wanted them to write messages for the theft ring."

"But why would he use such a pen on Langton's memo?" Joe inquired.

"He made a mistake," his father said. "I also found out he was stationed in San Diego for a while, and I suspect this was the headquarters of the gang for a long time."

"Al Ambrose is from San Diego!" Frank cried out.

Mr. Hardy nodded. "When the two got leery about being caught, they volunteered for service in the Antarctic. Now Muller is running the operation from here. I wasn't convinced that my theory was correct until I came here."

"You're right on target, Dad. When we left Byrd Base, Muller marked the location of Outpost I on our map. Later, the mark disappeared. We know the mark was in the wrong place to mislead us."

"We must have Muller arrested at once!" Joe urged.

"I've been working on that," his father said. "Unfortunately, the man left on an army transport plane for Punta Arenas this morning. Admiral Langton tells me it's all on the level, and that Muller was to go to San Diego on official business. But I suspect he'll use the opportunity to escape. Once we arrived on the scene, he must have sensed he was in great danger of being discovered. That's why he tried to get you two out of the way as fast as he could. I doubt he'll ever arrive in San Diego, but if he does, he'll be arrested."

"He must have radioed Al Ambrose before he left," Frank surmised. "Then, when we got here, Al realized that Muller's scheme to get rid of us had failed. So he tried on his own."

Mr. Hardy nodded. "We'll confront Ambrose

with the evidence in the morning. Right now I suggest we all get some sleep."

The trio huddled together, putting on every bit of clothing they could find to keep from freezing. Mr. Hardy turned the engine on every so often to warm up the cabin, but the rest of the night was far from comfortable for the Bayport sleuths.

In the morning, one of the men spotted the Sno-Cat through the window, and opened the door for them. After taking off their heavy clothing, they went into the dining room, where the crew of Outpost I was just arriving for breakfast.

Al Ambrose came in with a steaming pot of coffee. When he saw the Hardy boys, he stared at them as if they were ghosts, and the pot almost fell out of his hand.

"Morning, Al," Joe greeted him. "I can sure go for some ham and eggs."

"Especially after you kicked us out the door last night and we almost froze to death," Frank added. "If our father hadn't arrived in time, both Joe and I wouldn't be alive this morning!"

Ambrose gulped and began to tremble. Commander Noonan stared at him in surprise, then turned to the Hardys. "What on earth are you boys talking about?"

"I suggest that you put this man under arrest for

attempted murder of my sons, to which I was a witness," Mr. Hardy spoke up. "Then I'll tell you why I'm here."

Al dropped the coffee pot on the table and tried to run out of the room.

"Stop!" Noonan commanded. "Where do you think you're going? Out into the cold?"

Al realized that there was no way to escape. He meekly submitted to being handcuffed and was led out of the dining room.

The commander and Mr. Hardy disappeared into Noonan's private quarters and the detective reported what had happened. Noonan was dumbfounded and regretted deeply that one of his men was involved in the theft ring. An hour later, the three Hardys were on their way back to Byrd Base.

The Bayport detective drove his Sno-Cat with Ambrose locked in the rear. Frank and Joe followed in the vehicle they had brought to Outpost I.

Joe, who was at the wheel, commented, "It sure is easier going back than it was coming out. Of course, we know where we're going this time, and we have a better driver. Me."

"Don't run through a red light!" Frank quipped. "You might lose your Sno-Cat license."

When the group reached Byrd Base, Ambrose was taken into Admiral Langton's headquarters.

The young man confessed to being in league with Muller. He did not know, however, where Muller had gone.

"We tracked down the plane he was to take out of Punta Arenas," Langton said. "Apparently he never made the connection and disappeared."

"Well, it seems I have my next assignment cut out for me," Mr. Hardy said with a smile.

Langton nodded. "We're counting on you to find the man," he confirmed.

"Can we help?" Frank asked.

Mr. Hardy shook his head. "I can handle it on my own. Why don't you two go back to Santiago and see what you can find out about Julio Santana."

"We'll be glad to supply your transportation," Admiral Langton offered. "You've been a great help to us, and I regret that your lives were in such danger while you were here."

Frank grinned. "That's happened before," he said. "It's part of the job."

Early the next morning, the Hardy boys arrived in Punta Arenas. Before going any further, they decided to get in touch with Bertrand. The antique dealer told them that Santana had not been found yet.

"The police have had no luck so far," Bertrand said. "We're up against a blank wall. If you want to try again, why don't you come here and see what you can do?"

"We will," Frank promised. "But first we'd like to do a little sleuthing in Punta Arenas. Santana might be back here on his job as an oil driller."

After finishing the conversation with Bertrand, Frank called the local authorities and the company Santana had worked for. Nobody had seen or heard from the Easter Islander.

"What'll we do now?" Joe asked.

"We might as well go back to Santiago," Frank advised.

While waiting for a connecting flight, the boys walked through the lobby. Suddenly, Frank grabbed Joe by the elbow and pointed to a row of seats at the end of the room facing the wall. Two dark men were sitting on the aisle with passengers near them. They had their heads together and were holding an intense conversation.

"That's Santana!" Frank hissed. "And the other one's the guy who helped him overturn the bridge when we nearly fell into the gorge!"

14 Airport Chase

"What do you think he's doing in Punta Arenas?"
Joe whispered.

Frank shrugged. "Let's follow him. Maybe we'll
find out."

Adopting a casual air, the Hardys strolled across
the waiting room, bought newspapers, and sat down
behind Santana and his companion. They raised
their papers as if reading, and strained their ears to
hear what was being said.

However, the men were speaking Spanish in
such low tones that the only thing they could make
out was *Isla de Pascua*, which Frank knew meant
Easter Island.

Suddenly Santana rose to his feet and walked past

the Hardys without noticing them. They got up and followed him through the waiting room, screening themselves by mingling with the crowd and staying just close enough to watch him.

Santana walked to the elevator, where he punched the button for the mezzanine. Realizing he was going up one flight, the boys immediately ran up the stairs. They positioned themselves against a low wall overlooking the waiting room, again shielded by their newspapers, and waited to see what would happen.

The elevator door opened and Santana emerged, walking over to a row of lockers. He took a key from his pocket, opened one, and removed a leather case. Then he walked away.

"Maybe he has the idol in there!" Joe hissed.

The boys hurried after the man, who seemed to sense their presence and looked back over his shoulder. When he recognized them, he rushed to the opposite side of the wall overlooking the waiting room. Frank and Joe followed, but at that moment, passengers flooded into the mezzanine from a plane that had just landed. The crowd crossed between the boys and Santana, who raced to the wall, called out something in Spanish, and tossed the case to his companion below in the waiting room.

The man caught it, clasped it tightly under his arm, and ran out an exit, while Santana headed for the stairs on the opposite side of the mezzanine.

Still held up by the crowd, Frank and Joe followed as fast as they could.

When they reached the stairs, they could see the fugitive going through a revolving door leading to the runways outside. Vaulting down the stairway, they dashed to the door, only to be stopped by two small children who got there first. They wedged themselves in with their mother behind them and moved the door slowly.

At last, the boys found themselves outside the terminal. Many planes were being serviced and a few were taxiing into position for takeoff. One was coming in for a landing.

A small craft stood on the nearest strip. On its side were stenciled the words *Inca Chief.* The Hardys could see the pilot preparing to leave.

"He's Santana's pal!" Joe gasped.

A passenger, whose face they could not distinguish, sat behind the man. Santana, running at top speed, reached the plane while the pilot revved the motor. He jumped in and slammed the door shut, then tapped his friend on the shoulder, pointing through the window at Frank and Joe. Obviously, he was telling his friend to hurry. At once, the plane began to move. A rush of exhaust fumes and dust deluged the boys as they raced up. Then the craft gathered speed, became airborne, and zoomed off into the sky!

The boys stopped in disgust and watched it vanish into the clouds.

"We've lost him again," said Joe. "He's as slippery as an eel in Barmet Bay."

"Let's see if we can find out where he's going," Frank suggested. "The pilot had to file a flight plan with air traffic control."

They went into the control tower, where the man in charge spoke several languages, including English. Frank explained that the Santiago police were looking for the man in the *Inca Chief*, and asked for the plane's destination.

The official consulted the records. "According to the flight plan filed by Pedro Morena, the pilot, the *Inca Chief* is headed for Easter Island," he told them.

Thanking him, the Hardys went back to the terminal, and Frank phoned the police. The lieutenant they had spoken to earlier listened to his report on Santana.

"I will radio Easter Island at once," he promised. "Santana will be arrested as soon as his plane lands."

"Now what'll we do?" Joe asked after his brother had hung up.

"We'll try to get a flight to Easter Island," Frank said. "But first, let's tell Bertrand what happened."

The antique dealer was disappointed that Santana had escaped again, but agreed with the boys that they should follow him.

"I know Easter Island," he said, "so I can tell you what to do. Fly into Hanga Roa, the capital. Stay at the Hanga Roa Hotel, and go to the governor's residence and tell him why you're there. He'll help you with everything."

"Santana and his buddy should be in the lockup when we get there," Frank observed.

"I hope so!" Bertrand said fervently. "You boys have to retrieve our idol!"

Since there were no commercial flights to Easter Island, Frank and Joe found a charter pilot who was willing to take them. Before boarding, Joe bought a guidebook on Easter Island, while Frank selected a copy of Thor Heyerdahl's *Aku-Aku*.

"Easter Island's more than two thousand miles off the coast of Chile," Joe said. "From down here, it'll be even farther. We're in for a long flight."

After the pilot had taken off, the boys studied the guidebook. They discovered that Easter Island was quite small, only fifteen miles by eleven, with a population of about two thousand people. "It has a number of extinct volcanos," Joe announced, "the most important being Mount Rano Raraku where the natives got the volcanic stone from which they carved their giant figures."

Frank smiled. "That's one thing I've been wanting to see for a long time, and thought I never would. The stone heads of Easter Island!"

"I know one thing you won't see," Joe said. "Trees!"

"You mean there are none on the island?"

"That's right. Only grass. Sheepherding is one of the leading industries, but many natives make a living from the growing tourist trade."

"Well," Frank quipped, "in that case, the only place Santana can hide is in a volcano!"

15 The Wizard

As they were thundering along over the ocean, Frank flipped through the pages of *Aku-Aku*.

"This book is great," he said. "Tells about Thor Heyerdahl's expedition. He wanted to solve the mysteries of the island, which he did. Some of them, anyhow. Like that business of the long ears on the statues. He says the Incas who came from South America had long ears. So when they made the carvings, they gave them long ears."

"But why did they produce those big stone figures?" Joe asked.

"That's one mystery Heyerdahl didn't solve. He says no one knows why they created them or how they transported them from Mount Rano Raraku. Some weigh fifty tons! Look at this picture."

Frank pointed to an illustration of Heyerdahl sitting on top of a stone figure twenty feet tall. Other illustrations showed giant carvings lying on the ground near platforms on which they had once stood.

"Who knocked them over?" Joe wondered.

"Invaders from across the Pacific, Heyerdahl thinks," Frank replied. "They came from Polynesia and conquered Easter Island. To demonstrate they were the bosses, they pushed the statues off the platforms. That's the way it was when a Dutch sea captain discovered the island in the eighteenth century. Later, Captain Cook landed there during his voyage around the world. Finally, Chile annexed the place in the nineteenth century."

Their conversation was interrupted by their pilot, who offered them sandwiches that he had brought along.

"Oh, I'm so glad you thought of that," Joe said. "I'm starved!"

After their meal, they slept for several hours until at last Easter Island came in sight. The plane circled over the area, and the Hardys got a broad view of rolling, grass-covered terrain. They looked down into the craters of extinct volcanos and noticed that high cliffs fell off into the water along most of the coast.

Over the airfield, Joe commented, "No planes on

the ground. The *Inca Chief* must have left already. I hope they arrested Santana when he arrived!"

After landing, the Hardys went to the control tower and asked about Santana's plane.

"According to the flight plan of pilot Pedro Morena, that plane's overdue," said a man at the monitoring control board. "I'll see if I can raise him on the radio."

He lifted the transmitter and called, "Easter Island control to *Inca Chief!* Come in, please! Pedro Morena, come in, please!" He repeated the call several times, then set the transmitter aside.

"No answer," he reported.

"Will you let us know what happens?" Frank asked. "We'll be at the Hanga Roa Hotel."

"As soon as we know," the man promised.

"Thanks. Our names are Frank and Joe Hardy."

The boys retraced their steps just in time to catch the bus to the hotel at the southeastern end of Easter Island. They found the capital was a town of tiny houses, where most of the people on Easter Island lived. The hotel was small but modern. After being shown to their room, they debated their next move.

"There isn't much we can do tonight," Frank said. "But we should report to the governor right away. He's the one who can make sure Santana's taken into custody when the *Inca Chief* lands. Anyway, we'll have to let him know what we're doing here."

"You're right," Joe agreed. "Let's go find him. Shouldn't be too hard. Hanga Roa is a small place."

After getting directions at the hotel desk, the brothers walked to a bungalow south of Hanga Roa where the governor of Easter Island resided. Chile's flag flew from a flagpole, but there was no activity at the building

"I guess we're the only ones who have business with the governor tonight," Joe said. "Things are rather informal around here."

A servant showed them into the official's office. The governor was a middle-aged man wearing the uniform of a captain in Chile's army. He shook hands with Frank and Joe, gestured them to be seated, and settled down behind his desk.

"What can I do for you?" he inquired in fluent English.

The boys explained that they were looking for Santana and the stone idol. Frank showed him the photograph of the sculpture that Kimberley had given them.

"I know about this," the governor responded. "The police called me. I will interrogate Santana as soon as the *Inca Chief* arrives. The control tower at the airfield informs me that the plane is overdue. Of course, the pilot may have changed his plans or had trouble and set down somewhere else."

"Governor, do you know anything about the stone idol?" Frank inquired.

"I never signed a receipt for its removal from the island," the man replied. "In fact, I never saw it."

"We were told a Scandinavian collector bought it," Joe pointed out.

The governor shook his head. "I know nothing about this man or how he got the idol. I suggest you see a man named Iko Hiva, who's the leader of the people of Easter Island. He's considered a wizard, and if anyone knows anything about the idol, Iko Hiva does."

"We'd like to talk to him," Frank said.

The governor gave them directions to the man's home, and the following morning after breakfast, Frank and Joe walked to the outskirts of Hanga Roa. They stopped at a hut with a grinning skull over the front door.

"I wonder who that is," Frank muttered. "Or was!"

"No point asking him," Joe quipped. "He's not about to invite us in."

The boy knocked and heard a shuffling of feet approaching inside of the hut. Then the door swung open. The face of a hideous monster confronted them! Its eyes glared savagely, and its mouth was twisted in an evil leer!

Startled by the apparition, the boys stood rooted to the spot. Suddenly, the figure's right hand reached up and pulled the face off. An old man grinned at them. "Welcome!" he said.

Frank was flustered. "Eh, do you always greet your visitors in disguise, with that awful mask on?"

"It is the image of one of the ancient gods of Easter Island," the man said in English. He was slightly built with wrinkled brown skin and coal black eyes. He wore a checkered shirt, canvas trousers, and sneakers.

"I am Iko Hiva," the man went on without answering the question. "I can see you are Americans. I learned your language at school. Why have you come to see me?"

The Hardys introduced themselves.

"We want to talk to you about a stone idol," Joe explained.

Iko Hiva shrugged. "I know more about the idols of Easter Island than anyone else. Come in."

The boys entered the hut. They found themselves in a single large room with neither table nor chairs. Stone figures with misshapen features were displayed on shelves along the walls, and a number of hideous masks hung from strings attached to the ceiling.

A block of black, volcanic stone rose three feet from the floor under one window. On it lay a long

138

stone knife. A primitive fishing spear leaned at an angle against the block.

There was a musty smell in the room because, despite Easter Island's warm temperature, all the windows were closed and locked.

Frank thought to himself, the governor said this guy was a wizard. Weirdo's more like it!

Aloud he said, "A man named Julio Santana has the idol we're looking for. Do you know him?"

Iko Hiva stroked his chin. "I know him. He used to be an important man on the island, a defender of our gods and our traditions. He left to find work elsewhere. But I have communicated with him recently."

The Hardys stared at him. "You've corresponded with him?" Frank asked.

Iko Hiva shook his head. "I spoke to him in spirit."

The boys felt disappointed, but said nothing.

"Do you know the Scandinavian collector who brought the idol from Easter Island?" Joe asked.

"I do not. But so many collectors come to our island that it is possible I failed to notice him. He did not come to me. What is your interest in him?"

"He sold the idol to South American Antiquities, who commissioned us to find it after Santana stole it," Frank said.

Iko Hiva looked thoughtful. "We have many

stone idols. Describe the one you are looking for, and perhaps I can help you."

"We can do better than that," Frank replied and took the photograph from his pocket, handing it to Iko Hiva. The wizard frowned as he gazed at the face with the circular eyes, broad nose, and long ears.

"This is the guardian of the sacred cave!" he cried.

"Is that important?" Joe queried.

"Of course it is! The guardian was on the altar of the sacred cave for centuries. It disappeared but a short while ago!"

"Maybe an Easter Islander sold it to the Scandinavian collector," Frank suggested.

"Never! No one would touch it!"

"Why not?"

"The *aku-aku* would take revenge on him!"

16 Guardian of the Sacred Cave

A strange feeling came over the Hardys as Iko Hiva spoke. A tingling sensation ran up and down Frank's spine, and the hair rose on the back of Joe's neck.

"The *aku-aku* protects the guardian of the sacred cave," the man shouted. "None of our people would have taken the idol. It must have been stolen from the altar by an outsider. No one has any right to it. Do you intend to keep it from us?"

"No, we don't," Frank assured him hastily. "If what you say is true, we'll see the idol stays on Easter Island. But if the sculpture was legally sold by someone in authority, we have to return it to South American Antiquities."

"All we want right now," Joe put in, "is to find the

idol. Since you want to find it too, why can't we work together?"

Iko Hiva calmed down. "I will tell you what I will do. I will take you to the sacred cave and you can see for yourselves the altar where the idol used to stand."

The wizard led the boys out the back door to a corral where three horses were grazing. A number of saddles hung on the fence.

"Can you boys ride?" he asked.

"Sure. We ride a lot at home in Bayport," Joe replied.

"Well, then, saddle up and we will go."

When the mounts were ready, the old man set out at a quick canter, followed by Frank and Joe. The ride took them about two miles to the coast and then south along a steep cliff where they passed an extinct volcano with stone ruins near the summit.

"That is Mount Rano Kao," said Iko Hiva. "The ruins are those of Orongo, the place where our bird men used to celebrate their rites. Some of them still haunt Orongo," he added darkly.

The wizard pulled his horse to a stop on the edge of a steep cliff and pointed across the water to an island. "That is Motunui where the terns nest. The bird men used to race down from Orongo, across to Motunui, and greet the terns flying in. That was the source of their magical power. It still is."

The wizard dismounted a short while later and tied the reins of his horse to a stake driven into the ground. Frank and Joe did the same.

Then Iko Hiva led the way to a point where a rope ladder dangled down the cliff for about fifty feet. Frank judged it was a thousand feet from the end of the rope ladder to the pounding surf below. The ladder swung in the breeze, its rungs clattering against the cliff.

"Climb down until you see an opening in the wall," Iko Hiva instructed the boys. "That is the entrance of the sacred cave. Follow the tunnel in and you will find the altar. There is not sufficient room for three, so I will stay here."

Frank edged himself over the brink first. Getting a grip on the top rung with his hands, he found a lower rung with his feet and began the descent. Joe came after him. Rung by rung, they worked their way down the swaying ladder along the side of the cliff while the sound of the foaming surf echoed in their ears.

The mouth of the cave was directly to their left. Frank went in first with Joe right behind him. When they reached the tunnel, they had to get down on their hands and knees, and finally wriggled forward on their stomachs. Soon they were in total darkness.

"What's the point of this?" Joe muttered. "We

wouldn't be able to see the altar if we fell over it."

"Maybe the old man laid a trap for us," Frank said uneasily. "Wait—there's a light up ahead."

The way began to broaden until the boys were able to move on their hands and knees again. The light became stronger as they rounded a corner and saw a strange sight.

The passage ended in a circular opening too narrow for them to slip through. It was guarded by a circle of stone knives fastened into the rock. Beyond the knives there was a block of volcanic rock on which stood seven sputtering candles, three on each side and one in the center.

A shelf cut into the earth next to the Hardys held unused candles, wooden tongs for reaching them past the knives onto the altar, and long tapers for lighting the candles when they were in place.

Frank tried the edge of one of the knives with his thumb.

"Sharp as a razor," he declared. "Anyone reaching in there would sure give himself a shave."

"Well, *somebody* got the stone idol off the altar," Joe said, "and not with those tongs, either. They're not strong enough to hold it."

Agreeing there was nothing more they could learn in the sacred cave, the Hardys slowly backed down the tunnel until they reached the rope ladder.

Mounting it, they rejoined Iko Hiva at the top of the cliff.

"I replace the candles when they burn down too far," he told them. "The idol used to stand in the middle of the altar. I am desperate to get it back. Can you help me?"

"We'll try," Frank promised.

The wizard nodded. "I want you to see Rano Raraku. You will learn more about the traditions of Easter Island. It is ten miles away in the northeast."

The three climbed back in the saddle and rode around the base of Rano Kao before turning their horses onto a long trail up the coast. They passed natives and Chilean officials traveling on horseback, in jeeps, or on foot. Statues were lying on the ground beside stone platforms. Iko Hiva pointed out more caves where the ancient population used to hide from their enemies.

The Hardys recognized Rano Raraku when they spotted it from down the trail because many famous stone figures stood in the earth on the flanks of the extinct volcano.

The three reined in their horses and looked at the mysterious figures with their oval eyes, broad noses, pursed lips, and long ears.

"They are the sentinels of Rano Raraku," said Iko Hiva solemnly. "They have been here since the beginning of time. They are telling us that the ancient traditions of Easter Island must not be violated. I am in mystic communication with them," he added.

Maneuvering their horses between the uncanny stone giants, the three rode up the slope to the summit and peered over the edge into the crater that once hurled forth dense clouds of suffocating smoke and rivers of molten lava.

When the volcano had stopped erupting, the lava had cooled and become hard, black rock. The boys could see how the Easter Islanders cut the rock into blocks from which they carved their weird statues. Some half-finished sculptures still lay in the crater, reminders that work had ceased when the Polynesians conquered the island.

"How did those statues get all over the island?" Frank asked, remembering Thor Heyerdahl's account that they had been moved to different points.

"They got where they are by themselves," the wizard replied.

"But they have no legs!"

"They flew through the air. Some stayed near Rano Raraku. Others continued to the platforms built for them along the coast."

"Why were they thrown off the platforms?" Joe asked.

146

Iko Hiva scowled. "A witch did it. Her magic was too powerful for the statues. They fell and were unable to get up again. Fortunately, the sentinels of Rano Raraku were strong enough to repel the witch's spell. That is why they are still standing."

The Hardys surveyed the area, noting that there was a lake at the bottom of the crater. Several boys were either swimming in the water or paddling reed boats over the surface.

"All of the old fire mountains have crater lakes," Iko Hiva explained. "We get our water from them because there are no streams on Easter Island. Do you wish to see more?"

Frank shook his head, recalling that he and Joe should be getting back to the hotel to see if there was any word on the *Inca Chief*.

"I will help you as much as I can," Iko Hiva promised. "If you need a wizard's power, call on me!"

He turned his horse down the slopes of Rano Raraku and led the ride back to Hanga Roa. This time they passed flocks of sheep and saw shepherds guarding them.

At Iko Hiva's hut, the Hardys unsaddled their horses, thanked the old man, and walked to the Hanga Roa Hotel. Since there was no message at the desk, Frank phoned the airport.

"We still have not heard from the *Inca Chief*," he was told. "The pilot must have interrupted his flight. But not long ago a blip appeared on our radar, then vanished from the screen. If it was the *Inca Chief*, I fear it has crashed into the ocean!"

17 The Bird Man

"We are in the process of starting an air and sea search," the voice continued.

"Please keep us posted," Frank said, and with a troubled frown, hung up.

"If the *Inca Chief* went down," he said to Joe, "we'll never see Santana again."

"Or the stone idol, Frank. Anyway, we can't leave Easter Island until we know for sure."

The phone rang. "Maybe that's the control tower now!" Joe exclaimed as he lifted the instrument to his ear.

A muffled voice said, "Hardys, if you want to know about the stone idol, be at Orongo before dawn!"

Then there was a click and Joe put down the receiver.

"That was a quick one," Frank commented. "You didn't say a word."

"I didn't have a chance." Joe repeated what he had heard.

"Did you recognize the voice?" Frank asked.

Joe shook his head. "It sounded as if he was holding a handkerchief over the mouthpiece. He could be anybody who knows we're looking for the stone idol."

"Maybe he's an Easter Islander who can tell us about it but doesn't want anyone else to know," Frank conjectured. "Iko Hiva could have spread the word around that we're interested in the idol. Or a servant in the governor's residence might have overheard us mention the idol last night."

"It could also be someone who wants to get rid of us!" Joe pointed out.

"I know. But I still think we should go to Orongo."

The boys spent the afternoon strolling around Hanga Roa, then had dinner at the hotel. A message that the search for the *Inca Chief* had been fruitless was awaiting them.

"Perhaps they'll go out again tomorrow," Joe said.

Frank nodded morosely, then suggested that they

go to the governor and tell him of their plans to meet their unknown contact at Orongo.

"It could be a trap," the governor agreed. "I will send a policeman after you if you have not returned by early morning."

"That would be great," Frank said. "Thanks."

"Call me as soon as you get back from your mysterious rendezvous," the governor added, and the boys left.

They set their alarm for three o'clock, then went to sleep. Later, in the darkness, they walked to Rano Kao and climbed up to Orongo. By now a full moon flooded light over the ruins, casting weird shadows on the ground. A dark patch showed the entrance to a cave used by the bird men in olden times.

"The Easter Islanders sure were big on this kind of thing," Frank commented.

"Real cave men," Joe quipped.

They came to a jumble of massive rocks decorated with weird figures. Many were of men with the heads of birds, their bodies twisted out of shape, their heads uplifted to reveal their long curving beaks. There were cryptic hieroglyphic marks on some of the rocks.

"Our friend on the phone sure chose a spooky place to meet," Joe grumbled.

"Maybe he wants to be sure we're alone. Thor Heyerdahl found that most Easter Islanders would not come up here at night. They're afraid the spirits of Orongo would get them."

Joe looked at the sky. "I hope we don't have to wait too long. This place gives me the creeps."

"Not scared of the bird men, are you?" Frank joked.

"No, but there are lots of places I'd rather be."

The boys found a protected spot and sat down with their backs against an outcropping of rock. They discussed the strange phone call.

"I just can't make any sense of it," Frank said. "But we've got to wait here until—" He broke off suddenly as the moonlight threw a sinister shadow on the ground in front of them.

Jumping to their feet, they whirled around and saw a man with the head of a bird perched on the rock overhead!

Holding a black volcanic rock in each hand, the uncanny apparition leaped on the Hardys, struck each on the head, and knocked them to the ground! Then their attacker ran off into the darkness.

Frank and Joe lay stunned where they had fallen, but gradually recovered. Sitting up, they rubbed their heads, wincing as their fingers touched the bumps where the stones had struck.

"We were ambushed!" Joe groaned. "It must have been the guy on the phone!"

"He's trying to scare us away from Easter Island, I bet," Frank added. "No doubt he's afraid we'll find the truth about the stone idol!"

"That means we're getting warm. But I still don't see how."

"Neither do I. By the way, what happened to our bird man? He sure flew away in a hurry."

"Maybe not," Joe said in an undertone. He pointed to the mouth of the Orongo cave. "He could be hiding in there. Let's go see!"

Grabbing a rock to use as a weapon, he slipped into the cave and began to work his way on hands and knees through a narrow tunnel, using his flashlight to see ahead of him. Frank followed close behind.

"This place gives me claustrophobia!" Joe muttered. "Anyway, the bird man can't ambush us in here. There's no place for him to hide."

The tunnel was short and they came to the end in a couple of minutes.

"No one here," Joe called over his shoulder. "Reverse gears."

Frank backed up as rapidly as he could. Joe was slower. Suddenly a shower of rocks fell between the boys! Frank was safe near the mouth of the cave, but his brother was trapped underground!

Frantically Frank threw himself on the barrier. As fast as he could, he dug into it, throwing rocks over his shoulder. When he removed a big boulder near the top of the pile, he created an aperture through to the other side.

"Joe! Can you hear me?" Frank shouted.

"Loud and clear!"

"Hold on, I'll get you out." The young detective removed the rest of the debris, taking care not to start another rock slide. Finally Joe was able to wriggle through and they both emerged from the cave.

"Do you think the bird man did that?" Joe said after he breathed in a lungful of fresh air.

"I doubt it," Frank said. "I was already near the entrance and didn't hear or see anyone. I think the rocks just caved in. Maybe no one has used the cave in a long time, and the movement we made inside caused some of the ceiling to shift."

"Well, that's the last cave I'll ever go into!" Joe vowed. "The chances we take to find Santana!"

Just then, a voice sounded behind them. Whirling around, they went into a defensive stance and prepared to meet another attack by the bird man. Instead, a friendly Easter Islander was walking toward them. On his shirt, he wore an official-looking badge.

"He must be the policeman the governor promised to send after us," Joe said.

The man said something in his native dialect, ending with, "Santana?"

"Do you know about Santana?" Joe asked eagerly.

The man nodded. He pointed to the shore, gestured to the Hardys to go with him, and walked off.

"Maybe the *Inca Chief* arrived, or they found the wreck offshore," Frank surmised. "Let's see where he's taking us."

They followed the Easter Islander from Orongo to the cliff below. A narrow trail enabled them to reach the bottom where surf pounded over massive rocks. An outrigger canoe, with a spear and hand net inside, was drawn up to the shore.

"He's a fisherman," Joe said. "They probably don't even have full-time cops around here."

The man pointed to the island of Motunui across the water.

"Is Santana there?" Frank asked.

The man nodded. Pushing the canoe off the rocks into the surf, he climbed aboard and gestured to the Hardys to join him.

When they got in, he handed them a couple of paddles and took one himself. He sat up front and gave the boys a lead as the three dug their paddles into the water and started the canoe toward Motunui.

The small craft pitched up and down in the waves, maintaining its balance by means of the outrigger on one side, which stablized it and prevented it from turning over. The Hardys had experience with most types of boats, and had no trouble keeping up with the fisherman. The going got easier as they reached the placid water beyond the surf.

They crossed about a mile of open ocean before arriving at Motunui. Frank and Joe were preparing to jump out and help drag the canoe onto the beach, but the Easter Islander shook his head and pointed to a smaller island on the right. They turned in that direction, entered the surf of the little patch of land, and beached the canoe.

Curious, the Hardys followed their guide inland.

"Joe, be ready for anything," Frank warned. "Santana plays rough. He sure did with us in the Andes."

"I know. But I hope he's already in the hands of the police."

The man led them to a stone chapel, which had broken windows and grass growing around its foundation. The door hung crazily on one hinge.

"This place hasn't been used for years," Frank muttered.

"Where's Santana?" he asked their guide apprehensively.

The native pointed to an inscription on the stone above the doorway. The Hardys looked at it and read the words *Santa Ana*.

"Oh, no!" Joe groaned.

Frank grinned in spite of his disappointment. "He must have heard us talking about Santana when he walked up to us and figured this is what we wanted to see. Santa Ana and Santana do sound alike."

Suddenly a noise that seemed like a footstep came from within the building.

"Someone's in there!" Joe cried.

He and Frank rushed toward the door. As they reached it, a man with the head of a bird plunged between the boys, ran around the corner, and vanished!

18 *The* Inca Chief

The Hardys ran after the bird man. Rounding the abandoned chapel, they saw him dashing for the beach, where a reed boat was drawn up. Quickly they closed the gap and had almost overtaken him when he suddenly turned and tripped Joe.

The boy fell heavily to the ground, but Frank reached out and put a headlock on the fugitive. They struggled violently for a moment, then the man wrenched loose from his disguise. Frank was left holding the bird headdress and the man shoved him into the sand. Then the man jumped into the reed boat and paddled away furiously.

Frank got to his feet as Joe ran up to him. "Outwitted again," he muttered angrily. "There he goes, and all we have are his stupid feathers!"

"Did you recognize him?" Joe asked.

Frank nodded. "He's Pedro Morena, Santana's pilot!"

"That means the *Inca Chief* didn't crash after all!" Joe cried out. "Let's see if we can catch up with Morena in the canoe!"

The boys ran back to their guide, who still stood near the chapel, an expression of fear on his face.

Frank used a sort of sign language to explain that they wanted to pursue the fugitive, but the man shook his head. He pointed to the headdress in Frank's hand and waved his hand to indicate his refusal.

"He's afraid of the bird man," Frank interpreted. He was proven right when the Easter Islander would not let them into the boat with the bird man's feathers. Finally Frank put the headdress on the chapel steps and their guide reluctantly indicated he would take them back to Easter Island.

When they passed Motunui, Joe spotted something gleaming in the sunlight beyond the crest of a small hill. "Hey, Frank," he said and pointed. "I wonder what that is."

Frank shielded his eyes with his hand. "Let's check it out."

They signaled their guide to paddle ashore, then strode to the top of the hill and looked down on the other side. A small plane was parked at the end of a level plain below, and on its side were the words *Inca Chief!*

"So this is where Morena and Santana landed," Frank cried out. "They maintained radio silence and came down secretly on this deserted island. Easy enough for a small plane."

"It zipped right past the radar," Joe added. "They fooled the guy in the control tower when the blip went off the screen. We'll have to get back to Hanga Roa and tell the authorities."

"First let's give the *Inca Chief* the once over and drain the fuel tank in case Morena comes back to fly out after we leave."

The Hardys advanced cautiously toward the plane. When they got close enough, they saw through a window that it was empty. Pulling the door open, they got in and searched the interior.

Joe opened a leather case he found on the floor. "This is what Santana took out of the locker in Punta Arenas," he declared. "If the idol was ever in here, it sure isn't now. As a matter of fact, it isn't anywhere in the plane," he added after an exhaustive search of the cabin.

Finding the key still in the lock, Frank turned on the motor, which erupted into action for a moment and then died.

"Now I know why Morena left the key," the boy commented. "The fuel tank's empty. He must have just made it here. A few minutes more and both of them would have landed in the ocean."

Joe nodded. "But one thing puzzles me."

"What's that?"

"What was Morena doing on the island next door with that goofy birdman outfit?"

"I think I have the answer to that," Frank replied. "He was on the island for some reason of his own, and saw us approaching. Apparently he had his disguise with him, so he quickly put it on and tried his scaring act to frighten us away from the area and protect the hiding place of his plane."

The Hardys got out and scouted around the island, which was less than half a mile across in each direction. The lack of trees gave them a clear view, and they quickly realized that they and their guide were the only people on it.

"Let's make tracks for Hanga Roa," Frank suggested. "We don't have to leave a guard on the *Inca Chief*. It's not going anywhere."

They climbed back into the outrigger canoe and crossed over to Easter Island. After paying the fisherman with a handful of Chilean coins, they went directly to the governor's residence, where they were shown into his study.

"I am glad to see you safe and sound," he said with a smile. "Did my man find you?"

"He did," Joe replied. "He also helped us indirectly to find the *Inca Chief!*"

"What!" the governor was dumbfounded. "Our search was futile and we finally gave up looking for the plane!"

"The pilot landed on Motunui," Frank explained. "We almost caught him, but he escaped."

"What about Julio Santana?" the governor asked.

"He must be around here somewhere," Frank said. "But we have no idea where."

"There was also another passenger on board when they left Punta Arenas," Joe put in. "I don't know whether he was dropped off along the coast or whether he came here."

"Well, your investigation has been a success so far," the governor declared. "I will have the *Inca Chief* brought to the airfield and held there. And I will order a search for Morena and Santana and their passenger. I talked to the leading citizens of Easter Island. They are sure none of the natives stole the idol. That Scandinavian collector must have taken it himself!"

The Hardys promised to help the police in looking for the suspect, and then returned to the Hanga Roa Hotel.

"How about some chow?" Joe suggested. "We haven't had anything all day."

"Good thinking. Let's see what the chef can rustle up for us."

When they went and asked the man in charge of the kitchen, he smiled. "I see you are Americans," he said. "Perhaps you would like hamburgers? Most Americans do."

"Great!" Frank said. "And soda, if you have it."

"We have that, too. Every week we get supplies from Santiago."

Minutes later, Frank and Joe were on their way to their rooms. They sat down on their beds, placed their hamburgers and soda on the night table in between, and plunged into their meal with gusto.

After a while, Frank said, "What do you suppose Santana's up to? He's got the stone idol, but what's he doing with it? And why did he sneak into Easter Island like this?"

"He may have sold the stone idol," Joe pointed out. "We don't know for sure that he brought it here. On the other hand, he might be in cahoots with Iko Hiva. The wizard wants the idol back, and as long as Santana is willing to give it to him, Iko Hiva in turn might help our friend to get away from us."

Frank took a sip from his glass. "Santana can't hide for long on Easter Island. It's too small. And he can't get away either without his plane. By now, he must know we spotted Morena."

Joe munched his last bite of hamburger. "What about that passenger they had on the plane?" he asked. "Could he have anything to do with the stone sculpture?"

Frank shrugged. "I have no idea. I couldn't see his features at all. Perhaps he's another relative of Santana's."

"What'll we do next?"

"Let's walk around town and see if we can pick up a clue as to where Santana and Morena are hiding out," Frank suggested.

The young detectives scoured the area all afternoon, but found it difficult to communicate with the natives. And there was no sign of the two men anywhere.

In the morning, as they were coming out of the dining room after breakfast, they saw Iko Hiva sitting in the lobby.

"I have been waiting for you," the wizard declared. "I have something important to tell you."

"What is it?" Frank asked.

"The stone idol is back!"

19 Explanations

"What!" The Hardys were thunderstruck.

"The guardian once more stands on the altar in the sacred cave!" Iko Hiva went on. "I went in this morning to replace the candles and there it was. I hope you will come with me and see for yourselves."

"Of course," Joe agreed. "We've chased that sculpture a long way, and we don't want to leave without seeing it where it belongs."

"Good. A friend of mine has brought a car. He will drive us." Iko Hiva led the way outside, where he introduced the boys to another Easter Islander, who was at the wheel of a jeep. The newcomer did not speak English, but, with a friendly smile, he waved for the Hardys to climb into the back of the jeep.

When they arrived at the cliff, a crowd was gathered near the rope ladder. Two men were climbing up.

"The idol sure is popular," Joe commented.

Iko Hiva nodded. "The people are relieved to know it is back. They came down here as soon as I announced its return. Well, nobody is using the rope ladder now. I suggest you go into the sacred cave."

"Joe, what about your vow to stay away from caves?" Frank teased.

Joe grinned. "I've got the *aku-aku* on my side this time. That's good enough for me. I'll even show you the way, Frank."

Descending the ladder, the boys reached the entrance to the sacred cave. They crawled through the tunnel in the darkness until they saw the light at the opposite end. At last, they reached the opening guarded by the circle of stone knives.

Seven new candles were burning brightly on the altar, and the stone figure stood in front of the center candle!

A feeling of awe came over Frank and Joe as they gazed at the features they had seen before in the photograph. The circular eyes glinted at them in the flickering light, and the fierce scowl seemed to threaten them. The long ears reached to a level with the chin and looked more sinister now than in the office of South American Antiquities back in Santiago.

"You know something," Frank said, staring at the idol. "I don't think he likes us."

"I don't think he likes anybody," Frank muttered. "Let's get out of here before he puts the whammy on us."

They went back through the tunnel to the mouth of the cave and mounted the ladder to the top of the cliff. The crowd was growing bigger as more people arrived to view the stone idol. Frank and Joe climbed back into the jeep, and their driver started the return trip to Hanga Roa.

"So you see, the guardian of the sacred cave has come back to us," Iko Hiva declared.

"Who put it on the altar?" Joe inquired.

"The *aku-aku*," the wizard replied solemnly.

An *aku-aku* named Julio Santana, Frank thought.

"You will not try to take it away?" the old man went on.

"No," Joe assured him. "Not unless we can prove it was sold legitimately. But in order to do that, we'll have to find the Scandinavian collector who sold it to South American Antiquities. He didn't want his identity revealed, but at this point he has no choice."

The wizard smiled. "That is good. Now you do not have to fear the *aku-aku*."

Frank spoke up. "What if someone steals the idol again? The *aku-aku* couldn't prevent it before and might not be able to do it now."

Iko Hiva smiled. "Someone will always guard the cave in the future," he declared.

When they arrived at the hotel, the boys said good-bye to the wizard and his companion, then went inside. In their room, they discussed the latest developments.

"Santana must have put the idol back last night," Frank noted. "He was probably in the sacred cave while we were having our go-round with Morena at Orongo. The bird man stuff was a setup to get us out of the way. I bet it was either Santana or Morena on the phone who disguised his voice and tricked us into going to Orongo."

"Then perhaps Santana's not a thief, Frank! We thought he stole the idol after we found it because he wanted to sell it. Maybe he only wanted to bring it back where it belonged!"

"You're right," Frank said. "Someone else could have stolen it from Kimberley's bag in the hotel room, and hidden it in the secret compartment."

"And who took it from the sacred cave in the first place?"

Frank sighed. "For a minute, I thought we'd solved the puzzle, but now we have more questions than ever."

"Bertrand's still a suspect," Joe declared firmly. "He had the opportunity to take the idol in the hotel room. And he had a motive if he was trying to incriminate Kimberley and grab control of the business."

A knock on the door interrupted the discussion. Joe opened it up and gasped.

Julio Santana stood on the threshold!

"May I come in?" he asked pleasantly.

"Sure," Joe offered. "We were just talking about you."

"I can understand that," Santana admitted as he sat down. "Much has happened since we met in Santiago."

"Like you and Morena trying to knock us off the bridge into the gorge," Frank suggested.

"And fixing our brakes so we'd crack up in the Andes," Joe added. "Then you disguised your voice on the phone last night and sent your bird man to ambush us at Orongo."

"You're right," Santana admitted. "But I can explain everything. First of all, I did not tell Morena to attack you. I merely wanted him to frighten you away from Easter Island."

"Why?" Frank demanded.

170

"I thought you were here to steal the stone idol again. But Iko Hiva just told me you agree it must remain in the sacred cave. So I have come to apologize for mistrusting you. But you must understand that I felt *you* had stolen the idol when I saw you with it at South American Antiquities. I assumed you and Bertrand were going to sell it illegally. So I seized it and ran. I had to do everything in my power to protect it."

"Even if it meant killing us?" Joe challenged.

"When we followed you into the Andes, you decided to finish us off," Frank added.

"Remember, I thought you were thieves. Anyone who takes a sacred idol is not worthy of living. But the *aku-aku* knew better and protected you. So, you were never in real danger!"

"Why were you selling sculptures at the stand in your village square?" Frank inquired.

"I had watched you all the time," Santana revealed. "I saw you disguise yourselves at Ata Copac's house and set out for my village. I knew a shortcut and rushed home before you arrived. Then I asked Pedro to let me take over the stall."

"But what made you think we'd stop there?"

Santana smiled. "Anyone looking for a stone figurine would be interested in similar items. I intended to trap you by making you appear as thieves. The villagers have stern punishment for people like that. But you escaped and I went back to Santiago until Pedro could fly me here. He used to be in the Chilean air force and has his pilot's license."

"Why couldn't he take you right then?" Frank asked.

"He was in the process of buying the *Inca Chief*, which he will use for charters. I had to wait until the transfer was completed."

"What were you doing in Punta Arenas?" Joe inquired.

"Pedro had a fare to drop off first. Then we stopped along the coast before we came to Easter Island."

"How did you know the stone idol had been taken from the sacred cave?"

"Iko Hiva wrote and told me while I was working in the oil fields at Punta Arenas."

So Iko Hiva didn't communicate only in spirit as he said, Joe thought. He's a wizard who pushes a pen. I guess he didn't want us to know about it until he figured out what we were up to.

"You see," Santana went on, "I grew up here, knowing the stone idol as the guardian of the sacred cave. Only the sacrilegious would touch it. When I heard it was gone, I resolved to get it back at any cost. Since South American Antiquities handles more Easter Island artifacts than anybody else, I went to their office and applied for a job."

"And, fortunately, Bertrand needed a chauffeur," Joe said.

Santana nodded. "I took care of the company cars while trying to find the idol. You got it before I did. That is when I went into action."

"You didn't know it was in the possession of South American Antiquities before that moment?"

"No. I still don't know how they obtained it."

"Supposedly it was sold to Mr. Kimberley by a Scandinavian collector," Joe said.

Santana shrugged. "It's possible. But what I don't understand is why you pursued me. I thought you were doing research on the ancient Incas."

"That was our cover story," Frank told him. "We're really detectives. Mr. Kimberley hired us to find the idol, which had disappeared from his handbag."

"Now I understand," Santana said. "When I saw you at Punta Arenas airport, I thought Mr. Bertrand had sent you after me."

"So you had Morena fly you to Motunui instead of Easter Island," Joe surmised.

"Yes. I did not want you to intercept me and seize the idol before I could place it back where it belonged. But since you told Iko Hiva you will not take it away again, I decided to tell you the truth."

The Easter Islander took out a handkerchief and dabbed at a cut on the right side of his chin.

"That's a bad cut," Joe observed.

"I got it in a good cause. One of the knife blades protecting the sacred cave nicked me as I reached through the circle to replace the idol on the altar."

He put his handkerchief in his pocket and looked at the Hardys questioningly. "What do you intend to do now?" he asked.

20 The Final Clue

Frank and Joe looked at one another. They realized they were thinking the same thing.

"We understand why you gave us such a rough time," Frank spoke up. "We're not about to press charges against you. Or against Morena, either. It was just a foul-up in communications when he conked us at Orongo."

"But you'll have to tell the governor what you told us," Joe pointed out.

"I have no objection to that," Santana stated. "We can go at once."

The three walked over to the governor's residence. Admitted to his office, they found that he already knew from Iko Hiva about the return of the stone idol. Santana then explained that he had put the sculpture back on the altar during the night. He continued with an account of his part in the case. The Hardys added that they were not pressing charges.

"Then that ends it as far as I'm concerned," the governor said. "What are your plans now?"

"I shall stay on Easter Island," Santana replied. "But I hope you will allow Pedro Morena to fly his plane out again. He picked up a charter fare at Punta Arenas. The man wants to go to Santiago."

"Oh, he's the passenger we noticed sitting behind Morena," Frank said. "Why did he come to Easter Island with you if he wanted to go to Santiago?"

Santana shrugged. "He seemed to be afraid of someone. When Pedro told him he had to stop here first, he agreed to come along for the ride just to get out of Punta Arenas. He is an American, by the way."

Suddenly Frank had a hunch. "Julio, what's his name?"

"Sigmund Muller."

Frank and Joe stared at the man. "Muller!" Frank cried out. "He's wanted by the U.S. military for heading a widespread theft ring!"

Now it was Santana's turn to stare. "You mean this man is a criminal?"

"He sure is," Joe declared and quickly told about their mission in the Antarctic.

"Where is Muller now?" the governor demanded after Joe had finished.

"He is waiting for us to pick him up at the Beach Hotel," Santana replied.

"I shall have him arrested at once and brought here," the governor declared.

An hour later, two men with police badges on their shirts brought Sigmund Muller into the governor's office. His eyes bulged when he saw the Hardys and he tried to run, but the two men caught him at the door.

"What a surprise, meeting you here," Joe said. "I thought you were supposed to be in San Diego!"

Muller glared but did not comment.

"I bet you'd feel better if we had fallen into that crevasse on the way to Outpost I," Frank said. "Your pal, Al Ambrose, made another attempt on our lives, but failed. He was arrested and confessed everything!"

"I don't know what you're talking about," Muller said sullenly.

"Your theft ring is exposed and we know you're the leader," Joe told him. "No confession is necessary for your arrest."

Muller shrugged. "You'll have to prove it."

"Don't worry, we will. And I'm sure Admiral Langton will be happy that we found you."

"Governor, is there some way you can hold this man for the U.S. military?" Frank asked. "If you get in touch with Admiral Langton at Byrd Base in Antarctica, he'll arrange for the transfer."

"I certainly can," the governor replied. "We have a jail on the island, even though it is very small."

"Mr. Muller, I'm curious about one thing," Joe said. "Why did you stay in Punta Arenas a whole day, and then take a charter plane to Easter Island?"

Muller realized he was defeated. "I was looking for a friend, who I thought could help me," he replied. "Unfortunately, I didn't find him. When I spotted U.S. military police at the airport, I panicked. I didn't dare book on a commercial airliner, so I found Morena and decided to go with him no matter where he went."

"How'd you ever expect to get back to the United States?" Frank asked.

"I have contacts in Santiago who might have helped."

The governor called Byrd Base and spoke to the admiral, who promised to notify Mr. Hardy that Muller had been found. "I'll submit the necessary extradition papers for Muller and have him picked up," the commander added.

As Muller was led away, the governor turned to the boys. "We would be very happy to entertain you for a while on our island if you'd care to stay," he said.

Frank shook his head. "We still have work to do on the idol case. May I call Mr. Bertrand in Santiago?"

"Of course."

When the young detective spoke to the antique dealer, Bertrand was disturbed to learn that the idol had not been legitimately acquired from Easter Island.

"You'll have to find the Scandinavian collector who sold it to Kim," he told Frank. "I never spoke to the man. I suggest you fly back to New York and talk to my partner."

"If we could figure out who sent Mr. Kimberley that secret message about the sculpture's hiding place, it would help, too," Frank said.

"I questioned my staff, and they deny knowing anything about it," Bertrand said. "If you locate the collector, you might get the answer to this question."

The boys were on the next flight out of Easter Island. They spent the night in Santiago, then continued on to New York.

"I still wonder if Bertrand's on the level," Frank observed.

"So do I," Joe agreed.

"I wonder if he really wants us to find the collector. He seemed uneasy about the whole thing. He might know more than he told us."

"He might be afraid we'll discover that the two of them were in on the theft of the idol," Joe agreed. "The collector stole it, and Bertrand told him to sell it to Kimberley. Later Bertrand stole it from Kimberley. That's one theory anyhow."

"Perhaps he has reason to believe we'll never find the Scandinavian," Frank said. "And he's the only person who can expose the whole thing."

When they arrived at Kennedy Airport, the boys checked into a nearby hotel. The following morning, they phoned Kimberley, who told them to come to his office. They found that he had shaved off his beard.

Frank and Joe recounted the story of the stone idol, ending with the statement that it was permanently back on Easter Island.

"It looks as if the Scandinavian collector who sold you the sculpture is a crook," Frank concluded. "You've got to tell us who he is."

"I tried to find him myself in the meantime," Kimberley said. "Unfortunately, my investigation proves that he does not exist. The man who sold me the idol gave me forged documents and a phony name!"

Agitatedly, Kimberley began to scratch the right side of his chin with his thumb. "I was cheated!" he cried. "Fooled by a thief!"

Suddenly the truth dawned on Frank and Joe at the same time.

"You have a scar in the same place as Julio Santana!" Joe cried out. "He was cut by one of the stone knives in the sacred cave when he put the idol back on the altar. You got cut when you reached in and stole it!"

Kimberley turned ashen white and jumped up from behind his desk. Flinging Joe aside, he tried to push his way past Frank and out the door. But after a short scuffle, the boys subdued him and shoved him back in his chair.

Frank called the police, and soon two officers arrived. They handcuffed the prisoner and informed him of his rights, then Frank gave them the details of their investigation.

When he had finished, he turned to Kimberley.

"You forged the bill of sale for the idol after you returned from Easter Island, and you grew a beard to hide the wound you received from the stone knives!"

"Then you hid the idol in the secret compartment in Bertrand's office before you went to your hotel," Joe took up the story. "The sculpture was not in your handbag when you brought it to your room.

Then you waited to pick up your watch until Bertrand was there so he'd be alone with the bag and could be accused of the theft!"

"Prove it!" Kimberley snarled.

"We will. We know you made up the secret message by cutting words from a newspaper and pasting them on a sheet of South American Antiquities stationery. Then you gave us the note so we'd find the idol and have Bertrand arrested!"

An evil smile curled around Kimberley's lips. "All you have is a harebrained theory. Pure conjecture. I would have no reason to do what you accuse me of."

Suddenly Joe grinned. "But we can prove it. Iko Hiva saw you come up the rope ladder from the sacred cave. He says you were carrying the stone idol, and he'll be glad to identify you in court."

Frank realized his brother was bluffing, and took it one step further. "We also know what your motive was. Mr. Bertrand knows you've been stealing from the company. He'll testify to that. And he can prove it by the records you falsified!"

Kimberley fell right into the trap. His nerve broke and he began to confess.

"I was afraid Bertrand would find out that I faked our financial records," he said, his voice shaking. "So I decided to get rid of him and acquire control of the business."

"That's what you accused *him* of wanting to do," Joe observed.

"I had to ascribe a motive to him," Kimberley muttered, "in order to set him up. When everything was ready, I advertised for a detective because I needed someone who could read the false clues I left in Santiago."

"We followed them at first," Frank admitted. "Then Santana messed everything up for you by snatching the stone idol from us."

"That's when your scheme began to come apart," Joe added. "But it took us a long time to figure out what was going on. The razor did it."

"What razor?" Kimberley grated.

"The one you used to shave your beard."

Kimberley hung his head. "I grew the beard because initially the cut was obvious. But I found it very uncomfortable, so I finally removed it. I didn't think anyone would notice the scar."

"It is so slight that we wouldn't have," Frank admitted, "except you touched it just like Santana touched his fresh cut while we talked to him on Easter Island."

Kimberley shrugged. "Now it'll be easier for Iko Hiva to identify me."

"Actually, it won't," Joe said. "I only made that up in the hope you'd confess."

Kimberley jumped up and let out a string of curses, while the two officers looked admiringly at the boys.

"I also dreamed up the story about Bertrand discovering that you've been stealing from South American Antiquities," Frank added.

Kimberley was so crushed to learn the Hardys had tricked him into a confession that he offered no resistance when the two officers led him away.

The boys looked at each other. Both were relieved that the case was solved, but at the same time they were wondering if they would ever get another assignment that could top the one that took them to such exotic places as Easter Island and Antarctica.

Another mystery, *The Vanishing Thieves*, was to come up soon and would require their best sleuthing skills, even if it did not take them quite as far as the South Pole.

Just then the telephone rang. Frank answered. It was Bertrand from Santiago.

"Where's Kim?" he asked. "How come you're on the line?"

"Mr. Kimberley's at the police station," Frank replied. "He—"

"Good! Make sure he stays there!" Bertrand thundered. "He's been stealing from the firm for a long time. I just found out!"

Frank raised his eyebrows. "You did?"

"That's right. I checked our books. I suspected him ever since you boys told me how he hired you. But I couldn't say so because I had no proof."

"How did you get it?" Frank asked.

"I phoned Kim after you left Easter Island and demanded to know who the Scandinavian collector was. He was so evasive that I decided to go through our financial records with a fine-tooth comb. And there was my proof. He must be arrested at once!"

"Consider it done," Frank replied. "And thanks for the information."

"What information?" Joe asked as Frank hung up.

"Bertrand wants us to know Kimberley's been cheating him for a long time! How about that!"

The Hardy Boys® in

The Vanishing Thieves

Franklin W. Dixon
Illustrated by Leslie Morrill

The Vanishing Thieves was
first published in the U.K. in a single volume in hardback in 1982
by Angus & Robertson (U.K.) Ltd, London
amd in Armada in 1982

Contents

1 The Stolen Car

"Quick, eat the rest of the pizza!" Frank Hardy urged. "Here comes Chet!"

It was Saturday afternoon and Frank and his younger brother Joe were seated at a table in the Bayport Diner with Callie Shaw and Iola Morton. Iola's tubby brother Chet, who was known for his voracious appetite, and a slender boy of about eighteen had just walked in.

Frank's warning was too late. Chet had already spotted them, and was headed their way with his gaze fixed on the half-eaten pizza. His companion followed close behind.

Picking up a piece of pie, Chet said, "Umm, pepperoni and cheese, my favorite."

"You're welcome," Joe said with good-humored sarcasm.

After taking a bite, Chet turned to the other boy, and in a generous tone offered, "Have some pizza, Vern."

"No, thanks," Vern said, embarrassed.

"Chet, you might at least introduce Vern before eating up everything in sight," Iola admonished her brother.

"Oh, sure," Chet said. "This is our cousin, Vern Nelson, from Canada." He used his slice of pizza as a pointer. "Callie Shaw, Frank and Joe Hardy."

"Vern is visiting us at the farm," Iola explained.

Finishing his piece of pizza, Chet took another. "The matinee today is a monster movie," he announced. "Why don't we all go?"

The others agreed, and a few minutes later the six left the diner. As they emerged onto the parking lot, Vern Nelson suddenly stopped short. "Somebody's stealing my car!" he cried out.

A brand-new blue sedan was being driven out of the lot by a red-haired man. "Let's go after him!" Chet cried.

The young people raced to the Hardys' sports sedan and jumped in. Frank, Callie, and Vern sat in front, while the others squeezed into the back. Seconds later, Frank began following the blue sedan.

The thief had a head start of a block, but was

not driving fast. Frank soon reduced the distance between them to a quarter of a block. However, intervening traffic kept him from getting any closer.

The red-haired man obviously was unaware that he was being followed, because he kept well within the speed limit. He headed for the downtown section of Bayport. Frank gradually narrowed the distance between them until he was only fifty feet behind. At that moment, the thief seemed to realize he was being tailed. Suddenly he floored the accelerator!

There was a red light ahead. The man drove through it with a blasting horn, barely missing another car. Frank had to brake to a halt, and though the light changed a moment later, the stolen car was already more than a block away.

Frank saw the thief turn left into an alley. He went after him, but when he emerged at the next cross street, there was no sign of the blue sedan.

A huge eighteen-wheel truck was parked on the right, and the driver was closing the back door. Joe called out to him, "Did you see a blue sedan speed by here?"

The driver turned around. He was a squat, powerfully built man wearing a short-sleeved sport shirt that revealed tattooed arms.

"Zoomed by like an express train," he said. He pointed east. "Went that way."

"Thanks," Joe said, as Frank turned the car in that direction.

The thief, however, was nowhere to be found. They cruised up and down side streets for a time, then drove to the Hardy home on Elm Street. All thoughts of a movie matinee were now abandoned.

Aunt Gertrude was in the kitchen when the six young people trooped in the back door. Miss Hardy, sister of the boys' father, was a tall, angular, peppery woman, who was just taking a pie from the oven.

"Umm, smells like cherry," Chet said, moving towards the pastry.

"This is no time to think about food," Joe told him. "We have to call the police."

"The police!" Aunt Gertrude repeated. "Are you boys involved with criminals again?"

"Tell you all about it later," Frank promised, heading into the front hall.

He used the front hall extension to call Chief of Police Ezra Collig. Fenton Hardy came down the stairs as he was talking. The tall, middle-aged detective had once been with the New York City police force, but was now a world-famous private investigator.

"What's going on?" he asked Frank as his oldest son hung up.

Frank introduced Vern Nelson to his father and then explained about the car theft.

"That's quite a coincidence," Mr. Hardy said. "I happen to be investigating a car-theft ring, but not in this area."

"Where are they operating?" Joe asked.

"Mainly in New York City."

Chet said, "The funny thing is the way the car disappeared. Course that red light slowed us down, but we were only a little over a block behind when the thief turned into the alley. He should have still been in sight when we came out the other end."

"Particularly since that tattooed fellow told us which way he went," Vern Nelson said.

"Tattooed fellow?" Fenton Hardy asked, raising his eyebrows.

"A truck driver," Frank explained. "He was closing up the back of his truck when we drove up."

"What did he look like?"

"Sort of squat, but well-built."

"Did you happen to notice the design of his tattoos?"

The four boys and Iola had not paid any attention, but Callie Shaw said, "I saw the one on his right arm as we went by. It was a dagger with a snake wrapped around it."

"Crafty Kraft!" the detective exclaimed. "The

car-theft ring must be spreading, because he's one of its chief lieutenants!"

"You mean that driver's in cahoots with the gang you're investigating?" Joe asked in surprise.

Mr. Hardy nodded. "I've a feeling Vern's car disappeared into Kraft's truck. It's probably the type whose rear door lowers to form a driving ramp."

"Oh!" Vern said in exasperation. "I wish I could lay my hands on him and that redheaded thief who drove off in my new car!"

"The car thief was red-haired?" Fenton Hardy asked.

"Yes."

"Now I'm positive it was the gang I'm after," the detective said. "Red Sluice, one of the slickest car-heist artists in the country, works with Crafty Kraft."

Mr. Hardy listened to the group's description of the truck, and phoned the information to Chief Collig. When he hung up, Vern asked whether he thought there was a chance his car would be found.

"I doubt it," the detective said frankly. "So far not a single vehicle suspected of being stolen by this ring has been recovered. The theory is that they're either being repainted and sold in other states under fake registrations, or being stripped for spare parts."

"But the police have the truck's description."

The detective nodded. "But no license number, and there are hundreds of similar trucks on the highways."

Aunt Gertrude walked in from the kitchen and invited the boys' friends for dinner. They all accepted, and, after calling their parents, went into the dining room.

With Mrs. Hardy, there were nine around the table. Laura Hardy was a slim, attractive woman with sparkling blue eyes. She quickly put Vern at ease by warmly asking about his family and plans for his stay in Bayport.

Vern explained that he was an orphan who lived with an older sister in Montreal. An uncle on his father's side—no relation to the Mortons—had died in California and had left him a rare coin, a 1913 Liberty Head nickel. Only five of those were known to be in existence, and his Uncle Gregg, who had bought his eight years ago, had paid $100,000 for it. However, the coin had disappeared under mysterious circumstances before the will could be probated. Vern was on his way to California to look into the matter, and had stopped en route to visit the Mortons.

"Was the coin stolen?" Fenton Hardy asked.

198

"That's the mystery," Vern replied. "According to the will, it was supposed to be in a safe-deposit box in Los Angeles. But when the box was opened, it was not there. Only Uncle Gregg had a key, and the vault record showed that he had not visited it since the day he placed the coin in it eight years ago."

"That sounds like a case for the Hardy boys," Chet said. "Why don't the three of us go to California with you?"

"I no longer have a car to get there," Vern remarked.

"Maybe we could fly," Frank suggested.

"You're going to get involved with criminals again?" Aunt Gertrude asked in a worried tone. "Must you?"

"Don't worry about it, Aunt Gertrude," Joe said cheerfully. "We can take care of ourselves."

"So far. But someday you may get in more trouble than you can handle."

"We'll be careful," Frank assured her.

Laura Hardy asked, "Why are there only five of these coins in existence, Vern? Nineteen-thirteen isn't that long ago. I think I have a 1910 nickel in a drawer somewhere myself."

"They were not a regular issue and were never placed in circulation," the boy replied. "The story is that a group of VIPs was visiting the mint, and to show them how it operated, 1913 Liberty Head nickels were cast. As the government switched from the Liberty Head to the Indian Head nickel that year, no other Liberty Heads were ever minted. The coins were supposed to be destroyed after the demonstration, but half of them disappeared while the visitors were examining them."

"You mean they were stolen!" Mrs. Hardy exclaimed. "Who were these visitors?"

"All reputable men," Vern said with a grin. "They included a senator, a cabinet officer, and a general. Years later, five coins showed up in the estate of a well-known millionaire. Those five were sold by the estate, and eventually my uncle bought one."

A loud thud sounded, seeming to come from the front hall. Frank went to investigate. When he saw nothing amiss, he opened the front door.

The point of a large dagger was buried in the heavy oak, pinning a note to the wood. Penned in block letters was: IF YOU WANT YOUR FAMILY TO STAY HEALTHY, DROP YOUR INVESTIGATION, HARDY.

2 Hijacked!

When Frank shouted in surprise, everyone at the dinner table rushed into the front hall to see what was going on.

"I'll bet that was left by the car-theft gang," Joe remarked, after reading the note.

"Not necessarily," Mr. Hardy said. "That isn't the only case I'm working on. Let's see if the culprit left his fingerprints."

Using a handkerchief, the detective pulled the dagger from the door and carried it to his laboratory. The four boys followed, while the girls stayed to help Mrs. Hardy and Aunt Gertrude clear the table.

Holding the dagger with forceps, Mr. Hardy used .

a camel's hair brush to dust it lightly with a fine, dark powder. A set of prints appeared on the haft. He lifted them off with inch-wide transparent tape and transferred them onto a white card.

Then he took a number of case folders from a filing cabinet and compared fingerprint cards in them to the prints taken from the dagger. After checking the first folder, he shook his head.

"It isn't any known member of the car-theft gang," he said.

He examined several other folders without success. Finally he exclaimed triumphantly, "Anton Jivaro! I didn't even know he was still in the States. He was supposed to have fled to Canada."

"Who's Anton Jivaro?" Frank asked.

"An escaped mental patient. A clever man, but insane. Thinks he is the Maharaja of Kashmir, and has a nasty habit of hijacking planes to take him to India. I caught him once, that's why I have his prints on file."

"Maybe you'd better turn on the outside lights and the burglar alarm tonight," Joe suggested. "Just in case Jivaro decides to come back with another dagger."

"Good idea," Mr. Hardy said.

When they returned to the kitchen, Aunt Gertrude was horrified to learn that the dagger had been left by a madman.

"We'll all be murdered in our sleep," she declared. "Why do you take such cases, Fenton?"

"I'll turn the alarm and the outside lights on," her brother assured her. "Don't worry, nothing will happen."

While Mr. Hardy and the boys had been busy in the laboratory, Laura Hardy had hunted up the 1910 Liberty Head nickel she owned. She showed it to Vern.

After examining it, he said, "It isn't worth very much, Mrs. Hardy. Maybe fifty cents or a dollar. I could tell you exactly if I had my bible with me."

"Your bible?"

"The annual Guide Book of United States Coins. Coin collectors call it the bible."

"It's at our house," Chet said. "If we fly to Los Angeles, put it in your hand luggage. That way we can check our pocket change on the plane."

After some discussion, it was decided that Frank, Joe, Chet, and Vern would go to Los Angeles the next day. Everyone was very exhausted from the excitement of the day, and Frank and Joe drove all of their guests home. Filled with anticipation, both boys had trouble sleeping.

The following morning, as they waited in line at Bayport Airport, Chet called attention to a dark, furtive-looking little man who had bought a ticket.

"Hope they check that fellow for guns," he said

203

forebodingly. "He looks like a hijacker to me."

"You watch too many movies," Frank scoffed.

Walking over to the security checkpoint, they found themselves standing right behind the dark little man. When he passed through without causing the electronic metal detector to buzz, Chet was relieved. "I guess he doesn't have a gun on him after all," he said.

Then Chet passed through. A bulb lit up and there was a loud buzz. Immediately two security officers grabbed him. While one gripped him firmly from behind, the other patted his pants pockets, then reached into the left one. He drew out a metal box.

"Open it!" he commanded.

Sheepishly Chet obeyed. Inside was a large collection of nickels.

"Why are you carrying your change in a metal box?" the guard demanded.

"It's kind of my piggy bank," Chet replied with wounded dignity.

The guard shook his head, handed back the box, and passed the boy through. As the four friends moved toward the gate, Vern inquired why his cousin was loaded down with nickels.

"I didn't have time to check them last night, so I thought I'd do it on the plane. Did you bring your bible?"

"Sure. But what do you expect to find?"

"Maybe a 1913 Liberty Head nickel!"

On the plane Frank, Joe, and Vern sat in one row, while Chet's seat was across the aisle, next to an attractive, platinum blond woman of about thirty. Beside her, in the window seat, was the dark little man Chet had suspected of being a hijacker.

When they were airborne, Chet took out a handful of nickels and began checking their dates. After a while the platinum blonde asked curiously, "Do you mind telling me what you're doing?"

"Looking for a particular coin, ma'am."

"Oh."

Frank, who was on the aisle seat across from Chet, leaned forward with a grin and said, "He's a little odd, ma'am, but harmless. Don't mind him."

She smiled. "You four all together?"

"Yes, we are."

"Well then, let's get acquainted. It's a long flight. I'm Cylvia Nash."

"How do you do?" Frank said. "I'm Frank Hardy, and our friend next to you is Chet Morton. On my left are my brother Joe, and Vern Nelson."

"Glad to meet you," Cylvia Nash said. "You boys on vacation?"

"Not exactly," Chet said, dropping the nickels into an empty pocket and taking another handful out of his "piggy bank." "Didn't you recognize the names Frank and Joe Hardy?"

The woman shook her head, puzzled, while the man next to her openly stared at them.

"Fenton Hardy's sons," Chet explained.

"Oh, the famous private detective." She looked at Frank and Joe admiringly. "You often help your father, don't you? Are you on a case now?"

"We are," Chet replied. "You see, this valuable coin disappeared—"

"It's really not a case at all," Frank interrupted, giving Chet a sharp glance. "A relative lost something and we're going to try and find it. Since we haven't been to California in a long time, we're really looking forward to it."

"Yes, we want to get some sightseeing in," Joe added.

"You'll like it," Cylvia said. "Are you planning to visit the northern part of the state, too?"

"We don't know yet," Frank said. "Do you live near there?"

"No, L.A. I'm returning from vacation."

The dark little man on her right said, "Excuse me, madam, but do you know how to work this?" He held up his earphone for recorded music.

As Cylvia Nash showed him how to plug it in, Chet resumed examining nickels.

"Hey!" he exlaimed. "I found a 1901 Liberty

Head!" Leaning across the aisle, he said to his cousin, "That worth anything, Vern?"

"Let's see it," Vern requested.

Chet passed the coin across the aisle to Frank, who handed it to Vern. After studying the nickel, Vern took a small red book from his pocket and opened it.

"Twenty-six-and-a-half million of those coins were minted," he stated. "If it were a proof coin, it would be worth a hundred and thirty-five dollars. If you could find a buyer, that is, which is unlikely unless you're a dealer. A dealer would probably give you about half that."

"I'll settle for sixty-five dollars," Chet said eagerly. "Is it a proof coin?"

Vern shook his head. "The next grade down is uncirculated. That's worth seventy-two-fifty, again about half that from a dealer."

"Is it uncirculated?"

"No. Now extra-fine grade would bring about six dollars from a dealer."

"What grade is it?" Chet asked meekly.

Studying it again, Vern said, "It has some worn spots, so it can't be rated very fine, or even fine. Very good is the next rating down, but I don't think it's even that. I'd say it rates only as good."

"So what's that worth?"

"You might get thirty cents for it."

Chet made a face. "Big deal!" He took the nickel and dropped all of the coins into his metal box.

Cylvia Nash, who had been listening, leaned forward to Vern. "You seem to know a lot about coins, young man."

"My uncle was a collector, and he taught me. Are you interested in numismatics?"

She shook her head. "I know nothing about the subject."

Just then the little man next to her unplugged his earphone. "Thanks again for showing me how to use this," he said.

"You're welcome," she replied. "We haven't introduced ourselves. I'm Cylvia Nash."

"How do you do?" he said formally. "I am the Maharaja of Kashmir."

Chet stiffened. Trying not to show his excitement, he signaled Frank to meet him at the back of the plane.

Both boys pretended to go toward the restroom. As soon as they were beyond earshot of the others, Chet whispered, "That little guy is Anton Jivaro, the hijacker! I heard him tell Miss Nash he was the Maharaja of Kashmir!"

Frank stared at him. "Are you sure?"

"Of course I am."

"Then we better get word to the captain that there is a mental patient aboard," Frank decided.

"Well, at least he doesn't have a gun," Chet said. "He couldn't have sneaked it past that detector."

Jivaro had risen from his seat and stepped past Cylvia Nash into the aisle. In a loud voice, he said, "May I have everyone's attention?"

Most conversation stopped and all the passengers looked at him questioningly. He opened his coat, then slowly made a complete turn so that everyone could see the six long, brownish-colored tubes strapped to his waist.

"These are sticks of dynamite," he announced. He took hold of the loop at the end of a short lanyard attached to his belt and wrapped it around his hand. "If I pull this, the explosives will go off."

There was dead silence in the plane.

"If everyone behaves, I will not have to use them," he continued. "I don't wish to harm you. I only want to be flown to my native land. You see, I am the Maharaja of Kashmir."

Silence continued. The hijacker's gaze fixed on the flight attendant who had just emerged from the small galley at the rear of the plane.

"Stewardess!" he demanded. "Take me to your captain!" Turning to the passengers, he gently raised his hand with the lanyard wrapped around it. "Remember, don't anybody try anything. I can pull this in a second . . . and I'll blow us all up if I have to!"

209

3 Crash Landing

As the hijacker and the flight attendant disappeared
into the cockpit, Cylvia Nash said in a high voice,
"Kashmir? Where in the world is that?"

"On the northern border of India," Frank replied,
looking around at the stunned passengers.

Joe tried to break the tension. "My brother's
been reading up on the Far East," he spoke up.

"Yes? Well, who is the real Maharaja of Kashmir?" Chet asked.

"There isn't any. Kashmir used to be an independent nation ruled by an absolute monarch, but after
World War II, both India and Pakistan tried to take it
over. In 1956, India formally annexed it, but Paki-

stan still claims it. An assembly set up by the United Nations in 1949 abolished the monarchy. I don't know if the man who was maharaja at that time is still alive, but even if he is, he would be much older than Mr. Jivaro."

"Mr. who?" Miss Nash asked loudly, trying to make herself heard over the cries of some nearby passengers.

"Anton Jivaro is the hijacker's real name," Frank explained. "He's an escaped mental patient my dad's been trying to track down."

"What!" she exlaimed. "You mean we're in the hands of a madman?"

Just then the cockpit door opened and the hijacker and flight attendant emerged. The frightened burst of conversation that had broken out throughout the plane suddenly died.

A slightly shaken voice came over the intercom. "This is your captain. As you all know, the plane has been hijacked. Please stay calm. The hijacker has promised not to harm anyone if we all do as he says. He tells me he is the Maharaja of Kashmir. I don't want any heroes attempting to subdue him, because he is carrying dynamite. My instructions are to change course from Los Angeles to Miami. There we will refuel to fly, via Casablanca, to Kashmir. We are now on the way to Miami."

The hijacker spoke up. "All of you are to obey the captain and stay calm. We'll carry on just as though eveything was normal." He turned to the flight attendant. "Isn't it about time you served lunch?"

"Lunch?" she said, flustered. "Oh, yes. Ladies and gentlemen, we will now have lunch."

The strain of being in great danger left few of the passengers hungry, and some were so upset that they could not eat at all. The Hardys only picked at their food, and even Chet's appetite was diminished. Only the hijacker ate with gusto, standing at the rear of the plane.

Shortly after the meal, the captain's voice came over the intercom again. "Ground Control at Miami reports the airport closed in by fog," he announced. "Will the maharaja please come forward to discuss an alternate landing place?"

Jivaro walked up to the flight attendant. "Go tell him to make an instrument landing."

The young woman disappeared into the cockpit. When she came out a few moments later, she called to the hijacker. "The skipper wants to see you."

Jivaro moved forward, but when the flight attendant opened the door to the cockpit for him, he shook his head. "I want my eye on the passengers," he said. "We'll talk through the door."

The voice of the captain was heard. "It's too

dangerous to land at Miami, Maharaja. The south Atlantic and Gulf coasts are socked in by fog clear to Mobile. Ground Control recommends New Orleans."

"We will land at Miami," the hijacker insisted. "Unless you want to land right now, in pieces."

"Can't we talk about it?"

"No. You have instruments to land in a fog. Use them."

The captain sighed. "Close the door, Peg," he said to the flight attendant.

Jivaro returned to his position at the rear of the plane. Again the captain's voice came over the intercom.

"Ladies and gentlemen, in case some of you couldn't hear my conversation with the maharaja, we are going down at Miami despite the fog condition there. We will be landing in about one hour. Please don't be alarmed. We are equipped with instruments for a blind landing. While not quite as safe as visual landing, we'll make it. However, we will take certain routine precautions so you're not shaken up too much in case it gets a little rough. The flight attendant will instruct you."

Raising her voice, Peg said, "Please remove all sharp objects from your pockets. Women passengers should take off shoes with high heels. When the seat belt light goes on, fasten your belt loosely enough so that you can bend forward with your head between your knees, and cover your head with your hands."

With frightened expressions on their faces, the passengers followed her instructions. Nervously, Vern asked Joe in a low voice, "How safe is a blind landing?"

"Not very," Joe muttered. "The captain was just trying to prevent panic. If he comes in a few feet too low, we'll belly flop and skid maybe a quarter mile. The friction could set the plane on fire. If he comes in a few feet too high, we could hit the control tower."

Frank added reassuringly, "But on the other hand, instrument landings are often made without even shaking up the passengers."

An hour later, the "Fasten Seat Belts" sign went on, and the captain could be heard on the intercom. "We will be landing in five minutes. Please follow the instructions given you."

The passengers fastened their seat belts loosely, leaned forward, and gripped their heads between their knees with both hands. The hijacker took an empty seat in the back of the plane, and leaned into the aisle so that he could keep an eye on everyone. The cadence of the engines changed as the plane dropped. Suddenly, the wheels struck the ground hard. The plane bounced, came down again, and taxied smoothly along the runway.

Cries of relief filled the cabin. A few sobs were heard, and Chet looked so white that Frank was afraid his friend would pass out.

When the plane stopped, everyone got up and looked through the windows. Outside there was a blank wall of fog.

The captain said over the intercom, "All right, Maharaja, we're down. Now what?"

The hijacker, back on his feet, moved forward to open the cockpit door. Without going inside, he asked, "Do police have the plane surrounded?"

"I imagine so," the captain replied. "Do you want to talk to them?"

"No, I merely want them to keep their distance. Order the plane refueled."

"This plane isn't designed for overseas flight, Maharaja," the captain pointed out. "But we could make Casablanca with less weight. If you'd release the passengers and just keep the crew, we'd be better off."

After considering, Jivaro gave in. "All right, I'll let most of them go, and just keep five. It would lighten the plane even more to unload the baggage, so have that done, too. But no tricks. If any cops come aboard as baggage handlers, I'll blow us all up."

"They couldn't," the captain said. "There's only an outside door to the baggage compartment, and no way to get in here from there."

"All right. Have the stuff removed and the plane refueled. When that's finished, I'll release everyone but five hostages."

Some time passed before the captain announced that the plane was refueled and they were ready to take off.

Satisfied that everything had been carried out as he had requested, the hijacker walked back to the center of the plane and pointed to the Hardy boys, Vern, Chet, and Cylvia Nash. "You five stay aboard. Everyone else can get off."

As the passengers were leaving, Jivaro said to Frank and Joe, "I warned your father to get off my back. Because he didn't, you two are going to end up in Kashmir."

When everyone but the hostages and the crew were off the plane, Joe got to his feet and stepped past Frank into the aisle.

"What's on your mind?" the hijacker hissed.

"I don't think you'd blow up this plane, because you'd have to blow yourself up, too."

Opening his coat, Jivaro gripped the loop on the end of the lanyard. "Test me," he challenged.

After studying the six tubes strapped to the man's body, Joe suddenly grabbed him and threw him down into the aisle! The hijacker jerked the lanyard, and Cylvia Nash screamed in terror!

4 A Clever Escape

Frantically, the hostages and the crew dived behind seats in a desperate attempt to escape the explosion. But nothing happened!

As Joe fell on top of the hijacker, the little man squirmed like an eel from his grip and delivered a karate chop to Joe's neck that momentarily stunned the boy. Then Jivaro jumped to his feet and raced for the emergency exit. By the time the others cautiously peeked above the headrests, the fake maharaja had opened the emergency door. He slipped through it, letting himself down by his hands, and dropped the dozen feet or so to the ground.

Frank rushed after him to the door, but he could see nothing through the thick blanket of fog.

Meanwhile, the flight attendant ran to the cockpit and returned with the pilot, the copilot, and the navigator. When the captain, a large, ruddy-faced man, learned what had happened, he hurried back to the cockpit to radio the surrounding police.

By then Joe had recovered from the karate chop. Frank asked him why he had taken the chance of jumping the hijacker.

"I recognized his so-called dynamite as highway flares," Joe told him. "It was all a bluff!"

Police, led by a uniformed lieutenant, raced aboard the plane. After questioning the witnesses about the hijacker's escape, the lieutenant ordered the entire landing field sealed off and searched.

At once, his men left to put the order into effect, and the lieutenant turned to the flight attendant. "I suppose he gave a fake name, but how was this kook listed on the manifest?"

She went to get her clipboard. "John Smith," she reported.

"Figures," the lieutenant said glumly.

"His real name is Anton Jivaro," Frank volunteered.

The lieutenant looked at him in surprise. "Who are you?"

"Frank Hardy." He pointed to his companions. "This is my brother Joe and my friends, Chet Morton and Vern Nelson."

Nodding acknowledgment, the lieutenant asked, "How do you happen to know this screwball's name?"

"My father's been trying to hunt him down," Frank said. "He's an escaped mental patient."

"Who is your father?"

"Fenton Hardy."

The lieutenant looked impressed. "I've heard a lot about him. So you two are the famous Hardy boys."

"We're the Hardy boys," Joe said modestly. "I don't know about famous."

The lieutenant grinned. "Give me a description of Anton Jivaro," he said.

The boys told all they knew about the fake maharaja while the lieutenant made notes. Just then, a police sergeant returned to report that no trace of the hijacker had been found.

"The fog is so thick, he could easily have sneaked by the cordon," the officer said. "I'm having the terminal and hangars searched right now."

"Also put out an all-points bulletin," the lieutenant instructed. "The man's name is Anton Jivaro." He rattled off a description from his notes.

"Yes, sir," the sergeant said, and left again.

The lieutenant turned to the captain, "You may as well reload your passengers and continue to Los Angeles."

Even though the plane was already refueled, it took some time before it could start again. The passengers, who had not yet recovered from their fright, boarded reluctantly, and all the luggage had to be reloaded.

Shortly after they were airborne, Chet said, "I just thought of where that hijacker might be."

"Where?" Frank asked.

"In the baggage compartment!"

"Oh, my!" Cylvia Nash said. "You mean he could hijack us again?"

"No. There's no way to get from the baggage compartment into the cabin while we're in flight," Frank said reassuringly. "Didn't you hear the captain say that? Besides, Chet's brainstorms are usually not on target."

"I figured it out logically," Chet insisted. "In the fog the hijacker could have hidden under the plane, or maybe in one of the wheel housings. I read about a young boy stowing away in a wheel housing once. While the stuff was being reloaded, Jivaro could have climbed through the open door."

"Two things wrong with that," Joe said. "The door's too high above the ground, and the baggage handlers would have seen him."

"Not so," Chet said. "It's a low opening at the back of the plane, not up high like the passenger entrance. And the handlers had to make more than one trip to load all those suitcases. They wouldn't close the door between trips. He could have gotten aboard easily."

"Could he survive in there?" Vern asked. "I mean, is the baggage compartment pressurized?"

"Sure," Chet said. "They ship pets in there, don't they?"

"Well, there's no way to check now," Frank said. "You can't get into the compartment from here any more than Jivaro could get into the cabin."

The flight to California was uneventful. Chet checked the rest of his nickels, but found none of any real value. The others tried to relax, and Cylvia closed her eyes in a futile attempt to take a nap. At ten P.M. they landed at Los Angeles International Airport.

As the boys were starting to debark, a baggage truck manned by two handlers backed up to the plane and one of them unlatched the baggage compartment door. As they pulled it open, a small, dark figure suddenly dashed out, knocking the men down as he pushed past them.

Before the dazed baggage handlers realized what had happened, the hijacker jumped from the truck and raced off across the field toward a distant chain-link fence.

Joe had watched Jivaro's swift escape and ran down the gangway as fast as he could. "Chet was right!" he exclaimed. "Let's get him!"

The four boys rushed after the fugitive. However, the hijacker had gained too much of a lead. Reaching the fence twenty yards ahead of them, he climbed up and over it with the agility of a monkey. He dashed to the corner and hopped aboard a bus that had just stopped.

Frank and Joe started to scale the fence, but dropped to the ground when the bus pulled away. Grimly, they walked back to the plane which by now was swarming with security guards who were questioning the passengers. Cylvia Nash pointed to the young detectives excitedly. "Here are the boys who chased after the man when he jumped out," she said.

The chief security guard turned to the Hardys. "Was it the hijacker Miami wired us about?" he asked.

"Yes," Frank replied. "He climbed over the fence and caught a bus at the corner."

"We'll try to have that bus stopped," the security officer said, and immediately began talking into his walkie-talkie.

The passengers were finally allowed to leave, and the four boys found themselves behind Cylvia when they entered the terminal. She quickened her pace and was warmly greeted by a lanky, red-haired man waiting for her.

Joe watched the two curiously. "I've seen this guy somewhere before," he mused.

The other three turned to observe the man.

"No wonder he looks familiar!" Vern exclaimed. "I think that's the man who stole my car!"

The lanky redhead was now walking next to Cylvia, so that his back was turned to them. But the boys had gotten a good look at him.

"I'm sure it is," Chet confirmed. "Didn't Mr. Hardy say his name was Red Sluice?"

"That's right," Joe said. "Let's grab him."

"We can't," Frank demurred. "We have no proof. Let's follow him instead. You go get our luggage. I'll rent a car and pull up outside."

He hurried across the lobby to a rental desk while the other three headed for the baggage area. The rental cars were parked in a lot across the street. Frank got a four-door sedan and was waiting for the boys when they came out of the terminal carrying their suitcases.

"Miss Nash's luggage hasn't come down the chute yet," Joe said as they loaded their bags in the trunk. "We've got plenty of time."

He climbed in front next to Frank, while Vern and Chet settled in the back. Soon Miss Nash and Red Sluice emerged, the latter carrying a large suitcase. They crossed the street to the public parking lot.

"The exit is right there," Joe said, pointing ahead. "So we're in a good position to take up the chase."

In a few minutes, the red-haired man and Miss Nash drove off in a red sports car with its top down.

"That ought to be easy to tail," Frank said, shifting into gear.

Sluice took the San Diego Freeway north to the Ventura Freeway, then east a short distance to the Hollywood Freeway. Turning into downtown Los Angeles, he pulled up in front of an apartment house on Parkview, directly across from Douglas MacArthur Park. Frank parked a quarter of a block away, and quietly they watched Red Sluice follow Cylvia Nash into the building.

As they disappeared, Joe slipped from the car. "I'll go after them," he volunteered, and walked to the front entrance of the apartment house. He went in and almost immediately came out again.

As he climbed back into the car, he said, "Her name's listed in the lobby, Apartment 2B. Now what do we do?"

"Wait," Frank said.

Five minutes later, Red Sluice left the building.

He climbed into the sports car and drove off. Frank followed. The lanky redhead led them to a small house a dozen blocks away. He pulled into an open carport attached to the house, then went inside.

Frank again parked a quarter of a block away on the opposite side of the street, where there was no light.

"What now?" Joe asked.

"We'll wait a while to see if he comes out again to lead us somewhere else," Frank said.

"You know it's almost eleven?" Chet inquired.

"So?" Frank asked.

"That makes it two A.M. in Bayport. I'm getting sleepy."

"If nothing happens in fifteen minutes, we'll find a hotel," Frank promised.

Just then a small, furtive-looking man came into view on the opposite side of the street. As he passed beneath a light, Joe stiffened. "That's Anton Jivaro!" he blurted out.

The hijacker turned toward the house Red Sluice had entered. With bated breath, the boys watched him ring the doorbell!

5 The Plant

The door opened and Jivaro entered.

"Joe and I'll do a little spying," Frank said tensely, turning to Chet. "You and Vern stay here. You'd better get behind the wheel so we can take off fast if we run into trouble."

"Okay."

The Hardys got out of the car, crossed the street, and walked up to the house. They could not see into the front room because the drapes were drawn. Tiptoeing to the door, they listened, but heard nothing.

"You check to the left, and I'll go to the right," Frank whispered to his brother.

Joe nodded, and the two separated. There were

lights behind drawn drapes in windows on both sides, but they could not see in or hear anything. They met in the back, where all was dark.

"Any luck?" Frank asked in a low voice.

"No," Joe replied.

At that moment, a kitchen light went on and they noticed that the screened window was open. Tiptoeing over, they peered inside. Anton Jivaro was seating himself at the table, while Red Sluice turned on the gas under a kettle.

"All I got is instant," the lanky redhead said.

"It's all right," the hijacker told him.

Sluice put his hands on his hips and regarded the little man dourly. "If you weren't an old partner of mine, I'd turn you in. Course you're doing a good job of that yourself by making headlines all over the world with that silly hijack attempt. With all that publicity, you're easy to trace."

"I was just trying to collect my inheritance," Jivaro said sullenly.

"What inheritance? Will you get over the crazy idea that you're a maharaja?"

"But I am. My father was the son of Kashmir's last monarch, Maharaja Hari Singh."

"Your father was a used car salesman in Brooklyn."

"Just because he was a car salesman doesn't mean he wasn't the maharaja's son," Jivaro argued. "There are ex-kings working as waiters in New York

City. My grandfather went into exile and passed away twelve years later, making my father next in line. When he died, I became maharaja."

"I looked up Kashmir at the library," Red said impatiently. "The last maharaja's only son was Dr. Karan Singh, who was elected president after his father was deposed. You've got to stop telling people you're a maharaja."

The kettle whistled and Red made two cups of instant coffee. Then he sat down across the table from his old partner.

"What are your plans now?" he asked.

"I figured you'd put me to work at your plant."

"You're even crazier than I thought! You think I'm going to risk the whole operation by bringing a looney into the gang? I don't know what happened to you, but as long as you don't know your name, you can't work with me!"

"Would you rather I tipped off the cops to who robbed that bank in Boston?"

Red Sluice's eyes narrowed. "Blackmail?"

"Let's say you're going to hire me only because we go back a long time," the little man suggested.

After a period of silence, Red chuckled grimly. "Well, I guess we both have something on each other, then. All right, you can start in the morning. But you got to promise you'll forget this maharaja stuff."

"I won't tell anybody who I really am," Anton Jivaro agreed.

"Okay, we'll be leaving at eight, so we better get to bed as soon as we finish our coffee."

There was a meow right next to Frank and Joe, and both boys turned in the direction of the sound. A cat stood at the back door. While they stared at the feline, Red Sluice rose and opened the door. "Okay, kitty, come on in," he said, then spotted the two boys.

"Who are you?" he yelled, rushing at them.

Frank and Joe ducked around the corner of the house and ran off, with Sluice right behind them. Chet saw them coming and started the engine. Vern, who had moved into the front with Chet, leaned over and opened the right rear door. Frank and Joe dived into the car, and Chet gunned away so fast that the door slammed shut by itself.

The Hardys looked back to see Red Sluice standing in the street, shaking his fist.

"What happened?" Chet asked as he slowed to round a corner.

"He caught us listening at a window," Frank said.

"Did you find out anything?" Vern inquired.

"Sure did," Frank replied, and related what they had heard. "We'll come back in the morning to follow them to the plant Red Sluice mentioned," he added.

They went to a downtown hotel, where they got connecting rooms with twin beds. By now it was after midnight, and the boys went to sleep instantly.

The next morning they had a quick breakfast, then drove to Red Sluice's house. By seven-thirty, they were parked across the street. At eight, the lanky redhead and Jivaro came out and climbed into the red sports car. When they drove off, the gray sedan followed.

Frank, who was behind the wheel, kept a safe distance as the thief led them to a warehouse at the edge of Old Chinatown. Sluice parked in front, while Frank drove past and stopped a hundred feet away. Through the rear window, the boys watched Red and Anton Jivaro enter the warehouse.

Frank drove around the block and turned into an alley in back of the building. He told Chet to get behind the wheel while he and Joe investigated the warehouse.

There was a large sliding door at the rear of the building that was locked from inside. Next to it was a window about four feet from the ground. It was too dirty to see through, but Frank wiped clean a circular area with a scrap of newspaper he found and peered into a restroom.

"See if we can get in through the window," Joe urged.

Frank nodded and pushed up the lower part.

Since the room was empty, the two boys climbed over the sill, letting themselves down carefully on the other side. They tiptoed to the door across from the window, opened it a crack, and peered out into a large, barnlike room. It contained about twenty new and almost new cars! A dozen men in coveralls were working on them, systematically taking them apart.

"Why are they doing this?" Joe whispered.

"It must be for spare parts," Frank whispered back. "Remember Dad guessed they were either repainting the cars, or stripping them for parts to sell on the black market."

"Do you see Red and his crazy friend?" Joe asked.

Frank shook his head. "No one's looking this way. Let's poke around a little."

He eased the door open enough for them to slip through. Quickly they ducked behind a partially dismantled car and glanced around. They noticed a door centered in the wall to their right, and another open one on the left which led into a small office. Red Sluice and Anton Jivaro were inside. Apparently, Red was introducing Jivaro to the burly man behind a large oak desk.

"That big guy must be the boss of the operation," Joe whispered.

"Probably just the boss of the warehouse," Frank replied. "Dad said the tattooed guy named Crafty

Kraft was one of the ring's chief lieutenants, so he's probably in charge of the car thefts."

A man crossed over to the door in the right wall, opened it, and went through. A moment later, he returned carrying a wrench, closed the door behind him, and went back to work.

"Let's see what's in that room," Frank suggested.

"Right in front of those workmen?" Joe objected.

"With all the people around here, no one's going to notice. Where's your spirit of adventure?"

Joe shrugged. "I'm game if you are."

No one glanced their way as the Hardys casually sauntered over to the closed door. Frank opened it a few inches and peered into the room to make sure it was empty. Then the boys slipped inside and Frank shut the door behind them.

It was a small machine shop, containing a metal lathe, a planer, a drill press, and a number of other power tools. Hanging from the walls were assorted hand tools, such as wrenches and screwdrivers.

"They must use these to fix up the spare parts so they look like new," Joe surmised.

"Probably," Frank agreed.

"Well, let's get out of here before someone else comes for a tool."

But Joe's advice was too late. At that moment another workman came in. He was tall, thin, and

234

had a bald head. When he saw the boys, he raised
the large wrench he was carrying like a weapon.

"What are you doing here?" he hissed. "You don't
belong in this place!"

6 Caught!

Frank and Joe regarded the raised wrench warily.

"I said what are you doing here?" the workman repeated.

"We, eh, we're looking for jobs," Joe replied, hoping he could talk his way out of the situation. "The front door was locked and nobody answered, so we came in the back way. We thought this was the hiring office, but I guess it isn't."

The workman looked them over suspiciously. "What made you think we needed help?"

"We're auto mechanics," Frank put in. "Isn't this a repair shop?"

Another workman stepped into the room, and

came to a halt when he saw the baldheaded man holding the boys at bay with his wrench.

"What's going on?" he inquired.

"I caught these two nosing around. They claim they're looking for jobs and wandered in here because they thought it was the hiring office."

"Wandered in how? Both the front and back doors are locked!"

"The back door was open," Joe said, his heart pounding.

"What do you think?" the baldheaded man asked his companion.

"We better take them over to the office and let Big Harry handle it."

"Okay, you two," the man with the wrench ordered, gesturing toward the door. "March!"

Frank and Joe had no choice but to obey. They were herded across the big garage to the office on its opposite side. On the way, they saw Red Sluice and Anton Jivaro standing toward the front of the building with their backs turned, talking to one of the mechanics.

In the office, the burly man behind the desk looked up in surprise as the boys were shoved in by the two workmen.

"What's this, Slim?" he asked the baldheaded man.

"I found these two in the machine shop. They

claim they were looking for work and thought that was the hiring office."

Frowning at the boys, Big Harry asked, "How'd you get in here?"

"The back door was open," Joe said.

"Who left it unlocked?" Harry demanded in an accusing voice.

"Not me," Slim said. "I wasn't the last one in. Anyway, I think they're lying."

"Bruce, go check the door," Big Harry ordered the other workman.

Frank said, "It fell shut behind us. It might have locked itself."

Bruce paused in the doorway, looking at his employer inquiringly.

"Never mind," Big Harry said impatiently. He stared at the two boys. "What's your names?"

"I'm Joe Bayport," Joe said. "He's my brother Frank."

Just then Red Sluice walked into the office, took one look at the boys and exclaimed, "What are you two doing here?"

"You know them?" Big Harry asked.

"I sure do!"

"Slim and Bruce found them lurking around the machine shop. Who are they?"

"I don't know their names, but they were hanging around my house last night also. They were peeking in a window, getting ready to break in I think," Red explained.

"You sure they're the same ones?" Big Harry asked.

"Positive. Anton and I were having coffee in the kitchen when the cat meowed to get in. I opened the door and saw them because the light from the kitchen window was shining right in their faces."

"To make sure, go get your old friend," Big Harry suggested.

With sinking hearts, Frank and Joe realized that once Jivaro saw them, he would recognize them as the Hardy boys. As long as the crooks thought they were just thieves, they had a good chance of being let go with just a lecture. But if it was discovered they they were the sons of the private detective investigating the car-theft ring, they were in big trouble!

But Red Sluice gave them a brief respite. "My friend didn't see them," he admitted. They got away before he came out. I chased them until they jumped into a car and drove off."

"Okay, boys," Big Harry said to Frank and Joe. "Get out your I.D.s."

The boys winced inwardly. This was just as bad as being identified by Jivaro. Desperately, Joe stalled by saying, "I'm not carrying any."

"Neither am I," Frank added.

"Search them for wallets," Big Harry ordered.

Joe had kept an eye on the man with the wrench. When Slim let it hang at his side, feeling the boys would not try a break, the young detective suddenly reached out and grabbed it from his hand.

Tossing it into a wastebasket across the room, he yelled, "Come on, Frank!" and headed for the door.

Slim stepped in front of him, though, and delivered a roundhouse right. Joe ducked under it, drove a fist into the man's belly, then delivered an uppercut that sent his opponent reeling backwards.

Red Sluice swung at Frank, who ducked the blow. An instant later, Bruce knocked Frank down with a hard right to the jaw. But as he bore in to finish the boy off, Joe stuck out a foot to trip him. A moment later, Bruce was flat on his face.

As Frank recovered, Red Sluice rushed at him. Frank pushed him back into Big Harry, who had just come around the desk to join in the fray.

As the two workmen again moved in for the attack, Joe shoved Slim, Frank hit Bruce, and the two men crashed together, going down with a loud thud.

"Let's get out of here!" Joe yelled, leading the way through the door.

They were almost to the restroom when the four hoods recovered sufficiently to run after them. The boys darted inside and Frank slammed and bolted the door. They climbed out the window just as a heavy shoulder hit the door from the other side.

Chet started the engine and Vern leaned over to let the Hardys into the rear of the car. When Chet pulled away, the back door of the warehouse opened and the four hoods rushed out.

"After them!" Big Harry yelled.

Looking through the rear window, the boys saw the thieves jump into a green sedan parked behind the warehouse. Big Harry took the wheel, swung around, and raced after them.

Chet sped down an alley and turned right at the cross street before the other car came in sight behind them. Then he swung left into another alley. He continued this winding course for some blocks until he was sure they had shaken their pursuers.

"Now what?" he asked. "Back to the hotel?"

"May as well," Frank said.

Chet continued on for a few minutes, then pulled over to the curb. "Which way is it?"

"Are you lost?" Vern inquired.

"No, but I think the car is!" he joked, relieving the tension.

The four boys laughed and then looked carefully in all directions. Chet's winding course had confused everyone.

"I think it's that way," Joe said, pointing.

Chet started up again, but after a few minutes,

they realized they were driving deeper and deeper into Old Chinatown. The streets became narrow and buildings on both sides pushed right up to the sidewalks.

Glancing into the rearview mirror, Chet suddenly said. "Uh-oh."

The others turned around to look. A block behind them, the hoods had just turned a corner. Apparently, they had been randomly cruising side streets in search of the boys and had finally sighted them.

Chet turned right, then swung left into an alley, attempting the same zigzag maneuver as before. But the other car was too close behind this time. It followed wherever the boys went.

As they sped along one of the narrow streets, Chet sighed. "Hey, here's a whole block of Chinese restaurants."

"Want to stop for a snack?" Vern inquired sarcastically. Chet did not reply.

They went past a sign reading ROAD CONSTRUCTION AHEAD, and the pavement suddenly became slick with mud spewed up from a drainage ditch being dug to their right. On their left, a flimsy wooden guard rail edged a sheer twenty-foot drop into a rocky ditch.

The pursuing car put on a burst of speed and began to come up alongside the boys.

"They're going to run you into the ditch, Chet!"

Frank cautioned. "Give them a driving lesson."

Chet nodded and suddenly slammed on his brakes. He let the green sedan shoot past, then swung left, and gently prodded their opponents' bumper. Accelerating, he nudged the hoods' car forward and sideways so that they, instead of the boys, nosed over toward the ditch.

Finally, the green sedan came to a halt with its radiator buried in the mudbank. Chet swung back to the right in order to straighten his wheel. Just then he hit a patch of mud, skidded, and headed directly for the guard rail with the twenty-foot vertical drop beyond!

7 The Stakeout

Chet turned the front wheels into the direction of the skid. The car veered sidewise, but straightened out just as the left rear fender scraped the guard rail. Gritting his teeth, Chet fought for control, and was finally able to drive onto the right side of the road.

"Whew!" Vern muttered. "Was everybody as scared as I was?"

"I wasn't scared at all," Chet said, his voice shaking. "I've got nerves of steel." Then, exhausted, he slumped behind the wheel, resting his head against the window. Frank twisted in his seat to see what happened to the green sedan. Big Harry and

Red Sluice were angrily trying to push the car out of the ditch, but the harder they struggled the more embedded the vehicle became.

All four boys chuckled smugly, but not wanting to push their luck, they drove quickly back to the hotel, where they decided to phone Fenton Hardy in Bayport.

Frank dialed and Gertrude Hardy answered.

"Are you all right?" she asked anxiously. "We heard on TV about that terrible hijacking."

"We're all fine, Aunt Gertrude. Is Dad there?"

"No, he's gone away. He said it was a secret mission. You're to leave word where you can be reached, and he'll get in touch with you."

Frank gave her the telephone number of the hotel and their room numbers.

"Have you found Vern's nickel?" Aunt Gertrude asked.

"We haven't had time to look yet," Frank said. "Maybe we'll get to it this afternoon."

"All right. I'm glad that this time it's just a simple mystery, and you're not involved with criminals."

"Yes, Aunt Gertrude. Say hello to Mom."

When Frank hung up, Joe raised his eyebrows. "Dad isn't there?"

"No. He's on some kind of secret mission. I wish we'd been able to talk to him, so we could discuss our next move."

245

"That's simple," Chet said. "We call the police and tell them about that warehouse."

"That may not be a good idea just yet. If they raid the place, all they'll get is the small fry. We want the kingpin of the operation!"

"Maybe it's Big Harry," Chet said.

"I doubt it."

"So how do we get the chief?" Vern asked.

"We could stake the place out and photograph everyone who goes in or out with our pocket cameras," Joe suggested.

"Good idea," Frank agreed. "The big boss is bound to show up eventually and when he does, we'll have some real evidence to turn over to the police."

All four agreed that this was the best plan. They decided to watch the warehouse in shifts. Frank and Chet were to take the first one, while Joe and Vern would check up on the Liberty Head nickel. They all drove to the warehouse and parked a block away. Getting out of the car, the boys scouted the area.

No one was in sight as they approached the front of the building. A number of empty wooden crates and cardboard boxes were piled near the entrance. While the others kept watch, Frank picked out a large shipping carton that had contained a refrigerator. He used his pocketknife to make a door in the back of it, cutting only the top, bottom, and left side, and then bent the right side so that the door could be opened and closed. He set a small wooden crate into the carton to serve as a seat, then put a hole at eye level.

"This'll make a great 'guard house' for me in front," he declared, turning to his friends. "Now let's find a place for Chet to hide in back of the building."

They began walking toward the alley to pick a safe spot when suddenly Frank, who was in the lead, motioned for everyone to move out of sight. Big Harry was parking behind the warehouse. The sedan's radiator was caked with dried mud, but none of the occupants seemed to have been injured in the accident. They all got out and went into the building.

Frank watched them, gingerly peeking around the corner.

"What's going on?" Joe whispered.

"Nothing now," Frank said. He moved forward and motioned for the others to follow him. "The hoods who chased us just got back and went inside. None of them seemed to be hurt."

As they neared the sedan, Vern said, "Those guys must have had a tow truck rescue them. They couldn't have backed out on their own. They were nose-first in that mud bank."

There was a small shed right across from the rear

door of the warehouse on the other side of the alley. They found it unlocked and went in. It was empty. A dirt-encrusted window faced the building. When Chet scraped clean a spot about the size of a silver dollar, he had a perfect view of the door.

Handing him his pocket camera, Joe said, "Snap pictures of everyone going in or out. Okay?"

"When are you guys coming to relieve us?" Chet asked.

"Soon as Vern and I finish our business," Joe told him. "Shouldn't be later than one o'clock."

"You mean we have to wait until then for lunch?"

"It's not going to hurt you," Vern chided him.

Chet grimaced. "You skinny guys can talk, but it takes sustenance to maintain a muscular body like mine!"

"Oh sure, real muscular!" Vern teased his cousin, as he and the Hardys started back to the street. Frank quickly took up his station in the refrigerator carton, while Joe and Vern went back to the car.

Slipping behind the wheel, Joe asked, "Where to?"

"First, we ought to see the lawyer in charge of Uncle Gregg's estate," Vern suggested. "He's in the Nichols Building downtown. His name is Charles Avery."

The attorney had a plush office on the seventeenth floor. He was a plump, middle-aged, cheerful-looking man. Greeting the boys courteously, he asked them to sit down in comfortable chairs.

"As you know, your uncle had severe financial reverses shortly before he died," the lawyer told Vern. "Even his extensive coin collection had to be sold to satisfy claims against the estate. All, that is, but the 1913 Liberty Head nickel, which he left to you. Unfortunately, that has disappeared."

"How?" Vern asked.

"The president of the bank where your uncle had his safe-deposit box can explain that," Charles Avery said. "Let me phone Mr. Barton Laing of the Bunker Bank to make an appointment for you."

The lawyer called and was able to arrange an immediate meeting between Mr. Laing and the boys.

The bank was only two blocks from the Nichols Building, so they left their car where they had parked it and walked. Barton Laing, a tall, slightly stooped man with gray hair, shook hands with the boys and invited them into his office. When all three were seated, he leaned back in his desk chair and began folding and unfolding his hands.

"This is quite embarrassing to the bank, Mr. Nelson," he said to Vern nervously. "Of course, we have no legal responsibility for the missing coin. The only evidence that it was ever in your uncle's safe-deposit box is a statement in his will that on a particular date he placed it there. Nobody saw him do it, because what customers put in or take out of their boxes is their private business."

"Why would he say he put it there if he didn't?" Vern asked.

"I can't imagine."

Joe spoke up. "Could he have taken it out again and not changed his will?"

The banker shook his head. "He never opened the box after the day he deposited it."

"How can you be sure of that?" Vern asked.

"Our records show every visit. Whenever a customer uses his safe-deposit box, he must sign a card giving not only the date, but the exact time of day. Our files show no such visits after the date specified in his will."

"Could a bank employee have gotten into the box?" Joe asked.

Mr. Laing frowned. "Impossible. No one but the boxholder possesses a key. A boxholder's key, that is. There is, of course, the bank's master key."

"Master key?" Vern repeated.

"Let me explain the procedure. It takes two keys to open a box, the customer's and the bank's. The bank key fits all boxes. But it can't open a box by itself. The customer's key must be used along with it."

Vern said, "Then when Uncle Gregg put the coin in the box, somebody saw him do it."

"Not necessarily. Usual procedure is for the customer to carry his box into one of the curtained alcoves in the vault room, where he can transact his business in privacy. When he's ready to return the box, he calls the vault clerk, who uses both keys to lock it up again."

Joe spoke up. "But if Mr. Nelson had chosen not to use a private alcove, he could have put the coin into his box right in front of the vault clerk, couldn't he?"

"Oh yes, but there would be no record of whether or not he did that."

"Would there be a record of who the vault clerk was that day?"

"Of course. She signs the card."

"Has she been asked whether or not she saw Mr. Nelson put the coin into the box?"

Barton Laing gave Joe an indulgent smile. "It's hardly likely an employee would recall anything about a transaction that took place so many years ago. The person on vault duty may usher as many as fifty people to their safe-deposit boxes in a single day."

"Is the clerk still employed here?"

"I have no idea," Mr. Laing said. "But I'll find out."

Picking up his desk phone, he asked for the safe-deposit-box records to be brought to his office. A few minutes later, a young man delivered a metal file-card holder.

"Want me to wait?" he asked.

The bank president shook his head. "You can pick it up later."

As the clerk left, Mr. Laing began thumbing through the cards. Finally, he pulled one out.

"Here it is," he said. "Yes, she's still working here."

"Let's ask her if she remembers Mr. Nelson using his box that day," Joe suggested.

Shrugging, the banker again picked up his phone. "I doubt that she'll remember, but we'll try." Into the phone he said, "Send in the vault clerk, please."

After a few moments' wait, there was a knock on the office door.

"Come in," Barton Laing called.

The door opened and the boys gaped. Cylvia Nash stepped into the room!

8 Trapped!

"Why, hello, boys," Cylvia said in surprise. "What are you doing here?"

"You know these two?" Barton Laing asked.

"They were on the plane with me," she explained. "In fact Joe was the one who nearly captured the hijacker."

"They want to talk to you about Gregg Nelson's missing coin," the bank president said.

"Oh, are you the nephew?" Cylvia asked Vern. "That never occurred to me when we met."

Vern grinned. "It's a common name."

"Miss Nash," Barton Laing said, "You're registered as the one who admitted Mr. Nelson to the vault eight years ago when, according to his will, he put the coin in his safe-deposit box. Do you remember that day?"

"So long ago?" She shook her head.

"No recollection at all of seeing the coin?" Joe asked.

"I don't even remember signing Mr. Nelson in."

Mr. Laing shrugged. "I guess that settles that," he said. "Sorry."

"It's not your fault," Vern smiled wryly. "And after all, it's only a hundred thousand dollars."

As the boys walked back to the car, Joe said, "I might believe Miss Nash if we hadn't seen who met her at the airport. But people who associate with crooks are usually crooked too. For all we know, she was the one who stole your uncle's coin!"

"I don't see any way to find out," Vern said.

"Don't give up so easily," Joe advised. "We know where she lives. Maybe there's some evidence at her apartment."

"Well, we can't just break in!"

"Of course not. But I have a plan. Let's buy some coveralls."

Joe drove to a department store, where each bought a suit of work clothes. Next, they went to a hardware store and bought tool belts resembling those worn by telephone repairmen. They returned to the hotel long enough to change into their outfits and then drove to Cylvia's home.

They parked in front of the building, went inside, and rang the apartment manager's bell.

An elderly woman answered the door. Joe smiled. "Telephone company, ma'am. The tenant in 2B reported her phone out of order."

"She isn't at home days," the woman said. "I'll have to let you in."

Leading the way up to the second floor, the manager opened the door of 2B with a passkey.

"Set the lock when you come out," she told them.

"Yes, ma'am," Joe promised.

At the warehouse, meanwhile, Chet was getting tired of peering through the small clean spot in the dirt-encrusted window. He was also getting hungry, thinking about hot dogs, hamburgers, and pizza.

Just then, he saw a small Chinese boy about four years old meander by, clutching a dollar bill in his hand. A few minutes later the child came back, working a yo-yo with his right hand and licking an ice-cream bar on a stick in his left. Chet could not stand it any longer. He ran out the door and after the boy.

"Hey, kid," he called out.

The child stopped to regard him with large eyes.

Chet took out a dollar bill. "Do me a favor and I'll give you a quarter. Go back to where you got the ice cream and get me one, too."

"Eh?" the child said.

When Chet repeated himself, the little boy answered in a stream of Cantonese.

"Don't speak English, huh?" Chet said. He pointed at the bar, then down the alley in the direction of a delicatessen he'd seen earlier.

Smiling, the child held his ice cream up toward Chet's mouth.

"No, I don't want a lick," Chet said. "I want a whole one." Again gesturing in the direction of the delicatessen, he held out the dollar bill.

The little boy suddenly looked as though he understood. Smiling broadly and nodding his head, he accepted the bill.

He turned around and retraced his way toward the store while Chet slipped into the shed again and put his eye back to the peephole.

When he spotted the little boy on his way back, he hurried out into the alley. With a big smile, the child handed him a yo-yo and a quarter in change, spouted a friendly stream of Cantonese, and walked away. Chet stared after him darkly, his stomach rumbling.

Out in front, Frank was getting just as tired of

sitting in the refrigerator carton. His interest perked up when the warehouse door opened and Red Sluice came out with Anton Jivaro. The red sports car was parked only a few feet from Frank's box, and he could hear their conversation clearly as they walked toward it.

"You should have told me right away the Hardy boys were on that plane, instead of waiting until now," Red complained to his cousin.

"How'd I know that Fenton Hardy was investigating you too?" Jivaro asked. "Anyway, didn't your girlfriend just tell you over the phone that their being here has nothing to do with the car operation?"

The two climbed into the sports car.

"Yeah, she did," Red admitted. "When I called to bawl her out for not mentioning they were on the plane, she told me they're in town to check on some missing coin that one of their friends inherited. We'll get the details when we meet her at her apartment."

"Will she be able to get away from the bank?"

"She says she can make it on her lunch hour. The key's under a flowerpot, so we can get in."

Red started the engine, but did not immediately drive off because Jivaro said, "Wait a minute. You think I ought to go with you?"

"Why not?"

"She was on the plane. She's going to recognize me as the hijacker."

"She's not going to squeal on any friend of mine," Red told him. "Don't worry about it." With that, they took off in a cloud of dust.

At the apartment, Joe and Vern had searched everywhere except in the bedroom without finding anything of interest. Now, while going through a dresser drawer, Joe saw a bankbook under a pile of stockings. Opening it, he let out a whistle.

"What's the matter?" Vern asked.

"This is a savings account in Cylvia Nash's name, opened ten years ago. It shows regular deposits of twenty dollars every month, up to last month— except for one!"

Vern shrugged. "So she's a frugal woman. You can't blame her for missing one deposit in ten years."

"I didn't mean she missed one. She made a larger one. On April 12, eight years ago, she put in fifty thousand dollars!"

Vern took the book from his friend's hand to look at it. "Now there's a coincidence! Uncle Gregg put that coin in his safe-deposit box on March 22, just two weeks prior to her big deposit."

Suddenly, they heard a key turn in the front door. Joe hurriedly replaced the bankbook beneath the stockings where he had found it and closed the dresser drawer. Then he and Vern flattened themselves against the wall at either side of the bedroom door.

A male voice that sounded vaguely familiar to Joe said, "We may as well relax. She won't be along for at least fifteen minutes."

Another man grunted an unintelligible reply. The boys were relieved that it wasn't Cylvia who had entered. They would never have been able to pass themselves off as telephone repairmen to her!

Joe signaled to Vern and tiptoed toward the bathroom. When they were both inside, he closed the door as quickly as he could, and went over to the window. He raised it carefully and looked out. They were on the second floor, and the drop to the concrete courtyard was too great to risk.

"Guess we'll have to walk out the front way," the young detective grumbled. "I hope it isn't anybody that knows us. That one voice sounded familiar!"

"Not to me," Vern said. "But do you think we'll get away with it even if they don't know us?"

"Sure. We'll just have to brazen it out," Joe said with determination. "Just say the phone is okay now. If they ask how we got in, we'll tell the truth. The manager let us in."

"Maybe we better wait in here until they leave," Vern suggested.

259

Joe shook his head. "They're expecting somebody along in fifteen minutes, and it's a woman. Probably Cylvia Nash. If she sees us, it's all over."

Vern nodded. "Okay. Let's try it."

Joe eased open the bathroom door. Deliberately rattling some tools on his belt, he said in a loud voice, "The phone's working all right now. What's our next stop?"

Vern mumbled an address, as they walked into the front room.

"Your phone's—" Joe started to say, but came to an abrupt halt when he saw Red Sluice and Anton Jivaro seated in chairs.

Sluice jumped to his feet instantly. "Those thieves again!" he shouted.

The boys raced for the door, but Sluice got there ahead of them and, with his back firmly planted against it, pulled out a knife!

9 The Bomb

Anton Jivaro followed the group. "Thieves?" he said. "What do you mean by that?"

Red pointed his knife at Joe. "That's one of the kids who tried to break into my house last night. Then we caught him in the machine shop at the warehouse this morning. I don't know who the other one is."

"I'll tell you! First of all, they're not thieves!" the hijacker exclaimed. "That's Joe Hardy, and the one with him is named Vern Nelson."

Joe whispered to Vern, "You take the little guy and I'll handle Red."

"You'll handle who?" Red said, raising his knife threateningly.

Suddenly, Anton rushed at Vern and landed three quick blows before the boy could get set. As Vern reeled backward, Joe undid the buckle of his heavily laden tool belt and tossed it at Red. A heavy wrench smashed into the man's toe.

"Ow!" Red yelled, dancing on one foot in pain.

Vern recovered, grabbed Jivaro by both arms and hurled him across the room. The little man crashed into Red and both went down in a tangle.

Joe scooted out the door with Vern right behind him. The boys were running down the stairs four at a time before Red and Anton picked themselves up and took off in hot pursuit.

The elderly woman who managed the apartment house was supervising a gardener weeding the lawn when the boys rushed outside. Both she and the gardener gazed after them in surprise, and almost failed to notice Red Sluice and Anton Jivaro dash out the door. The two hoods stopped suddenly when they saw they would have witnesses. Red hurriedly put away his knife before the manager and the gardener turned around to look at them.

The young detectives jumped into the gray sedan. Joe started the engine, and they took off as fast as they could.

"Sluice and Jivaro are walking to their car real easy," he reported looking back. "Guess they don't want to chance the manager calling the police."

Joe turned a corner before the red sports car started to move. He ducked through an alley, then drove a zigzag course for several blocks. When he was sure he had lost his pursuers, he returned to the hotel.

As they approached their rooms, Joe felt in his coveralls pockets and said, "Uh-oh! Guess what."

"What?"

"My room key was in a section of that tool belt. If they find it, they'll know where we're staying, because the tag on the key shows the hotel."

"I still have my key," Vern said. "I'll let you in my room, and you can go into yours through the connecting door. But we should change hotels once we get Frank and Chet."

After changing back into their regular clothes, the boys drove to the warehouse to relieve their friends. En route they picked up a sack of hamburgers and soft drinks for lunch.

Joe gave a code signal with his horn when they passed the front of the warehouse, then parked down the street. As they walked up the block, Frank emerged from the refrigerator carton and started toward them.

"It's about time," he said as he neared. "Chet's probably half dead of starvation."

Joe grinned. "We've got something to save him," he said, waving the bag of hamburgers. "We'd have been back sooner, if we hadn't run into some problems. Anything happen here?"

"Nothing important. Red Sluice and Anton Jivaro came out and drove off in the sports car. I overheard them talking before they left. They were headed for Cylvia Nash's apartment."

"Wish we'd known that," Joe said ruefully. "We were searching the place when they walked in, and had to fight our way out."

"Searching it? Why?"

"Cylvia's the bank clerk who checked Vern's Uncle Gregg into the vault the day he put the Liberty Head nickel in his safe-deposit box. We found a bankbook in her name showing a fifty-thousand-dollar deposit two weeks later."

"Maybe she stole the coin!" Frank exclaimed.

"Maybe. With the system the bank has, I don't see how she could have, but the timing of that deposit is certainly suspicious."

Together the three walked cautiously around to the alley. Chet was in the shed, looking through the eyehole and playing with his yo-yo absentmindedly. He turned around as they entered.

"Where'd you get the toy?" Joe asked.

"Through a failure in communication. I'd rather

not talk about it." Eyeing the sack Joe was carrying, he sniffed appreciatively. "That smells like hamburgers."

"Five of them," Joe said. "Two for you and one each for the rest of us. Plus four sodas."

As the boys opened the bag to begin eating, Joe asked Chet if he had anything to report. The boy said nothing had happened except that half a dozen workmen had emerged from the warehouse at noon and walked down the alley in the direction of the delicatessen. A half hour later they returned. Chet assumed they had gone for lunch.

After they finished eating, the boys exchanged cameras. Vern was to take over stakeout duty at the rear of the warehouse, while Joe would station himself in the refrigerator carton in front. Chet and Frank decided to return to the hotel.

Leaving Vern in the shed, the Hardys and Chet walked to the car. "Be careful," Joe cautioned. "I left my room key in the tool belt when we were getting away from those hoods, and if they find it, they'll know where we're staying."

As the two drove off, Joe went to the refrigerator carton, settled himself on the wooden box, and put his eye to the view hole.

An hour passed without anyone going in or out of the warehouse. He was getting bored when he heard someone opening the cardboard door behind him.

Jumping to his feet, he whirled with his hands raised in karate stance, then relaxed when he saw it was Vern.

In a low voice Vern said, "Remember that tattooed truck driver your father said was named Crafty Kraft?"

Joe nodded.

"He backed his truck up to the sliding door. I couldn't see what he unloaded, because the hood was right in front of me, but I'll bet it was stolen cars, and I wouldn't be surprised if mine was among them!"

"Maybe we'd better take a look," Joe suggested.

They walked around to the alley. Kraft's truck was still parked there, but the sliding door was closed. After looking both ways to make sure no one was watching, Joe raised the restroom window and peered inside. Seeing it was empty, he climbed in. Vern followed.

Cautiously, Joe peered out into the big, barnlike garage. When he spotted no one nearby, he opened the door far enough for Vern and him to slip through. They crouched behind the same partially dismantled car where the Hardys had concealed themselves earlier.

The office was open and no one was inside.

Glancing around, Joe spotted neither Big Harry nor Crafty Kraft.

Three relatively new cars were parked right next to the back door. Excitedly Vern pointed to a blue sedan. "That's mine!" he whispered.

Suddenly the boys had to crouch low because a workman was headed their way. He went by without seeing them and entered the restroom.

"When he comes out, he'll spot us," Joe pointed out. "We'll have to find another place to hide."

"How about between those cars?" Vern suggested.

Nodding, Joe stood up, glanced toward the crew to make sure no one was looking, and led the way to the newly delivered cars. At that moment, Crafty Kraft and Big Harry rose to their feet right in front of them! They had been in a crouched position, examining the underside of one of the cars. They spotted the boys instantly.

"Hey, you!" Big Harry shouted in a threatening voice, starting toward them.

Joe and Vern bolted for the restroom door, only to find it locked from inside. Before they could run in any other direction, Big Harry grabbed Joe in a bear hug and Crafty Kraft collared Vern. Fighting hard, the boys broke free and began to trade blows with their opponents. Moments later, a number of workmen, alerted by the commotion, converged on them. The young detectives were grabbed and held motionless by a dozen hands.

"Take them into my office," Big Harry ordered.

Frank and Chet, meanwhile, discussed Joe's warning as they rode up in the hotel elevator.

"If they found the key, they could be waiting for us when we walk into our room," Chet said with trepidation. "They could take us off somewhere, and we'd never be seen again."

"You sound like Aunt Gertrude," Frank said. "They wouldn't try to kidnap us here."

"Why not?"

"Because a hotel is too public a place for that kind of thing. How would they get us across the lobby? More likely they'd just bug our rooms so they'd know what our plans are."

"Then we'll look for bugs," Chet concluded with relief.

The boys entered each room cautiously, examining everything with great care. They even checked the heating vents, and unscrewed both the mouthpieces and earpieces of the telephones to make sure no microphones had been planted in them.

"The place is clean," Frank declared finally.

"When do we have to relieve Joe and Vern?" Chet asked.

"We won't. We'll just pick them up about five. I

figure that's when the gang'll close down for the day. If the big boss hasn't appeared by then, he probably won't show up at all. There's no point in staking out the warehouse all night. We'll start again in the morning."

"Suits me," Chet said, flopping down on his bed.

"I'm going to take a shower," Frank announced, and walked through the connecting bathroom into his own room.

His suitcase lay on a small bench against the wall. Deciding to take out some clean clothes before showering, he opened the bag. Instantly there was a puff of smoke, a blinding flash, and a thunderous explosion!

10 Captured

Chet rushed in and saw Frank sitting on the floor with a stunned expression on his face.

"Are you hurt?" the boy asked anxiously.

Frank climbed to his feet. "No, I'm fine." He went over to look into the suitcase. "It was just a scare tactic, I think. All noise and no damage."

Picking up a note that was lying next to the remains of the fake bomb, he read it, then passed it on to Chet. In block letters was printed: GO BACK TO BAYPORT, OR THE NEXT ONE WILL BE REAL!

"They mean business," Chet said nervously.

"So do we," Frank stated in a grim tone. "We won't be going back to Bayport. We'll just make them think we did."

"How can we do that?" Chet inquired.

"After we pick up Joe and Vern, we'll check out of here and go to another hotel."

At five o'clock the two friends drove to the warehouse and Frank gave the code honk. Parking down the street, they waited. When Joe and Vern did not appear, Frank walked back to check the refrigerator carton. It was empty, but his camera was lying underneath the wooden crate.

Frank was about to leave when he heard a car drive up. Peering through the view hole, he saw a distinguished-looking man getting out of a Lincoln Continental. Frank took his camera and snapped a picture through the view hole as the man let himself into the warehouse. Then he pocketed the camera.

He returned to their rental car, leaned in the window, and said to Chet, "Joe isn't there, but a guy I'm betting is the kingpin of this operation just went into the place."

"Where do you suppose Joe is?" Chet asked.

"Probably back in the shed with Vern."

Chet got out of the car and they sneaked around to the alley. An eighteen-wheel truck was parked next to the sliding door, but no one was in the shed.

"Maybe they got hungry and went to the deli," Chet suggested.

"We'll check," Frank said with a frown. "But I don't think they'd both take off."

They hurried to the delicatessen, but Joe and Vern were not there. Frank described the two boys to the Chinese proprietor, but the man couldn't remembering seeing anyone who resembled Joe and Vern.

Outside Chet asked, "What do you think?"

"I think they're in trouble, maybe being held prisoner in the warehouse."

"We can't go in there."

"Why not?" Frank asked, heading back up the alley. "Joe and I got in there this morning."

"You got into trouble, too," Chet said. "That place is full of hoods."

Frank stopped next to the warehouse's restroom window. "You stay in the shed, then," he suggested. "I'll go in alone."

The window was already open. Frank made sure the room was empty, then climbed inside. Stealthily, he crept over to the door that opened into the main room.

Hearing a grunting noise behind him, he spun around. Chet was just pulling himself over the sill.

"I thought you didn't want to come," Frank whispered.

"I didn't. But I hate to be alone."

Opening the door a crack, Frank looked into the garage. Workmen were putting down their tools and preparing to go home.

Frank whispered over his shoulder. "They're quitting work. We better move before they start coming in to wash up."

He opened the door far enough to slip through and led the way to the three new cars parked near the back door. The boys crouched out of sight between two of them.

"That's Vern's!" Chet hissed, jerking a thumb at the blue sedan to their left. "It must have been delivered by that truck out there."

"Which means Crafty Kraft's around here somewhere," Frank replied in a low tone.

The boys had left the restroom just in time, since workmen began heading toward it to wash up. Frank and Chet lay low until the last of them had finished and had exited through the front door.

When the big garage was empty, Frank rose to his feet, looked in all directions, and then tiptoed toward the office. Through the open office door, he could see Big Harry behind his desk, talking to two men seated in front of it. One was the tattooed truck driver Fenton Hardy had identified as one of the chief lieutenants of the car-theft ring, Crafty Kraft. The other was the distinguished-looking man who had arrived in the Lincoln Continental.

Frank retreated behind the cars again, where he was out of sight from the office, and motioned Chet to follow him. Quietly, they moved along the rear wall, then made their way around to the office door. They stopped just before they reached it and positioned themselves so that they could hear everything, but not be seen.

A voice that Frank guessed belonged to the distinguished-looking man said, "Who, may I ask, are they?"

"According to their I.D.s, they're Joe Hardy and Vern Nelson," Big Harry replied.

"Joe Hardy! That's one of Fenton Hardy's sons. I thought he was in town on other business."

"So did Red Sluice," Big Harry said. "He told me those kids were here to find some coin that disappeared, but this is the second time we've caught this one prowling around. The first time he was with a different guy, and they both escaped."

"Probably his older brother," a third man said in a raspy voice. Frank assumed this was Crafty Kraft. "I hear they're always together."

"Well, what do you want us to do with these two, sir?" Big Harry asked.

The *sir* told Frank that he had guessed right about the newcomer being the big boss of the car-theft ring.

"They'll have to be kept out of circulation until we finish stripping this shipment," came the reply.

"After that it won't matter, because we can move to another location. But if we turn them loose now, they'll run straight to the police."

"I've got an isolated cottage over on Catalina Island," Big Harry offered.

"That would be excellent. You own a boat, too, don't you?"

"Yes, sir."

"Then run them over there and hold them until further notice. Oh, and while you've got them, you may as well squeeze out any information you can about how much Fenton Hardy has learned about our operation."

"Yes, sir," Big Harry repeated.

There was the sound of a chair scraping. Frank and Chet made a beeline for the nearest hiding place. They hid themselves behind a partially dismantled car and an instant later, the distinguished-looking gentleman stepped from the office.

As he started toward the front door, it opened and Red Sluice came in with Anton Jivaro. The three met halfway across the garage, near enough for Frank and Chet to overhear them.

"Who is this, Red?" the boss asked sharply.

"My old partner, Anton, sir. He started work here today."

Frowning at the little man, the boss said, "You

know my rule about thoroughly checking all prospective employees, Red."

"But he's a very old friend, sir," Red protested. "I can vouch for him."

"I hope so, because we already have a serious security problem. Big Harry and Crafty caught the younger son of Fenton Hardy and a companion inside the warehouse this afternoon."

"Again! Both Hardys were here this morning, but they got away. Who was Joe's companion?"

"Someone named Vern Nelson."

Red and Jivaro looked at each other. "The same pair!" Red said.

"What do you mean?" the boss asked.

"We almost had them earlier today. Did they get away again?"

The boss shook his head. "Not this time. They're trussed up in the machine shop."

"What were they after?"

"I haven't interrogated them, because I prefer not to have my face seen by people outside the organization."

"The older Hardy boy is still around somewhere," Red said, "and so is another friend named Chet Morton."

The boss frowned. "They could be lurking around here. You better search the whole area."

"I think they'd be too scared," Anton Jivaro spoke up. "We left a warning in their hotel room to go back to Bayport."

"Look anyway," the boss instructed.

He continued out the front door while Red and Jivaro went into the office. Frank motioned for Chet to follow him, and the two tiptoed over to the machine shop. They slipped inside and closed the door behind them.

Joe and Vern lay on the floor, tied and gagged!

"I'll take care of them," Frank whispered to Chet. "You'd better open the door just a crack and watch if anyone's coming."

Chet nodded. While Frank removed the gags from the prisoners' mouths, the chubby boy silently turned the doorknob to peek out. Then he gasped.

He was staring directly into Red Sluice's face!

11 Overboard!

Chet tried to close the door, but Red kicked it open with his foot, and the boy jumped back in order to avoid being batted.

Then Red Sluice, Anton Jivaro, Crafty Kraft, and Big Harry poured into the room. Frank had not yet succeeded in loosening either Joe's or Vern's bonds, so it was four against two. There was a fierce struggle but the hoods finally subdued the young detectives, tying their hands behind them.

When the boys were safely bound, Red declared with satisfaction, "You two saved me the trouble of hunting you down."

Crafty Kraft asked, "Now what?"

"Untie the feet of those two so they can walk," Big

Harry ordered, pointing to Joe and Vern. "Then load all four of them on your truck."

"Are we going over to the island now?" Crafty asked.

Big Harry shook his head. "We have to wait until morning because I can't get away tonight. But I want them out of here. They'll be safe tied up on the boat."

Red scowled. "I'd rather get it over with tonight."

"Can you run the boat?" Big Harry countered.

Red shook his head, and then looked hopefully over at his partners. Crafty Kraft and Anton both admitted they knew nothing about boats either.

The boys were put in the rear of the eighteen-wheel truck. Sluice and Jivaro got in with them as guards, while the tattooed Crafty drove.

"Where are we going?" Frank asked Red as the truck began to move.

"Terminal Island," Red told him.

"I thought that was a prison," Joe said.

"There's a federal prison there, but the Los Angeles Harbor's there too."

"What kind of boat does Big Harry have?" Anton Jivaro asked Red.

"A thirty-six-footer with twin diesel engines. Sleeps six and has a cruising range of one thousand miles."

"Will we be going that far?" Chet asked, worried.

"You'll only be going about three miles out," Red told him.

Chet gulped.

"He's only trying to scare you," Frank whispered in the plump boy's ear.

"Speak up if you have anything to say," Red said sharply. Frank fell silent.

They rode for about an hour. When they finally stopped, Crafty Kraft opened the rear door.

"All clear," he announced. "Nobody in sight."

Red and Anton jumped out, and immediately ordered the boys to move. They were parked on a dock containing dozens of boat slips. It was still light enough for them to see that the nearest boat was a large cabin cruiser with *Sea Scorpion* lettered on its bow.

"I have to get the truck off the dock," Crafty Kraft said to Red. "I'll come back with Big Harry in the morning."

He climbed into the vehicle and drove off, while the boys were taken aboard and herded down into the main cabin. Inside there were only two double bunks, but through a hatch they could see that the galley next door contained benches that could be converted into two more bunks.

Red and Anton shoved the boys into the galley

and ordered them to sit down. Then Red pulled out a table that folded into the wall and lowered it between them.

"Chow time," he announced, and began rummaging in the refrigerator. "Nothing but bacon and eggs and bread," he grumbled.

Taking all the ingredients out, Red cooked an unappetizing dinner. He and Anton quickly ate, and then fed the prisoners, whose hands were still tied behind their backs.

After they had eaten, the young detectives were herded back into the main cabin. Red assigned Chet and Vern the two lower bunks, and told Frank and Joe to climb into the upper ones.

"You'll have to untie us before we can make it," Frank objected.

"No way," Red said. "You guys have gotten away from us twice, and I'm not taking any risks. Anton, help me lift them up."

The two men shoved the brothers into the upper bunks and hogtied them securely. In addition, the boys were bound to wall stanchions behind them so that they could not roll from their beds.

When they were finished, Red and Anton went topside, leaving the cabin lights on.

"What do you think they're going to do to us?" Vern asked.

"Take us over to Catalina Island, I guess, where

Big Harry has a secluded cottage," Frank said optimistically. "They're only going to hold us until they finish stripping the cars they have at the warehouse, then they're going to move to another location. As soon as they do that, they figure it will be safe to turn us loose."

"That isn't what Red Sluice said to Chet," Joe stated.

"He was just trying to scare us. We overheard the big boss giving instructions. He wants them to squeeze out of us what Dad has learned about the theft ring so far."

"You saw the big boss?" Joe asked.

"I even took his picture," Frank replied. "I don't know who he is, but he's a kind of rich-looking guy. I just hope those crooks don't take my camera out of my pocket."

Chet said, "I remember him telling Big Harry to get information from Joe and Vern, but he didn't say anything about us."

"We hadn't been captured then, superbrain," Frank told him. "What all of us should keep in mind is that if they make any threats, it's just a bluff to get us to talk. They aren't going to do any more than the big boss ordered them to do."

About nine o'clock, Red and Anton came down again and checked the boys' bonds. Finding them secure, they made up the two bunks in the galley for themselves and turned out the lights. Within minutes both were snoring.

Unable to change position, the four boys slept fitfully. Sometime in the early part of the morning, they heard footsteps on deck. Moments later, Big Harry and Crafty Kraft came below.

Sticking his head into the galley, Big Harry woke his companions.

When Red and Anton were up and dressed, the boys were untied one at a time and told to wash up. Then they were allowed one sweet roll each from a sack Big Harry had brought along.

After their meager breakfast, the young detectives were left sitting in the galley, with only their wrists bound, under the watchful eyes of Red and Anton. Big Harry and Crafty went above and started the engines. About ten minutes after the boys felt the boat pull away from the dock, Crafty called down from above, "The skipper says to bring them topside."

Red and Anton herded the boys on deck. They saw that the boat, with Big Harry at the helm, was headed well out to sea. "Sit with your backs to the rail!" Red ordered. Frank and Chet lowered themselves on the portside, while Joe and Vern leaned against the starboard rail.

Standing over Frank and looking down at him, Crafty Kraft began the interrogation. "How much does your father know about our operation at the warehouse?"

"How could he know anything?" Frank inquired. "He lives in Bayport."

"He sent you and your brother here," the tattooed man said impatiently. "And I'm sure you've phoned him since you found out about us."

"We came here on our own," Joe spoke up. "And we'll give you our word that we haven't talked to him since we arrived."

Crafty turned around to face the boy. "You feel like talking?"

"I have nothing to talk about!"

Crafty told Anton to follow him, and the two went down into the cabin. Shortly they reappeared with two small, rowboat-size anchors.

They dropped them on the deck near the boys' feet. Then, while Anton joined Red and Big Harry at the bridge, Crafty went below again.

When he came back, he was carrying a coil of thin wire in one hand and a pair of wire cutters in the other. Dropping the wire near the anchors, he snipped off four lengths of about four feet each.

"What's that for?" Chet inquired fearfully.

"Nothing, if your friends talk," Crafty told him. "If they don't, we're going to see how well you boys can swim with anchors tied to your bodies."

"Hey, that's murder!" Chet protested.

"So, try calling a cop!" Crafty snarled.

Dropping the wire cutters next to the anchors, the tattooed man went forward to confer with his companions.

The wire cutters were closer to Joe than to any of the others. Glancing toward the bridge, he whispered, "Keep watch and warn me if any of them look this way."

He had just started to inch forward when Frank hissed, "Watch out!"

Joe hurriedly slid back against the rail, just as Crafty Kraft came back to stand over him again.

"Your last chance," he said. "Would you rather talk or go overboard?"

"I have nothing to talk about," Joe said evenly.

The tattooed man kneeled down before the boy and passed a piece of wire around his waist, twisted it tight and fastened an anchor to it. Then he rose to his feet. "I'll let you think about it a while. Soon as we're three miles out, I'll ask you again."

He went to the bridge. As soon as his back was turned, Joe again inched forward on the seat of his pants. Then he swung around and gripped the wire cutters with his right hand. He twisted the jaws of the cutters toward the rope binding his wrists, but found it too awkward in a seated position. Slowly he struggled to his feet.

At that moment, Big Harry spotted a log floating

in the water just ahead and made a sharp turn to port. Frank and Chet both slid toward the starboard rail. Joe started to lose his balance, almost recovered, but then Chet's sliding body crashed into him.

Joe's knees hit the rail and, head first, he pitched overboard!

12 Turned Tables

The younger Hardy took a deep breath just before
he hit the water. He sank swiftly, as the weight of
the anchor pulled him down. Frantically, he twisted
the wire cutters around until the blade gripped the
rope binding his wrist. Desperately, he squeezed
the handle.

The rope parted, but he was reaching the point
where he had to release his breath, and he was still
sinking rapidly. Then, as he brought the wire
cutters around in front of him, they slipped from his
grasp!

In a last-ditch effort, he reached out with his left
hand, felt his fingers close over the blades, and
guided the tool into his right hand to regrip the

handle. Slowly letting out air from his lungs, he shoved the blades of the cutters around the wire and squeezed the handle.

As the anchor dropped away, Joe let go of the wire cutters and thrust himself upward. He had been dragged down so deep that his lungs emptied while he was only halfway to the surface. Rapidly scissoring his legs and using a powerful breast stroke to propel himself upward, he fought the terrible urge to inhale.

He was losing the battle and was on the verge of breathing in water when he suddenly broke the surface. Gasping, he drew in air, released it, and inhaled again. He treaded water as his breathing gradually returned to normal.

The *Sea Scorpion* was a couple of hundred yards away by now, slowly circling, as the men looked for him. He waved one arm and yelled, but it was too far for anyone to see or hear him. He started to swim toward the boat, but it circled farther and farther away. Finally the skipper gave up and continued out to sea.

As the *Sea Scorpion* disappeared from sight, Joe looked around. There was nothing but unending water in all directions. Fortunately the sea was relatively calm, though the water was cold.

Joe guessed that he was three to five miles from shore. If the sea did not get any rougher, he figured he could swim it, providing he stopped for frequent rests and kept in the right direction. He knew the coast was due east, and positioning himself by the sun, he hoped to avoid swimming in circles.

It was still early enough in the morning for the sun to be fairly low. Joe began swimming directly at it.

Meanwhile, aboard the *Sea Scorpion*, there was considerable confusion. Frank, Vern, and Chet anxiously kept shouting out for Joe, horrified at what might happen to him. As Big Harry circled around in search of Joe, he screamed at Crafty Kraft for allowing the accident to happen.

"It was you who made that sudden turn," the tattooed man objected vehemently.

"Why'd you have to tie that anchor to him?" Big Harry yelled.

"I was just trying to scare him."

"We'll see who gets scared when I report this to the boss," Big Harry said grimly. "He didn't want anything like this."

Frank and Chet took advantage of all the confusion and still calling out Joe's name, put their backs together as though to search for him in opposite directions. Determinedly, they began to pull at each other's wrist bindings. But as Big Harry gave up circling and resumed heading out to sea, Red Sluice noticed what was going on.

"Hey, those two are getting loose!" he shouted.

Red ran over to check Chet's bonds, Crafty bent over Frank, and Anton checked Vern. Frank had moved his back against the rail again so that the tattooed man had to approach him from the front. As he leaned forward to swing Frank around by the shoulders, the boy drew his knees to his chest, planted both feet in the man's stomach, and kicked as hard as he could. Crafty was thrown clear across the deck, hit the opposite rail, and did a back flip into the ocean!

"Man overboard!" Red Sluice yelled. "Turn around!"

As the boat began to circle, Anton grabbed a life preserver and tied a line to it. Frank and Chet swung their backs to each other again and Frank frantically picked at the knot binding Chet's wrists. Anton and Red were too busy looking for Crafty over the side to notice.

Frank loosened the knot and the rope fell away. Chet turned around and quickly untied Frank, while Red and Anton still hung over the railing, calling to their partner.

"All right, Harry!" Red shouted. "Slow down!"

Big Harry throttled the engine until the boat was barely moving, and Anton tossed the life preserver overboard. The man in the water grabbed it and Red began to reel in the rope.

Frank whispered to Chet, "Body blocks. Pretend you're on the football field."

Nodding, Chet crouched as though on the scrimmage line. Frank did the same.

"One—two—three, hike!" Frank said.

In unison they drove forward to throw body blocks into the men at the rail. Screaming loudly, both hoods went overboard to join Crafty Kraft in the water.

"Untie Vern," Frank said to Chet in a low voice, and headed for the bridge.

Big Harry, with his back to the action, had not seen his companions go overboard, and the noise of the engine had drowned out the screams and splashes. He seemed to sense, however, that something was wrong, and looked over his shoulder just as Frank came up behind him. Releasing the wheel, he started to spin around, but Frank managed to land a karate chop at the base of his neck.

Without making a sound, Big Harry pitched forward on his face, unconscious. Quickly the boy searched him for weapons. Finding none, Frank took the helm, while Vern and Chet stood at the rail, looking at the hoods in the water.

"Tell them to hold on to the life preserver," Frank called out. "We'll be back for them after we look for Joe."

While the crooks clung to the life ring, Frank steered the *Sea Scorpion* back into the sun, fervently hoping that Joe had been able to free himself with the wire cutters.

A mile to the east Joe had stopped to rest for a time floating on his back.

Out of the corner of his eye he caught sight of something sliding past him in the water, but did not get a good enough look to identify what it was. Letting his feet down until he was treading water, he turned in the direction the thing had moved, but saw nothing marring the gently rolling surface of the water. He decided it must have been his imagination and started to swim toward the sun again.

Then a movement to his left brought him to a halt. Treading water, he looked that way. A large gray fin broke the surface and swam widely around him.

With his heart pounding, Joe watched the fin going around again, this time in a narrower circle. The shark had spotted him when it originally went by, and was now closing in.

He submerged in order to get an underwater look at the beast. An enormous man-eating white shark over twenty feet long passed him no more than a dozen feet away.

Surfacing, Joe watched as the great fin cut the

water in a wide arc that took it fifty yards beyond him, then swung back in his direction. This time it moved in a straight line, directly toward him!

As the fin neared, he dived in a desperate attempt to swim beneath it. But the shark had a fix on him now. It dived too, opening its enormous jaws wide!

13 Dolphin Rescue

Joe froze in terror. The shark was almost upon him, when he suddenly saw a dark shape on his right, streaking in like a torpedo. Thinking it was another shark, Joe gave up all hope. But the shape, instead of attacking him, struck the shark's midsection. The monster veered aside, and even underwater Joe could hear a loud click as the enormous jaws snapped shut only inches away from him.

The dark shape moved away as fast as it had come in, only to be replaced by another torpedo-like object. It too drove into the shark's side at breakneck speed, then scooted off again. In rapid order, four more speeding forms bludgeoned the maneater's side, making it flounder almost onto its back before it fled in panic.

Joe surfaced to see the gray fin moving away at express-train speed. It kept going until it disappeared from sight.

Then a graceful, hard-snouted figure arched through the air ten feet over Joe's head and came down in such a perfect dive that it hardly made a splash. Five similar shapes performed the same acrobatics, their crescent-shaped mouths seeming to grin down at Joe as they soared above him.

It was a school of six dolphins, the mortal enemies of sharks, but friends to humans. Joe remembered reading how dolphins occasionally attacked sharks by butting them at high speed with their hard snouts, sometimes even killing them by rupturing their hearts.

The dolphins continued to cavort about him, playfully showing off their acrobatic skill. Joe raised his hands above water to applaud loudly.

Meanwhile, Frank had headed the *Sea Scorpion* into the sun.

"You don't think Joe could have drowned, do you?" Chet asked, shivering at the thought.

"He had the wire cutters in his hand when he went overboard," Frank said, his face drawn and his eyes clouded with fear. "If he acted fast, he could have cut both the rope and the wire around his waist in time. We can only hope."

Chet glanced around. The lump in his stomach

began to ache violently and his voice trembled. "Even i-if he got free of that anchor, how would we find him way out here? We could pass fifty yards from him without spotting him."

"We'll start circling when we get back to where he was knocked overboard."

"If you can figure out where that is. I couldn't."

"I don't think we sailed more than a mile beyond him," Frank said. "I admit our starting point will be a blind guess, but we'll circle from there in wider and wider loops. We ought to hit the right spot eventually."

"Suppose we don't?"

"We'll run in and call the Coast Guard. They'll send up helicopters to scour the whole area. From the air, he'll be a lot easier to see."

When they came to the spot where Frank figured Joe had been thrown overboard, he throttled down until the boat was barely moving.

"Okay," he said to Chet. "You and Vern take posts on opposite sides of the boat and start looking."

Chet moved back amidship to relay this instruction to Vern. Chet took the starboard side and Vern the port side as Frank steered the boat in everwidening circles. Both boys strained their eyes intently looking out over the water.

When the circle had reached a half mile in diameter with no sign of Joe, Frank became discouraged. "I guess we better leave it up to the Coast Guard," he said, his face ashen white.

"Wait. There's something over there!" Vern suddenly called out.

He pointed into the distance, and at once Frank reversed engines to bring the boat to a halt.

"It's not Joe," Chet said glumly. "It's something jumping in and out of the water. In fact a lot of somethings."

Frank squinted his eyes, and peered under his hand to see what Chet was talking about.

"Sea lions?" he asked.

"Why don't we go see?" Vern suggested.

Advancing the throttle, Frank steered the boat in the direction of the jumping animals.

As they neared, Chet said, "It's a school of porpoises."

"Dolphins, I think," Frank said.

"What's the difference?"

"Dolphins are porpoises, but porpoises aren't necessarily dolphins," Frank explained. "It's like a nickel is a coin, but a coin isn't necessarily a nickel."

Vern said, "He means dolphins are a special kind of porpoise."

By now, they were within fifty yards of the cavorting dolphins. Chet exclaimed, "Hey, there's something in the water they're jumping over!"

Frank pulled the boat in closer.

"Hey, look! It's Joe!" Chet yelled to the others.

Either the approach of the boat, or the boys' relieved shouts, frightened the dolphins away. They raced off in formation, arcing in and out of the water as though they were riding some invisible roller coaster.

Frank slowed the *Sea Scorpion*, reversed engines, and came to a stop within a few feet of his brother. Joe swam over and was pulled aboard by Chet and Vern.

"We thought you were a goner," Chet said happily, pounding his friend on the back.

"I will be, if you keep that up," an exhausted Joe told him, moving out of range.

"Too bad we scared off your friends," Vern said. "It looked like you were all having a good time."

"They saved my life by running off a shark," Joe declared. "How'd you manage to turn the tables?"

"Brains, pure brains," Chet said, tapping his forehead.

"Yeah, but not yours," Vern said. "It was Frank's." He told Joe what had happened.

Frank headed the boat back to the spot where they had left their attackers, while Joe went below in search of dry clothing. He did not find any, but discovered a pair of sneakers that fit him. He would just have to put up with being wet until he got back to the hotel.

Soon the *Sea Scorpion* pulled up near the trio in the water.

"Like to come back aboard?" Chet invited.

"Please," Red Sluice said in a frightened voice. "I can't swim."

"Want us to throw you one of these anchors?" Chet asked.

"Cut the comedy, Chet," Frank called over his shoulder. "Bring them aboard one at a time, and tie each one up before you pull out the next."

"Roger," Chet said. "Come on, Red."

"But first bring out that knife you carry and hold it up," Vern added.

Red let loose of the life ring with one hand to get his knife.

"Drop it," Vern ordered.

Red released his grip and the knife sank into the water.

"You have any weapons, Maharaja?" Chet asked.

"No," the little man said.

"How about you, Crafty?"

The tattooed man shook his head.

"We'll check both of you when you come aboard," Chet warned. "If either of you have anything, we'll toss you back in the water."

"We're not carrying anything," Crafty insisted.

"Okay," Chet called to Frank.

Frank maneuvered the boat right next to the trio.

Chet leaned over to offer Red Sluice a hand. As he pulled him aboard, he twisted the man's right arm behind his back. Vern took hold of the left one and they forced Red face down. After binding his wrists with one of the pieces of rope that had been used on them, they searched his pockets but found no gun or other knives.

"You're next, Crafty," Chet said, leaning over the rail to offer the tattooed man a helping hand.

When Crafty was aboard, they bound his hands and searched him in the same manner. He was carrying no weapons, either.

Finally, they pulled up Anton and gave him the same treatment. Then Chet reached down to retrieve the life preserver and dropped it on the deck.

After arranging the three with their backs to the rail, far enough apart so that they could not untie each other, Chet and Vern went forward to Big Harry, who was still unconscious. He began to wake up just as they finished binding his wrists behind him. Then Frank headed the boat in.

It was close to noon when he berthed the *Sea Scorpion*. After it was tied up, the boys walked a few yards along the dock beyond earshot of the four captives in order to discuss what to do with them. Chet was for turning them over to the authorities immediately.

"We decided not to call in the police until we knew who the big boss of the car theft ring is," Joe reminded him.

"Chet and I did find out," Frank said.

"You only saw him," Joe insisted. "You don't know who he is."

"I snapped his picture from inside that refrigerator carton. I had been looking for you when he drove up in a big car and went into the warehouse."

"How do you know it was the big boss?" Vern asked.

"We sneaked into the warehouse and overheard him talking to Big Harry and Crafty Kraft. That's how we learned you guys were tied up in the machine shop."

"But you don't know his name," Joe said.

"That doesn't matter," Frank told him. "When I get the film developed, I'll turn it over to the police. They should be able to find out who he is. In the meantime, we can't keep those four guys tied up, and we can't let them loose, either. Seems to me we have to turn them in."

"I guess so," Joe agreed. "Wonder if there's a phone around here."

Vern pointed to a large building at the edge of the dock area, about fifty yards away. "Maybe there."

"You guys go check," Frank suggested. "I'll stand guard over our prisoners."

Joe, Chet, and Vern headed for the large building. As they neared, they saw that it was a boat tackle shop. Chet stuck his head in the door and asked a clerk if he had a public phone.

"Out back," the clerk told him.

The three went around the building and found a phone booth. Joe took a dime out of one of his wet pockets, dialed the operator, and asked for the police.

At the dock, Frank stood alongside the boat, occasionally glancing at the prisoners to make sure they were in the same positions. After a time, he decided to go back aboard.

As soon as he stepped on the deck, he realized they had not searched the prisoners as thoroughly as they should have. Crafty Kraft's right pant leg was pushed up above his knee to disclose a leather sheath strapped to his calf. The sheath was empty and he held an eight-inch hunting knife in his hand!

He had already cut the prisoners' bonds, and now all four jumped to their feet and rushed at Frank!

Big Harry and Red Sluice were in the lead. Frank ducked under a looping right thrown by Big Harry, grabbed the man's wrist, and flipped him over his shoulder onto the deck. Whirling to face Red, he fended a blow and shoved him into Crafty and Anton, who were right behind the redheaded man.

While the three were untangling themselves,

Frank thought quickly. He knew there was no way he could win against these four opponents. Just as he saw Big Harry painfully climb to his feet, he took a running jump onto the dock and, picking himself up, raced away.

Big Harry chased after the boy, and the other three hoods followed in hot pursuit.

But Frank had a good lead. When he was halfway between the boat and the tackle shop, Joe, Chet, and Vern came around the corner. Immediately seeing Frank's predicament, they ran up as fast as they could.

The hoods were too tired to stomach another fight, though, and turning, they rushed back toward the boat.

By the time Chet, Vern, and Joe reached Frank, Big Harry was jumping aboard. Seconds later, he started the engine, while his partners were hastily casting off lines.

"Come on!" Frank shouted. "Don't let them get away!"

The four boys raced for the boat. But Red, Anton, and Crafty hopped aboard just before the boys got there, and the *Sea Scorpion* backed from the slip.

The foursome halted at the edge of the dock and watched in frustration as Big Harry swung the boat around and opened the throttle wide!

14 A Magical Disappearance

As the boat disappeared from sight, Joe asked, "How'd they get loose?"

"We didn't search them well enough," Frank said. "Crafty had a knife strapped to his leg."

"Well, at least that settles the argument about whether or not to turn them over to the police," Chet said philosophically.

"Did you call them?" Frank asked Joe.

His younger brother nodded. "They said they'd be right over."

The boys walked back to the boat tackle shop to await the arrival of the police. A paddy wagon and a squad car showed up a few minutes later. Two uniformed officers got out of the car, one middle-aged and wearing sergeant's stripes, the other a young rookie.

"Which one of you phoned in?" the sergeant asked.

"I did," Joe said.

"Your name's Joe Hardy?"

"Yes, sir," Joe said and introduced the other boys.

"I'm Sergeant Kelly and my partner's Jim Olsen." The officer looked from Joe to Frank. "Are you the famous detectives?" he asked.

"Our father's Fenton Hardy," Frank admitted.

"I've heard a lot about him, and you two also. Where are these kidnappers?"

"They got away," Frank confessed. "It was my fault because I was guarding them. One of them had a knife strapped to his leg that we didn't find when we searched him. He cut himself and the others loose and they sailed off in the boat."

"Maybe you'd better tell us the whole story," Sergeant Kelly suggested. He turned to his companion. "Looks like we won't need the paddy wagon, Olsen. Tell Ralph he can take off."

"Sure, Sarge." The young policeman went over to deliver the message to the driver, who left immediately. Running back to the group, he listened to their story.

The boys told everything that had happened, going back to the theft of Vern's car in Bayport.

When they finished, Sergeant Kelly said, "This is a matter for the auto-theft division. But first, I want you to describe the kidnappers and their boat so the Coast Guard can begin a search."

The boys related every detail they could remember, and the sergeant radioed their report to headquarters.

When he hung up the radio mike, he said, "Now we'll take you to Parker Center to talk to someone in the auto-theft division. Okay?"

"Can we stop at our hotel on the way?" Joe asked. "I'm soaking wet."

The sergeant grinned. "You do look like a drowned rat. Sure, we'll give you time to clean up."

The young detectives crowded into the back seat of the squad car and were driven to their hotel. Since they had slept in their clothes, they all decided to change. Sergeant Kelly told them to take their time.

"There's no rush," he said. "The whole police force plus the Coast Guard are looking for the kidnappers, and that warehouse you told us about won't go away."

"Then we have time for lunch," Chet said, his eyes lighting up. "It's almost two P.M."

"Good idea," Jim Olsen said. "We haven't eaten either."

Chet gave him a delighted look, and Vern

laughed. "You just made a lifelong friend, Officer Olsen."

To save time they ordered from room service. The boys had all finished cleaning up and dressing when the food arrived.

After lunch, they were driven to Parker Center, the police administration building. The officers took them to the auto-theft division squad room on the third floor and left them with a tall and somewhat stiff detective named Lieutenant Harold Frisby.

When they repeated their story, he asked them to describe the exact location of the warehouse. Then he picked up his desk phone and asked the switchboard operator to get him the district attorney.

"Hi, Jud," he said into the phone. "I finally have a lead on that nationwide car-theft ring we've been after for so long. I need a search warrant." He gave the address of the warehouse.

As soon as he hung up, he called the Metro division, asking for a squad of a dozen uniformed policemen to accompany him on a raid. "I won't need them for about an hour, because I'm waiting for the district attorney's office to send over a warrant," he added.

When he hung up the second time, Frank asked, "Can we go on the raid?"

The detective shook his head. "No civilians

allowed. There may be shooting. I'll have you dropped back at your hotel."

"Our car's parked near the warehouse," Frank said. "We'd rather be dropped there."

"All right," Lieutenant Frisby agreed.

"As long as we're right there, can we watch the raid from outside?"

The detective gave him an amused look. "You're determined to get in on it one way or another, I see. All right, you can watch from across the street. But you're not going to talk me into letting you participate in the raid."

When the search warrant arrived, Lieutenant Frisby and the four boys took the elevator to the basement garage, where they found three carloads of uniformed policemen with riot guns. The boys got into a fourth car with Lieutenant Frisby, and he led the way to the warehouse at the edge of Old Chinatown.

When they reached the street fronting the warehouse, Frank pointed to the building and said, "That's it." Then he indicated the gray sedan a block beyond the warehouse. "And that's our car."

Lieutenant Frisby parked behind the sedan and the three squad cars pulled up next to him. Everyone got out, and the lieutenant addressed the uniformed sergeant in charge of the riot squad.

"Post five men in the back and five in front," he ordered. "Then you and I'll go in."

"Yes, sir," the sergeant said.

Picking five officers, he told them to walk around to the alley and cover the rear of the building. After another five were selected to cover the front, only one was left. The sergeant designated him to accompany him and the lieutenant inside.

Lieutenant Frisby gave the men time to get into position. While waiting, he told the boys to move in back of the parked police cars in case there was any shooting. The young detectives crouched behind the two nearest to the warehouse.

The lieutenant checked his watch. "Okay, let's go now," he said to the two officers. Quickly, the lieutenant and his companions crossed the street.

He tried the front door and looked surprised when he found it unlocked. Opening it, he drew his gun and stepped inside. The two men followed.

Ten minutes passed with no sound from the warehouse. The boys heard one of the men ask uneasily, "Think we should bust in there?"

"The lieutenant said to wait," another one answered.

Then Lieutenant Frisby and his two companions reappeared. He no longer had his gun in his hand, and the two men carried their riot guns pointed downward. They recrossed the street, slowly.

"False alarm, fellows," the sergeant said. "Head back to Parker Center."

Apparently, he had already told the men out back that the raid was called off, because they came around from the alley and climbed into the squad cars. The young detectives watched open-mouthed as all three cars drove off.

"I don't get it," Joe said to the lieutenant.

"Follow me," the detective said peremptorily.

He led them across the street, opened the warehouse's front door, and they all went in. The boys gaped in astonishment. The big, barnlike main room was completely empty!

The lieutenant crossed to the door to their left and opened it.

"This the machine shop you mentioned?" he asked.

Crowding around the door, the boys stared in at the empty room.

"It was," Frank said, a sinking feeling in his stomach.

The lieutenant led them to the office. A skinny old man smoking a corncob pipe sat in Big Harry's chair with his feet up on the desk.

"Back again, Lieutenant?" he said with a grin.

"This is Mr. Jonas Moapes," Lieutenant Frisby said. "Mr. Moapes, would you mind repeating to these four what you told me your job was here?"

"Sure," the old man said agreeably. "I'm the caretaker."

"And how long have you held that job?"

"Three months, ever since the last people who rented the place went out of business."

"What's been in here since?"

"Nothing," the old man said. "The place has been empty."

"That's a lie!" Chet blurted out. The caretaker merely shrugged.

15 Spare Parts For Sale

All four boys were in a state of shock as they left the warehouse with Lieutenant Frisby. Outside he halted and, looking from Frank to Joe, said, "If you two weren't the sons of such a famous father, I would arrest you for filing a false report."

"But the crooks *were* using this warehouse," Joe protested. "Somehow they must have known we were coming."

"We didn't just dream this, Lieutenant," Vern spoke up. "How do you explain our being kidnapped and being taken aboard that boat?"

"I think you dreamed that too," the lieutenant said shortly, and strode toward his car.

After watching him drive away, the boys disconsolately walked up the street to their own automobile. There was dead silence as they returned to the hotel. Upstairs they gathered in the Hardys' room.

"Maybe we did dream the whole thing," Chet suggested.

"Don't be silly," Frank said. "That old man is in with the crooks. They knew the jig was up when we got away, unless they discredited us with the police. And they were clever enough to do it. While Lieutenant Frisby waited for that warrant, they cleared the place out and installed the fake caretaker."

"Let's go back and question Mr. Moapes," Joe said. "Maybe we can shake his story."

"First, let's change hotels," Chet said. "After our encounter with those crooks, I don't feel safe here anymore."

All agreed that this was a good idea. Checking out, they drove to another hotel a few blocks away and again moved into connecting rooms.

When they were settled, Joe suggested that they phone home to report the change, so that their father would know how to get in touch with them if necessary. Frank made the call and his mother answered. She said Fenton Hardy was still on his secret mission, but that she was expecting a call at any time, and would relay this new number to him.

Driving back to the warehouse, the boys parked

315

and tried the front door. It was locked, so they drove around to the alley. They found the back door locked too.

Joe tried the restroom window, which was open. "I wonder why they don't ever lock this too. We've used it twice already," he commented as he climbed over the sill, followed by Chet and Vern.

Frank went in last. Examining the window, he answered Joe's question. "The latch part of the lock is missing!"

The elderly Jonas Moapes was no longer in the building.

"I knew he was a plant," Frank said. "They stuck him in here just long enough to con the police into believing we were crazy."

The boys examined the building thoroughly, ending up in the office where Joe began opening desk drawers. All were empty except the top center one, and the only thing it had in it was an empty matchbook cover. Joe shut the drawer and tossed the matchbook cover on the desk.

Frank picked it up to look at it. On the front was an advertisement for the Admax Wholesale Auto Parts Company of Studio City.

"Hey, look at this," he said, handing it back to Joe.

After reading the ad, Joe said, "It could be a lead.

Maybe it's the outlet for their stolen spare parts!"

Chet and Vern examined Joe's find, too. "It must be," Chet said with enthusiasm. "They have to have some place to get rid of the stuff they steal."

"Let's visit the Admax Wholesale Auto Parts Company," Frank suggested.

The store was on a quiet street off Ventura Boulevard, near Laurel Canyon. It was a long, one-story building with ADMAX WHOLESALE AUTO PARTS painted on a plate glass window.

Parking across the street, Joe told the others to wait while he scouted around. He went to peer in the window, then immediately returned.

He said, "It's the gang's outlet, all right."

"How do you know?" Frank asked.

"Red Sluice is behind the counter!"

At that moment, a chauffeured limousine drove up before the store and a bent old man in expensive clothing got out and went inside.

"Let's sneak around back and see what we can find out," Frank said to Joe.

"Here we go again," Chet said. "I suppose you want me behind the wheel in case we have to take off fast."

"You got it," Frank said with a grin.

There was an alley running alongside the building. Frank and Joe walked to the rear and saw a truck entrance with a sliding door, similar to the one in the back of the Old Chinatown warehouse. It was partially open.

The boys peeked into a large room running the full width of the building. Obviously it was the storeroom, because it was full of auto parts, including complete engines. Parked against the right wall were the three almost new cars, including Vern's blue sedan, that had originally been unloaded at the warehouse.

Crafty Kraft and Anton Jivaro were placing small parts on shelves along the left wall, and the elderly Jonas Moapes was sweeping with a push broom, his back turned toward the boys. He finished just as they looked in, and disappeared through a door that presumably led to the store in front.

Seeing no one else, the boys quietly moved inside and bent down low as they crept along an aisle formed between a row of car engines and stacks of radiators.

In addition to the door straight ahead, which led into the store, there was a second door off to their right. It stood wide open, and through it they noticed the elegantly dressed, bent old man who had arrived in the chauffeured limousine. He was seated before a desk with his back to the door, facing someone the boys could not see.

They moved up alongside the door to listen, hidden from view by a stack of radiators.

The old man said in a creaky voice, "The Merriweather Auto Repair Shop chain is almost nationwide, Mr. Knotts. Surely you've heard of us."

"Sorry, Mr. Merriweather," Big Harry replied in an apologetic tone. "I don't recall seeing your ads."

"Probably because California is one of the four states where we have no shops. We plan to correct that by opening a dozen next month. That is going to require a tremendous supply of parts."

"I'm sure we can serve you satisfactorily," Big Harry said, his tone suddenly becoming ingratiating.

"I didn't make my fortune by beating around the bush," the old man creaked. "So I'll get right to the point. The Merriweather shops are able to undercut all competition because we buy our spare parts cheaper. I ask no questions about where they come from, and I don't care if they're new, so long as they look new. Do you follow me?"

"I think so," Big Harry said cautiously.

"But I pay only half the regular wholesale price."

"We're a discount house, Mr. Merriweather. I'm sure we can make a deal."

"My main need in the beginning is reconditioned

319

engines that will pass for new," the old man said. "Got any in stock?"

"I'll show you," Big Harry offered.

There was the sound of chairs scraping back. Hurriedly the boys ducked. Big Harry and the old man emerged from the office and slowly moved along the aisle, their backs to the two boys.

Big Harry said, "As you can see, we have a large selection. And the way we clean them up, I doubt that even an expert mechanic could tell they're not brand new."

Taking out a small notebook, the old man peered at an engine and wrote something down. Slowly moving along the line, he continued to make notes.

Finally putting away the notebook, he said, "I guess that's enough of a list for now. I'll go over it with my chief parts buyer, and let you know tomorrow how many and what type engines we'll need."

Suddenly, the boys were grabbed from behind. With a gasp, they tried to turn and face their attackers, but they were held so tightly that moving was impossible!

16 Outwitted

Looking over his shoulder, Frank saw that it was the powerfully built Crafty Kraft who held him in a bear hug. Again he struggled, but was unable to break loose.

Anton Jivaro had a half nelson on Joe, but the little man was no match for his larger opponent. Raising his right foot, Joe slammed his heel into the man's knee. With a howl of pain, Anton broke his grip and backed away.

Hearing the commotion, Big Harry and his aged customer both turned around. As Joe started to go to Frank's aid, Big Harry rushed at him.

Suddenly, the old man clutched his chest. "My heart!" he cried, falling down.

He collapsed in a way similar to an illegal football clip, against the back of Big Harry's legs. The big man lost his balance and landed flat on his face.

Joe got a headlock on Crafty Kraft from behind and pulled him away from Frank. As he released the headlock, he punched the tattooed man in the back, causing him to trip over Big Harry.

Then the boys ran for the door, dashed out, and hurried along the alley to the front. They were across the street and in the car by the time Big Harry and Crafty Kraft burst into sight.

Chet had started the engine when he saw his friends coming, and pulled away before the pursuers could cross the street.

"Good work, Chet," Frank said.

"Head for Parker Center."

Chet turned up Laurel Canyon Boulevard toward the Ventura Freeway. "What happened?" he asked.

"We got caught poking around. All four kidnappers are there. Vern's car is too. Even old Mr. Moapes is there. I have no doubt that the Admax Company is the outlet for what the crooks steal."

Joe added, "Incidentally, we learned Big Harry's last name. It's Knotts."

At Parker Center they found Lieutenant Frisby in the auto-theft division squad room. Frowning at the boys, he said, "You four again?"

"We solved the mystery of the empty warehouse,"

Frank said, handing him the matchbook cover. "They moved everything to this place."

After examining the advertisement, the lieutenant shook his head. "How does this fit in with the warehouse being empty for the last three months?"

"The old man lied," Joe said. "He's the janitor at Admax. The crooks stuck him in the warehouse just to discredit us."

Frank added, "Not only that, but all the men who kidnapped us are at this very minute working at Admax."

"Maybe you better tell me the whole story," Lieutenant Frisby suggested.

When Frank and Joe finished, he looked less doubtful but was not yet completely convinced.

"I'm not going to go off half-cocked by setting up another raid," he told them. "But I'm willing to check it out. You boys can lead me there in your car."

They took the elevator to the basement garage, and the lieutenant drove them around to where they had left their car on the visitors' parking lot. From there he followed them to Studio City.

The five entered the wholesale parts store together. A plump man the boys had never seen before was behind the counter. Lieutenant Frisby showed him his I.D.

"Your manager in?" he asked.

"Just a moment," the plump man said, and disappeared into the back.

"Is he one of your kidnappers?" the lieutenant asked when the clerk was out of sight.

The boys shook their heads. "He wasn't here before," Joe said. "Red Sluice was waiting on customers."

The clerk came back with a tall, gangling man. Offering a handshake to the lieutenant, he said, "I'm Osgood Admax, Lieutenant, the store's owner. What's the problem?"

Lieutenant Frisby turned to the boys. "Is he one of them?"

They shook their heads again.

"Mr. Admax," the officer asked, "you employ a janitor named Jonas Moapes?"

In a puzzled voice the man said, "I don't even know anyone by that name. Except for a part-time bookkeeper, my only employee is Melvin here." He nodded toward the plump clerk. "What's this all about?"

Indicating the boys, the detective said, "These young men have made some serious charges against you. They claim this place is an outlet for auto parts stripped from stolen cars."

"That's a lie!" Admax objected indignantly.

"Mind if we take a look at your storeroom?" Lieutenant Frisby asked. "Or do I need a warrant?"

"I don't mind at all. We have nothing to hide."

Raising a hinged section of the counter to let the officer and the boys through, Admax led them into the back room. Frank and Joe gazed around in consternation. The three stolen cars were gone, and all the engines had disappeared. Everything else that had been there previously, however, still seemed to be in place.

"They've moved out the hottest stuff!" Joe exclaimed. "They knew we'd go to the police, so they got rid of it fast."

"What are you talking about, young man?" Osgood Admax inquired.

Pointing to the side wall, Joe said, "An hour ago three stolen cars were parked there."

"And over a dozen engines were lined up here," Frank added. He pointed to the spot. "You got them out of here because you knew the serial numbers would prove they were stolen!"

Drawing himself up with dignity, the store owner said, "I have invoices for every item in this place. Lieutenant, you are free to examine my records."

"They won't show anything," Joe said angrily. "Invoices are easy to forge. They got everything out of here that had serial numbers on it, so there's no way to prove the rest of this stuff is hot."

The lieutenant's voice was just as angry when he

said, "What kind of game are you boys playing?" He turned to the gangling man. "Accept my apologies, Mr. Admax."

"Of course," the man said graciously. "You were only doing your duty." He frowned at the young detectives. "I don't know why you are trying to cause me trouble, but if you try it again, I'll sue you for defaming my character."

"Let's get out of here," Joe muttered in disgust. "I don't think he has any character."

Outside Lieutenant Frisby said in a grim tone, "Now I want you four to come with me."

As they followed the detective's car, Chet asked worriedly from the back seat, "Think he's running us in for filing a false report?"

"How could he?" Frank said. "We haven't filed any."

"He seems to think we have," Chet said.

But the lieutenant was not leading them back to Parker Center. Instead he drove to the warehouse on the edge of Old Chinatown. He parked in front and Frank pulled in behind him.

When they got out of the car, Frank said, "I've got a feeling we're in for another surprise."

The lieutenant tried the front door and found it unlocked. As they went inside, Joe said to Frank, "I have a feeling your feeling is right."

They headed for the office. The elderly Jonas Moapes was seated behind the desk with his feet up, again smoking his corncob pipe.

"Why, hello, Lieutenant!" he exclaimed cordially. "What is it this time?"

"Nothing," the officer said, and, turning abruptly, he stalked out of the place.

The lieutenant climbed into his car and drove off. The four boys looked at each other.

"Now what?" Chet asked.

"Now that he's discredited us again," Frank said, "that old man won't stick around here long. Let's tail him wherever he goes."

Since they did not know whether Jonas Moapes would come out the front or the back door, Frank drove the car to the side street and parked so that they could see up the alley. Then Joe posted himself at the corner, where he could observe the front and signal to the others if the old man should appear.

About fifteen minutes later, Frank lightly beeped the horn. Joe hurried to the car and climbed in next to him. Looking up the alley, he saw Crafty Kraft's eighteen-wheeler backing up to the sliding door.

As they watched, the tattooed man lowered the ramp, and three coveralled workmen emerged. Using a dolly, they began unloading car engines and wheeling them into the warehouse.

When they were finished, Crafty pulled the truck

out of the way, but left it in the alley. The vehicle had blocked the boys' view of what was beyond it, but now they saw that the three stolen cars were parked there, waiting for the truck to move. They were driven into the warehouse by Sluice, Jivaro, and Big Harry Knotts.

Joe got out of the car.

"Where're you going?" Frank asked.

Pointing to the delicatessen right across the street, at the edge of the alley, Joe said, "To call Lieutenant Frisby."

There was a pay phone on the wall of the small shop. Dropping in a dime, Joe dialed Parker Center and asked for the auto-theft division.

A voice answered, "Lieutenant Frisby."

"This is Joe Hardy," the young detective said. "We're still at the warehouse. Those stolen car engines were just unloaded from a truck, and the three cars were driven in there a few minutes ago. The crooks must figure that since you've already checked the warehouse twice, you won't check it again."

"They're right about that," the detective said and hung up.

Joe walked back to the car, discouraged and frustrated. As he climbed in, Crafty Kraft started the truck. It was facing their way, and while it was too far for the driver to notice the four boys, he would be able to see them once he got to the mouth of the alley. Frank hurriedly pulled away.

"We'll circle the block and come in behind them," he said. "What did the lieutenant say, Joe?"

"He didn't believe me," Joe said glumly. "Who's in the truck?"

"Everybody, including old Mr. Moapes. They locked up the building."

Vern said, "If Lieutenant Frisby isn't going to do anything, what's the point of following the truck? He won't react when we tell him where it went, either."

"I guess you're right," Frank agreed. "We may as well go back to the hotel. It's getting late anyway."

Some time later, they all gathered in the Hardys' room to discuss their next step.

"Let's wait until we hear from our dad," Frank suggested. "We'll give him all the information and let him contact Lieutenant Frisby. Hopefully, the lieutenant will believe *him*."

There was a knock on the door. Joe went to open it, and gaped in surprise.

Standing in the hall was the well-dressed, bent old man, Mr. Merriweather!

17 The Old Man

Without a word, the old man moved into the room.
Joe regained his composure. "I thought you'd be in
the hospital, Mr. Merriweather," he said.

Merriweather shut the door behind him and said
in his creaky voice, "I had a miraculous recovery
from my heart attack."

Then he laughed and straightened up. He pulled
off his white wig and false white eyebrows, and used
a handkerchief to wipe away the makeup that made
him look wrinkled.

"Dad!" Frank and Joe cried out. "How did you
find us?"

"I went to your previous hotel," the private

detective said. "When I found you'd checked out, I phoned home."

"B-but what were you doing at Admax, Mr. Hardy?" Chet asked.

"Getting evidence against the car-theft gang! When you saw me writing in my notebook, I was taking down the serial numbers of engines. I just phoned the Division of Motor Vehicles in New York State, and all of them are from stolen cars. What were *you* doing there?"

The boys related the results of their investigation, and how the crooks had managed to trick the police into thinking they were lying.

"If only Lieutenant Frisby had gotten to the warehouse about fifteen minutes later this afternoon," Chet said. "He would have caught them moving the stolen goods back in."

"I doubt it," Mr. Hardy disagreed. "The timing was deliberate on the part of the crooks. Probably they were waiting somewhere with that truck and the three stolen cars for an all-clear phone call from the phony caretaker."

"And now Lieutenant Frisby won't even talk to us anymore," Joe complained.

"I think he'll listen to me," Mr. Hardy said.

Dialing Parker Center, he asked for the officer, holding the phone so that the boys could listen in.

When he got Lieutenant Frisby on the line, he explained who he was.

"Oh, yes," the lieutenant said. "I've heard a lot about you, sir. But I'm afraid I've been having some trouble with your sons and a couple of their friends."

"I know, Lieutenant. I'm calling from their hotel room. The gang has been cleverly fooling you. Everything the boys told you was true."

"But the evidence against their story was overwhelming," the detective protested.

"Nevertheless, it was false evidence. As the boys told you, those stolen cars and things *were* at Admax. I not only saw them, but by pretending to be a crooked buyer, I got the serial numbers of the engines. I just checked with the New York State DMV, and all are listed as stolen. Right now, the three cars that have not been stripped yet and the engines are at the warehouse in Old Chinatown."

"Your word is good enough for me," the lieutenant said. "My search warrant for that place is still good, so I won't have to wait for a new one. Can you meet me there right away?"

"I'll be glad to."

Mr. Hardy, who had turned in his rented limousine, had come in a taxi, so they drove to the warehouse in the boys' car. Lieutenant Frisby was already there with a half dozen policemen.

After shaking hands with Fenton Hardy, the lieutenant said, "The rear doors are locked. I guess we'll have to break in."

"There's a restroom window around back with a broken lock," Frank said. "I can climb in and open the door for you."

"Good idea," the lieutenant agreed. "That'll save smashing in a door. But just in case anyone is inside, I'd rather send a policeman instead of you."

He designated one of the officers to go to the back and enter through the restroom window. A few minutes later, the officer unlocked the front door.

"Nobody in the place, sir," he reported.

Lieutenant Frisby led the way into the warehouse. When he saw the three cars and the row of engines, he stopped short and stared. "Well, I'll be," he muttered, then turned to the boys. "My apologies, gentlemen."

"We don't blame you, Lieutenant," Frank said. "The gang was so clever, at one point they almost had *us* believing we imagined the whole thing."

The officer looked at his wristwatch. "After five-thirty. It's unlikely any of the gang will return here tonight, and Admax will be closed by now. I'll have both places watched. We'll nab the crooks as soon as they show up in the morning."

"We know a couple of stakeout points, one in front and one in back," Joe said.

"Good."

The boys showed the officer the cardboard refrigerator carton near the front door and the shed across the alley. The lieutenant posted a man with a walkie-talkie in each place and told them he would have a backup force of several squad cars waiting nearby. They were to move in as soon as the stakeouts reported that the gang had arrived the next morning.

Frank spoke up. "There are a couple of other places you ought to watch, too, Lieutenant. We know where Red Sluice lives, and have the address of his girlfriend's apartment. I think Anton Jivaro is staying with Red."

"The hijacker?" the lieutenant said. "We want him as badly as the gang members."

"He *is* a gang member," Vern said as Frank gave the officer the two addresses, which he wrote in a notebook.

"Maybe you ought to keep all four places under surveillance and hold off making arrests for a few days," Fenton Hardy suggested. "If you move in right away, you may miss the kingpin of the operation. But if you maintain a stakeout, he might show up. If he doesn't, one of the gang members might lead you to him."

"In the meantime, they'll tear apart my car," Vern said ruefully.

"You can identify the big boss from the picture I took," Frank said. "I'll have it developed tomorrow and turn it over to you."

The lieutenant looked doubtful. "I'd rather not wait to move in at any of the locations, but we won't tip our hands. We'll stay out of sight and nab them as they show up. That way none of them will have the opportunity to spread the alarm. Of course, they'll know something's up when people start disappearing. Still, it should only take a few days to net all of them."

Mr. Hardy smiled. "I guess my investigation of the theft ring is over. Lieutenant, I'll give you the information I have, including the descriptions of all known gang members. That should wrap it up. From there on it will merely be a matter of nabbing them."

"I certainly appreciate your help, Mr. Hardy," the lieutenant said.

"You're welcome. Boys, are you ready to fly back to Bayport with me tonight?"

"I don't think so," Joe said. "We still have the mystery of Vern's coin to solve. Up till now, we haven't had much time to concentrate on that."

"Besides," Vern added, "I want to hang around to

wait for my car. When can I have it back, Lieutenant?" he asked eagerly.

"Tomorrow," the lieutenant replied. "It will be in the police impound lot."

"Well, boys," Mr. Hardy said, "perhaps you can take me to the hotel to pick up my baggage, and then drive me to the airport."

He shook hands with the lieutenant and said good-bye. The officer told the boys to phone him the next day. "I'll let you know how successful the stakeout was," he promised.

In the morning, Frank took his film to a twenty-four-hour developing service. Then, he phoned Lieutenant Frisby from their hotel room, holding the receiver so that the other boys could hear the conversation.

"So far we've had only partial success," the lieutenant reported. "A number of small frys were arrested at the warehouse, but they were just workers employed to strip the stolen cars. At Admax, we nabbed the man who claimed to be Osgood Admax, and who turned out to be a wanted forger named Calvin Renk. His clerk, Melvin, apparently was just an employee, and didn't know the items they sold were stolen."

"You haven't gotten Big Harry, Crafty Kraft, Red Sluice, or Anton Jivaro yet?" Frank asked.

"No, nor the big boss. Neither Sluice nor Jivaro has been near Red's house, Red hasn't visited his girlfriend, and none of them have shown up at either the warehouse or the store."

"You think they were somehow tipped off?"

"No, I suspect they are simply being cautious. They are a cagier group than I thought. Probably they just went underground for a few days to make sure they really had me fooled. I'm suddenly not too confident that we'll get them anytime soon."

"Why, Lieutenant?"

"Before they surface, they'll take the precaution of phoning the store to speak to Calvin Renk, and the warehouse to ask for one of the workmen there. When they can't get hold of either, I think they'll run!"

18 A Surprising Discovery

Vern said to Frank, "Let me speak to the lieutenant before you hang up."

"Hold on, Lieutenant," Frank said. "Vern Nelson wants to talk to you."

He handed the phone to his friend.

"When can I get my car back, sir?" Vern asked.

Come down and sign for it anytime you want. Check in here first and I'll have the papers ready for you. But not before 2:00 P.M., because I'm leaving for lunch."

"All right," Vern said. "We'll see you at two."

The boys ate at the hotel coffee shop, then drove to Parker Center. They found Lieutenant Frisby in the auto-theft division squad room. When Vern had signed the necessary papers, the lieutenant gave him a release form to present at the impound lot in return for his car.

"One other thing, Lieutenant," Vern said. "Do you think we could get a look at a certain case file?"

"Which one?"

"A missing 1913 Liberty Head nickel that disappeared. It was left to me by my uncle, Gregg Nelson, but wasn't in his safe-deposit box when it was opened."

"That would be a case for the burglary division," the lieutenant said, picking up his phone.

After a short conversation, he hung up. "No such complaint was ever filed," he announced.

The boys looked at each other. Joe said, "Maybe we'd better ask the lawyer who handled your uncle's estate about that, Vern."

The boys thanked Lieutenant Frisby, then got Vern's car released from the impound lot. Since they did not need two cars, they turned in the rented one.

"What's our next move?" Chet asked as they drove away from the rental agency.

"There's nothing more we can do about the gang," Frank said, "so we're free to concentrate on Vern's nickel. Who is this lawyer Joe mentioned?"

"Charles Avery in the Nichols Building," Vern

said. "It sure sounds fishy that he never reported the coin missing."

They found Charles Avery in his seventeenth-floor office. Vern introduced Frank and Chet, and the plump attorney invited them all to sit down.

Vern said, "We just came from the police, Mr. Avery. How come you never reported that the coin was missing?"

"Because there was no evidence that a crime had been committed," the lawyer said smoothly. "For all we know, your uncle hid the nickel somewhere other than in the safe-deposit box."

"But his will said he put it there."

Mr. Avery nodded. "On the other hand, there was no evidence of the box having been tampered with. Did you talk to Bank President Laing?"

"Yes."

"And he was no help?"

Vern said ruefully, "He explained to us how impossible it was for anyone but Uncle Gregg to get in that safe-deposit box."

"Actually that only increases the mystery, doesn't it? I don't see how the police could have done anything, even if I had reported it."

"They could have checked coin dealers to see if the nickel was offered for sale," Joe suggested.

Pursing his lips, the lawyer said, "I hadn't thought of that."

"We could check them now," Frank suggested. "Let's make a list of all coin dealers in the area, and visit every one of them."

"You can use my telephone directory," Charles Avery offered.

The boys looked in the yellow pages and copied down a list of names.

"This is going to take a long time," Chet said, as they finished.

"Perhaps you ought to start with the dealer through whom Mr. Nelson bought the coin," the lawyer suggested. "I have it in my file." He rose to get a folder from a cabinet and leafed through it. "Here it is," he commented. "Everett Fox on Wilshire Boulevard."

"I thought he bought it from a fellow collector in Massachusetts," Vern spoke up.

Mr. Avery nodded. "But it was handled through a local dealer on a commission basis. Such sales usually are."

He wrote the address of Fox's shop on a scrap of paper and handed it to Vern.

As they left the building, Chet said darkly, "That explanation of why he didn't make a police report sounds fishy to me. I think he's the one who swiped the coin."

"We'll need more evidence before we make any accusations," Frank said.

342

They drove to the address on Wilshire Boulevard. There was a barred plate-glass window with FOX COIN AND STAMP COMPANY lettered on it. Inside, two long counters ran from front to rear on either side of the store. A fussy-looking little man with gold-rimmed eyeglasses stood behind one of them, waiting on a fat woman.

"Be with you gentlemen in a minute," he said as the boys came in.

"No hurry," Frank told him.

The two counters were glass-topped. The one on the right contained displays of postage stamps. The left one was devoted to coins.

Chet studied the display. It consisted mostly of single coins, but in some cases there were complete collections in flat, plastic-covered folders.

"You know," Chet said, "this is a hobby that could be a lot of fun."

Joe whispered to Vern, "Here we go again. Chet's going to develop a new interest."

"Does he do that often?"

"About once a month. He gets all enthusiastic about something, then drops it."

Looking over his shoulder, Chet asked, "Are you guys talking about me?"

"I was just betting your cousin that you're about to become a coin expert," Joe replied.

"Not in a big way. I thought maybe I'd just collect

343

some ordinary coins, like this penny collection here."

He pointed to a pair of three-section folders lying open. When the other boys crowded around to look, they saw that they were Lincoln Head pennies.

"There can't be more than a hundred and fifty pennies there," Chet said. "I can afford a dollar and a half."

Vern said, "You don't get a collection like that at face value, Chet. Count on it costing a lot more."

"I suppose coin dealers have to make their profit," Chet conceded. "I don't mind paying a fair premium."

The woman customer left and the fussy little man came over to them.

"I'm Everett Fox," he said. "How may I help you gentlemen?"

Pointing to the penny collection, Chet said, "I'm interested in that."

"A fine collection," the coin dealer said, rubbing his hands together. "That's the Lincoln penny with wheat ears on the reverse, minted from 1909 to 1959. One hundred and forty-three coins altogether."

Frank said, "It was only fifty years from 1909 to 1959. How come so many coins?"

"There are different mint marks, because they

were struck at different mints. For instance in just the first year there were four: the 1909 V.D.B.; the 1909 S, V.D.B.; the plain 1909; and the 1909 S."

"What do all those letters mean?" Chet asked.

"V.D.B. are the initials of the designer, which appeared on only two issues. S is the San Francisco mint, and when there is no mint mark, it means the coin was minted in Philadelphia."

"I see," Chet said. "How much for the whole collection?"

"These are all either proof coins or uncirculated," the dealer said. "Sold individually they would cost you about eight. As a complete collection, naturally their value increases. I'm asking eleven."

"Eleven dollars?" Chet said dubiously. "For only a dollar-forty-three cents worth of pennies? I don't know."

"Not eleven dollars," the coin dealer said, elevating his nose. "Eleven thousand."

Chet gulped.

Frank chuckled. "I can loan you ten bucks, Chet. You could put the rest on your credit card."

Joe said to Vern, "That's a record. He had this hobby for less than five minutes."

Frank addressed Mr. Fox. "Actually, we came in to talk about a 1913 Liberty Head nickel."

"Oh, are you making a bid?" the dealer asked.

"A bid on what?"

"The nickel currently being offered for auction by the DuBois estate in Paris."

"We hadn't heard about that," Frank said. "When did DuBois acquire the coin?"

"Oh, it's been in his collection for over fifty years."

The boys looked at each other. "I guess that rules out it being Uncle Gregg's," Vern said.

The coin dealer said, "If you want to make a bid, I will be glad to forward it."

"How much would we have to bid?" Frank asked.

"The last auction for such a coin was eight years ago, and a man named Gregg Nelson got it for a hundred thousand dollars. He outbid the next-highest bidder by only two thousand."

"Who was that?" Joe asked.

"A local banker and avid coin collector named Barton Laing!"

19 The Big Boss

"Barton Laing!" Vern exclaimed.

"You know the man?" Everett Fox asked.

Vern nodded grimly.

"Strange thing," the coin dealer said. "Naturally, I contacted him when this auction was announced, and he expressed no interest at all."

"Maybe because he already has a Liberty Head nickel," Joe muttered under his breath.

"Beg pardon?" Mr. Fox asked.

"Just talking to myself," Joe replied.

Frank spoke up. "What would you do if someone walked in and offered you a 1913 Liberty Head nickel?"

"Have him arrested," Mr. Fox said promptly. "There are only five known to exist, and I know who the owners of all of those are. It would have to be stolen."

"Any other dealer would have the same reaction?" Frank persisted.

"Any honest one." After a pause Mr. Fox said reflectively, "I doubt that even a dishonest dealer would take a chance. The moment he offered it for sale, *he* would be arrested."

"Then actually there wouldn't be much point in stealing such a coin, would there?"

"Not for profit. An unscrupulous collector might steal one for his own collection."

"Thank you for the information," Frank said. "Let's go, fellows."

Outside, Joe said, "Seems pretty obvious who stole Vern's coin. I don't think we have to waste time visiting any other dealers."

"But how are we going to prove it?" Chet asked.

"I have an idea," Frank said. "I noticed a little park only about a block from here. Let's go sit on a bench and talk about it."

"That's Pershing Square you're talking about," Vern said. "Down that way." He pointed left.

They walked to Pershing Square and found a vacant bench.

"Okay, guru," Chet said to Frank. "We await your words of wisdom."

Frank smiled. "Barton Laing has never met me or

Chet. Suppose Chet phoned him and pretended to be a fellow bank president? He could say he has a son interested in coins, and ask if Mr. Laing would be kind enough to show the young man his collection."

"And you're the son?" Joe asked.

"Right."

"Two objections. Barton Laing probably knows most of the other bank presidents in town. If we used a real name, it might be a personal friend of his. If we gave a fake name, he might catch on, knowing the bank and the name of the president."

"That's only one objection," Frank said.

"I know. The other is that Chet's voice sounds too young to belong to a bank president."

"No problem," Frank said. "He can pretend to be calling long distance from somewhere like San Diego, and he can make his voice low."

"Laing still might know the names of all the banks in the state," Joe said. "And probably he has a directory that lists their presidents. He'd be almost sure to look it up after the call."

"So let's pick an actual San Diego bank and use the real name of its president," Vern suggested. "We'll take the chance that Laing doesn't know him personally."

They all looked at him. "How do we do that?" Chet inquired.

"It's simple," Vern said. "Just follow me."

He led the way up Fifth Street to the Los Angeles Public Library only a block away. There he went to a shelf of telephone directories.

"They have one for every major city in the country," he said. "I found out the library had them when I was visiting my uncle once and wanted the address of a friend in Vermont. He sent me down here."

Vern took the San Diego directory and carried it to a table. From the yellow pages they picked out a bank called the Bouchercon Trust Company, and Vern wrote down the number.

"Anybody got a couple of dollars worth of change?" he inquired.

The boys searched their pockets and came up with three dollars in nickels, dimes, and quarters.

"That should be enough," Vern said. "It's only a little over a hundred miles."

There were several public phones in the library, and he called the San Diego bank.

"Will you tell me the name of your president, please?" he asked when a woman answered.

"Certainly, sir. It's Mr. Jason McGuire. Do you wish to speak to him?"

"Not right now, thanks," Vern said, and hung up.

"A piece of cake." He grinned. "The president's name is Jason McGuire."

"You may as well phone from here, Chet," Frank suggested. "Let's hear your executive voice."

In a low, false bass Chet said, "This is Jason McGuire, Mr. Laing."

A passing librarian gave him a sharp look, and Joe chuckled. "You sound more like a bank robber disguising his voice. We better go outside to practice."

Several people were seated on the library lawn, reading. The boys moved out of earshot of everyone, and Chet practiced several different voices. They all sounded false, but suddenly Joe had an idea.

"Why don't you develop laryngitis?" he suggested. "That way, if Laing happens to know Mr. McGuire, you'll have an excuse for your voice being different."

In a hoarse, rasping tone Chet said, "Sorry if I'm hard to understand, old chap, but I've got laryngitis."

"That's perfect," Frank said approvingly.

They went back in and Chet phoned the Bunker Bank, asking for Barton Laing.

"Who's calling, please?" the switchboard operator asked.

"Jason McGuire, of Bouchercon Trust in San Diego."

"Just a moment, please."

351

Then a hearty voice sounded in Chet's ear. "How are you, Jason, old man?"

Barton Laing was obviously acquainted with the San Diego bank president and for a moment threw Chet off balance. The boy almost answered in his normal tone, but just in time he remembered and said hoarsely, "Fine, except for laryngitis."

"You sound terrible," Laing said with sympathy.

"I'll keep it brief, Bart, because it's hard for me to talk. Do you know my son Frank?"

"Not unless he was at some bankers' convention with you. I've never been in your home."

Chet was relieved. "Frank has the same hobby you do, coin collecting. He's driving up there from San Diego this afternoon, and I wonder if you'd do me the favor of letting him see your collection."

"I'll be glad to," Barton Laing said, apparently pleased. "We coin nuts like nothing better than to show off our treasures. When will he be here?"

"He's leaving now, so it shouldn't be more than a couple of hours. It's not quite three. He should make it by five."

"Maybe he'd like to drop over for dinner about seven, Jason? We'd love to have him."

Chet panicked and almost choked. "Ah, no, ah, he has a dinner date with friends. Could he come later?"

"Sure," Barton Laing said. "Tell him to make it

eight, then." He gave an address in West Los Angeles.

"Thanks very much," Chet said. "He'll be there."

"Take care of that laryngitis," Laing said, "and good-bye."

When Chet hung up, Joe slapped him on the back. "You did a wonderful job!"

"Thanks," Chet rasped. Then he looked surprised. "I-I think my voice stuck!"

"A soda should fix you up," Frank told him.

Chet cleared his throat and said in his normal tone, "I've recovered, but I'll still take that soda."

They found a small restaurant on Fifth Street, across from Pershing Square, and sat in a booth. Over cold drinks they discussed the coin case.

"Even as bank president," Vern said, "I don't see how Laing could have gotten into that box, because Uncle Gregg's key was needed."

"He didn't necessarily have to steal it himself," Joe pointed out. "Maybe he just bought it from the thief."

"You mean Cylvia Nash?"

"It makes more sense than Laing personally taking it," Joe said. "Suppose Cylvia, knowing that her boss would do nearly anything to get the coin for his collection, slipped it out of your uncle's box after he handed it back to her to lock it up. She could have taken it while she was walking away from him with the box and her back was turned to him. He wouldn't know it was missing because he never checked the box after that."

"I think you've got it," Frank said. "That fifty-thousand-dollar deposit in Cylvia Nash's savings account must be what Laing paid her for the coin. It all fits."

"All except her being the girlfriend of Red Sluice," Chet said. "How does *he* figure in this?"

"He doesn't have to fit into the coin theft," Joe told him. "Birds of a feather flock together. Probably they met each other because they travel in the same circles."

The house in West Los Angeles was an expensive home on an exclusive street. Vern parked a quarter block away and Frank got out alone.

"I shouldn't be long," he said. "As soon as I spot your coin, Vern, I'll make an excuse to leave and we'll drive straight to Parker Center."

He mounted the steps to the wide veranda and rang the bell.

The door was opened by a distinguished-looking man, and Frank gaped. It was the same man he had photographed entering the warehouse!

20 The Missing Coin

Trying to control his expression, Frank asked, "Mr. Laing?"

"Yes," the banker said cordially, holding out his hand. "You must be Frank McGuire."

"Yes, sir," Frank said, shaking hands. Barton Laing led him through a front room into a library and offered him a seat. Frank took a leather-covered easy chair, while the banker sat behind a desk.

Tapping his fingers on the wood surface, the man said, "So you are a collector, too."

"Not on the same scale as you," Frank said modestly. Then, using some of the knowledge he had picked up that afternoon, he made himself sound like an expert. "My only complete set is

Lincoln Head pennies with the wheat ears on the reverse. I have all one hundred and forty-three in uncirculated coins."

"That's quite a start for a young man your age," the banker said, impressed.

"May I see your collection?" Frank urged.

Rising from his chair, Barton Laing went over to an oil painting on the wall, slid it aside to disclose a safe, and opened the box with a key. He removed a stack of blue coin folders, but left one in the safe.

Laing set the folders on the desk and carefully relocked the safe. Since nothing was left in it but a single folder, the boy couldn't help wondering why he was being so cautious.

Standing alongside of Frank, the banker now opened the folders. In descending order he displayed collections of silver dollars, half dollars, quarters, and dimes, then set them aside.

"Now come my favorites," he said, opening the first of the remaining covers. "I specialize in nickels. I have everything from the first nickel coined in the United States in 1866, the shield type, through the latest Jefferson nickel. With one or two exceptions, the sets are complete."

Looking at a folder containing Liberty Head nickels, Frank said, "This is complete except for 1913."

Barton Laing smiled. "That's not hard to under-stand, is it?"

"Not considering that there are only five in existence," Frank agreed. "Did you know that the DuBois estate is offering one for auction?"

"Yes, I heard that," Laing said. "But bidding for that is a little out of my class."

Since Frank knew the man had bid ninety-eight thousand dollars for a Liberty Head eight years ago, he figured the real reason Laing was not going to bid was that he already had the coin.

"I noticed you left one folder in the safe," Frank pointed out. "Is that something special?"

"Just an empty cover."

The doorbell rang and Barton Laing went to answer it. Frank got up to try the safe door, but it was locked tight. Quickly, he resumed his seat when he heard the banker returning.

As he entered the room, Laing said, "I have some unexpected company. Have you finished looking at everything?"

"Yes, thanks," Frank said, rising to his feet.

The banker replaced the coins in the safe and locked it. Then he gestured for Frank to precede him to the front door.

As they started through the living room, four of the five people seated there gaped at Frank.

357

Angrily, Big Harry Knotts, Crafty Kraft, Red Sluice, and Anton Jivaro jumped to their feet! Cylvia Nash was the only one who remained seated as the men rushed at Frank, grabbing him before a single word was said.

"What's the matter with you?" Laing asked indignantly. "How dare you manhandle my guest!"

"Do you know who he is?" Big Harry challenged.

"Certainly. Frank McGuire, the son of a colleague."

"You've got the first name right, but the last name's Hardy!"

"What!" The banker glared at Frank in outrage. "Frank Hardy! You came here to spy on me!"

Frank saw no point in replying.

"Wait here," Laing ordered his gang. "I'll be back in a minute."

He disappeared into the kitchen and returned carrying a coil of rope. "Follow me!" he said as he went past.

He led the way into the library while Frank's captors forced the boy along. Cylvia trailed after the group, her face tense.

Laing pointed to a straight-backed chair. "Tie him to that!" he ordered.

When the boy had been bound hand and foot, the banker said, "His brother and his two friends are probably nearby, too. Search the neighborhood and

don't let them get away. Cylvia and I'll keep our eyes on this one."

The four rushed out. Frank could hear the front door open and close. Meanwhile, Laing and Cylvia were standing side by side, watching him closely. Frank started to feel panic. How could he possibly get out of this situation? Just then, he saw a window behind his captors being pushed up slowly.

To divert their attention, he said to Cylvia, "How did a nice lady like you get involved with this gang of crooks?"

"None of your business!" Laing snapped.

"I don't get it," Frank went on. "I just don't. When we met on the airplane—"

He kept talking on and on in a loud voice, while the window was being raised all the way. Joe noiselessly threw a leg over the sill, pulled himself inside, and tiptoed up to Barton Laing. Vern was right on his heels and Chet followed.

Frank was still talking when Joe and Vern suddenly grabbed the bank president from behind. Chet ran to the doorway to block Cylvia Nash's escape in case she tried to run.

Laing struggled to get out of the boys' grip, but in vain. Vern had pushed a handkerchief into the man's mouth so he could not scream and alert his companions.

360

Cylvia was too scared to make a sound. She stood motionless, watching the boys subdue her boss.

"Okay, Miss Nash," Chet said. "Untie him." He pointed to Frank.

The woman gave the banker a frightened look, and went up to Frank. When he was freed, Joe and Vern forced Barton Laing down into the chair and bound and gagged him.

Then Joe turned to Cylvia. "You behave, and we won't have to do the same to you."

"I'm not going to make any trouble," she said meekly and sank into a leather love seat.

Suddenly, they heard the front door open and close, and several sets of footsteps moved their way. Chet and Frank hid on one side of the door, Joe and Vern on the other. Big Harry and his gang filed into the room. When they saw their subdued leader, they whirled to face the boys.

Frank ducked a blow from Big Harry, cracked him on the jaw, and sent him reeling backward to crash into the wall. Joe grabbed Crafty's wrist when the tattooed man swung at him, and flipped him over his shoulder onto his back, while Vern traded punches with Red Sluice.

Chet tossed little Anton Jivaro face down on the floor and sat on him. Then Big Harry bore into Frank again, swinging both fists. Frank blocked the blows, feinted, and landed another hard crack on Knotts's jaw. This time, Big Harry went down and stayed there.

Crafty started to get up, but collapsed on his face when Joe hit him with a judo chop on the side of his neck. Sluice knocked Vern off his feet and tried to kick him in the stomach. Grabbing his ankle, Vern up-ended him onto the seat of his pants. Then the Hardys grabbed the redhead and held him tight.

It wasn't until the boys had all four hoods bound securely that anyone noticed Cylvia Nash was gone!

"We should have tied her up," Chet muttered.

"Don't worry about it," Frank said. "The police will find her." He used the phone in the library to call Lieutenant Frisby. When he hung up, Vern asked, "Did you see my coin?"

"He didn't show it to me, but I think I know where it is," Frank replied. He got the safe key from the banker's pocket, unlocked the box, and lifted out all the folders except the last one. After putting them aside on the desk, he took out the remaining cover and opened it.

It contained only a single coin, a 1913 Liberty Head nickel!

"My uncle's coin!" Vern cried out.

"Well, I guess that solves both mysteries," Frank declared.

"But we haven't found the big boss of the car-theft ring yet," Joe pointed out.

"Oh, I didn't tell you? It's Laing. I was quite shocked when I came here and realized he was the man whose photo I took."

Just then, the police arrived and took the prisoners away. "We'll be on the lookout for Cylvia Nash," Lieutenant Frisby promised the boys. "Meanwhile, congratulations. You've done a great job. Sorry I didn't believe you at first. You turned out to be better detectives than we have in the department. Want to join the force?"

The boys laughed and Frank shook his head. "We'd like to know whether you get hold of Cylvia, though."

"Call me tomorrow," Frisby replied.

Cylvia Nash was arrested when she returned to her apartment that night, and the boys left town after breakfast the next morning.

"I hope you don't run into another mystery right away," Chet told the Hardys as they drove along in Vern's car. "Can't we just have some simple, plain fun for once?"

Frank and Joe grinned. "Maybe," Joe said. None of the boys knew that almost as soon as they returned to Bayport, they would find themselves involved in *The Outlaw's Silver*.

The Hardy Boys® in

The Outlaw's Silver

Franklin W. Dixon
Illustrated by Leslie Morrill

The Outlaw's Silver was
first published in the U.K. in a single volume in hardback in 1982
by Angus & Robertson (U.K.) Ltd, London
and in Armada in 1982

Contents

1 The Devil Doll

"Boy, this heat is really getting to me!" Chet Morton declared. "I need a banana split in the worst way!"

Joe Hardy laughed. "It seems to me your mother packed you an adequate lunch."

"How could she pack a banana split? Listen, I've been slaving all morning, burning up energy, and those sandwiches were just not enough to stoke up sufficient body fuel."

"I guess not," lanky Biff Hooper teased. "After all, you've got plenty of storage capacity."

The boys had been unloading bricks at a construction site for Tony Prito's father and had worked up hearty appetites. Even though they had brought sandwiches, they were looking forward to dessert at a downtown ice-cream parlor.

"Let's get a booth," said Frank Hardy and added, "Hey, watch it!" as someone jostled him roughly just before they reached the little restaurant.

Dark-haired and eighteen, Frank tended to be calmer and more even-tempered than his younger brother Joe. But his good-looking face flushed with anger as he slapped away a hand groping in his jacket pocket.

"What's the matter?" Tony Prito asked.

"Pickpocket!" Frank exclaimed, turning to scowl at the person who had just passed him. He had caught only a fleeting glimpse of a tall man with beetling brows and a drooping black mustache, but he was ready to chase after the culprit if anything had been stolen.

Quickly, Frank reached in his pocket to feel for the familiar shape of his wallet, but his hand closed on an object pressed against the soft leather. Instead of taking something, the alleged pickpocket had left behind a memento!

In the ice-cream parlor, Frank took out the object to inspect it more closely. It was a weird little plastic figure, resembling a kangaroo with bat wings and a spear-pointed devil's tail.

"What's that?" Chet Morton inquired.

"Search me." Frank frowned as he studied the tiny devil doll. "That guy I thought was a thief must've stuck it in my pocket!"

"Oh, oh, here we go again!" Biff grinned. "Another mystery for the Hardy Boys!"

"Maybe that's why he put it in your pocket," Tony suggested, then broke off as the waitress began serving their orders.

"What do you mean?" Frank asked, after she had left.

"Well, there could be some mysterious curse attached to the thing—it sure *looks* devilish enough!"

"You can say *that* again!" Chet muttered between mouthfuls of ice cream.

"Anyhow, say he recognized you as one of those famous young detectives, Frank and Joe Hardy. So he planted the devil doll in your pocket, hoping you'd unravel the curse." Tony sounded half joking, half serious.

Frank smiled wryly. "Aw, knock it off."

"If you ask me, he might just be right," said Biff.

Joe Hardy nudged his brother's arm. "Get a load of that flat-nosed guy in the corner booth."

Frank put the devil doll on the table in front of him and glanced over at the tough-looking man Joe had referred to. He was thickset with short, bristly hair and the twisted, broken nose of a boxer who had stopped a straight punch. He was eyeing the Hardys and the weird figure intently.

"Big eyes and big ears," Joe muttered.

Suddenly, the man seemed to realize he had been noticed. He averted his gaze and busied himself with his food. A minute or two later he snatched up his check and walked hastily to the cashier's counter.

The place was overflowing with noontime business. Amid the comings and goings of customers, the Hardys soon forgot the flat-nosed busybody.

Suddenly, there was a muted crash of breaking glass somewhere at the rear of the ice-cream parlor.

"What in the world was that?" Biff exclaimed.

"Either someone dropped some glassware or broke a window," Tony guessed.

Moments later, smoke began to billow out of the kitchen.

"Great!" said Tony sarcastically. "Now it looks like someone started a fire!"

As the smoke increased, patrons began to cough and mutter anxiously. Some called out to the counterman and waitresses nervously, trying to figure out what to do. Suddenly a voice shouted, *"Fire!"* and the stampede was on.

Chairs scraped as people jumped up from their tables to head for the door. There was angry jostling as other customers squirmed out of their booths to join in the exit rush.

"Come on!" Frank said to his friends. "Let's try to help evacuate people. This could be a disaster if we don't!"

Calling out loudly to the patrons, the boys worked their way through the crowd.

"Please form a line to prevent injuries!" Frank commanded. "There will be plenty of time for everyone to get out as long as you don't create delays at the door. Please stay in line and walk quickly without pushing the people ahead of you!"

He was gesturing to a group of women in the back of the room while Joe and the others had worked their way toward the exit, trying to keep people calm. Frank's clear voice had a soothing effect on the frightened patrons, and they did their best to cooperate.

The din subsided a bit and the ice-cream parlor gradually emptied. When there were only a few people left, the boys went toward the door. Biff and Tony held the bandannas they had been wearing around their necks to their noses as makeshift smoke filters. The others could only keep their heads down, pinch their nostrils, and grope blindly through the fumes.

By the time Frank neared the door, the smoke was so thick it was almost impossible to see. Sud-

denly he was hit on the head from behind! The blow was only glancing, but it was hard enough to stun him. Eyes smarting and head swimming, Frank sank to the floor, bumping into a table as he fell.

Someone's going through my pockets! he realized. He struggled groggily to fight off whoever was bending over him. But another clout, this one on the side of the head, left him too dazed to resist.

Outside the restaurant, people stopped and gathered to stare at the emerging customers and ask what was going on. A fire siren shrieked in the distance.

"Someone must've called in an alarm," Biff said.

"Hey, where's Frank?" Joe exclaimed, running a hand through his blond hair.

The four realized that the older Hardy boy was still in the ice-cream parlor. Without hesitating, Joe plunged back into the reeking interior, followed by Tony, Biff, and Chet.

Despite the dense smoke, they were able to make out Frank's prostrate form and carry him outside, where he soon revived after a few whiffs from an oxygen inhalator supplied by the firemen.

"Want us to call an ambulance?" one asked.

"No thanks, I'm okay," Frank assured him.

As the firemen moved on to other tasks, Joe turned to his brother, his brow puckered in a slight frown. "What happened in there, Frank? Don't tell me you just passed out from the smoke?"

"No, I didn't. Someone conked me on the head."

Joe whistled and the other boys stared in amazement as Frank related the attack in the ice-cream parlor.

"Two pickpockets in one morning," Tony commented. "This town isn't safe any more!"

"The first man wasn't a pickpocket," Frank reminded him. "And maybe the second creep was after the devil doll that the first guy left."

"Are you kidding?"

"No way. It's too big a coincidence to assume the two events aren't connected."

"Maybe you'll never know," Chet said. "Now that the thing's been stolen."

"Don't worry, it's safe." Joe grinned and pulled his hand out of his pocket to reveal the sinister little figure. "I grabbed it off the table when we all got up to leave."

"Nice going!" Frank congratulated his brother. "Actually, I wasn't too sure whether the guy who slugged me had taken it, or I'd left it behind."

"What do you mean, 'nice going'?" Chet said uneasily. "If the crooks want it that much, you might get conked again!"

The fire crew was already coiling up the hoses, preparing to depart, and the smoke from the ice-cream parlor seemed to have cleared considerably. The boys now realized they had seen no flames.

"What caused all this?" Joe asked the fire captain.

"Smoke bomb. Someone tossed it through the kitchen window. There was no fire at all."

The Hardys looked at each other, both wondering the same thing. Had the smoke bomb been thrown on purpose to give the sneak thief a chance to steal the devil doll from Frank? If so, the trick had failed.

"Did you see that flat-nosed guy come back in the place?" Joe asked his brother.

Frank shook his head. "No, but he could've sent someone else in to conk me. If our hunch is right, *he* probably threw the bomb."

Joe dropped his brother off at home to rest before the boys went back to the construction site to finish their jobs. When the younger Hardy finally came back from work, he was greeted by his tall, thin Aunt Gertrude, who handed him a special delivery letter. Scrawled in ink on the envelope was THE HARDY BOYS, followed by their house number on Elm Street in Bayport, but there was no return address.

"Wonder who it's from?" Joe asked just as Frank came downstairs from their bedroom.

"What is it?" the older boy asked.

His aunt clucked impatiently. "Why not open it and find out?" Gertrude Hardy was the unmarried sister of the boys' father, the famed investigator Fenton Hardy. She lived with the family and was known as the best cook in town. Although she worried and constantly nagged Mr. Hardy and his sons about the dangers of detective work, she took a keen interest in all their cases.

Frank smiled as he realized she was as curious about the contents of the letter as he was. "Good idea, Aunty," he said and slit open the envelope.

The hall telephone rang. Joe answered it.

"You one of the Hardy boys?" said a gruff voice.

"That's right. What can I do for you?"

"Keep your grubhooks off my treasure, boy! Someday I'm coming back for that load of silver plate—and it better still be where I left it, y'understand? If it's gone, there'll be the *devil* to pay!"

"Who is this?" Joe demanded curtly.

"The Outlaw of the Pine Barrens!" came the reply, followed by a burst of maniacal laughter. Then a receiver clicked at the other end of the line.

2 A Mystery from History

Joe put down the phone with a bewildered expression.

"What was that all about?" Aunt Gertrude demanded sharply. He turned and saw that she had been eavesdropping discreetly on the brief conversation.

"Search me," he shrugged. "Something about a load of silver plate. Sounded like some nut. He called himself the Outlaw of the Pine Barrens."

"If he was telling the truth," Frank spoke up, "you've been talking to a dead man."

Joe stared at his brother. "What do you mean?"

"Take a look at this." Frank held out a sheet that he had taken from the envelope and unfolded.

Joe studied it with curiosity. It appeared to be a photostat of an old letter, crudely written in an outdated style of handwriting, with many of the words misspelled.

MARCH 3, 1781

HOPE THIS REACHES YOU TU. WILL SEND IT BY INJUN PETE CUZ HE NOES OUR HIDEOUT ON CEDAR KNOB AND SAYS HE WILL STOP THERE ON HIS WAY BACK TO PARSONS FORGE. ALSO HE CAINT READ, SO HE CAINT TELL NOBUDDY WHUT I HEV WRIT. BLACK JACK WAS TOOK BAD AND DIED. BURIED SILVER UNDER HIM FISH-HOOK TEN PACES NORTH AS CROW FLIES. COME QUIK AND WE WILL SPLIT TREASURE. GOOD LUCK, MATES.

JEM TAGGART

Joe looked up at his brother in blank amazement and passed the letter on to his aunt, who scanned it intently through her gold-rimmed glasses. "What do you make of it, Frank?" he asked.

"First tell me exactly what that weird caller said," the older Hardy boy countered.

After Joe finished, Frank puzzled over the events thoughtfully. "Both the phone call and the letter concern a silver treasure. That has to be more than a coincidence, right?"

Joe nodded. "Just like that sneak who stuck the

devil doll in your pocket, and the other sneak who tried to swipe it."

"What was that?" put in Aunt Gertrude, frowning at the boys suspiciously. "What devil doll are you talking about?"

Joe produced the tiny plastic demon to show her, and Frank briefly related the incidents Joe had referred to.

Miss Hardy shook her head as she examined the ugly little figure. "I don't like this a bit!" she fretted. "Looks absolutely nasty to me—like something right out of a horror movie!"

"I wasn't too crazy about the whole business myself," Frank replied dryly, "but I'm not sure what we can do about it, Aunty."

Turning back to Joe, Frank resumed their discussion of the letter and phone call. "You'll notice the letter also speaks of *our hideout*."

"Which sure sounds like a gang of crooks."

"Exactly! Add it all up and I'd say the chances are Jem Taggart is—or *was*—the Outlaw of the Pine Barrens."

"That figures, all right," Joe agreed. "The timing alone makes it look as though the letter and the call are connected somehow. But who's behind it all?"

"Good question. For that matter, we don't even know if this letter's authentic or a fake."

"Oh, I almost forgot!" Miss Hardy exclaimed.

"Forgot what?" asked Joe.

"You two had another call this morning while you were out, right after that special delivery letter arrived."

"Who was it?" Frank queried.

"I don't know. He didn't give me any name. In fact, he was rather gruff and impolite. His voice was sort of muffled, or—well, *distant*, as if he were rasping at the phone from far off."

"Sounds like the nut I just spoke to," said Joe. "Probably trying to sound like a ghostly voice from the grave."

"Another thing," Miss Hardy went on, encouraged by her nephews' obvious interest. "There was a car parked down the street all morning. I couldn't see who was in it, but I'm sure there was someone at the wheel. And I noticed a few moments ago when I looked out the window that it's gone. Mighty suspicious, if you ask me."

"You could be right," Frank said thoughtfully. "The driver may have parked there to watch for the special delivery. Then he could have radioed the person who made the call. Or, if he had a car phone, he could have phoned himself. When you told him we weren't home, he stuck around till he saw us come back and called again."

"That makes sense," Joe said. "The call came

right after we got here. But why? You think some-one's playing a joke on us?"

"That's possible," Frank said dubiously, "but if so, the joker has a strange sense of humor."

"And he's sure going to a lot of trouble to set us up for laughs," Joe added wryly.

Frank nodded. "We'd better check it out."

"Okay. But where do we start?"

"Well, let's see. The Pine Barrens are in southern New Jersey, I think—" Frank paused, frowned, and scratched his head. "But don't ask me what went on there in 1781."

"Hmph! You young folks still get American history in school, don't you?" Miss Hardy cut in. "Why not ask your history teacher?"

"Say, that's a good idea!" Joe exclaimed.

"Well, don't look so surprised," she retorted. "Is there anything all that strange about me getting a good idea?"

Both boys burst out laughing.

"Not a thing, Aunty," Joe replied, giving her an affectionate hug.

The boys promptly phoned their high-school history teacher, Miss Degan, who said she would be glad to give them whatever help she could. She turned out to be an excellent source of information. During the summer, she was studying to complete her master's degree at nearby Bayshore University. Ultimately, she hoped to achieve the degree of Ph.D. and become a college professor herself, specializing in American history of the Revolutionary period.

"Now then, what's this all about?" Miss Degan inquired when the Hardy boys were seated in her study.

Frank handed her the letter and, when she had read it, asked, "Ever hear that name before?"

"Jem Taggart? Of course. He was the famous Outlaw of the Pine Barrens."

The Hardys felt a thrill of satisfaction on hearing Frank's hunch confirmed.

"What can you tell us about him—and about the Pine Barrens, Miss Degan?" put in Joe.

The teacher smiled. "That's a pretty large order, but let me try to give you a brief answer. To begin with, New Jersey has the greatest population density—that is, the most people per square mile—of any state in the Union. Yet it also has the hugest tract of undeveloped timberland east of the Mississippi—namely, the Pine Barrens."

The northern half of the Atlantic coast, she went on to explain, was so built-up and industrialized that the stretch from Boston to Richmond was almost like one continuous city. Yet sprawled right in the middle of it, almost within sight of New York's towering World Trade Center, stretched a vast expanse of wilderness called the Pine Barrens—hundreds of thousands of lonely, sandy acres of pines, oaks, and cedars.

"It's no good for farming," Miss Degan continued, "so the early settlers left it untouched. But it did have bog iron, which they forged into cannons and cannonballs during the Revolution and the War of 1812. It also bordered the ocean and had a lot of creeks and inlets, so it offered a perfect hiding place for smugglers, not to mention Tories who disagreed with the rebels, and Hessian deserters, as well as various fugitives from the law."

One of the latter, it seems, was Jem Taggart. He pretended to be both a Tory and a rebel, depending on whichever suited his nefarious plans of the moment. He preyed on both sides during the war.

"But he was finally brought to justice," Miss Degan ended. "This book will tell you about it."

She plucked a volume from her bookshelf, found the right page, and handed the open book to her two young visitors. Together, the Hardys read how Taggart and the surviving members of his dreaded gang had been captured and hanged in 1781.

"Wow! That's the same year as the date on this letter!" Joe commented.

"And it says he's supposed to have left a buried treasure, which was never found," said Frank, "consisting of a cargo of silver plate from a captured British merchant ship. Do you suppose that's the silver Jem mentions in his letter?"

"It's possible," Miss Degan said cautiously, "and I must admit the letter looks very convincing. But remember, this is only a photostat of the original, so there would be no way to test the document scientifically. I suggest you get an opinion from an expert."

"Anyone in particular you can refer us to?"

The teacher hesitated. "Well, let me see. You might try Mr. Caleb Colpitt. He's a dealer in old maps and manuscripts."

She consulted the telephone directory for his address, which she wrote down on a slip of paper and handed to the boys. Frank and Joe thanked her and left.

Frank was at the wheel of their car as they headed homeward. The boys were discussing their visit to Miss Degan, when Frank suddenly jerked his head and muttered, "I wonder what this creep's up to now?"

"What are you talking about?" Joe inquired.

"See that black station wagon? I think he's been tagging us all the way from Bayshore. Now all of a sudden he's in a big hurry!"

"Oh, oh," Joe said, alarmed. He turned back just in time to see the wagon roaring up behind them at high speed.

"Hey, Frank! I think the driver is that flat-nosed guy from the ice-cream parlor!"

"Are you sure?" Frank asked tensely, glancing in the rearview mirror for a moment. Then he trod hard on the accelerator. "I hope we can get away from him." He looked at the lonely stretch of coastal road, ideal for a possible ambush. The sudden appearance of the flat-nosed man might have been purely accidental, but both boys doubted it.

"I bet he was following us," Joe declared. "I wish I knew what he's after!"

"We might find out sooner than you think unless we can get away from him," Frank replied. "Personally, I'd rather avoid a confrontation at this spot! It's a little too isolated for me." He drove as fast as he could, trying to outdistance the black car.

But it soon became clear that their pursuer had no intention of letting the Hardys get away. The station wagon was a powerful, eight-cylinder model, and Flat Nose was recklessly floorboarding his gas pedal. Bit by bit, he drew abreast of the Hardys' sports sedan.

Suddenly there was a loud clash of metal, and their car lurched, jolting both boys to the right.

"The dirty rat's sideswiping us!" Joe blurted.

Frank nodded grimly. "Trying to force us off the road!"

From the window of the station wagon racing alongside them, they saw Flat Nose bare his teeth in a nasty grin of vindictive glee. Again he side-swiped them—*and again!*

On their right, the shoulder of the road dropped off sharply in a cliff sheering down to a gully below. Tight-lipped but calm, Frank eased his foot off the pedal and tried to slow down, but it was no use. Whether he dropped back or sought to forge ahead, Flat Nose kept them tightly penned in.

In desperation, Frank jammed his own gas pedal to the floor, hoping their sports car might have enough zip in the showdown to leave the wagon behind. But at that same moment, the black station wagon leaped ahead and cut in front of them! Frank turned the wheel and stamped on the brakes to avoid a collision. The yellow sports sedan spun out of control toward the shoulder!

3 A Face in the Crowd

There was a screech of tires and a clatter of gravel!
The Hardys froze with fear as the steep drop-off to
the gully below yawned beneath their front wheels.
Fleeting instants seemed drawn out into agonizing
minutes before their car came to a shuddering halt,
teetering on the very brink of the cliff!

The boys stared at each other, then slowly released their tension in long, gusty sighs.

"Wow!" Joe gasped. "That's what I call too close
for comfort!"

As he reached for the door handle, his brother
warned tensely, "Don't get out. You might tip us
over."

Joe turned pale. "Can you back up?"

"I'll try." The engine had stalled, but Frank keyed it back to life and cautiously eased the gearshift lever into reverse.

The car groaned and the wheels spun gravel, but aside from a momentary jerk there was no movement.

Joe looked uncertain. "What do we do now?"

"Call a tow truck, I guess." Frank switched on their CB radio and was soon able to contact a wrecker cruising for business. He described their location, and the tow truck driver promised to be there in ten minutes.

The black station wagon that had caused the accident had disappeared, much to the Hardys' relief. But Joe had had the presence of mind to memorize its license number, and while the boys waited for assistance, he reported it by radio to the State Police.

The wrecker soon arrived. Its driver maneuvered into position so that the rear end of his truck was only a few feet away from the Hardys' car. Then he hooked a chain to their back bumper and within a few moments pulled them to safety.

"Thanks!" both boys exclaimed, getting out.

"What were you trying to do?" their rescuer asked with a grin. "Play rocking horse?"

"Far from it," Joe retorted. "Some wise guy forced us off the road."

The Hardys' car radio buzzed. Joe went to answer it while Frank paid the tow truck driver. The call was from the State Police, reporting that the license number that Frank had taken down belonged to a station wagon that had been stolen only an hour or so earlier, and had just been found abandoned on a highway near Bayport.

"Thanks, Sergeant, that was fast work!" Joe replied. He passed the news on to his brother, adding in disgust, "So much for our chances of identifying Flat Nose!"

"Don't worry, something tells me we haven't seen the last of him," Frank said dryly as they started home again. "But one thing we know for sure—those guys play rough!"

When they arrived home, the boys learned from their slim, attractive mother that they had had a telephone call from a newspaper reporter named Grimes.

"What did he want, Mom?" Frank asked.

"To interview you and Joe. I didn't encourage him, because I know how you and your father feel about publicity. But he was very persistent and said he'd drop around anyhow."

The Hardys had not long to wait. Less than half an hour later, the doorbell rang. Their visitor, a curly-haired man in his thirties, dressed in a rather rumpled suit, introduced himself as Nate Grimes.

Frank let him in, more out of politeness than from any desire to be interviewed.

"You write for the *Bayport Press*?" he asked the reporter.

"No. Atlantic News Service. I'm what they call a stringer, more or less a freelance correspondent."

"What can we do for you?" Joe said, trying to keep the interview as brief and as businesslike as possible.

"Is it true that you have a clue to a famous treasure? I mean the silver that was buried by the Outlaw of the Pine Barrens a couple of hundred years ago."

There was a moment of startled silence. Frank's eyes narrowed as he asked, "Where did you hear that?"

"An anonymous phone tip. I figured it might be good for a feature story, so I called to ask for this interview." Grimes studied the boys' faces intently before pressing, "Well, is it true?"

"In a way, yes," Frank admitted. "We've received a copy of an old letter that may have been written by Jem Taggart to other members of his gang, and it does mention some buried silver."

Grimes was watching Frank's expression eagerly. "Do you think the letter's on the up and up?"

Frank shrugged. "Hard to say. It looks authentic, but we're no experts."

"What about your father?" Grimes pressed. "Can't he tell if it's phony or not?"

"Perhaps. But he's busy with his own case load."

"Hey, that's right," Grimes said. "You two seem so young to be detectives, I keep forgetting you've grown up in the business, so to speak. Must be exciting, being in on all of those sensational cases he investigates. What's he working on now, by the way?"

"Sorry, we're not allowed to discuss that."

Fenton Hardy had once been an ace manhunter for the New York Police Department. Later he retired to the pleasant seaside town of Bayport to become a private investigator. Many of his cases had made national and even international headlines, but Frank and Joe had long since learned to emulate their father's tight-lipped "no comment" attitude on such matters. By his own example, the famed sleuth had taught them the importance not only of preventing security leaks, but also of safeguarding clients' privacy.

If Nate Grimes was put out by the boys' evident distaste for publicity, he gave no sign of it. Instead, he kept pelting them with questions about the Pine Barrens mystery.

"What's your own opinion, Mr. Grimes?" Joe said, deftly turning the focus of the quiz on their interrogator. "Do you think there's really a valuable treasure hidden out there in the woods?"

The newsman chuckled and ran his fingers through his curly hair. "You've got me there, pal—and, incidentally, make it Nate, please, not Mr. Grimes. To tell you the truth, I'd never even heard of this Outlaw character until I got that anonymous phone call. Guess I'll have to read up on him before I write my story."

"Might be a good idea," Joe commented dryly.

"Do you think that letter of Taggart's will start you off on a treasure hunt?" Grimes went on.

"I doubt it," Frank said. "But anything's possible."

In case they actually did decide to search for the outlaw's silver trove, they did not want to volunteer any information that could stir up a swarm of other treasure hunters.

After probing a bit more, Grimes asked permission to snap a few pictures of the boys and finally left.

"Nosy guy, wasn't he?" Joe remarked as they watched their visitor drive off.

Frank grinned wryly. "Guess that's what makes a good reporter."

"Hmph! If you two have nothing better to do than stare out of the window, I have a good suggestion," a tart voice broke in. "The front lawn's about a week overdue for mowing, and the bushes could do with some trimming, too!"

"Okay, we get the picture, Aunt Gertrude," Joe said, adding a surprise kiss and squeeze that left Miss Hardy tut-tutting sharply, but unable to repress a pleased smile at her nephew's obvious affection.

"If you think that'll get you an extra big slice of devil's food cake tonight, young man, you're absolutely right!" she muttered.

Twenty minutes later, as the power mower was humming across the grass and the hedge trimmer clipping away busily at the shrubbery, a white station wagon pulled up at the curb.

"Hey, it's Iola and Callie!" Joe exclaimed, stopping the mower.

The blond girl at the wheel smiled and waved, while her pert, dark-haired companion brandished several pink tickets as the Hardy boys hurried over to greet their girlfriends.

"What've you got there, Iola?" Joe asked.

"Tickets to the Turnerville Three concert tonight, over in Shoreham," the pixie-faced brunette informed him. "Want to come? You're both invited."

"You bet!" Frank said. "How'd you get the tickets? We heard they were sold out."

The Turnerville Three was a popular recording group. Iola, who was Chet Morton's sister, explained proudly that she had sold the group one of her driftwood sculptures. The musicians had been so enthusiastic over her work that they had tipped her with three pairs of tickets to their local concert. Iola had been spending the summer polishing and mounting her driftwood creations, which she sold from a stand in front of the Morton farm.

She blushed a little in spite of herself as Frank's date, Callie Shaw, spoke up. "You two didn't know we had such an artistic genius in our midst, did you?"

"Oh, yes, I did," Joe said, patting Iola gently on the shoulder. "That's really great. Is Chet coming?"

"No, he can't be bothered," Iola replied. "He's too busy with his latest hobby, so we asked Biff and Karen."

"Great! What time should we call for you?"

"You won't have to. Callie's mom said we could have the station wagon. That way we can all go in one car."

"I'll honk at seven," put in Callie. "Be ready."

"Have I ever kept you waiting?" Frank chuckled. "Don't worry!"

That evening, after the young people left the Hardy home, traffic seemed unusually heavy as the white station wagon moved along in the line of cars on the highway to Shoreham.

"I must be watching too many mystery shows on TV," Callie murmured.

"How come?" Frank asked.

"I have this strange feeling that we're being followed," she replied with a nervous giggle.

"Probably some secret admirer who wants to ask you for a date," Joe suggested jokingly.

"Not while I'm around," said Frank. "What kind of a car is this romantic creep driving, Callie?"

"Oh, I don't know! I'm not even sure what color it is. I just keep seeing the same windshield and grille in my rearview mirror every so often!"

The Hardy boys exchanged quick glances, both thinking uneasily that Callie's suspicions might not be due only to her imagination. However, neither wanted to say anything that might alarm their companions and perhaps spoil their evening. Instead, they began watching the traffic, alert for any possible tail car. But none appeared.

It was not yet seven-thirty when the three young couples reached the downtown section of Shoreham. Callie parked the station wagon in a nearby lot, and they walked to the Strand Theater where the concert was to take place.

A sign announced that the doors would open at ten minutes to eight, but a noisy crowd had already gathered outside and seemed to be growing larger every moment. Fans not lucky enough to have purchased tickets were bidding for them at inflated prices. Hawkers elbowed their way about, offering T-shirts bearing likenesses of the Turnerville Three, as well as posters, fan magazines, and other souvenirs.

"What a madhouse!" exclaimed Iola. She had to raise her voice to make herself heard.

"Let's hope it's quieter inside," Joe responded, "or we won't even be able to hear the concert!"

"Don't worry," said Biff. "Once they turn on the amplifiers, the sound'll be booming off the walls!"

Frank was about to add a good-natured wisecrack about the advisability of wearing earplugs, when he caught a glimpse of a face that froze him to instant attention. The crowd was mostly composed of young people, but the face he had just seen was that of an older man with beetling brows and a drooping black mustache.

"Hey, Joe!" he hissed, clutching his brother's arm.

"What's up, Frank?"

"See that guy with the black mustache?"

"What about him?"

"I think he's the one who stuck the devil doll in my pocket!"

The man was trying to worm his way through the crowd toward the Hardys. Frank eyed him intently,

feeling there was something strangely familiar about him.

But suddenly the man's face registered alarm. He turned abruptly and ran back the way he had come!

"I'm going after him!" Frank exclaimed and began pushing in pursuit.

4 A Sinister Suspect

Frank looked back over his shoulder as he ran, wondering what had caused the man to turn around and flee. He caught a glimpse of a red-haired fellow who was holding a folded-up newspaper and pointing it toward the mustached man in front of him.

As the fugitive broke away from the crowd, Frank heard something whiz past his ear, followed by a sharp thump just ahead. He stopped short with a gasp as he saw a deadly looking steel dart burying itself in one of the big framed posters on the gate leading to the theater parking lot.

The boy felt a chill run down his spine at the sight of the lethal missile. Had it been aimed at him or the stranger with the black mustache? Either way, he was convinced he had narrowly escaped a serious injury, or death!

By now the crowd was milling about more excitedly than ever, even though most of the people had no idea of what had happened.

Frank made a desperate effort to go after the man with the black mustache, but the fellow was already lost to view.

Finally, the young detective got clear of the crowd and darted down the street, glancing in every direction. It was no use. The mustached man had disappeared.

Disgusted, Frank went to rejoin the others. As he approached his companions, the theater doors opened and the eager fans began pouring inside. Frank met up with Joe, Biff, and their dates to the right of the entrance.

"Good grief! What was that all about?" Callie asked him anxiously.

"Tell you later," said Frank, squeezing her hand, not wanting to worry her. "Come on, we'd better go inside before the concert starts, or some of these eager beavers may grab our reserved seats!"

The dart, he turned around to check, was gone. He guessed that the red-haired assailant had plucked it out of the poster as Frank pursued the man with the dark mustache.

The cheering inside the auditorium made it

nearly impossible to carry on a conversation, and once the concert started, the amplifiers boomed as loudly as Biff had predicted. The Hardys and their friends had to shout in each other's ears to be heard. Frank and Joe were just as glad to postpone their explanation to the girls, knowing the story might stop them from enjoying the performance.

Not until the concert was over and they were parked in a hamburger drive-in on the road to Bayport, did the young detectives tell Callie, Iola, and Karen the whole story.

"Oh, my goodness!" Iola gulped. "I had no idea it was that serious!"

Callie, too, had turned pale. "Do you believe the dart was meant for you, Frank?"

The older Hardy boy shook his head. "No. The more I think about it, the more I'm convinced it was fired at that man with the black mustache. He knew the red-headed guy had spotted him. That's why he turned and ran away. The funny thing is, I have a feeling I've seen that mustached man before somewhere."

"You mean, before he stuck that devil doll in your pocket?" Karen inquired.

Frank nodded, frowning thoughtfully. "Don't ask me why, but his face just looked familiar, somehow. For that matter, I have a hunch we've seen the other guy before, too."

"The redhead?" Joe shot a glance at his brother.

"Yes. In fact, I seem to connect them up in my mind, as if I saw them about the same time—"

His voice was trailing off when suddenly his eyes widened and he snapped his fingers. "Now I remember! I saw him at the ice-cream place. He was one of the customers who came in after that flat-nosed guy left!"

"Wow! Then the two of them could have been in cahoots on the smoke-bomb caper!" Joe said.

"Sure. He probably was sent in to shout 'Fire!' in order to set off a panic when smoke started billowing out of the kitchen."

"But why are they still trailing us?"

"Maybe they're hoping to get back the devil doll," Frank theorized. "Or wait, come to think of it, maybe they even figured that sooner or later we'd lead them to the man with the black mustache!"

Both Joe and Biff looked startled.

"In that case," Biff said, "they sure figured right!"

When Frank and Joe arrived home that night, they were surprised to find their mother and Aunt Gertrude waiting up for them. Mrs. Hardy looked uneasy, and even her sharp-tongued, stiff-necked sister-in-law seemed a trifle disturbed.

"Anything wrong, Mom?" Joe asked.

"I hope not, dear, but Gertrude and I had a

notion that someone was spying on the house tonight."

"It was more than a notion, Laura," Miss Hardy corrected. "We both saw that fellow skulking in the shadows!"

"Whereabouts, Aunty?" asked Frank.

"First we sighted him across the street, standing by that big, old elm tree on the corner. Later on we glimpsed him going through the alley, peering over the back fence."

"What did he look like?"

"It was too dark to tell, but I'm sure it was the same man."

Both ladies admitted they were worried. But they had decided against calling the police, since the prowler could no longer be seen and had evidently given up his vigil for the night.

"We'd better make sure," Frank said, and Joe agreed.

The two boys armed themselves with powerful flashlights and searched around the vicinity of the house, but found no one. Switching on the burglar alarm system, they then turned off all the downstairs lights and settled down for a vigil of their own, keeping a lookout through various windows. No prowler appeared, however, so the boys finally went to bed.

After breakfast the next morning, Frank and Joe drove to the shop of Caleb Colpitt, the dealer in old maps and manuscripts whom their history teacher had mentioned.

His place of business was located in a weather-beaten frame building in one of the older sections of Bayport. Several ornate maps, one of them dating back to the early 1700s, were displayed in glass cases in the window. The Hardy boys guessed that these were removed frequently or shifted to different positions, so as not to expose them to too much sunlight.

Colpitt himself was a tall, spare, balding man who wore sleeve garters and was dressed in a rather old-fashioned way. When Frank and Joe introduced themselves, he recognized their names at once and said that he had helped their father some years ago on a case involving a stolen rare map.

"That's great, Mr. Colpitt," said Frank. "Then maybe you won't mind helping us, too."

"Be glad to, if I can."

"First," Frank handed him the photostat of Jem Taggart's letter, "would you say the letter this was copied from was authentic?"

"H'm." Caleb Colpitt proceeded to study the sheet carefully for two or three minutes, using a large, square magnifying glass to aid in his examination. "It certainly *appears* to be genuine," he announced cautiously at length, "or if not, then it was forged with a great deal of expertise. For example, the way certain letters of the alphabet are formed here would require the forger to know a good deal about the handwriting of the period, or at any rate more than the average person knows. I'm afraid there's no way to tell for sure, however, without seeing the original parchment and subjecting it to various tests."

Looking up with a slight frown, he added, "Of course, even without the original, you could probably get a much more reliable opinion from a trained examiner of questionable documents."

"Your opinion's good enough for us, Mr. Colpitt. At least it'll serve for the time being," Frank replied. "Next, would you have an old map in stock showing the Pine Barrens area of New Jersey during Colonial times?"

The elderly map dealer looked startled. "How odd that you should ask me that!"

"How come, sir?" Joe asked.

"It so happens I did have a detailed map of that very area that was drawn for the Continental Army in 1778."

"That sounds just like what we need! Where is it now, Mr. Colpitt?"

"I wish I knew! Someone broke into my shop the night before last and stole it!"

5 *The Angry Visitor*

The same suspicion struck both of the Hardy boys. The map might have been stolen by someone who was hoping to find Jem Taggart's buried treasure!

Caleb Colpitt saw the look that passed between them. "You're wondering if the theft may have anything to do with that letter you just showed me, aren't you?" he inquired shrewdly.

"How did you guess?" Joe blurted.

"The whole story's in the morning paper."

The boys realized the map dealer was referring to Nate Grimes's report of their interview.

"As you can see," Frank pointed out to Mr. Colpitt, "this letter says the gang's hideout was on Cedar Knob. Well, we've looked in Dad's big atlas at home and also on an automobile map of New Jersey, but neither one shows any place by that name."

"For that matter," Joe added, "neither one shows Parson's Forge, either. We did find the name in a book about the Pine Barrens that our history teacher showed us, but even the map in that book didn't have Cedar Knob on it."

Mr. Colpitt nodded. "A good many old names die out, especially in an area as lonely and off the beaten track as the Pine Barrens."

"How would the thief have known you had such a map?" Frank asked.

Colpitt explained that it had recently been on display in his shop window.

"Was anything else taken?"

The map dealer shook his head. "Just that one item."

"That sure does sound as if the thief knew exactly what he was after," Joe agreed. "And the robbery occurred the night before last?"

"That's right. I discovered what had happened when I came in yesterday morning."

"Then if there *is* any connection, the burglar must have known about Taggart's letter before Joe and I got this copy by special delivery yesterday."

"Wouldn't be too surprising," the elderly map dealer remarked dryly. "After all, if the letter's

409

authentic, it was written two centuries ago, so a good many people may have seen it by now."

"True," Frank said, "but I have a hunch it may have come to light just recently."

"Getting back to the geographic question," Joe put in, "do you have any other maps that might show the New Jersey Pine Barrens?"

"H'm. Well now, I do have one that might be worth checking." Colpitt disappeared into the back room and soon returned, bringing a map enclosed in transparent plastic. It had evidently been drawn during the Civil War period to show the area of military operations in Virginia and Pennsylvania, but also included the southern portion of New Jersey.

Colpitt and the boys scanned it eagerly. Joe was the first to spot the landmark. "There it is!" He stabbed his finger at the name CEDAR KNOB inscribed on the map in tiny letters.

The Hardys were jubilant, feeling they had now taken the first successful step toward finding the lost treasure.

"Mind if we copy this, Mr. Colpitt?" Frank asked.

"Not at all. Here's a piece of paper."

Joe whipped out a pen and sketched enough of the surrounding terrain and place names to enable them to find the spot without difficulty.

Frank, meanwhile, had another spur-of-the-moment inspiration. Pulling the devil doll out of his pocket, he showed it to the old map dealer.

"Ever see anything like that before, sir?"

Colpitt picked up his magnifying glass again to study the ugly little plastic figure.

"No, can't say I have," he said at last. "But it looks like some sort of heraldic beast."

"You mean like you see on coats of arms?"

"That's right, like unicorns and dragons and griffins, that sort of thing. There's a woman named Mrs. Amanda Hertford who traces people's genealogy and family coats of arms. She might be able to help you. Don't know her address, but you can find her in the phone book."

The Hardys thanked the elderly map dealer and left the shop. Before driving off, they called their three buddies, Chet Morton, Tony Prito, and Biff Hooper, and arranged to meet them for lunch at the Bayport Diner.

Chet was already ensconced in a booth, munching on a cheeseburger, when Frank and Joe arrived.

"Hope you don't mind my ordering before you got here," the plump youth said between mouthfuls. "I was really famished!"

"So what else is new?" Frank said, grinning at his brother.

"This story, for one thing," Chet retorted. Taking a rolled-up newspaper from the seat beside him, he flipped it out flat on the table so the Hardys could see their picture and Grimes's account of their interview on the front page. "Boy, you guys really have a knack for making news."

"We didn't ask the reporter to come around," Joe informed their friend as Biff and Tony walked in. "Somebody tipped him off."

The boys listened avidly as Frank filled them in on everything that had happened.

"Another mystery case!" Chet exclaimed, wiping his mouth with a napkin and signaling the waitress. "I knew it right off when Iola told me about that dart business last night!"

"You think there's any connection between this treasure letter and the devil doll?" Tony asked after the waitress had taken everyone's order.

Frank shrugged. "We don't have any evidence so far, except for the timing."

"And don't forget Flat Nose tailing us after we left Miss Degan's place," Joe put in.

But Frank shook his head doubtfully. "That doesn't prove anything. He could have shadowed us all the way from Bayport. Whatever's behind it all, though, it's pretty strange, getting mixed up with *two* sets of weirdos at the same time!"

"Well, anyhow, we do have one clue," said Joe.

"What's that?" Biff asked.

"We've located the place where the Outlaw of the

Pine Barrens and his gang hid out. So would you like to go treasure hunting with us?"

"Sure! How soon do we start?" Biff asked, and Tony exclaimed, "Count me in!"

"Me, too!" Chet said enthusiastically.

"Joe and I would like to get going tomorrow," Frank told them, and the five Bayporters hastily laid plans for the expedition. When they finally returned to Elm Street, the Hardys saw a flashy-looking, high-powered car parked in front of their house. A tall, balding man, presumably its driver, was standing on the porch, engaged in an argument with Aunt Gertrude.

As the boys approached, the man turned and glared at them. "Oh, so there they are!" he growled belligerently.

Ignoring him, Frank asked his aunt what was going on.

"A loud, unpleasant nuisance, that's what!" Miss Hardy snapped. "This rude individual came blasting away at the doorbell as if I was deaf, and then he demanded to see you boys. When I told him you weren't here, he tried to bully his way inside and threatened to make a scene unless I told him where he could get hold of you!"

Frank stared at the man coldly. "Well, here we are. What is it you want?"

"That letter of Jem Taggart's you two smart alecks

filched from my client!" The stranger was red-faced with anger as he hissed out the words.

"Watch what you're saying," the elder Hardy boy retorted. "I don't let anyone get away with calling us thieves. Before this goes any further, maybe you'd better tell us who you are."

"Verrill. Ambrose Verrill, attorney-at-law!"

"If you really are an attorney, then you ought to know better than to go around making wild accusations. It could either get you a lawsuit for slander or a punch in the mouth. Now if you can calm down and tell us what this is all about, come on inside and we'll listen."

Frank himself was angry enough to come to blows with their unpleasant visitor, and he could sense that Joe's quick temper was even nearer to the boiling point. On the other hand, he was eager to hear what the man had to say in the hope that his story might yield a clue to the mysterious sender of the Outlaw's letter.

Verrill swallowed hard, trying to get himself under control. "Very well," he huffed. "I'll give you a chance to clear this up, but you'd better come clean and talk fast!"

Joe could barely wait till they were seated in the front room to reply in a sizzling voice, "For your information, we have nothing to come clean about! You're the one who'd better talk fast!"

"According to the morning paper," Verrill began, "you have a letter, dated March 3, 1781, from the Outlaw of the Pine Barrens to other members of his gang. Correct or incorrect?"

"The story's accurate," Frank said curtly. "What about it?"

"You have no right to that letter! It's none of your affair!"

"Apparently you didn't read the news report very carefully. We don't have the original letter. What came to us through the mail was a photostat."

"Copy or not, makes no difference. What counts is the information contained in the letter. I don't want that circulating to every Tom, Dick, and Harry. So hand it over!"

At this outburst, the Hardys merely looked at each other and maintained a scornful silence.

Verrill rose to his feet, his face more flushed than ever. "For the last time, I want that letter. It belongs to my client, and it's my responsibility!"

"So you keep telling us," Frank replied. "I don't know if you take us for simpletons, but we'll need more than your word for that. The way you've been acting, it's hard to believe you're even a lawyer. Have you any idea who sent that copy of Taggart's letter to us, or why?"

"I don't have to answer any questions, young man! You're the ones in possession of stolen property. You'd better clear that up first, if you know what's good for you!" Ambrose Verrill shook his finger at the boys to emphasize his point. "Have you got some half-baked notion of hunting for that treasure?" Verrill paused, and when the boys did not answer, repeated more loudly, "Well, have you?"

"We don't have to answer any questions, either!" Joe blurted, stung by the man's hectoring tone.

"Let me tell you right now," Verrill ranted, "if you poke your noses into the Pine Barrens, interfering with my client's search, you'll be sorry!"

Frank sprang up from his chair, his eyes blazing. "Don't threaten us, Mr. Verrill! We've heard just about enough from you."

"Just remember what I said!" Verrill blustered and went out the front door and down the porch steps. A moment or two later they heard his car speed off.

"Well, I never!" Gertrude Hardy sniffed. She had been listening discreetly to the conversation from the archway leading into the dining room. "If that man's a lawyer, he should be disbarred!"

"I'd like to disbar his nose!" Joe gritted, clenching his fists.

"Are you two really going to look for the Outlaw's treasure?" their aunt added, curious.

"We'll give it a try!" Frank told her with a grin, "but don't worry about Verrill."

"Hmph!" Miss Hardy sniffed. "Loudmouthed bullies like him don't worry me. But there may be more to this treasure business than meets the eye!"

"We'll be careful," Joe promised. "And now we'd better make a list of all the items we need for our expedition."

Frank nodded. "We'll have to get our camping gear together. Our sleeping bags are still at Biff's house. I'll call him and tell him to pack them."

"Didn't you say there was a rip in your tent?" Aunt Gertrude inquired.

Frank snapped his fingers. "That's right. I forgot all about it."

"I'll fix it for you," his aunt offered.

Frank gave her an affectionate hug. "Aunt Gertrude, you're the greatest. What would we ever do without you?"

"I wonder." Aunt Gertrude chuckled.

When the young detectives had all their equipment ready, Frank telephoned Mrs. Amanda Hertford, the lady whom Caleb Colpitt had mentioned, and asked if they could see her. After shopping for supplies, the Hardys drove to her house.

She turned out to be a gray-haired woman with an open, pleasant manner. When Frank showed her the devil doll, she studied it carefully, then shook her head and frowned. "No, I don't believe this represents any heraldic beast. Still, it does seem familiar somehow. Wait a minute."

Mrs. Hertford took down several large books of heraldry and began leafing through them, looking for a picture of any similar creature, but without success.

Suddenly she stopped short and snatched up the little plastic figure. Her eyes lit up as she looked at it again. "Of course! Now I remember where I saw this before!"

6 Art for Sale

"Where, Mrs. Hertford?" Frank asked eagerly.

"It was a roadside stand, not very far from here. Let me see now, where was it?"

"You mean, someone was *selling* a devil doll like this?" Joe broke in.

"No, it wasn't this small. It was a ceramic statuette, maybe about a foot high."

"But the same sort of creature?" Frank pursued.

"Yes, definitely, with bat wings, just like this one has, and a devil's tail and the same kind of snout and claws. If only I could place it!"

The Hardys glanced at each other in surprise, while Mrs. Hertford knit her brows, trying to recall the exact location of the roadside stand.

"Old Orchard Road, that's it!" she exclaimed suddenly. "Somewhere on the right side. I saw it as I was driving into Bayport this morning. I'm afraid I can't be much more specific than that."

"That's specific enough, Mrs. Hertford. You've been a big help!" Frank exclaimed gratefully.

The boys thanked her and hurried back to their car. Just as they were about to start out for Old Orchard Road, the dashboard radio buzzed and a red light blinked, indicating a transmission on their special frequency.

The caller proved to be Aunt Gertrude.

"What's up, Aunty?" Joe queried.

"You boys have a client. Male, well-dressed, about forty. Sounds as though his case might be important."

"We'll be there in ten minutes. Over and out."

Postponing their business on Old Orchard Road temporarily, the Hardys drove straight home to Elm Street. Their client proved to be a quiet-mannered, pipe-smoking man in a tweed jacket who gave his name as Ogden Price.

"How can we help you?" Frank inquired as he and Joe sat down on the sofa, facing their visitor.

"By finding my cousin, Rupert Price."

"Is he missing," Joe asked, "or have you just lost touch with him?"

"He disappeared twenty years ago."

"How come you waited so long to trace him?"

"Because an uncle of ours died recently, leaving him a valuable inheritance, which he'll lose if he's not found. Also, I read in the morning papers that you may be going to the Pine Barrens, and I've a hunch that's where Rupert's hiding."

Frank frowned. "Hiding from what?"

"The law—or so he thinks. Actually, he's been in the clear for years."

"Maybe you'd better tell us the whole story."

Ogden Price nodded, rubbing the bowl of his pipe against his cheek and staring unhappily at the carpet. "It started when my cousin was accused of killing a man. They'd had a bitter quarrel over a business deal and the police proved that Rupe had been in the man's office just a short time before he was found dead. The evidence seemed pretty overwhelming. In fact, there was a warrant out for Rupe's arrest. When he came to me for help, I turned him down."

There was a moment's silence before Joe said, "You didn't believe he was innocent?"

"No. I was convinced he was guilty. On top of which, we'd never gotten along with each other, so I didn't want any part of the whole mess. I advised him to give himself up. Instead, when the police came to arrest him for the murder, he gave them the slip and disappeared."

"But since then, you say he's been cleared?" Frank questioned.

"Yes. Later on the real killer confessed. He was convicted and my Cousin Rupert's name was cleared. Trouble is, the case was a couple of years old when it was finally solved, so at that time it didn't get nearly as much attention in the press as it did when the murder was headline news. Rupe probably has no idea the police have stopped looking for him."

"What makes you think he went to the Pine Barrens?"

Ogden Price shrugged. "It's just a hunch. But Rupe went canoeing there several times, and I remember him remarking what a vast, lonely, unspoiled region it was, and how a man could hole up there as long as he liked. Rupe loved the wilderness and the outdoors, you see. That's why it seems natural that he'd go there to hide out."

Joe said, "How about the inheritance you mentioned?"

Price paused to relight his pipe before replying. "Well, it consists of both money and property. I can't give you an exact figure, but my uncle's lawyer estimates the estate will amount to over a million dollars."

Joe whistled. "Wow! That's a lot of money!"

"Indeed, it is," Price agreed.

"How much of that will go to your cousin?"

"I'm to get two hundred and fifty thousand. The rest will go to Rupert, to help make up for the injustice and unhappiness he's suffered. But if he doesn't show up to claim his bequest, then I'll inherit everything, since neither Rupe nor my uncle have any other living relatives."

"So if we find him," Frank pointed out, "it'll cost you three-quarter of a million dollars."

"That's one way of looking at it, I suppose."

"A lot of people wouldn't want to give away that big a fortune," Joe said. "If you don't mind my asking, how come you feel differently?"

Again their visitor shrugged. "If you want the truth, I'm ashamed of myself for not helping Rupe when he was first accused of the murder. At least I should have been willing to give him the benefit of the doubt. Since I didn't—well, the least I can do for him now is to find him and see that he gets his share of my uncle's estate." Ogden Price puffed on his pipe, then added with a dry smile, "As for the money itself, two hundred and fifty thousand is quite enough for me, thank you. I never married, and so I don't have a family to worry about."

The Hardys were silent for a few moments, mulling over the details of the case.

"How'll we know your cousin if we do find him?" Frank asked at length. "He may have changed a good deal in twenty years, let alone the fact that he's probably going under an assumed name."

"That's true," Ogden Price conceded. "All I can do is show you the last photograph I have of him."

He took a snapshot out of his pocket and handed it to the boys. It showed a lean, dark-haired young man in the uniform of a United States Navy medical corpsman.

"Rupe enlisted while he was in college," Price explained. "He was hoping to save up enough money to put himself through medical school. But instead, he found himself facing a murder rap only a few months after he got out of the service. It was a tough break, all right—I just hope it hasn't broken his spirit."

"Can you think of any other clues or leads that may help us identify him?" said Joe.

"Well, let me see." Ogden Price frowned thoughtfully as he shook the cinders out of his pipe into an ashtray. "His favorite pastime was whittling and woodcarving. That's not much to go on, but it's about the only thing that comes to mind."

"Okay, Mr. Price, we'll see what we can do," Frank promised. "Where can we reach you if we do turn up any information?"

Price wrote out his address, then shook hands with the Hardys and left. A few minutes later, after telling their mother and Aunt Gertrude about the new case they had just taken on, the boys hurried out to their yellow sports sedan and headed for Old Orchard Road.

They had driven only a short distance when Frank suddenly gasped and stepped on the brakes. "Joe! Do you see what I see?"

"I'll say I do! The greatest sculptor since Michelangelo—and I do mean greatest! In size, that is."

As Joe spoke, Frank was already swinging left into the driveway of the Morton farm.

On a stand nearby were several examples of Iola's driftwood sculpture, and a red ceramic statuette in the likeness of the devil doll! At a separate wooden table, Chet was molding a bust out of wet clay. He was wearing an artist's smock and a French beret.

A large sign tacked to the display stand said:

HAVE YOURSELF IMORTALIZED BY
A FAMOUS SCULPTER—$2.00!
ARTIST WILL POSE FOR SNAPSHOTS
WHILE HE WORKS—25¢

Chet greeted the Hardys as they jumped out of their car. "Want me to make busts of you guys?"

"Are you kidding?" Frank exclaimed. "One joke is enough around here!"

Chet's moonface fell. "Of course, if you don't appreciate art, that's your business," he said huffily.

"Just don't make fun of what you don't understand!"

The tubby youth perked up, however, as Frank picked up his red devil doll to admire it. "Not bad, except that you brought us here on a wild-goose chase."

"How come?"

"A lady told us about this, and we thought we had a hot lead on the real devil doll. When'd you make it, Chet?"

"Yesterday afternoon. Then I had it baked and glazed over at the Fair Hills Kiln. Pretty good likeness, just working from memory, huh?"

"Very good, I have to admit. You may be a sculptor yet, pal—if you can just learn to spell the word. And, incidentally, there should be two *m*'s in *immortalized*."

Chet flushed slightly with embarrassment, "Listen, you can't expect an artist to be talented at *everything*!"

With his eyes twinkling, Joe asked, "Any takers yet on your offer to pose for snapshots?"

"Not yet—but plenty of people slowed down to stare at me! And one wise guy snapped me without even paying!"

The Hardys burst out laughing and Chet looked surprised. Then he grinned good-naturedly. "Why don't you come in for a snack?" he offered, and the young detectives accepted gladly. After refreshing themselves with some pie à la mode, the Hardys started home.

That night, shortly after everyone had retired, the burglar alarm went off at the Hardy house. Frank and Joe were out of bed in an instant.

Both grabbed heavy, powerful flashlights. Not only would their beams blind an intruder, but in an emergency, the devices could be wielded as defensive weapons.

Outside their father's study, the boys paused for a moment while Frank gently took hold of the doorknob. Then he turned it suddenly and flung the door wide open, while they flashed their beams into the room.

A tall figure who had just finished climbing through the window, froze in the brilliant glare!

Frank gasped as he recognized the intruder. He was the person who had thrust the devil doll into his pocket and later had appeared outside the theater where the concert was being held—*the man with the drooping black mustache!*

7 El Diablo

There was a moment of tense silence as the boys stared at the intruder. Then the man slowly reached up to his mustache and pulled it off!

Seconds later, his bushy black eyebrows had also been peeled away!

"Dad!" Joe exclaimed.

"Right, Son!" Fenton Hardy, tall and strongly built, chuckled and held out his arms as the two boys rushed to share his hearty embrace.

"It's great to see you, Dad!" Frank said.

Hearing the happy outburst of voices, the women ventured downstairs and were soon caught up in the excitement of Mr. Hardy's return, while Joe quickly went to turn off the alarm.

"Why'd you slip that little devil doll in my

pocket, Dad?" Frank asked when he was able to make himself heard.

"Well, it's a long story, Son—"

"And you're not going to tell it till you've had a chance to sit down and catch your breath!" Miss Hardy interrupted in her usual sharp, scolding voice. "So I suggest you all adjourn to the kitchen while I make some cocoa!"

"Sounds like a mighty good idea, Gertrude!" The detective grinned, winking at the two boys, and slipping an arm around his wife's shoulders.

Later, as they sat around the table, Mr. Hardy began, "As you've gathered by now, I've been operating strictly undercover lately. It's all part of a coast-to-coast manhunt for a deadly international crook known as El Diablo."

"That's Spanish for 'The Devil,' isn't it?" Mrs. Hardy asked.

"Right, Laura. According to most accounts, he's Latin American, which explains the Spanish nickname—and believe me, he's really earned it!"

"What's he accused of?" Joe broke in.

"Among other crimes, large-scale smuggling, the infiltration of foreign spies into the U.S.A., disposing of stolen goods overseas, illegal exporting of technical electronic gear, and—well, I could go on with quite a list, but that'll give you the general idea, I believe," Mr. Hardy replied.

A nationwide dragnet by the FBI, Mr. Hardy related, had so far proved fruitless, so they had called him in to aid their search.

"Any leads to go on?" asked Frank.

"So far, just one that amounts to anything, at least in my opinion. Recently, a crook named Kerric, who's been on the FBI's 'Most Wanted' list, was picked up in the New Jersey Pine Barrens under odd circumstances."

At mention of the Pine Barrens, Frank and Joe exchanged startled glances, but neither wanted to interrupt their father's story.

"A state trooper happened to pull into a gas station down there," Mr. Hardy went on, "when he saw this fellow walking along the road. The trooper spotted him as Kerric and arrested him. Now, I'd already picked up some underworld rumors indicating that Kerric was mixed up with El Diablo. When they questioned him, Kerric absolutely refused to talk—they couldn't break him down, but they did find that little devil doll in his pocket."

Frank hurried out of the kitchen to get the sinister plastic figure and laid it on the table for everyone to see.

"How scary looking!" Mrs. Hardy murmured.

"This El Diablo character may be the head of a band of devil worshipers!" her sister-in-law declared. "Have you considered that possibility, Fenton?"

"Not very seriously, Gertrude. But I can tell you this. I've flashed that ugly little doll a number of times in various dives and hangouts where members of the underworld tend to congregate. Whenever I do, it seems to startle everyone who sees it, and more than once I've heard the name *El Diablo* being whispered behind my back."

"Have you tried to get any crooks to talk about it?" Frank asked. "Just casually, I mean."

"I have, in all sorts of ways," Mr. Hardy replied, "but invariably they clam up. It's obvious they're scared out of their wits for fear Diablo or one of his gang may spot them as squealers."

Mr. Hardy explained that after letting himself be seen carrying the devil doll and mentioning the name, El Diablo, in a big-city café frequented by mobsters and other known crooks, he found himself being stalked by two hoodlums—one red-haired, the other easily spotted by his flat nose.

"They even trailed me here to Bayport," the private investigator told his anxious listeners. "I figured they were about to jump me. But if it came to a fight or a gun in my back, I didn't want to risk them getting away with the devil doll—especially since that was the only clue I had. When I happened to see you boys with your friends, I decided the safest bet was to try and slip it into one of your pockets."

"The only trouble was, those two hoods saw you do it," put in Frank, "probably because I reacted so sharply. I thought you were a pickpocket!"

Mr. Hardy frowned with concern as his two sons gave him a full account of their recent adventures. He was particularly alarmed when he heard of the house being spied on after dark.

"That settles it!" he declared, thumping his fist on the table. "I'll call Chief Collig in the morning and ask him to provide round-the-clock police protection when I'm not home!"

Because of Kerric being nabbed in the Pine Barrens, Mr. Hardy said he also believed that Diablo's gang might have their hideout there. "A spot near the coast would be an ideal base for smuggling, and of course the wilderness would give them perfect cover. So when I read in the paper that you might go to the Pine Barrens, I decided to risk coming home after dark."

"We *are* going, Dad," Frank told him. "Matter of fact, we were planning to leave tomorrow."

"In that case, keep your eyes and ears open. See if you can spot any signs that the gang is operating in that area."

"Will do," Frank and Joe promised.

Next day the five boys headed for the New Jersey timberland. Tony and Chet rode in Biff Hooper's van, which was loaded with most of the camping gear, while Frank and Joe led the way in their yellow sports sedan.

The sky was sunny and cloudless as they sped southward along the Garden State Parkway. Nearing the northern fringe of the Pine Barrens, they turned inland and soon found themselves in a vast, sandy forest world of evergreens stretching away in all directions as far as the eye could reach.

"Wow!" Joe murmured in an awed voice. "Who'd expect a wilderness like this so close to New York City!"

The silence and loneliness were impressive, compared to the busy highway they had just left behind. The only visible landmarks in the piney sea were an occasional distant tower, rising above the treetops.

After passing through the little town of Chatsworth, known as the capital of the Pine Barrens, the boys turned southward. But after following a zigzagging road for mile after mile, they realized they had lost their way.

The next habitation they came to was a weatherbeaten building standing near a cranberry bog that was dammed along the sides with turf. An old pickup truck was parked in front of the building.

Maybe we can get directions here," said Frank,

and pulled off the road. Biff's van stopped behind the Hardys' car.

As the boys got out to stretch their legs, a sun-tanned, white-haired man in shirtsleeves emerged from the building to greet them.

"Can I help you fellas?" he inquired, a friendly grin crinkling his face.

"We'd sure appreciate it," Frank said. "We were heading for Cedar Knob, but we've lost our way."

"Just keep on the road you're going for about three more miles, then turn left at the next dirt lane you come to. You can't miss it."

"Thanks." Frank took out the snapshot of Rupert Price. "By the way," he added, "we were told this fellow might be living in the Pine Barrens, and if he is, we'd like to find him. Have you ever seen him?"

The white-haired man took one look at the snapshot. His grin faded. "Nope," he said, and turning on his heel, went back into the building. The door slammed shut behind him.

"Sufferin' snakes!" Chet said. "What got into him all of a sudden?"

"Good question," Frank murmured thoughtfully. "Maybe strangers are only allowed to ask directions. Get any nosier, and the natives clam up!"

Driving on, the boys reached their destination with no further trouble. Cedar Knob proved to be a wooded hill overlooking a crystal-clear lake. Prowling around to pick a campsite, the youths discovered the moldering, wooden remains of what might have been a lean-to.

"Wow!" Joe exclaimed. "This might have been the spot where Jem Taggart's gang took shelter in bad weather!"

The five boys set about unloading their gear from the van and pitched their tents. Later they heard a vehicle approaching. It was an old pickup truck. As the driver slowed and waved, they strolled down the slope to chat with him.

"Gonna camp here a spell?" he inquired.

"Sure are," Biff said. "Looks like we picked a great spot for it, doesn't it?"

"Mighty pretty." With a smile, the man added, "Just don't go startin' any forest fires!"

"Don't worry, we'll be careful," Frank promised. Once again he produced the snapshot from his pocket. "We'd sure like to find this man. Ever seen him, by any chance?"

"Listen, boy!" The man's face hardened. "This is no place for nosy strangers! If ya know what's good for ya, you'll mind your own business!"

8 Weird Booms

The man slammed his truck into gear and drove off without another word. His abrupt, angry departure left the boys startled and momentarily speechless.

"Another nice, friendly Piney," Chet mumbled.

"Something tells me they just don't like outsiders asking questions about their neighbors," Joe guessed.

"That may be the explanation," Frank agreed. "Whatever their reason is, they do get uptight when I show them this picture of Rupert Price."

Since everyone was hungry by now, Frank and Joe volunteered to go shopping, while Chet busied himself with building a stone fireplace and Biff tried the lake for fish. Tony went with the Hardys to acquaint himself with the general "lay of the land."

Twenty minutes of exploratory cruising brought them to a crossroads store. The proprietor, a paunchy, baldheaded man, served them in a friendly fashion and seemed quite talkative, perhaps because there was no one else in the store when they walked in.

"You lads expect to be campin' there on the Knob fer a week or two?" he inquired as he toted up the bill.

"We're not sure how long," Frank replied.

Fishing in his pocket, he felt the devil doll. He set it out on the counter and asked, "Got any idea what that's supposed to be?"

"Sure have." The storekeeper chuckled. "That's the Jersey Devil!"

The boys were thunderstruck by this reply.

"The what?" Joe echoed.

"The Jersey Devil."

"What's that?" Tony asked.

"Well now, that's a long story, young fella." The storekeeper hooked his thumbs behind his suspenders and grinned, pleased to have such an attentive audience. "In fact, you might say it's two or three different stories, dependin' on which one you believe."

"Which one do *you* believe?" said Frank.

"Well, the usual version is that a woman livin' in

these parts, named Mother Leeds, had twelve children—all of 'em normal, human-type kids—but when it turned out another one was on the way, somehow a curse got laid on it. And on account of that curse, her thirteenth child turned into this awful-lookin' devil creature with wings, which flew up the chimney."

Frank smiled at the elderly proprietor. "Quite a yarn. Are the other versions more sensible?"

"Not much. Accordin' to one, the mother got cursed by a gypsy because she wouldn't give him any food. And another story claims the curse was laid by a preacher who'd been mistreated somehow."

The storekeeper paused to tamp a pinch of snuff beneath his lower lip. "Mind you, all these yarns go back to the 1700s, when folks were a lot more superstitious than they are now. But that don't mean the critter itself is just moonshine. Wherever it came from, the thing's been seen by all sorts of witnesses, and there are people right today in these woods who'll swear the Jersey Devil really exists!"

During the past two hundred years or more, the storekeeper related, there were reports of the creature being seen all over South Jersey. It was said to devour livestock and even attack people.

"But the biggest scare," he continued, "came in

1909 when hundreds of people in at least thirty different towns reported seein' the critter in the same week. Some of the witnesses were policemen, and over near Camden a whole trolley car full of passengers saw it flappin' around."

The boys listened attentively, fascinated by the colorful local folklore.

"It sure doesn't sound like a joke when you tell it like that," Tony remarked. "Has the thing been seen in recent years?"

"Yep. Lots of times. Folks have reported hearin' it screech or seein' its tracks, and not too long ago a farmer had a whole flock of ducks and geese mauled by some sort of weird critter. He called a cop, who found strange tracks leading off into the woods."

The three Bayporters learned that the best guess as to the real nature of the Jersey Devil was that it might be a sand hill crane. But privately Frank and Joe suspected that the legend would persist for at least another two hundred years and would no doubt grow with every telling.

In any case, the Hardys were more interested in learning where the tiny plastic devil figure might have come from. But to this question, the storekeeper could offer no answers.

"I'll tell you one fella, though, who made up an image of the Jersey Devil," he went on, "and that was old Jem Taggart."

"You mean the Outlaw of the Pine Barrens?" Joe queried in surprise.

"Yep, only his wasn't any itty-bitty doll like this. It was a great big metal figure forged out of bog iron. He hung it up in a tree near Cedar Knob to scare folks away from his gang's hideout."

"What happened to it?" Frank asked.

"Dunno. It disappeared a while back. Probably got carted off by tourists for a souvenir."

Despite his willingness to talk about the Jersey Devil, however, the storekeeper proved as close-mouthed as any of the other Pineys when shown the snapshot of Rupert Price. He frowned and shook his head, then turned his back on the boys and stalked off into the back room of the store.

Returning to camp, the trio were greeted by Chet and Biff with an air of excitement.

"Wait'll you see what I found!" their chubby pal announced.

He led them to the remains of the robber gang's old lean-to and pointed to a carved inscription. The letters were barely legible in the dank, rotting wood but could still be made out: FISHHOOK X.

"Wow!" Joe exclaimed. "That word 'fishhook' also occurs in Jem Taggart's letter!"

The Hardys got out the letter, which had been packed with their camping gear, to show their three friends. Biff's eyes widened as he read the sentence

441

in question: BURIED SILVER UNDER HIM FISHHOOK TEN PACES NORTH AS CROW FLIES.

"Hey!" he blurted. "Does that mean the treasure may be buried right around here somewhere?" The three boys thoughtfully studied the inscription.

Frank shook his head regretfully. "Can't be," he reasoned. "The way it's written, Jem sent this letter to two other gang members who were here at Cedar Knob, saying he wants them to come and join him. Which means he must have stashed the silver someplace else."

After supper, as the shadows lengthened among the evergreens, they sat around talking over the campfire. Both Chet and Biff were keenly interested in hearing about the Jersey Devil.

"That's the wildest yarn I've heard in a long

time!" Biff commented with a chuckle. "I guess some people will fall for anything."

"What's so strange about that?" Chet replied uneasily. "I bet if you heard weird screeches out in the woods after dark, you'd start believing in the Jersey Devil, too!"

That night, the Hardys were awakened in their tent by an odd, booming sound. As Joe strained his ears, it came again suddenly: *Boooom!*

"Did you hear that?" he muttered to Frank.

"Sure did!"

The brothers emerged cautiously to look around. In the glow from the dying embers of the campfire, they saw Chet also peering nervously from his tent.

"Y-y-you guys heard it, too?" he quavered.

The Hardys nodded, listening alertly.

"I've heard it about half a dozen times," Chet babbled. "How can anyone get to sleep with noises like that going on? No wonder the Pineys talk about devil monsters in these woods!"

Frank got his flashlight and was about to start exploring for signs of any animal or human intruder on the wooded hillside when a bird came diving out of the darkness straight toward their camp. As it spread its wings to pull out of the dive, another *boooom!* resounded in the night air!

Joe burst out laughing in relief. "It's a night-hawk!"

"Diving for insects," Frank added. "We can all go back to sleep, Chet, with nothing to fear."

The stout boy snorted grumpily. "The Federal Aviation Agency should cite those things for causing sonic booms!"

Next morning, as the boys were cooking breakfast, a motorcycle rider stopped and greeted them with a friendly wave. "Mornin'!" he called out and slowed to a halt.

The boys talked to him for a while, then Frank pulled out the snapshot of Rupert Price. The young detectives were amazed when the man's manner did not change.

"Sure, I know that guy," he admitted promptly. "I can take you right to him!"

9 Grave Evidence

The stranger's response was so unexpected that at first the Hardys wondered if he might be joking or making fun of them.

"Are you serious?" Frank asked sharply.

"'Course I'm serious," the man retorted. "Why should I lie to you?"

The Hardys studied him for a moment before replying. He was rather thin and bony in build, with a freckled face and sparse, sandy hair. His expression seemed open and friendly.

"I guess we just weren't expecting such a stroke of luck." Joe grinned. "Got time for a cup of coffee?"

"You bet!"

"Great. We haven't had breakfast yet, but if you can wait for a few minutes and then take us to the man we're looking for, we'll sure appreciate it."

Frank, Joe, Tony, and Biff bolted down their food, excited at the prospect of meeting Rupert Price and hearing his story. They were eager to see his reaction to the news that he was no longer wanted by the law. Chet agreed to stay and watch the camp while the others accompanied the motorcyclist.

The boys piled into the Hardys' car and followed the man, who led them on a zigzag route, over several unpaved roads and rutted forest trails, to an ancient, weather-beaten cabin.

"Doesn't look like anyone lives here," Frank remarked as the procession came to a stop and the boys got out.

"You're right, no one does," the thin man said grimly. "Not any more, anyhow."

Without another word, he led them to a shallow, oblong mound at the edge of the clearing. It was overgrown with weeds and wildflowers, but there was no doubt that they were looking at a grave, as evidenced by a wooden cross stuck in the ground at one end. The cross bore a crudely carved inscription, RUPERT PRICE, with a date underneath the name.

"He came down with pneumonia and died last winter," their guide explained.

All four boys were saddened by Rupert's fate. They had been looking forward to greeting him with the news of his vindication.

"Is that where he had been living?" Frank inquired with a frown, gesturing toward the cabin.

"Yup, lived there quite a few years."

The thin, sandy-haired man walked with them to the weather-beaten shack. Inside, it was divided into two rooms, both largely empty now, except for such items as a rusty stove, a sagging metal bedstead, and a battered, overturned table with one leg off.

The only traces of Price's occupancy were a threadbare, once-white towel stenciled with the name R. E. PRICE, USN; a similarly stenciled, cracked plastic toilet case now containing only a well-worn toothbrush and the twisted remnant of a tube of shaving cream; and a yellowing snapshot tacked up on one wall. The photo showed Price in a navy uniform with a shipmate in some Oriental city, presumably while on liberty in port during a Pacific cruise.

"Is this all he left?" Joe asked.

Their guide shrugged. "It's all that's left *now*. I guess folks who come by have helped themselves to anything they figured they could use. He never did have much, far as I know."

The boys thanked him for his help and returned to camp.

Chet Morton's moonface sagged sympathetically when he heard the news. "Too bad. You guys better have one of my sassafras milkshakes to cheer you up."

"What's that? Don't tell me you're off on another one of your nutty fads," Tony said suspiciously.

"Fad my eye!" Chet replied. "Nature's full of tasty tidbits, if you're a real woodsman who knows how to live off the wilderness."

The others grinned warily. But after sampling Chet's milkshakes, they all drank down the concoction with hearty smacks of appreciation.

"Not bad, Chet!" Frank said. "But I'm not so sure we need cheering up."

"How come? You mean you halfway expected Price might be dead by now?"

"Not really. I'm not convinced he *is* dead!"

The chubby youth stared in puzzled surprise. "But you just told me you saw his grave!"

"We saw *a* grave, or something that looked like a grave," Frank replied. "But that doesn't prove Rupert Price is buried there."

"Wasn't there a wooden cross with his name on it?"

"Yes. But I've a hunch that was stuck there later, just to mislead us. The grave was sunken in and pretty overgrown with grass and weeds, as if it had been there for a while. But the marker didn't look nearly that old. The wood was all weather-beaten, but that doesn't prove anything. It could have been taken from somewhere else. What counts was the lettering on it, and that looked to me as if it had been newly carved."

Both Tony and Biff had been frowning thoughtfully as they listened to the conversation, and Tony nodded in agreement. "Yeah, now that you mention it, I noticed that, too."

"The cabin didn't look as if it had been lived in very recently, either," Frank pointed out. "If you ask me, it hasn't been lived in for a lot longer than just last winter."

"That figures," Biff said.

"Another thing," Frank said, "was that broken table leg. If that had happened while Rupert Price was there, he'd have fixed it. But it looked as if it had rotted off a long time ago, while the cabin was vacant."

"So what are we going to do about it?" Biff asked.

"I vote we go back for another look," Joe said, "without our helpful friend on the motorcycle watching us."

The boys were eager to accompany the Hardys

and probe deeper into the mystery, but it was decided that Biff should stay behind this time to guard the camp.

The four Bayporters retraced the route over which the motorcyclist had led them. Presently they stopped at the tumbledown shack and got out.

"First, let's examine the grave again," Frank suggested, "and see if we can spot any clues."

"Look here," Joe pointed out when they stood before the wooden cross. "The hole's at least a quarter of an inch bigger than the marker!"

"Couldn't that just be due to the marker sagging or getting blown over a bit by the wind?" said Chet.

"Maybe—only this marker isn't sagging. It's been pounded down hard, yet there's extra room in the hole on each side of it."

Joe glanced at his brother. "You mean as if this were a new marker, and the original were bigger?"

"Right. Which brings up another point. If the marker had been here very long, that hollow space would probably have filled in, just with windblown particles or by gradual shifting of the soil."

As he spoke, Frank began tugging at the wooden cross and soon pulled it up enough to expose the lower part that had previously been hidden from view. Then he brushed away bits of the sandy soil still clinging to the wood.

"No difference in weathering, above and below ground," Joe exclaimed. "I'd say that proves this marker's just been stuck in recently."

Moments later, they heard a triumphant cry from Tony Prito. He had poked about in the underbrush after hearing Frank's deductions about the grave marker.

"Look what I found!" Tony announced, holding up another wooden cross.

As he brought it over to show the others, they saw that the name on it was "Ezekiel King" and the carved burial date was more than ten years before Rupert Price's alleged death! Moreover, the upright member of this cross was about a quarter of an inch wider than that of the present marker, so it would have fitted the hole perfectly.

The wood of the newly found cross was also whiter, and even though its inscription showed obvious signs of weathering, the letters were still sharply visible.

"It's made from heart of pine," said Frank. "I remember Dad telling me about this stuff once. It never rots."

Joe suddenly clutched his brother's arm and hissed, "Sh!"

There was a rustling noise from among the trees on their right.

"Someone's spying on us!" Chet whispered.

His legs went into action as he ran in the direction of the sound. The other boys followed. They could hear footsteps now, pounding away in the distance, and caught a fleeting glimpse of a running figure before he was lost to view among the densely clustering pines.

"Spread out!" Frank shouted to his companions.

They did so, hoping to trap the fugitive if he tried to veer sharply to shake them off. Before they could overtake him, however, the thunderous *vroom!* of a motorcycle engine echoed through the woods. The sound of the bike soon dwindled in the distance.

"Gnats!" Joe growled, clenching his fists in angry frustration. "I'll bet it was that skinny, sandy-haired guy who tried to con us!"

"Probably," Frank agreed. "But never mind. The guy just outsmarted himself."

"How do you mean?" said Tony.

"He must've planted that new grave marker to convince us Rupert Price was dead. But now that we know it's phony, I'd say it's a safe bet Rupert Price is still alive."

"And probably hiding out in these woods," Joe reasoned.

Considerably heartened, the four Bayporters drove back to camp. As they climbed out of the car, they heard a moaning sound coming from one of the tents.

"Something's wrong with Biff!" exclaimed Frank.

They ran to his tent and found their friend sprawled on his sleeping bag, rolling his eyes and clutching his midriff.

"Biff, what's the matter?" Joe cried.

"I picked some wild grapes and ate them," Biff explained between moans, "but they must have been rotten. They tasted awful! I couldn't even keep them down!"

"Sure they were grapes?" Frank asked.

"Well, they *looked* like grapes. What else could they be?"

"Where are they growing?"

After listening to Biff's reply, Frank went off to investigate. He soon came back, holding a cluster of dark, purplish-black fruit. "Is this what you ate?"

Biff nodded, his cheeks pale and sickly hued.

"No wonder! These aren't grapes. We have some climbing our back fence. Aunt Gertrude calls them moonseed." Frank squeezed one of the fruits to show its crescent-shaped pit and added, "You're lucky you didn't keep the stuff down. You could've poisoned yourself!" Quickly, he boiled some water and gave Biff a mug of tea to soothe his stomach.

Later, after attending to various camp chores, the

Hardys pored over several books on the Pine Barrens which they had brought along, and studied their case notes.

Suddenly, Joe snapped his fingers and exclaimed, "Hey, Frank! I have an idea!"

10 Danger Trail

Frank looked up. "I'm all ears. Let's hear your idea."

"It concerns that crook named Kerric that Dad told us about," Joe said.

"The one who was picked up in the Pine Barrens with the devil doll in his pocket?"

"Right. Remember how it happened?"

"Sure. Dad said he walked up to a gas station, and there was a state trooper who recognized and arrested him."

Joe nodded. "Now why do you suppose Kerric would have been *walking* to a gas station down here in the boondocks?"

Frank hesitated. "Maybe he ran out of gas—or his car broke down."

"Right!" Joe burst out. "And if he did—or it did—then maybe his car is still standing where he left it."

"Wow!" Frank's eyes lit up with excitement as his brother's words sank in. "I'd say that's worth checking out! If the car *is* still there, it may contain an important clue!"

"Just what I'm thinking. But first we'll have to find out where the gas station is located."

"Dad can probably tell us. Let's call him on the radio."

Fenton Hardy soon responded to the transmission. He showed immediate interest on hearing Joe's idea. "Good thinking, Son. In an area as isolated as the Pine Barrens, a car could easily stand by the road for several weeks before anyone reported it to the police. By all means, have a look."

Luckily, the detective was able to give his sons precise directions, which enabled them to locate the gas station on their road map. He also described Kerric, in case they had to question anyone about the crook's movements.

Snores were now coming from Chet's tent, while Biff and Tony busily assembled a metal detector. They had rented it in Bayport and planned to run it over the area around the camp in order to check for signs of hidden treasure.

After telling them where they were going, the Hardys headed southwest from Cedar Knob.

It was late afternoon when they finally reached the gas station. Frank pulled in and asked the mechanic attending the pumps to fill their tank. Afterward, the boys bought three sodas from the soft drink machine, offered one to the mechanic, and engaged him in friendly conversation.

"I hear some crook the FBI was after got picked up at your place," Frank remarked casually.

"Yup. I saw it happen," the mechanic replied.

"Any fireworks?" Joe inquired.

"Nope. A state trooper was here getting a busted fan belt replaced on his patrol car. He was in plain clothes, and his car was up on the lift in the garage, so the guy didn't realize he was walking right into the clutches of the law. The trooper had a gun on him before he even knew he'd been spotted!"

"What was he doing down in the Pine Barrens?"

"Search me." The mechanic pointed down the highway to the left. "He just came hiking along the road, and two minutes later he was wearing handcuffs!"

The Hardys finished their drinks and drove off in the direction that the mechanic had indicated. They stopped a short distance from the service station and got out of the car.

"Let's split up and each take one side of the road," Frank suggested. "We'll have to proceed slowly because I have a feeling Kerric hid his car well. Otherwise the authorities would have found it."

Joe nodded. "I'll take the right, you take the left."

Carefully, the young detectives worked their way through the underbrush and trees, stirring up gnats and mosquitoes. I hope we find this car before I get eaten up alive, Joe thought, swatting a bug on his forehead.

Frank lost his footing a couple of times and stumbled, barely avoiding a fall. His arm scraped against the bark of a tree and tore the skin. But he plodded on determinedly.

After a half hour of searching, Joe suddenly called out, "Frank!" He ran through the brush to the road, yelling Frank's name a few more times. Finally he was near enough for his brother to hear him.

"Did you find anything?" Frank exclaimed, fighting his way through the heavily wooded area.

"I sure did. Come over here!"

It took a few moments for Frank to scramble over to Joe's side. When he reached his brother, he whooped with joy.

A car had rolled down the sandy shoulder from

the blacktop highway and come to a stop among the pine trees. It was so well concealed that it could only be seen from a vantage point between two bushy evergreens.

"This could be it, Joe!" Frank cried.

"I sure hope so," his brother replied. "I'm exhausted from looking for it!"

The boys examined their find, an expensive-looking, gunmetal-gray two-door sedan. It was in such a lonely spot that evidently the driver had not thought it necessary to lock up. This also seemed to indicate that he had expected to return soon.

A buzz sounded as Joe opened the door, and he noticed the key had been left in the ignition. Then he saw a piece of paper lying on the passenger side of the front seat.

"Hey, look at this, Frank!" he blurted, snatching it up. The paper bore a rough sketch map in pencil with the words:

KERRIC—FOLLOW THIS ROUTE.

"Jumpin' catfish! We really struck gold!" his brother murmured.

On the back seat was a portable, battery-powered ultraviolet sunlamp. The only other item of interest was a matchbook lying on the dashboard bearing an advertisement for a restaurant called the Pirate's Tavern, together with a diagram showing its highway position on the edge of the Pine Barrens near the coast.

The Hardys examined the paper closely for several moments before Frank muttered, "It shows the road we're on, Joe. It even has the gas station marked back there."

"You're right," Joe said, "and this looks like some kind of road about a mile ahead where he was supposed to turn off. I bet Kerric was on his way there when his car conked out on him!"

"The big question is, where would this route have taken him?"

Joe grinned. "There's one way to find out!"

Twenty minutes later, their yellow sports sedan was tooling down the road toward the turnoff. This proved to be little more than a rough, rutted track leading in among the pines. The boys followed it cautiously, jouncing up and down even though the car was moving at a very slow speed.

"Wow! Let's hope our springs hold out!" Joe said.

By now, the sun had sunk behind a cloud bank in the west, and the lengthening shadows, added to the natural forest gloom, gave the woods a sinister atmosphere. Twilight was falling fast as they reached a point where the trail became too narrow and brushy for the car to proceed.

"Now what?" Joe muttered in a hollow voice.

Frank had a sudden hunch. He got out, took the

sunlamp from the back seat, switched it on, and shone it all around. Both boys gasped as they saw a blaze mark glow into view on a nearby tree.

"Must be painted with fluorescent dye!" Joe exclaimed.

"And it points to the right," Frank added.

Joe got out of the car to join his brother, and the two boys pressed on through the deepening darkness, guided by other blaze marks every ten yards or so.

The trail wound on through the forest. Frank swung the sunlamp back and forth, so that its ultraviolet rays would miss none of the markers.

Suddenly, both boys stopped short in shock. Ahead of them, a ghastly glowing figure had just materialized out of the darkness.

"It's the Jersey Devil!" Joe cried out.

11 Colonial Ghost

For an instant, the Hardys were frozen with fright. The grotesque, glowing creature with its outspread bat wings looked as if it were about to fly straight down and attack them!

Then Frank sighed with relief. "Relax! That thing's not real, Joe!"

"You're right," his brother murmured huskily. "It's not moving. But what is it?"

Frank was equally puzzled at first. But as he stepped forward and nerved himself to touch the scary-looking image, the answer suddenly clicked in his memory. "I'll tell you what it is!" he exclaimed. "It's that devil figure made out of bog iron that the

storekeeper told us about! The one that Jem Taggart's gang used to frighten away snoopers!"

"You're right again," Joe concurred as he, too, fingered the metallic monster. "What's it doing here, though?"

"Good question." Frank brooded a moment before adding, "One thing's certain. Taggart's gang never coated it with fluorescent paint!"

"That's for sure. They didn't even have such a thing in those days. I'd say it's Diablo's gang who supplied the fluorescent touch, wouldn't you? At least that's how it looks, if we assume they're the ones who blazed that trail through the woods with all those fluorescent tree markings."

The older Hardy boy nodded. "That has to be the explanation. Which means they must also be the ones who moved the thing here from Cedar Knob."

But why? Neither boy could offer a convincing answer.

Joe glanced about uneasily. "It'll be pitch dark soon, Frank. Maybe we'd better not hang around here."

"I second the motion."

Only the glowing marks on the tree trunks enabled the Hardys to find their way back to the point where the weird trail began. Frank started the car and shifted into reverse. Joe guided him backward along the rutted track until they came to a place where there was enough room between the trees to turn the car around.

During the long drive back to Cedar Knob, the Hardys discussed the mystery and talked over their latest discovery. But the conversation trailed off as both boys became more aware of the gnawing hollow between their ribs due to lack of food.

"Let's hope the gang's whipped up something good for supper," Frank muttered as they whizzed along the road.

"You said it. And if they did, let's also hope that Chet hasn't gobbled it all up already," Joe quipped wryly.

An unpleasant disappointment was in store. As the Hardys pulled up at the edge of camp and got out, the expressions on the faces of their three friends who came to meet them was a plain announcement of bad news.

"Hey, what's wrong?" Joe demanded.

"Plenty!" Chet blurted. "Some dirty crook swiped all our chow!"

"We were out searching for treasure with the metal detector," Tony related. "We got so engrossed we didn't get back to camp till twilight. Then, when we started to get supper, we suddenly discovered there was no food!"

"Somebody raided the camp while we were gone and cleaned us out completely!" Biff added, with a look of angry exasperation.

"Sure it was a human thief?" Frank asked.

"You can bet your life it was no raccoon, if that's what you're thinking!" Biff retorted. "Whoever did it even opened our ice chest and pinched our milk cartons and bottles of soda! Boy, if I could get my hands on that dirty sneak, I'd wring his neck!"

"Me, too! I'm starving!" Chet grumbled.

"Any clues?" Frank pursued.

"We're stepping on most of them," Tony said, "if you can call them clues." He shone his flashlight at the sandy soil around the open door of Biff's van, where the supplies had been kept. "See those brush marks?"

The Hardys nodded glumly. "He must've used a pine bough to brush away his footprints," Frank declared. "But I'll see if I can get some fingerprints off the van. We can have them checked out later."

He managed to lift two clear prints, and when he was finished, Biff said, "Who do you suppose did it?"

Frank's face was serious as he shrugged. "It could have been El Diablo's gang—which may mean we're closer to them than we realized. On the other hand, it could also have been our friendly treasure-hunting competitor, Ambrose Verrill."

"For that matter," said Joe, "it could even have been that skinny guy on the motorcycle who tried to trick us into believing Rupert Price was dead. Since that didn't work, maybe now he's going to try and *starve* us out!"

"Yeah, that sure figures," Tony Prito said.

"Never mind all the fancy theories," Chet cut in plaintively. "The important thing is, what're we going to do for supper tonight?"

Frank grinned and threw an arm around the chunky youth's shoulder. "Relax, pal—there's more food where that stolen grub came from. That general store's probably still open."

"By the way," Frank added as he and his brother headed toward their car, "did you guys have any luck with the metal detector?"

"We got a few buzzes," Biff reported, "but they turned out to be empty cans or old rusty auto parts—junk like that."

"Too bad. At least we've learned a lesson, though. From now on, we'd better never leave the camp without someone to guard it."

"You said it!"

Luckily, when the Hardys reached the general store, its windows were still lit. Inside, the bald, paunchy proprietor was engaged in an after-hours, yarn-spinning conversation with several friends.

"You fellas must have right hearty appetites!" he

467

remarked with a chuckle, as the boys replenished the camp's supplies. "Weren't you in here just yesterday, stockin' up on vittles?"

Frank was about to report the robbery, but after a quick glance at Joe, he decided against it. He feared that the storekeeper and his cronies might take offense at the idea of outsiders implying a local Piney might be responsible. Instead, he merely replied, "We did, but we had an accident and lost some. By the way, we had a visitor this morning. We'd like to look him up again if we could find him, but we forgot to get his name."

"What'd he look like, Son?"

"Sandy hair, freckles, sort of thin and bony. He was riding a motorcycle."

"Oh, that musta been Willard Bosley," spoke up one of the men who were lounging in the store.

"Any idea where we can find him?" Joe asked. "We're camping on Cedar Knob."

"Sure, Willard lives about four, five miles southwest of there." The man proceeded to give the Hardys detailed directions for finding Bosley's cabin.

He had barely finished speaking when the door burst open and a wild-eyed man in a plaid flannel shirt and worn corduroy pants rushed into the store.

"What in tarnation's wrong with you, Pete?" the

468

storekeeper asked. "You look like y' just seen a ghost!"

"Right the first time!" the newcomer blurted excitedly. "That's exactly what I saw!"

His words and manner brought the group lounging around the counter to rapt attention.

"Are you kiddin'?" one of the men asked.

"Naw, I'm not kiddin'!" Pete replied. "And it wasn't just *any* ghost—it was *Jem Taggart's ghost!*"

The startling announcement aroused the boys' curiosity.

"Someone's pulling your leg, Pete," another man joked. "What'd he do—sneak up behind you and yell *boo!* in your ear?"

"Listen, wise guy!" Pete flared back. "This was no joke—and it was no live man, either!"

"How d'you know?"

" 'Cause he was all dressed up in old-time Colonial duds, that's how—includin' knee britches! And his face was dead white! If that wasn't a ghost, I'll eat your hat!"

The store loungers were taken aback by these unexpected details. But most of them still seemed to think Pete's imagination was running away with him. The Hardys listened to the wisecracks and speculation that continued for a while longer, then quickly paid their bill and left.

"Wow! What do you make of *that* story?" Joe asked his brother as they loaded the supplies into their car.

"Beats me," Frank said. "But I've got a hunch it may be connected to this mystery we're trying to solve."

Joe agreed. Back at camp, their three friends listened avidly to Frank and Joe's account of the strange incident. Chet Morton looked a trifle uneasy, but his nervousness soon gave way to a hearty appetite as the smell of baked beans, beef stew, and roasting potatoes filled the night air.

After they had finished clearing away the remains of supper and washed up the cooking utensils, the five boys retired to their tents and sleeping bags. Some time later Frank and Joe were awakened from a deep slumber by eerie wailing noises.

"That's no nighthawk!" Joe exclaimed.

"You can say that again," Frank agreed, squirming out of his sleeping bag.

Flashlights in hand, the boys hurried outside. Tony had already emerged from the tent he shared with Biff, and the other two appeared moments later, pulling on their jeans. All were tense and wide-eyed as they listened to the spooky wails.

"They're coming from there," Tony said, pointing westward along the shore of the lake.

"Could be that same joker who raided our camp!" Joe conjectured.

"Yes. Let me at him!" growled Biff, casting about for a stout stick. "If it *is* him, he'd better get ready to do some fast talking!"

Chet was as eager for revenge as the others.

"Might be a good idea if we all took sticks," Frank suggested. "Whoever he is, he could be a bit nutty—and he may have a mean streak!"

The boys started down the hillside and fanned out, hoping to surround their tormentor. In the moonlit darkness, with brush bordering the lake, they were soon lost to each other's view. But a sudden scream from Chet brought Frank, Joe, and Tony rushing to his side.

"What's up, Chet?" Joe exclaimed.

"Th-th-the ghost!" stuttered the fat boy.

"*What* ghost?" Frank demanded sharply.

"*Jem Taggart's ghost!* The one that guy at the store was telling you about—with knee britches and all! And that dead white face! I saw him right over there through the trees!"

Chet's hand shook as he pointed. His three listeners exchanged startled looks, hardly knowing what to make of his story.

Next moment, another yell split the darkness!

"Hey, that's Biff!" cried Frank. "Something's *really* wrong!"

12 Pirate's Tavern

The four boys started back to camp on the run.
Hearts thudding, they pounded up the hillside,
trampling their way through the heavy undergrowth.

Frank's flashlight picked out Biff's face in the
darkness. He looked both angry and rattled.

"What's going on?" Frank asked.

"We've been had, that's what!"

"How come?" Tony blurted.

"When we were fanned out in the woods, all of a
sudden I remembered what Frank said about never
leaving the camp unguarded. So I came back to
keep an eye on things, and that's what I found!"

Frank swung his flashlight in the direction Biff

was pointing. The yellow beam settled on the van. Its door was hanging open again. The ice chest had been lifted out, and various other items lay scattered on the ground.

"We've been raided again!" Chet moaned.

"Was anything taken?" Joe inquired as the boys hurried to inspect the van more closely.

Biff shrugged. "I don't think so, but I'm not sure yet. I've a hunch whoever it was searched our tents first. Then he was poking around in the van. When he heard me coming back, he scrammed."

After a hasty check, the Hardys and their friends concluded that nothing was missing. Frank, however, was glad that he had been carrying the devil doll with him in the pocket of his jeans. Also, much to his and Joe's relief, the raider had not taken the ultraviolet sunlamp and other items that the two brothers had removed from Kerric's abandoned car in order to safeguard them until they could be turned over to the proper authorities.

"Looks to me like our midnight visitor didn't have time to go through *our* car," Joe commented.

Frank nodded glumly. "That's one consolation, I guess. But I could kick myself for not realizing those spooky wails were just a trick to lure us away from camp."

"Listen! That ghost I saw was no trick!" Chet declared. "It was there, plain as anything!"

"What ghost?" Biff asked.

"Jem Taggart's ghost!" Chet described the white-faced figure in Colonial costume in great detail.

"What makes you so sure that wasn't part of the trick?" Tony demanded. "Somebody could've dressed up like that just to make the wailing seem even more spooky."

"Why would they go to all that trouble?" Chet retorted. "The wailing noises worked all by themselves, didn't they? They were enough to decoy us out in the woods. Besides, where would anyone get clothes like that on short notice?"

"Chet's got a point there," Frank agreed. "I'm not saying he saw a real ghost, mind you, but whatever it was—or whoever it was—may not have had anything to do with the raid on our camp."

The boys discussed the night's events for a while longer. Finally, they went back to their tents, and once again the camp was wrapped in silence as they drifted off to sleep.

Next morning, following the directions they had obtained from the Piney at the general store, the Hardys drove to Willard Bosley's house. This proved to be a shingle shack covered with peeling tar paper. Nearby lay two rusting, wheelless cars, a litter of cranberry boxes, and a stack of cordwood. The owner's motorcycle was leaning against the front wall of the shack.

As the Hardys' car jounced up the rutted path and drew to a halt, Bosley himself and a little girl appeared in the doorway to see who was coming. The girl, who was about six years old and evidently his daughter, was barefoot and had shimmering reddish-gold hair. Clutching a wooden doll in one arm, she skipped out eagerly, openly admiring the sleek and shiny vehicle.

"Your car is the prettiest I've ever seen!"

"Well, you're pretty, too, honey." Frank smiled. "What's your name?"

"Della," the little girl replied, and added gravely, "I probably look okay now, but last spring I was real sick and I must'a looked awful!"

"No kidding?" Joe said sympathetically. "What was the matter?"

"Well, I don't know exactly, but it was pretty bad. Daddy thought I was never gonna get well, and maybe I never would've except for—"

"That'll be enough out of you, Della," her father interrupted, kindly but firmly. "These fellas didn't come here t' hear about your health."

The thin, sandy-haired Piney had been hanging back in the doorway with a rather sullen air, as if reluctant to face the two boys after what had happened the day before. But now he stepped outside defiantly and flung an arm around his daughter's shoulders, drawing her close to him.

Since he showed no sign of going off to work, Frank and Joe assumed that Bosley must be an odd-job laborer, who followed the regular Pine Barrens work cycle they had read about—gathering sphagnum moss in the spring, picking blueberries in the summer and cranberries in the fall, and then chopping wood during the cold winter months.

Frank hesitated before speaking, not quite sure how to begin. "Mr. Bosley," he said finally, "my brother and I are anxious to find Rupert Price. We have some important news to tell him."

"I've already told you he's dead," Willard Bosley responded in a curt voice.

"I know that's what you said." Frank hesitated again uncomfortably, not wanting to accuse Bosley of lying. "But we're pretty sure—well, anyhow, we think you may be mistaken. We have a hunch he may still be hiding out because he thinks the law is after him."

"But he doesn't have to worry about that any more," Joe said. "He was cleared of that murder charge a long time ago."

"Right," Frank went on. "And now he's inherited a lot of money from his uncle, and his Cousin Ogden's trying to find him, because if he doesn't come forward to claim his inheritance, he'll lose out on his share of the money."

Bosley's freckled face had taken on a frown while

the boys were speaking. He stared at them intently for a moment, but finally shook his head. "I'm sorry, but you two have got it all wrong. You can believe whatever you like, but I'm telling you Rupert Price died of pneumonia last winter."

Joe started to argue, pointing out that the grave Bosley had shown them was obviously not that recent. But Frank cut his brother short, realizing they had no way of forcing Bosley to stop covering up for the missing man.

"We're telling you the truth about that inheritance," the older Hardy boy declared bluntly. "And if you're a real friend of Rupert Price, or know any friend of his, I hope you'll see that he gets the news."

Turning to his brother, Frank added, "Come on, Joe. Let's go."

As they drove off, Joe waved to little Della Bosley. In the rearview mirror, Frank saw her father staring after them with a troubled expression.

"What's your guess?" Joe asked his brother. "Was he lying to us?"

"He doesn't trust us, that's for sure," Frank replied. "I'd be willing to bet he's trying to protect Rupert Price."

'Wonder if he'll pass on the news like you asked?"

Frank shrugged. "Guess we'll just have to wait and see."

Arriving back at camp, the Hardys announced their intention of checking out the Pirate's Tavern, the restaurant advertised on the matchbook cover they had found in Kerric's abandoned car. Chet elected to go with them.

They found the place after a lengthy ride. It was a large, white, frame building just off the Garden State Parkway, with a parking lot in front.

The waitress who came to serve them kept staring at Frank and Joe as she took the boys' orders. "Say, aren't you two the Hardy boys?" she blurted.

The brothers nodded. "Guilty as charged," Frank said.

"How'd you guess?" Joe added.

"I saw your picture in the paper," the young woman said brightly. "I thought your faces looked familiar but I couldn't place you. Then I remembered that news story about how you were hunting for treasure here. Did you find it yet?"

"Not even a plugged nickel!" Frank chuckled. Partly to evade further questions on the subject, he asked if she had recently seen a chunky, hoarse-voiced man with bristly black hair, wearing a short-sleeved, tan safari jacket. This was the description of Kerric that Fenton Hardy had given the boys.

"Hey, yes! I do recall someone like that coming in here," the waitress exclaimed, "especially when you mentioned his hoarse voice. The guy sounded like a bullfrog! That was about a week or two ago."

"Anyone with him?" Joe asked.

"No, I think he was alone."

Two men were talking intently in a nearby booth. One paused to unzip a black bag. Frank was startled as he saw him take out a portable sunlamp.

Nudging Joe, Frank drew the waitress's attention to the pair. "Are those fellows regular customers, by any chance?" he murmured.

She shot a quick glance in their direction. She seemed to sense at once that Frank's question was prompted by a mystery case the boys were working on, and the Hardys guessed that she was thrilled at the chance to help out in such an investigation. "I'll need a better look before I know for sure," she replied. "Wait a minute."

The waitress walked back to the kitchen to deliver the boys' order. As she returned, she glanced casually at the two men in the booth, then looked at the Hardys and shook her head.

"Don't think I've ever seen them before," she reported. "From the sneaky way they've got their heads together, it wouldn't surprise me if they were deerjackers."

"Deerjackers?" said Chet. "What's that?"

"Poachers who shoot deer out of season for meat. Often they do it on order for contractors who make a business out of selling venison."

479

Presently the waitress brought their hamburgers and french fries. As the boys ate, they kept an eye on the two men. After a while, one of them, who had a tanned face and whitish-blond hair, got up from the booth and left.

"I'm going after him," Frank muttered, "to see if I can get his car license number before he drives away."

Joe nodded and watched the man's partner, who had remained seated in the booth. His back was turned to the Bayporters, but as he finished his coffee and glanced idly around the dining room, Chet heard the younger Hardy boy gasp.

"What's the matter, Joe?"

"Take a look at that guy. Isn't that Flat Nose?"

"Hey, I think you're right!"

By this time, Frank had been gone for several minutes. As they waited for him to return, both Joe and Chet began to get worried.

"Wonder what's keeping him?" the chubby youth murmured.

"Maybe we'd better find out!" said Joe, springing to his feet.

Leaving enough money on the table to cover their bill and tip the waitress, the two boys strode off to check on Frank.

A narrow corridor led from the dining room to the small lobby. Halfway along was a turnoff leading to the restrooms and a phone booth. Joe stopped short as he saw a dark-haired figure crumpled inside the booth.

"It's Frank!" he exclaimed.

13 Sun Flashes

Joe and Chet hurried toward the telephone booth. Frank was already stirring back to consciousness as they reached him.

"Wow! What hit me?" he moaned, opening his eyes and getting his bearings.

"I don't know *what* hit you," Joe replied, "but I can make a good guess *who*."

"So can I," Frank muttered wryly. "Something tells me it was that hood I tried to follow." He struggled to his feet and stepped out of the booth, while the other two supported him by the arms until he felt steady enough to stay upright under his own power.

"What happened?" Chet asked.

"What you're probably thinking. By the time I

got across the dining room and into the corridor, the guy was nowhere in sight. I figured he was already out in the parking lot, getting ready to drive off, so I made a dash for the lobby. It never occurred to me that he might be laying in wait for me. When I came past the turnoff—*wham!*—I got conked over the head and was out like a light. After that, I suppose he dragged me into the booth so nobody would spot me before he made his getaway."

Frank gingerly rubbed the sore spot on his head as he spoke.

"Never mind," Joe said tensely. "His buddy's still in the dining room—and he looks like Flat Nose!"

"You mean he *was* there when you two got up."

"Where else would he be?" Chet asked. "I haven't seen him leave while we've been talking to you."

"This isn't the only way out," Frank said.

"You're right!" Joe exclaimed. "If the guy knew he was being followed, they must have spotted us! Flat Nose sure won't sit around waiting to be arrested or tailed!"

The three hurried back into the dining room. Chet groaned irritably as Frank's hunch proved correct. The booth previously occupied by the two suspects was now empty!

"He probably slipped out the back door while we were gone," Joe conjectured. The waitress, who had served the three boys confirmed his guess.

The Hardys and Chet ran out to the parking lot with the slim hope that the men might not have driven off yet, but there was no sign of them. Glumly the trio returned to their car.

"Wait a minute," Frank said suddenly. "Maybe we're passing up a lead."

"Like what?" Joe asked.

"That tow-haired guy I chased took the ultraviolet lamp when he left."

Joe whistled. "Just like Kerric!"

Chet looked from Frank to Joe with a baffled expression and mumbled, "I don't get it."

"Kerric had one of those sunlamps for a certain purpose. We think it had something to do with him coming down here to the Pine Barrens, and also with the fact that he was dodging the law. If so, maybe that bleached-blond creep is a wanted criminal, too!"

"Won't hurt to check on him," Joe added. "You guys stay there. I'll call Sam Radley."

Radley was one of Fenton Hardy's most trusted operatives and had often assisted the sleuth's sons on other mystery cases. Joe hurried to the phone booth in the restaurant and dialed Sam's number.

"Whitish-blond hair, deeply tanned skin, height about five-ten, weight one-seventy," Sam repeated as he jotted down the description Joe had just given him. "Doesn't ring a bell offhand, but I'll see if he has a record."

"Thanks, Sam. If you turn up anything, call us right away on the car radio, please."

"Will do."

Frank and Chet were waiting in the car. "Now what?" asked the stout boy as Joe joined them.

"I think we ought to take a look at the Jersey Devil figure in the woods by daylight," Frank proposed, "especially after seeing another sun-lamp."

"Right," Joe agreed.

As they whizzed along the highway en route to the turnoff spot where the blaze-marked trail led deep among the pines, the boys recounted their discovery of the night before for their friends' benefit. Chet was keenly interested. But when they finally reached the turnoff, he made no objection to staying in the car to answer the radio in case Sam Radley transmitted any information.

Frank and Joe, meanwhile, started into the woods on foot. It was not as easy to follow the fluorescent tree markings in the daytime as it had been in the twilight and gathering darkness. However, beyond the point where the rutted trail became too indistinct to follow, tramped underbrush helped guide them in the right direction.

At last, their steps slowed to a halt as they came

in sight of the hanging metal demon figure. Even with the afternoon sun in full view above the treetops, the grotesque, bat-winged, iron monster retained its sinister aspect.

"Charming creature, isn't it?" Frank remarked wryly. "The question is, why did Diablo's gang hang it here?"

Joe looked around thoughtfully. "Maybe for the same reason Jem Taggart's bunch—" His voice broke off with a sudden gasp.

"What's the matter?" Frank asked sharply.

"That tree! Take a look!" Joe pointed to a tall oak nearby.

Metal spikes had been driven into its trunk, apparently as footholds for climbing!

As the boys' gaze followed the trunk upward, they saw a wooden platform or tree house on the upper branches, where the oak's crown reared above the surrounding pines.

"Must be some kind of lookout post!" Frank exclaimed.

Joe was about to climb up, but Frank restrained him. "Hold it! Let's make sure no one's up there, first."

The Hardys moved some distance away and circled about the oak, shading their eyes and peering at the platform from all directions until they were reasonably certain it was unoccupied. Then they scaled up the trunk, spike by spike, with Frank in the lead.

The planking that formed the floor of the platform was enclosed by a rickety wooden railing, with four corner-posts to support a flimsy roof that looked somewhat newer than the rest of the structure. A stout wooden box had been provided, evidently for whoever manned the lookout post to sit on. But Frank noticed that its cover was hinged. Inside was a hand mirror and a pair of binoculars in a case.

Joe eagerly tried out the latter, swinging the glasses in all directions. "Wow! What a view! You can even make out ships offshore!"

As he handed the binoculars to his brother, both boys blinked in a sudden dazzling glare.

"Hey, someone's flashing sunlight at us!" Joe blurted.

"Signaling," Frank exclaimed a moment later as the flashes continued. "Joe, I bet that's what the mirror in the box is for!"

"You're right. But it's not Morse."

"Some private code, probably." As he trained the binoculars on the source of the flashes, Frank found himself focusing on a large gray vehicle parked off the highway some distance to the west. "The signals are coming from a big motor camper," he reported.

"Oh, oh!" Joe muttered uneasily. "If they've got binoculars, too, they can probably see us up here.

In fact, I bet that's why they started signaling!"

"Right! They probably parked there just to keep watch. They must've been expecting someone to show up in this lookout post."

"Let's hope they can't see our faces clearly, or they'll know we're not members of the gang!"

The sun flashes had stopped momentarily, but then resumed faster than ever.

"If they get wise," Frank said, "they may come looking for us. And they might discover Chet in the car!"

"Why don't we take the hand mirror and signal back?" Joe suggested.

"How can we? We don't know their code."

"So what? They'll probably just think we made an accidental goof. While they're trying to figure out our message, we'll have time to get back to the car."

Frank was dubious, but agreed.

Joe promptly snatched up the hand mirror and began beaming sun flashes in the direction of the camper, trying to repeat the pattern he had just seen.

When he paused, the boys waited anxiously, but there were no further signals in response.

"They've clammed up," Frank muttered. "I'm not sure I like that."

Neither did Joe. But before he could say anything, both were startled by sounds from below of someone moving through the underbrush.

"Hear that?" Joe hissed to his brother.

"I'll say I do! Whoever it is, they're coming this way. Let's get out of here."

Fearing they might be trapped, the Hardys hastily clambered down the oak trunk and sought cover among the dense shrubbery and forest brush.

Within moments they could hear at least two persons moving about and beating the undergrowth with sticks.

"They're searching for us!" Joe whispered.

Frank nodded. "They didn't have time to come from the camper, though. These guys must have been on their way here already!"

The boys dared not raise their heads to see what was going on, but voices reached their ears.

"We saw 'em climbing down!" one searcher growled. "They must be around here somewhere!"

"I know. They didn't have time to get away," the other one agreed, and poked his stick deep into the shrubbery.

"Where's the dog?" the first man asked.

"On the boat. Why?"

"Because we're wasting our time. He could rout out those snoopers in seconds. Let's go back and get him—and we'll pick up some gas grenades while we're at it. If the Doberman can't sniff 'em out, we'll see how they like a dose of Mace!"

"That's a good idea, but what if they disappear while we're gone?"

"H'm. Tell you what. You stay here while I get the dog. If they stir somewhere, just follow them. Turn your walkie-talkie on so you can tell me where they are, okay?"

"Right."

The boys heard a set of footsteps retreating, while the other man kept walking around the area with his stick. When he was some distance away, Frank whispered to Joe.

"We can't wait until that other creep comes back with the Doberman!"

"You're right. Should we run for it while this guy's a little bit away from us?"

"No, we've got to jump him, otherwise he'll alert his partner with his walkie-talkie. Wait until he comes closer again. We've got to make sure he doesn't get away!"

Soon the footsteps became louder and the boys could hear the *swish* of the man's stick against the foliage.

"Now!" Frank hissed.

Both boys jumped up and caught the stranger by surprise. Before he had a chance to swing his weapon, Frank barreled into him and swung a fist at the man's jaw. With a grunt, the crook fell backward. Frank threw himself on top of the man and wrested the stick from his hand. At that moment the stranger rolled quickly to the right, throwing Frank off balance. But before the man had a chance to regain his feet, Joe hooked an arm around his neck and pushed him down again.

"I've got a good hold on him," Joe called to his brother. "Find some vines so we can tie him up!"

Frank quickly ripped out stout vines from the ground and bound the man's wrists and ankles. Then he took the scarf the stranger was wearing around his neck and gagged him with it.

"This way he can't alert his buddy over the walkie-talkie," the boy declared. "Come on, Joe, let's get out of here now!"

The brothers bolted away from the area of the tree platform and rushed toward their car.

Suddenly, Joe tripped and fell headlong on the ground.

Frank, who was slightly ahead of his brother, heard Joe's muffled scream and turned back. "Did you hurt yourself?" he asked anxiously.

Joe was about to get up, but fell back in pain. "I twisted my ankle! I don't think I can stand!"

Suddenly, in the distance, both boys heard vicious barking. Visions of the Doberman's angry jaws danced before their eyes. Determinedly, Frank reached for his brother, realizing the barking was becoming louder and louder!

14 A Warning in Red

"Come on, lean on me!" Frank panted and pulled Joe to his feet.

The younger Hardy let out a groan, but stayed up, his arm around Frank's shoulder. With his brother's support, he hobbled toward the car as fast as he could.

When they arrived, Chet Morton stirred from his comfortable, dozing position and opened the door for them. "What's wrong?" he asked.

"Joe's hurt his ankle and the crooks are after us with a Doberman!" Frank said.

"What!"

Just then the boys heard the dog again. He seemed to be getting angrier every second. Frank slid behind the wheel while Chet pulled Joe into the front seat. "Let's get out of here!" the chubby boy yelled. Frank had already started the motor, and with a cloud of exhaust the yellow sports car sped down the road.

"Now tell me what happened," Chet demanded.

Joe related their adventure at the lookout post, rubbing his ankle with both hands.

"Wow!" Chet blurted. "If they'd caught you guys, I might've been next!"

Joe grinned. "Unless that doggie would have picked up your scent on the way and gotten you first!"

Chet made a face. "I shudder just thinking of it. What about that camper? Could you see where it was parked?"

"Yes, we should be coming to it soon," said Frank. "From the treetop, it looked as if it was about half a mile or so beyond that cranberry bog we just passed. It was close to a point where the road makes a sharp turn to the right."

"Here's the turn," Joe muttered.

As Frank swung the wheel, he caught a glimpse of Chet's chubby-cheeked face in the rearview mirror. The stout youth looked tense and apprehensive at the prospect of a possible confrontation with whatever trigger-happy crooks might be lurking in the camper. But he had the heart and build of a bear, and Frank knew he could be counted on in any tight spot.

As it turned out, however, the big, gray camper van was nowhere in sight!

"Hey, what's that red stuff on the road?" Joe exclaimed.

Blood was the thought that immediately came to all three boys' minds. But as Frank stepped on the brake and slowed for a closer look, they saw that big red letters had been painted on the blacktop surface of the highway:

HARDYS—YOU'LL GET YOURS!

Just above the warning was a crude skull and crossbones!

Chet gulped. "Looks as if you found the right place!"

"And it also looks as if whoever was here had good binoculars to recognize our faces," Joe remarked grimly.

"No doubt we're up against El Diablo's gang," Frank added.

Just then a buzz sounded from the dashboard radio, and a red light blinked, indicating an incoming call. Joe answered and heard Sam Radley's voice over the speaker.

"What's up, Sam?"

"I finally got a 'make' on that guy you called

about. If I'm right, his name's Francis Jerome Waulker"—the private operative spelled out the last name—"better known as 'Whitey' Waulker. There's a fugitive warrant out on him. He's wanted for a long list of crimes, including car theft, armed robbery, and felonious assault."

"Jupiter! Sounds like he could be real bad news," said Joe, thinking of Waulker's attack on his brother.

"You better believe it! What's more, he's a three-time loser. If he gets convicted one more time, he could get sent up for life. So don't expect him to surrender meekly to the law, if you run into him again."

"Thanks for warning us, Sam."

"Just don't take any chances, that's all. But say, here's a bit more pleasant news, if you're interested," the detective went on. "Do I understand you fellows are looking for that old-time pirate's treasure while you're in the Pine Barrens, the one that got written up in the newspaper?"

"Trying to, anyhow," Joe responded with a dry chuckle, "though I can't say we're making much progress. Why? Got any hot leads for us?"

"Well, I don't know how hot it is, but this might be of some help. There's a local historical society in a coastal town called Tuckerton that keeps tabs on all sorts of folklore and historical records relating to the Pine Barrens. The secretary of the society helped me out on a case a couple of years ago. You might try him for information."

"Sounds like a great idea!" Joe said enthusiastically, and took down the man's name and address.

"Wait a minute before you sign off," Frank exclaimed suddenly. Taking the microphone from his brother, he asked, "Sam, would you ever have heard of a lawyer named Verrill—Ambrose Verrill?"

The boys were surprised at the short, harsh laugh over the radio loudspeaker. "I'll say I have. What do you want to know about him?"

"Anything *you* know."

"Well, I've run into him half a dozen times at the county courthouse when I've gone there to testify at trials. Verrill's more of a shady ambulance chaser than a reputable attorney. Matter of fact, he is under investigation by the State Bar Association."

"How come?"

"One of his clients accused him of absconding with a valuable old document, which he was supposed to have put in a safe-deposit box. Verrill claims it was misplaced by accident, but the Bar Association doesn't buy his excuse."

Frank whistled, then told Sam about their investigation. "No doubt that valuable old document was Jem Taggart's letter," he concluded.

"I'm sure it was," Sam agreed.

After Frank had replaced the microphone, he

turned to Joe. "No wonder Verrill got so upset when he heard we had a photostat of the letter. Whoever made that copy might be able to prove the letter was in Verrill's possession!"

"Which could land Verrill in jail if he swiped it from one of his clients," Joe said.

Finally the trio arrived back at camp. The pain in Joe's ankle had subsided quite a bit and he was able to limp around.

Frank proposed an early supper, since he had a theory that he wanted to check out that very evening.

Over charcoal-broiled steaks and fries, he told the others, "I've got a hunch that one of the Diablo gang's rackets may be helping wanted crooks to get out of the country."

Joe grinned. "Something tells me our minds are working in the same groove."

"Kerric was one of the gang's customers, right?"

The younger Hardy boy nodded in agreement. "And now Whitey Waulker's another."

"What do you mean 'one of their customers'?" Biff Hooper broke in.

"Kerric probably paid the gang plenty to smuggle him out of the United States before the FBI could nab him," Frank explained. "But a state trooper spotted and arrested him just as his disappearing act was about to get started."

"How was it supposed to work?"

Frank took the little plastic devil doll out of his pocket as he replied, "Let's say every customer gets one of these Jersey Devil figures when he first shells out money to the gang. They tell him to go to the Pirate's Tavern on the edge of the Pine Barrens and use the doll for identification."

"Another gang member meets him at the tavern," Joe conjectured, "and gives him an ultraviolet lamp and a map showing how to get to the trail through the woods."

"Right." Frank nodded. "So he waits till it gets dark and then uses the lamp to follow the fluorescent blaze marks on the trees, which eventually lead him to the big, spooky Jersey Devil figure, marking the gang's lookout post."

"What happens then?" Tony Prito asked.

"There's a river or creek close by that must run clear to the coast," Joe said. "We glimpsed stretches of it from the tree platform, and we also heard those guys who were searching for us today talk about going back to the boat."

"Exactly," Frank said. "So when the crook gets to the lookout post, one of the gang meets him there and takes him downriver by boat. From there he's whisked out to sea and aboard a ship headed for some foreign port."

"Pretty neat!" Chet exclaimed.

·"That's not all," Frank went on. "We saw Whitey Waulker with a lamp at the Pirate's Tavern today. He probably had a map, too. If our theory's correct, he may show up tonight at the turnoff to the secret trail."

Tony grinned. "And you figure if he does, we can nail him!"

Not wanting to leave the camp deserted, it was decided that Joe and Tony should remain behind. Joe's ankle still hurt him somewhat, but he was hoping that if he stayed off it as much as possible, he would be all right in the morning.

Dusk had fallen by the time Frank, Biff, and Chet reached the turnoff point to the trail through the woods. Chet, who was at the wheel, drove deep in among the trees on the opposite side of the road, so that the car would be out of sight to anyone approaching along the highway from either direction. Then the three boys got out and made their way through the underbrush to a point where they could keep watch and go into action quickly.

"What happens when he shows up?" Biff asked.

"We'll give him a chance to turn off onto the trail," Frank replied. "Then we follow him on foot and grab him as soon as he gets out of his car."

"I have an idea," Chet said, surveying a tree next to him. "I'll climb up to get a better view of the road. This way I can warn you when I see him!"

Before Frank could object, Chet had already pulled himself into the bottom branches of the tree.

"Don't go too high," Frank warned. "It'll take you too long to come down!"

"I won't," Chet replied. "I figured just about ten feet—"

Crunch! There was the noise of a breaking limb, and the next moment Chet hit the ground with a thud and an involuntary cry.

"*Shh!*" Frank urged, worried that they would be heard. "You can't be hurt. You didn't fall very far, so stop advertising that we're here!"

"Sorry," Chet mumbled.

Biff couldn't help but chuckle. "And here we were worried that you wouldn't come down fast enough!"

"Go ahead, laugh," Chet grumbled. "I was only trying to help!"

Suddenly, Frank held up a hand. They heard the sound of a car in the distance.

"That may be Waulker!" Chet hissed.

Sure enough, the vehicle came closer and slowed almost to a halt at the turnoff. But as it was about to pull onto the dirt trail, a brilliant spotlight suddenly blazed out of the darkness. At the same time, a loud voice shouted, "Keep going!"

15 The Spooky Glow

An instant later, a loud volley of warning shots pierced the air! Instead of turning, the car speeded up and continued along the highway!

For a moment, the boys were dumbfounded. Then Frank said angrily, "The crooks must have heard us, so they told the guy to scram. Let's go after him!"

The three ran to their car and piled in, afraid to be shot at any moment. But nothing happened as Frank slid behind the wheel, gunned the engine, and swiftly maneuvered out from among the trees.

"I guess they didn't see us," Chet murmured. "But they know we're around! Did anyone get a good look at the driver?"

Biff shook his head. "Not me."

"Neither did I," said Frank, "but it had to be Waulker. Who else would be turning onto that trail after dark?"

The getaway car, a dark-colored Chevy, was barely visible far ahead. The engine of the Hardys' yellow sports sedan, however, was tuned for maximum power and acceleration, and by skillful driving Frank steadily narrowed the distance between them.

"What if this guy's armed?" Biff muttered.

"Don't worry, we won't do anything stupid, or try any dumb heroics," Frank assured him. "Sam Radley warned that Waulker could be dangerous. I just want to trail him to wherever he's going and maybe help the police round him up."

Even at closer range, it was difficult to make out the exact color or model of the car. And the sudden glare of the spotlight back at the trail turnoff had momentarily blinded the boys, preventing them from identifying either the driver or his vehicle. Nevertheless, Frank switched on their dashboard radio to call the Red Lion barracks of the State Police west of the pine woods, hoping that roadblocks might be set up to trap the fugitive.

Just then, he saw something hurtle backward from the driver's window of the getaway car. A sound of breaking glass was heard and jagged bottle fragments glittered in their headlight glare. Frank swerved desperately, but at high speed it was impossible to avoid the scattered road hazard just ahead.

Blam! There was a momentary report as one of the front tires punctured, and the yellow sports sedan went into a terrifying spin!

Both Hardy boys had been well taught by their father how to react in a driving crisis. Frank steered and braked in such a way as to bring the car to the quickest, smoothest halt possible. Even so, it wound up broadside across the road, with its rear end only inches from the trees bordering the shoulder.

"Nice going, pal!" Biff congratulated Frank after all three boys had collected themselves.

Frank shrugged bitterly. "There go our chances of nabbing Waulker!"

They got out to inspect the damage. Luckily, only the left front tire had gone flat, but twenty minutes would be lost by the time they put on the spare. Not knowing what evasive route Waulker might have taken, much less his car's precise description or license number, the boys realized there was little use in contacting the police.

"We do know one thing, though," Frank reflected when they finally headed back to camp.

"What's that?" Biff queried.

"If Diablo's gang was going to smuggle Waulker out of the country tonight, they'd expect whatever ship they planned on using to be there."

"Hey, good thinking!" Chet said. "If you're right, the ship may heave to somewhere close offshore during the next twenty-four hours and wait for their signal."

"Right. And if we tell my father," Frank went on, "maybe he can alert the Coast Guard to keep watch for it, or take other steps to get the goods on Diablo."

"Call him right now, Frank!" Biff advised.

The Hardy boy transmitted the secret code signal which he and his brother used to contact their father in emergencies. But there was no reply. As they approached a crossroads gas station, which was closed for the night, Frank saw a telephone booth outside and pulled up beside it.

"I have an idea" he announced. "I'll call Jack Wayne. If we can't reach Dad, maybe we can get Jack to fly us offshore so we can try spotting the ship ourselves."

"Good idea!" Chet said. Jack Wayne was a charter pilot in Bayport who often flew Fenton Hardy and his two sons on special assignments.

Frank hopped out, plugged the pay phone with coins, and placed a call to Jack Wayne's company, the Ace Air Service, at the Bayport airfield. Presently, he returned to the car, shaking his head. "No luck. The girl in the office says Jack's in Dayton and won't be back till tomorrow."

"At least we've tried," said Biff. "If Waulker doesn't escape tonight, the gang probably won't try to smuggle him out to the ship during the daylight hours. Maybe there'll still be time to look for him tomorrow."

Arriving back at camp, the trio told their two friends everything that had happened. Joe and Tony, who had no news of their own to report, listened eagerly to the exciting account of the evening's events.

"Wow! Sounds like you guys had all the fun!" cracked Tony.

"If that's the right word for it," Frank said wryly.

The boys soon turned in as the nightly silence settled over the camp, broken only by the drowsy chirp of crickets and the occasional explosive boom of a diving nighthawk. But presently other, more mysterious noises made them poke their heads out of their tents.

"Did you guys hear that?" Chet hissed.

"We sure did," Joe replied. "Sounded like a low foghorn."

"Jumpin' catfish! Look at that!" Biff gasped, pointing as he spoke.

A weird greenish light could be seen glowing

among the trees near the foot of the hillside!

This time the boys had no intention of being decoyed away from the real scene of action. After a hasty conversation it was decided that Biff and Chet would remain behind to guard the camp, while the others would investigate the weird glow. Joe's ankle barely hurt any more, and he was eager to join his brother and Tony.

Cautiously the trio made their way down the slope, each clutching a stout stick with which to defend himself from possible attack.

As they approached the source of the illumination, the light suddenly went out—but not before Frank saw something that made his blood boil.

"Look out!" he shouted to his companions. "It's a trap!"

At the same moment, Joe tripped on a trailing vine, lost his footing, and stumbled forward!

16 Gallows Clue

There was no way Joe could stop himself from falling. Tony, too, had heard Frank's warning cry. He thrust out his hand in time to grab Joe's arm and jerk him out of the danger zone.

Joe landed on one knee, gasping. The yellow glow of Frank's flashlight revealed what he had almost stumbled into—*a steel-jawed bear trap!*

Joe swallowed hard. "That thing could break a guy's leg!" he whispered.

"And don't think those teeth wouldn't gouge into your flesh and muscle!" Frank added grimly.

At that moment, a sneering laugh rang out in the darkness. The sound brought the three boys instantly to attention, and Joe sprang to his feet.

"It came from over there!" Tony pointed.

As he spoke, they saw a figure break from cover and dart through the darkness. Frank swung his flashlight and pinned the fugitive in its glare.

"It's Verrill!" he cried.

The three youths angrily took after the man. With his long legs, Verrill might well have gotten away, but the boys' pursuit of him was fueled with burning rage. A mere dirty trick to lure them away from camp was one thing, but a deliberate attempt to cause them serious bodily harm was another. They were determined to catch the lawyer, even if it meant running both him and themselves to the point of exhaustion.

Verrill plunged through dense thickets and zig-zagged back and forth among the trees, trying desperately to shake them off, but the Hardys and Tony closed in relentlessly. Never for more than a few moments at a time could he evade the probing beam of Frank's flashlight.

Soon Verrill was far more winded than the boys. His chest was heaving and his legs were rubbery when Frank lunged through the air and finally brought him down with a flying tackle.

"Let go of me!" Verrill blustered as Joe and Tony joined in his capture, each of them pinning one of his arms.

"Do you realize what might've happened if one of

us had walked into that bear trap?" Frank gritted. "My brother nearly did!"

"I ought to punch you right in the nose for that!" Joe added.

The lawyer looked sullenly from one boy to another as they jerked him roughly to his feet. "I don't know what you're talking about," he muttered.

"Oh, no?" Frank's eyes drilled into him coldly. Then maybe you'd rather have us get the State Police so you can explain to them. If I remember correctly from what Dad told us about criminal law, there's a felony charge called 'reckless endangerment,' and the penalty if convicted can be pretty severe."

"Don't try to bluff me, Sonny!" Verrill's voice took on a deep, courtroom boom as he sought to impress his captors. "False arrest is also a serious charge, and that's what you'd be facing if you try any such nonsense. I'll remind you you're talking to an experienced *attorney*!"

Much to his astonishment, the Hardys laughed in his face.

"Tell us about it!" Joe said. "We've had you checked out, Mr. Verrill. You're in serious trouble with the Bar Association!"

Verrill's bluster suddenly evaporated. His open-mouthed dismay showed how completely the Hardys had demolished his false front.

Frank followed up fast. He had noticed that in addition to his flannel shirt and khaki pants, Verrill was wearing athletic shoes with heavy rubber soles of the kind that always have a distinctive pattern of cleats.

"No wonder you were so careful to brush away your footprints the other day when you raided our camp and stole our food," he remarked. "But we got enough fingerprints off the van to prove our case—if we need to, that is. You were probably heading for your car when we nabbed you just now, so it must be parked somewhere near here. It wouldn't surprise me if we found some of our stuff still stashed in it."

Again Verrill's expression showed that Frank's guess had hit home. The final blow came when Tony suddenly exclaimed, "Hey, look!" and pounced on a pale, oblong object lying among the trampled grass and brush.

"That's mine!" Verrill cried and tried to snatch it away from Tony, only to have his arms quickly pinioned again by the Hardys. "It fell out of my pocket when you fellows struggled with me!" the man whined. "Give it back to me!"

"Well, well, well," said Frank as he looked at the

transparent plastic envelope containing a weather-beaten, yellowed old document. He removed it and unfolded it in the glow of the flashlight.

Frank whistled, and Joe whooped triumphantly. "That's the original letter from Jem Taggart to his gang!"

"Which you stole from a client," Frank said accusingly to Ambrose Verrill. "This is clear evidence that you committed a crime!"

Verrill's face seemed to crumple, almost as if he were on the verge of tears. His hands jittered and his manner became cringing. "Look, boys, do we have to make such a big thing out of this? The fact is that the letter got misplaced. It just turned up this morning among a bunch of other papers in my briefcase. I was going to return it to my client as soon as I got back to Bayport. I'll admit it was, well, pretty high-handed of me, raiding your camp and all, but you must remember, I've been under terrible emotional strain! As for this prank to-night—"

"Some prank!" Joe cut in sarcastically.

"It was ill-judged, I see that now," the lawyer said. "Had one of you been hurt, no one would have been more upset than I. Put it down to the pressure I've been under."

Verrill paused to pull a flashlight out of his pocket, to show the boys how he had wrapped green cellophane over the lens to produce the greenish glow. "You see, it was just meant as a joke—a harmless joke—though in poor taste, I'll admit. As for Jem Taggart's treasure, you fellows feel free to go right on looking for it! I see no reason for any conflict between us at all. Perhaps we might even join forces and search for it together. I'm sure my client would agree. Then, if we find it, we can all split the fortune. What would you say to that?"

"Nuts," Frank responded bluntly. Verrill's face fell as the elder Hardy boy went on. "For the time being we'll hang onto Jem Taggart's letter until we can turn it over to the police as criminal evidence. It'll be up to your client to decide whether or not he wants you prosecuted for theft."

Verrill slunk off dejectedly and the boys returned to their camp. Early next morning, the Hardys drove into the pleasant seaside town of Tuckerton to consult the local historical society. The address Sam Radley had given them turned out to be a fine, beautiful house, more than a hundred years old, now occupied by a retired businessman named Soames who acted as secretary of the society.

He greeted the boys with a pleased twinkle in his eyes as they shook hands. "Matter of fact, I've been wondering if you fellows might come around. I read that newspaper item telling how you were interested in looking for that load of silver plate supposedly buried by the Outlaw of the Pine Barrens."

"Do you think it really exists, Mr. Soames?" Joe asked.

"Well, I can only say there's no reason to believe it's ever been found."

Frank said, "Do you have any information relating to Jem Taggart?"

"Oh, yes, indeed!" The elderly secretary nodded. "We have a whole file drawer full of material, such as photostats of old courthouse records and so on, which you're welcome to look at."

He led the boys into a large adjoining room filled with bookcases, file cabinets, and glass display cases containing historical relics.

Frank and Joe were excited when they saw the contents of the file drawer. Mr. Soames helpfully pointed out the most pertinent documents, then left the boys alone to glean through the material.

They learned that Jem Taggart himself had been captured near Tuckerton on March 4, 1781. "The day after he wrote that letter!" Joe exclaimed.

His two cronies, Xavier and Whaleboat Charlie, were nabbed on March 5th and 6th at different places near the coast.

"Which means they must have gotten caught when they tried to join Jem for the purpose of splitting the treasure," said Frank.

"And apparently they didn't have any of the silver on them," Joe added.

All three were tried and condemned for various serious crimes. According to an old newspaper account, just before mounting the gallows, Jem uttered a mocking laugh and chuckled to the attending parson, "You'll find another dead man ten paces north—if you're lucky!"

Joe frowned as he read the old newspaper story for a second time. "Those words 'ten paces north' tie in with the letter, which says 'ten paces north as crow flies.' But what exactly does that mean?"

Frank shrugged. "Search me. But I bet the letter X that Chet spotted on the lean-to stands for that one member of the gang named Xavier!"

"If we only could find out what *'fishhook'* means," Joe said.

Mr. Soames could offer no clues either, but promised to get in touch with the boys if he thought of anything. The Hardys thanked him and headed back to camp.

On the way, they stopped at Bosley's cabin.

"You two back again?" the man grumbled.

"We're hoping you passed on what we told you," Frank said, "about Rupert Price being cleared of that murder charge and inheriting a lot of money."

"I've told you, Rupert died of pneumonia!"

Joe threw his brother an exasperated glance and

shrugged. As they turned away, Della ran up. "Do you have to go so soon?" she asked, disappointed.

"I think your daddy wants it that way, honey," Frank said. Then he noticed her hugging her hand-carved wooden doll, and suddenly remembered that Rupert Price had enjoyed whittling and wood-carving.

"My, that's a pretty doll you have," he told Della. "Where did you get it?"

"Go on inside, Della," Bosley said sharply. "These boys have to be getting on."

His daughter obeyed reluctantly, and the Hardys got back into their car and drove off.

"That just about clinches it," Joe said. "Bosley knew why you were asking Della, so he—"

A buzz sounded from the dashboard and he switched on the radio. A familiar voice crackled over the loudspeaker. "*G calling H-1 and H-2. Do you read me?*"

17 *The Silver Fishhook*

"H-2 here," Joe replied. "We read you, Aunt Gertrude. Come in, please."

Aunt Gertrude's tone was sharp as mustard. "Are you all right? And where's H-1?"

"Sitting right beside me. Why, what's up?"

"We just had a phone call from Jack Wayne. He says Frank tried to get hold of him last night. Your mother and I were worried one of you boys might've strayed off and gotten lost in the wilderness, so you needed a plane to help look for him from the air."

Joe chuckled. "No, it was nothing like that, Aunt Gertrude. We think there's a smuggling operation going on down here that ties in with Dad's case.

Frank wanted Jack to see if he could spot the smugglers' ship offshore."

"Hmph! Sounds dangerous to me. You boys better be careful, understand?"

"Yes, ma'am. Over and out." Joe signed off with a grin. Despite Aunt Gertrude's constant fretting over her nephews' safety, he knew she was secretly proud of their work.

Frank detoured to the nearest gas station to return Jack Wayne's call. Jack himself answered, and the young detective explained the situation.

"Is there any place around here where you could pick us up?" Frank ended.

"Sure, there's a small airfield the fire wardens use right there in the Pine Barrens."

Jack Wayne described its location. By consulting their map, Frank saw that the field was only about a twenty-minute drive from their camp at Cedar Knob. A time was fixed later that afternoon when the plane would land and then take off with the brothers for a survey flight just offshore from the coastal edge of the Barrens.

As Frank hung up and left the phone booth, Joe was paying the service station attendant who had filled the tank of their yellow sports sedan.

"By the way," Frank said casually, "my girlfriend collects dolls. I'd like to bring her one from the Pine

Barrens as a souvenir. We've heard there's a skilled woodcarver down here. Would you by any chance know who he is, or where we could find him?"

"Oh, sure," said the attendant, "you mean Rube Peters. He's always whittling dolls for little kids."

The attendant gave the Hardy boys exact directions for finding the woodcarver's cabin. They thanked him and drove off.

"Nice going," Joe congratulated his brother. "That's got to be more than just coincidence—him having the same initials as the guy we're looking for. 'Rube Peters' must be the alias Rupert Price has been going under."

"Sure sounds that way," Frank agreed hopefully. "But let's wait and see."

After lunching with their pals at the camp, the Hardys drove to the cabin that the gas station attendant had described to them. It was set well back from the dirt road they were following, behind a pleasant screen of dogwoods and berry bushes. Small and with a veranda in front, it was covered with cedar shakes and looked somewhat neater than most of the weather-beaten houses and tar-paper shacks that the boys had seen deep in the forest.

But their hearts sank when a fat, scowling man came to the door in answer to Joe's knock. He looked nothing whatever like the snapshot Ogden

Price had shown them of his cousin in navy uniform.

"Mr. Peters?" Frank said lamely.

"Who wants to know?" the fat man growled.

"We do," Joe spoke up. "We heard you were quite a woodcarver, so we came to see your work. We'd like to buy something if any of it is for sale."

"I've nothing to sell," was the gruff reply. Then the door slammed in their faces.

The Hardys looked at each other, then reluctantly turned away from the house.

"He sure didn't look like that picture of Rupert Price!" Joe muttered under his breath.

"No, and I don't think he *is* Rupert Price—or even Rube Peters!" Frank replied in a low voice.

"How come?"

"Willard Bosley may have warned Rupert that we're still looking for him—maybe even that we spotted a wooden doll he'd carved. Rupert might have arranged for someone to take his place, if any strangers came looking for the local woodcarver."

"Something tells me you could be right," Joe murmured glumly. "But if he's hiding inside, and using that fat guy to front for him, how do we flush him out?"

Instead of replying, Frank suddenly appeared to catch his foot among some matted weeds. He lost his balance and fell headlong!

"Hey, are you all right?" Joe exclaimed as his

brother gave a loud groan and rubbed his hand gingerly over one leg.

Frank struggled to get up, only to utter another cry of pain, then flopped back on the ground. "I—I think my leg may be broken!"

"Don't try to stand on it! Just stay there until I get help!" Joe instructed him and hastily turned back to the house.

The fat man was scowling at them from the window. He had the door open even before Joe had time to knock. "What's the matter?" he demanded gruffly.

"My brother fell and thinks he's broken his leg," Joe said. "Can you give me a hand?"

The fat man stood glaring in the doorway with his mouth open, obviously uncertain of what to say. As he hesitated, Joe heard another voice from inside the cabin. "Maybe I can help, Gabe."

"But—" Gabe began to object.

"It's okay. I'll handle this."

A lean, muscular, dark-haired man now emerged into view, as if he had been standing somewhere just inside the doorway. He patted the fat man, who was evidently named Gabe, on the shoulder and came out of the cabin.

"Let's take a look at your brother's leg," he said calmly.

Frank, who was still lying on the ground, watched

as the two walked down the footpath toward him. "Mr. Price?" he inquired.

The dark-haired man stopped short with a frown. "Don't tell me your broken leg was just a trick?"

"I'm afraid so, sir," Frank confessed, standing up easily. "I understand you were a navy medical corpsman and planned to become a doctor. I had a hunch you wouldn't feel right about letting an injured person go without first aid, just so you could stay in hiding."

There was a moment of exasperated silence. The Hardys wondered if Rupert Price might give way to an angry outburst. Instead, his expression gradually relaxed into a wry smile. "Well, it looks as though you guessed right, Son," he conceded. "I suppose you two are those young detectives, the Hardy boys?"

"Yes, sir. I'm Frank and this is my brother Joe."

They shook hands, and Price explained, "There isn't much available in the way of medical care down here in the Pine Barrens, so I've tried to help out whenever I could. Actually, I've learned a lot from the old-timers around here—I mean, about Indian medicines and herb remedies you can make from plants growing wild in the woods. Anyhow, the people in these parts are loyal friends, and they're grateful for whatever little doctoring I've done, so they've tried to cover up for me, even though they know I'm wanted by the law. I hope you won't hold that against them."

"Don't worry about that, Mr. Price," Frank assured him. "There's nothing to hold against them because you're no longer wanted by the law. That's what my brother and I tried to tell your friend, Mr. Bosley, but he wouldn't believe us."

Rupert Price nodded. "He told me. But I'm not sure *I* believe it."

"It's what your cousin, Ogden Price, claims. He said you both have an uncle, who recently died and left an estate worth over a million dollars—most of which will go to you. He's only supposed to get about two hundred and fifty thousand dollars of that, but he'll inherit the whole estate if you don't show up to claim your share."

Frank went on to explain that Ogden now felt remorseful for not having helped Rupert prove his innocence years before when he was wrongfully accused. So now he was trying to ease his conscience by finding his cousin and making sure he received his full inheritance.

Rupert Price looked somewhat dazed on hearing all this, but his expression soon settled into a worried frown. "H'm, you've certainly given me food for thought," he said. "But I'm still not certain I trust Ogden. We never did get along. For all I know, this could be a trick on his part to make me give myself up, and then maybe forfeit my inheritance by being sent to prison for a crime I never committed."

"I doubt that very much," Frank said. "Anyhow, we're not going to send the police after you. We did take Ogden's story at face value, but we'll check it out, and if it turns out your cousin has lied to us, we'll do everything we can to help clear your name."

"Thanks for that, boys." Rupert Price smiled and gave both of the Hardys a warm handshake.

Before leaving, they told him about their hunt for Jem Taggart's secret treasure and asked if the word clue, 'fishhook,' meant anything to him.

Rupert thought for a moment. "I've a feeling I've heard that name before, from some of the old-time Piney woodsmen," he said. "My guess would be that it's a place name—maybe for one of the old ghost towns in the Pine Barrens. But that's about all I can tell you."

Frank and Joe drove to the fire wardens' airfield. A short time later, the pilot, Jack Wayne, landed there in his sleek, twin-engine plane, *Skyhappy Sal*, and the Hardys took off with him to scout for any sign of the ship Diablo's gang was expecting.

The plane winged coastward, giving the boys a magnificent view of the vast pine forest. Far ahead they could make out the blue-green expanse of the ocean, dotted with fishing boats.

Suddenly, Joe grabbed his brother's shoulder and pointed downward. "Look!" he exclaimed.

Below, among the trees, could be seen the silver outline of a creek or river. *It was curved in the shape of a fishhook!*

18 Ten Paces North

Frank gasped with excitement as he saw how the stream curved through the wooded terrain. "That could be the 'fishhook' Jem Taggart meant in his letter to the rest of the gang!"

"I'll bet anything it is!" Joe declared. "And that means we must be somewhere over the treasure right now!"

"Any place you could land around here, Jack?" Frank asked.

The pilot scanned the scene below them, then shook his head. "No way. I don't see any spot within miles that's bare enough or smooth enough to use for a landing strip."

"Then we'll have to jump!" Frank decided.

Jack Wayne flashed the boys a worried glance. "Sure you know what you're doing?"

"It's the quickest, simplest way," Joe argued. "We could waste hours trying to find the fishhook if we had to hike in from the nearest road!"

"What about your dad—would he approve?"

"I'm sure he would," Frank told the pilot. "He taught us skydiving himself."

"I suggest you go back to the airfield and get our car," Joe said. "Would you mind driving to the road point nearest to the stream, so we can join you later?"

Jack grinned. "Will do. And I expect you to find the treasure, hear?"

Skyhappy Sal carried parachuting gear as part of her regular equipment. The Hardys zipped themselves into coveralls, strapped on backpack chutes, then donned goggles, helmets, and gloves. Their high-laced hiking boots would serve for the jump.

Jack Wayne banked and circled to the right, maneuvering the plane into position, then headed into the wind directly over the fishhook-shaped stream. One by one, in quick succession, Frank and Joe poised in the open doorway and launched themselves into the air.

Both dropped in "stable-fall" position—face down, body arched, arms and legs spread out and slightly bent. Moments later, as each pulled his

ripcord handle, the parachute popped out, opening the canopy with a jolt. Presently, the two boys felt the exhilarating thrill of floating down through wind-swept space toward the earth below.

By "slipping" their chutes expertly, the Hardys steered themselves toward their target. They landed close together on the same bank of the stream, touching down feet first. They whirled fast as they fell forward so as to take the main shock in a sitting position, with a quick hand tug on the risers to help cushion the blow.

Scrambling to their feet, the boys unsnapped their canopies and pulled off helmet and goggles to exchange satisfied grins.

"Not bad, I must say!" Joe declared.

"I think Dad would have approved our form," Frank agreed, smiling.

They waved at *Skyhappy Sal*, watching Jack Wayne circle and dip the wings, then head toward the airfield. Then they stripped off their gloves, harness, and coveralls and rolled up their chutes with practiced skill before turning their attention to the problem of the treasure.

"You know, I was thinking on the way down," Frank remarked, "trying to put the whole picture together, and I've got a hunch about the way things happened."

"Great! Let's hear it," Joe said eagerly.

"Well, first of all, that carving Chet discovered on the lean-to . . . 'Fishhook X' . . ."

"You figured the X stands for Xavier," Joe broke in.

"Right. Let's say that's his signature. But why did he carve the word 'Fishhook'?"

"As a message?"

"Right." Frank nodded. "That's my guess too. Maybe Whaleboat Charlie, the other member of the gang, wasn't with him at camp when the Indian runner brought the letter from Jem Taggart. It's not likely Xavier would be carrying any paper or ink with him, so he just carved the word 'fishhook' to let Charlie know where they were to meet the gang leader and divide the treasure."

"And when Charlie got back, he saw the message and followed Xavier," Joe chimed in eagerly. "But they all got caught before they could dig up the treasure."

"We hope!" Frank concluded with a wry grin.

As the boys surveyed the area where they had landed, they saw that the point of the fishhook was located at an opening in a rocky outcrop where the stream emerged from some underground source, probably draining from higher ground.

"Let's count off ten paces north, like the letter says, and see where it takes us," Joe proposed.

Starting from the point of the hook, they measured the distance. From their aerial inspection of the terrain, they already had a fairly precise bearing, but they used Joe's pocket compass to check and make sure their steps were heading north.

This maneuver brought them in among the trees fringing the bank of the stream, and it was immediately apparent that they had correctly followed the directions of the Outlaw of the Pine Barrens.

Just ahead lay a rectangular plot of slightly sunken ground. It was topped by small rocks, probably plucked from the streambed. Staring at the rock configuration for a few moments, the boys suddenly realized that if a few of the rocks shifted position slightly, they would form the letters *BJ*!

"Black Jack!" Joe exclaimed. "The guy that Jem said in the letter *'was took bad and died'*!"

Frank nodded again dryly. "What took him bad was probably a cutlass blow from Jem Taggart, or a bang over the head with a rock."

"One person less to share the treasure with," Joe conjectured. "Or maybe Jem suspected Black Jack was planning to double-cross him."

"Whatever the reason was, it looks as if Jem planted him here for keeps." Frank paused and rubbed his jaw thoughtfully before adding, "And the letter says the silver plate was buried under him."

Joe looked at his brother uncertainly. "So what do

we do—get some sticks and start digging?"

"Pretty slow way to tackle the job. We actually need shovels," Frank said. "Do you really want to dig up Black Jack's grave?"

"Not much." Joe's face showed a total lack of enthusiasm, even at the prospect of eventually finding a load of silver plate under the remains of the old-time outlaw.

"Neither do I," Frank admitted. "Besides, now that we've found where Jem buried Black Jack, I'm not so sure I trust Taggart's letter."

Joe frowned, puzzled. "What do you mean?"

"Well, we know Taggart was a real scoundrel. He even killed one member of his own gang. Why trust the other two? If he told them where the treasure was buried, he'd be taking a risk they might get here first and do him out of his share."

"You may have a point there. On the other hand, maybe Black Jack really became ill and died, and Jem buried him."

Frank shrugged. "I doubt it. From all we've read about Taggart, it sounds more like him to pull some dirty trick and try to either get rid of or mislead his own pals."

"It sure does," Joe agreed thoughtfully. "Come to think of it, that could be why that line in the letter—'ten paces north as crow flies'—sounds so funny."

"Not only funny, but downright phony," said Frank. "Maybe a deliberate attempt to mislead Xavier and Charlie. I mean, if the distance is as short as ten paces, why say *as the crow flies?*"

Joe frowned and puckered his brows. "Search me. What's your guess?"

"Yeah, let's hear it, smart boy!" a harsh voice suddenly called out.

The Hardys whirled to see who had spoken. Four men had just stepped out into view from among some trees. The boys' hearts sank as they recognized two of them—the flat-nosed thug whom they had first encountered at the ice-cream parlor in Bayport, and his redhead accomplice!

The third man, much to their surprise, was the curly haired reporter, Nate Grimes, who had come to the Hardys' home on Elm Street to interview them about the treasure of the Outlaw of the Pine Barrens.

But it was the speaker on whom their gaze finally settled—a tall, dark, hook-nosed man. Both Frank and Joe sensed that here was the mastermind whom their father was hunting!

19 Smugglers' Hideout

"El Diablo!" Joe gasped.

The dark-haired, hook-nosed man threw back his head and laughed, displaying brilliant white teeth that seemed even brighter by contrast with his deeply tanned, olive-complected face.

"Smart boy!" he exclaimed in a voice that bore a faint trace of foreign accent. "Seems like Fenton Hardy's two brats take after their old man when it comes to brains—eh, *amigos*?"

His three companions grinned and agreed sarcastically with their leader.

"It almost looks as though you were expecting us," Frank said levelly, fishing for information.

"You might put it that way, kid." Diablo smiled and fingered a pair of high-powered binoculars that hung from a strap around his muscular neck. "Grimes here spotted you two as the Hardy boys when we first saw you floating down from the sky. He recognized you through these glasses, even with your helmets and goggles on."

Nate Grimes blushed slightly as the boys' glances flicked toward him.

"Some newspaper reporter!" Joe muttered scornfully.

"No cracks out of you, kid, if you want to stay healthy!" Grimes shot back. "And don't blame me just 'cause you and your wise-apple brother got suckered so easily!"

"How?" Frank needled. "You mean the way we took you at face value and assumed you really *were* a newspaperman?"

"I'm a reporter, all right—don't worry about that," the curly-haired man retorted. "I'm talking about the way you two swallowed the bait when I sent you that copy of Jem Taggart's letter!"

Diablo's gang, the Hardys now learned, had become suspicious of Ambrose Verrill when he first showed up in the Pine Barrens, fearing he might be a detective or lawman working in cooperation with Fenton Hardy. So they had searched his camp secretly and found the original Taggart letter.

Diablo, however, was not convinced that the letter was authentic. He thought the document might be a fake, which Verrill was merely using as a cover to explain his snooping about the woods.

The crooked journalist, Grimes, had come up with the bright idea of photographing the letter and sending a copy to the Hardy boys—and then interviewing them to get their reaction.

This would give him a chance to find out if they took it seriously as a possible clue to Taggart's long-lost treasure. If so, Diablo's gang would know that Verrill was probably not working with Fenton Hardy.

In the event the Hardy boys actually came to the Pine Barrens to search for the silver hoard, so much the better from Diablo's point of view. This would give the gang a chance to keep an eye on them—perhaps even to nab Fenton Hardy himself if he came to visit his sons' camp.

"And if you happened to *find* the treasure," Grimes ended with a nasty smile, "who could ask for anything more?"

"Looks like they found it, all right!" Diablo chuckled, flashing his white teeth again. He had closed in on the boys to see what they were examining when the gang surprised them, and now he pointed triumphantly at the stones loosely forming the letters *BJ*. "Black Jack's grave!"

The other three crooks pressed forward eagerly to see for themselves.

"Hey!" Grimes exclaimed, his eyes lighting up greedily. "If Taggart's letter means anything, the treasure's down there, right underneath Black Jack's bones!"

Diablo turned and barked out orders to Flat Nose and the red-haired thug. "Go get some spades from the camper!"

Frank and Joe glanced at each other, both realizing he was evidently referring to the big gray van they had seen from the lookout tree before responding to the sun flashes. Too bad they had not spotted it from the air before parachuting down this time, but no doubt it was parked somewhere well out of sight among the pines.

Flat Nose and Red finally returned with spades, and the crooks began to dig. But after they had gone down more than six feet, it became clear to everyone that the pseudo-grave was empty!

Diablo was furious—especially when he noticed Joe grinning contemptuously at him and the other baffled, sweating crooks. "You punks think you're smart, wasting our time with this foolishness!" Diablo leered. "Well, let me tell you something, my fine young brats—you may be laughing out of the other side of your mouths when I get through with you!"

The Hardys' hands were tied behind them, and the two boys were marched off through the forest to the gang's camp. It was situated near the sandy bank of what Frank guessed must be a deep tidal inlet. Dusk was already falling. In a small clearing behind the gray camper van, two men were cooking steaks on an outdoor grill. One of them had whitish-blond hair and a tanned, seamed face. Joe gasped, and both Hardys recognized him as the crook they had seen at the Pirate's Tavern.

Whitey Waulker!

An unpleasant smile spread over his face as he saw the boys. "So you caught the junior detectives, Diablo? Nice going!" Waulker rasped. "They loused things up for us last night, but something tells me that's the last time they'll interfere with one of your business deals—right?"

"You can count on that, *amigo!*" El Diablo responded in a voice that sent a chill down the boys' spines.

Evidently Waulker had found some way to make contact with the gang after the Hardys had kept him from following the fluorescent blaze-marked trail to the pickup point in the woods. And from the next few remarks, it became obvious that Frank's theory had been correct—Waulker was now waiting for the gang to smuggle him out of the country, beyond the reach of federal law.

Various tools and implements lay scattered about the camp, including a heavy automotive jack. There were also several discarded supply cartons filled with empty cans, bottles, and other trash, as well as two large tires, which looked as though they had been removed from the camper.

Rather than eat in cramped quarters inside the van, the crooks proceeded to wolf down their supper outdoors. Just before they fell to, another man came rushing out to join them. Apparently he had been manning the camper's radio gear.

"The freighter just heaved to offshore, boss!" he told Diablo. "They'll send in their load as soon as it gets dark enough!"

"Good! Tell the skipper I'll be sending the boat back to his ship with an extra load we weren't expecting!" As he spoke, the gang leader shot a vicious look at the Hardy boys, and ended with a menacing chuckle. "Once they've disappeared out of the country, Fenton Hardy will have to do whatever I tell him, if he ever hopes to see his two brats again!"

Frank and Joe looked on hungrily while the gang ate. They had been shoved down into a sitting position among the trash—Frank with his back to the cartons, and Joe leaning against the two big van tires.

Just before being shoved down, Joe had noticed a

shiny glint in the badly worn treads of the top tire. In the circle of light from the camper, his keen eyes had quickly detected the cause—a shard of glass protruding from the tire casing!

By feeling around cautiously behind his back, Joe managed to notch his wrist cords in between the piece of broken glass and the tread. Then he began sawing back and forth.

It was slow, nerve-wracking work, having to start and stop every time he thought one of the crooks might be noticing what he was up to. But finally he felt the last strands of rope beginning to give way.

Nate Grimes was the first of the gang to finish eating. At Diablo's order, he took a pair of night glasses from the camper van and headed seaward on foot along the bank of the inlet to keep watch for the freighter's boat.

Joe sawed frantically, trying to finish cutting the bonds around his wrists. He had no plan except for a desperate hope that once he himself got free, he might be able to pull the piece of glass out of the tire and cut Frank's ropes also.

Suddenly a shout was heard. "Hey, boss. The boat's coming in from the ship!" Grimes hurried back to the camp out of the darkness.

Diablo, who was still chewing on a mouthful of steak, merely waved in response.

Just then, Joe's wrists came free. Desperately, he

tried to think of a way to cut Frank's ropes, too, without being seen.

But as Joe glanced at his brother, he saw Frank grin. There was no need to cut his bonds—he already had them nearly sawed through, using the jagged edge of a tin can in the trash carton!

Diablo belched, wiped the back of his hand across his mouth, and rose to his feet. "Okay, *amigos*," he said. "Get ready to heave those brats in the boat as soon as we unload the goods they're bringing in!"

The other crooks got up, one by one, and turned to look at the Hardys. Red and Flat Nose started toward the two boys.

"Now!" Frank hissed to his brother. Joe groped for a lug wrench lying near the tires, and Frank's fingers closed around the neck of a bottle in the trash carton.

"On your feet, punks!" Red ordered gruffly.

The Hardys rose together, and their hands came out from behind their backs. Each swung hard at the crook nearest him!

20 Treasure Tree

Joe's lug wrench caught Flat Nose on the side of the head, knocking him to the ground! Meanwhile, Frank smashed the bottle against the red-haired thug's temple, and he, too, went down.

"Keep fighting, Joe!" the older Hardy panted. "Maybe the Coast Guard'll spot us!" Both boys realized there was always a chance that the Coast Guard might notice the smugglers' boat and trail them to the cove. It was a slim hope, but enough to inspire the young detectives with an extra measure of courage as they turned back to face their foes.

El Diablo roared with anger when he saw what had happened to two of his men. "Grab those punks!" he shouted.

Nate Grimes and the two other gang members moved fast to obey their chief's command. Whitey Waulker also looked eager to join the fray if more help was needed to subdue the brash youths.

The Hardys fought like wildcats, swinging their makeshift weapons in all directions. Grimes yelped with pain as the lug wrench hit him on the arm, and the gang's cook staggered backward, half stunned by a glancing blow from Frank's second bottle!

The muffled thrum of a boat engine had been growing steadily louder, and presently a heavily laden motor launch thrust out of the darkness to beach itself in the sandy bank of the cove.

"Come on! Give us a hand with these brats!" Diablo yelled and gestured to the two seamen aboard the launch.

With their desperate tactics, Frank and Joe had so far managed to keep their attackers at bay. But now, with El Diablo himself and the two smugglers surrounding them and starting to close in, there seemed little chance that the Hardy boys could go on battling much longer.

Just then fresh voices were heard. Five more figures swarmed into the little clearing. But it quickly became obvious that these were no allies of the gang. Fists flying, they flung themselves on the crooks, grabbing them by the arms or shoulders and swinging them around so that punches could be landed more effectively!

"Dad!" Joe exclaimed joyfully as he caught sight of Fenton Hardy's grim-jawed face. Jack Wayne, Chet, Biff, and Tony were with the big, broad-shouldered detective!

In a few minutes the fight was over. El Diablo tried to draw a weapon with each hand, but a hard right to the jaw by Fenton Hardy sent him sprawling among the trash!

In all, five of the crooks had been knocked off their feet and now remained stunned or cowering on the ground. The others had their hands in the air as the famed private investigator held them covered with Diablo's own gun.

"Find some rope!" Mr. Hardy told his companions.

It was several moments before his sons, winded and panting, could catch their breath enough to speak.

"What a terrific break, you guys turning up when you did!" Frank blurted happily.

"How did you all get here?" Joe added.

Jack Wayne said he had known that dusk would be falling by the time he drove back on the road to a point near where Frank and Joe had parachuted down, and that he would need help to find the fishhook-shaped stream in the gathering darkness.

So he had radioed the young detectives over the CB in Biff's van to meet him at the airfield. Mr. Hardy, who had come to the Pine Barrens to search for El Diablo's gang undercover, had gotten in touch with Jack shortly before he landed, and had promised to be at the airfield as soon as he could.

After they had all met, they had driven as close to the fishhook as they could. Then, using flashlights and lanterns, they had found the stream, and from there the trail of the gang and their captives had been easy to follow to the campsite.

One by one, the crooks were bound and handcuffed. Fenton Hardy used the gang's own communications gear inside the camper to summon the New Jersey State Police. The motor launch was found to contain stolen merchandise smuggled in to avoid customs payment or seizure.

A Coast Guard cutter was dispatched to board and take command of the smugglers' ship, which was lying offshore without lights.

"Now a few things become clear in my mind," Frank said while the young detectives and Mr. Hardy were watching the prisoners. "Flat Nose and Red were following you all around Bayport and Shoreham. You were getting in their way. That's why Red fired a dart at you at the concert."

Mr. Hardy nodded. "Unfortunately, they caught on to my disguise."

"Did they steal Mr. Colpitt's map of the Pine Barrens?" Joe asked, telling his father about their visit to the map dealer.

Mr. Hardy shook his head. "I don't think so. The smugglers were not actively looking for the treasure."

"Then it must have been Verrill!" Frank declared.

"Sam told me about Verrill when I last talked to him," Mr. Hardy said. "Verrill's the one who was after the treasure, so I'm sure he wanted the map."

"And I bet he was the one who played Jem Taggart's ghost, too!" Joe put in.

Mr. Hardy smiled. "No. That was me. I wanted to contact you that night, but then I noticed someone prowling around your camp and chased him."

"Verrill again," Frank guessed. "But why'd you walk around the woods in that getup, Dad?"

"It was a good way to scare away snoopers while I was roaming around and watching El Diablo's gang," the detective replied.

Next morning, while Mr. Hardy was briefing the FBI on the outcome of the case, Frank and Joe decided to return to the fishhook site with their buddies. On the way, Joe called Sam Radley on their car radio to verify Ogden Price's story about his cousin.

"I'll check it out for you and call you back as soon as I have the answer," Radley promised.

"Thanks, Sam," Joe replied.

When the boys arrived at their destination, Frank and Joe were eager to try out a new theory about the location of the treasure.

As they moved the shovels they had brought out of the car, Chet asked, "Where do we start digging?"

"First, we have to count off ten paces north," Frank replied.

"I thought you already did that yesterday."

"That was ten paces north from the tip of the fishhook," Joe explained. "This time we'll pace them off from the phony grave."

As Frank did so, the others watched and followed eagerly. To everyone's disappointment, they failed to find another clear-cut clue like the initials *BJ* formed with pebbles. The ten paces merely brought them to a fallen hollow oak tree.

"Now what?" Biff murmured blankly.

"Wait! Look there!" Joe cried suddenly and pointed to a round, wooden structure nailed to the trunk. It was half hidden among the brush where the tree had fallen.

"It's a crow's nest from an old sailing ship, where the lookout used to stand!" Tony Prito said.

"Right!" Joe went on excitedly. "Jem Taggart could have gotten it off some old shipwrecked hulk on the beach—or maybe from the very ship they plundered to get the silver. And that could be what he meant by that tricky wording in the letter—*as the crow flies!*"

Frank's pulse began to pound as a thought struck him. Directly below the crow's nest, he had noticed an opening in the hollow tree trunk. And now, as he stooped down and peered up inside the trunk, he saw his hunch confirmed.

"Look what's in the tree!" he exclaimed to the others.

As they joined him and peered inside the trunk, Chet shuddered and gulped, "Jumpin' Jupiter! It's an old skeleton!"

"*Black Jack's* skeleton!" Frank declared.

"And the letter says the silver was buried underneath him!" cried Joe.

"Right! Which means it's somewhere inside the stump!"

Leaping to his feet, Frank turned and began pushing aside the weeds and creepers with which the old hollow tree stump was now densely overgrown. A moment later, as the others gathered around him, he shouted triumphantly, "*Look! There's the treasure!*"

Together, the boys pulled out a heavily loaded

metal chest containing dishes, platters, and other items of silver plate. Though darkened and oxidized by the passage of time, they were much more valuable now than when the Outlaw of the Pine Barrens had cached the treasure inside the hollow oak two centuries earlier—guarded by a dead man!"

The Hardy boys and their friends transported the treasure by car to the State Police post.

On the way, the radio buzzed. It was Sam Radley, confirming that Rupert Price had long ago been cleared of the murder charge against him.

"I'm so glad," Frank said. "Let's tell Rupert as soon as we deliver the silver plate."

The sergeant, who relieved them of the treasure, looked at them admiringly. "You've done a great job," he said with a smile. "By the way, we arrested Verrill this morning. We're holding him until his client decides whether he'll press charges against him for stealing the letter."

"Good," Frank said. "We're glad you rounded him up."

"Your father left a message for you," the sergeant went on. "He'll be in later to talk to Captain Torelli, and he wants you to meet him here."

"Thanks," Joe said. "We have some business to attend to, but it shouldn't take very long."

The boys left the State Police headquarters and drove to Rupert Price's cabin. When they arrived, they noticed a number of cars parked in front, and three men were standing in front of the door.

The boys got out of their sports sedan and walked up to them. "We'd like to speak to Mr. Price," Frank said. "We have a message for him."

"He ain't here," one of the men growled.

Frank and Joe looked at each other. Both boys had the feeling Price was there, but was barricading himself in the house with his friends guarding him against possible arrest!

"Look," Frank said, "it's important that we talk to him. He's a free man and he does not have to hide from the law any longer!"

"I suggest you leave!" one of the Pineys said. "Right now!" He walked toward the boys menacingly, followed by the others. One of them called, "Hey, Charlie, Cleve! We need help!"

Instantly the door opened, and a few more men came out. All advanced toward the boys, looking hostile and ready to fight.

"Get lost!" one commanded.

Joe was angry enough to argue, but Frank pulled his brother by the arm. "No sense starting anything." Turning to the men, he calmly said, "Mr. Price has a decision to make. I realize he doesn't know us, and we can't prove it to him right now, but he's a free man. He can either believe us or go on hiding."

550

Shrugging, he led the way back toward their car. They were about to pile in, when the door of the cabin opened again and Rupert Price rushed out.

"Frank! Joe! Wait!" he called.

"What—" His friends began objecting all at once, but he waved for them to listen. "It's okay," he said. "I just got a call that those boys were right. I *am* a free man!"

He walked up to the Hardys and began shaking their hands. "Thanks, fellows! I really owe you a great deal, and I apologize for not completely trusting you. But you must understand that I didn't want to go to jail a second time for a crime I never committed!"

"We understand," Frank said. "How did you find out that we were telling the truth?"

"Oh, I know a few fellows around here, and one of them checked with the authorities, not mentioning, of course, that he knew where I was. My friends were ready to take me away and hide me, but I wanted to know, so I insisted that I wait until I got the word."

"I'm glad we could help," Joe said with a grin.

Price gave each of the boys a warm handshake. "Thanks to you, I'm a free man—and a mighty rich one!" he added with a twinkle in his eyes.

"What are you going to do, now that you have all of their money?" Tony asked.

"Take a cruise around the world?" Biff suggested.

"Not on your life!" Rupert replied. "I'll stay right here and open a modern medical clinic for my friends and neighbors, the Pineys!"

"That's wonderful," Frank said, and the others agreed enthusiastically. The men, who had guarded Price so loyally, cheered and applauded. Now that they realized the boys were not enemies but had done Price a great favor, their hostility disappeared and they, too, shook hands with the Hardys and thanked them.

Finally the young detectives got into their car, saying good-bye to Rupert Price and his neighbors. On the way back to the State Police headquarters, both Frank and Joe had a vague feeling of anxiety in the pits of their stomachs. Would this be their last case, or would something else turn up in the future? Something would, called *The Submarine Caper*, and it would require all the sleuthing skill they had.

Suddenly, Frank brightened up. "Hey, I just had a great idea," he said to his friends. "What say we donate the Outlaw's treasure to Rupert Price's cause, fellows?"

The Bayport High gang cheered and agreed.

"That reminds me, I'm famished," Chet Morton put in. "Let's get some burgers and milkshakes before we meet Mr. Hardy. If we don't, I may need medical attention myself!"

The Hardy Boys Mystery Stories

by Franklin W. Dixon

Have you read all the titles in this exciting mystery series? Look out for these new titles coming in 1987:

No. 41 **The Mysterious Caravan**
No. 42 **Danger on Vampire Trail**
No. 82 **Revenge of the Desert Phantom**
No. 83 **The Skyfire Puzzle**

Armada

'JINNY' BOOKS
by Patricia Leitch

When Jinny Manders rescues Shantih, a chestnut Arab, from a cruel circus, her dreams of owning a horse of her own seem to come true. But Shantih is wild and unrideable.

This is an exciting and moving series of books about a very special relationship between a girl and a magnificent horse.

FOR LOVE OF A HORSE
A DEVIL TO RIDE
THE SUMMER RIDERS
NIGHT OF THE RED HORSE
GALLOP TO THE HILLS
HORSE IN A MILLION
THE MAGIC PONY
RIDE LIKE THE WIND
CHESTNUT GOLD
JUMP FOR THE MOON
HORSE OF FIRE

Armada

The Three Investigators

Brilliant Jupiter Jones, athletic Pete Crenshaw and studious Bob Andrews make up the Three Investigators. Read more about their baffling mysteries in these new titles, available from Armada in 1987:

No. 38 The Mystery of the Smashing Glass
No. 39 The Mystery of the Trail of Terror
No. 40 The Mystery of the Rogues' Reunion

Armada

Have you read all the adventures in the "Mystery" series by Enid Blyton?

The Rockingdown Mystery

Roger, Diana, Snubby and Barney hear strange noises in the cellar while staying at Rockingdown Hall. Barney goes to investigate and makes a startling discovery . . .

The Rilloby Fair Mystery

Valuable papers have disappeared – the Green Hands Gang has struck again! Which of Barney's workmates at the circus is responsible? The four friends turn detectives – and have to tackle a dangerous criminal.

The Ring O'Bells Mystery

Eerie things happen at deserted Ring O'Bells Hall – bells start to ring, strange noises are heard in a secret passage, and there are some very unfriendly strangers about. Something very mysterious is going on and the friends mean to find out what . . .

The Rubadub Mystery

Who is the enemy agent at the top-secret submarine harbour? Roger, Diana, Snubby and Barney are determined to find out – and find themselves involved in a most exciting mystery.

The Rat-A-Tat Mystery

When the big knocker on the ancient door of Rat-A-Tat House bangs by itself in the middle of the night, it heralds a series of very peculiar happenings – and provides another action-packed adventure for Roger, Diana, Snubby and Barney.

The Ragamuffin Mystery

"This is going to be the most exciting holiday we've ever had," said Roger – and little does he know how true his words will prove when he and his three friends go to Merlin's Cove and discover the hideout of a gang of thieves.

Armada

Horror Classic Gamebooks
by J. H. Brennan

Now you can bring your favourite horror characters
to life in these spinechilling gamebooks.

Dracula's Castle

Deadly traps and evil cunning await Jonathan Harker on
his arrival at the forbidding Castle Dracula. The choice
is yours whether to play the fearless vampire-hunter or
his arch-enemy, the vampire count himself. Will you
have the stamina to survive?

The Curse of Frankenstein

Enter the ghoulish world of Frankenstein and his
monstrous creation. But be warned, you will need skill,
luck and nerves of steel to endure this bloodcurdling
adventure.

Armada

Have you read all the "Secrets" stories by Enid Blyton?

THE SECRET ISLAND

Peggy, Mike and Nora are having a miserable time with unkind Aunt Harriet and Uncle Henry – until they make friends with wild Jack and discover the secret island.

THE SECRET OF SPIGGY HOLES

On a holiday by the sea, Mike, Jack, Peggy and Nora discover a secret passage – and a royal prisoner in a sinister cliff-top house. The children plan to free the young prince – and take him to the secret island.

THE SECRET MOUNTAIN

Jack, Peggy, Nora and Mike team up with Prince Paul of Baronia to search for their parents, who have been kidnapped and taken to the secret mountain. Their daring rescue mission seems doomed to failure – especially when the children are captured and one of them is to be sacrificed to the sun-god.

THE SECRET OF KILLIMOOIN

When Prince Paul invited Nora, Mike, Peggy and Jack to spend the summer holidays with him in Baronia, they were thrilled. By amazing luck, they find the hidden entrance to the Secret Forest – but can they find their way out?

THE SECRET OF MOON CASTLE

Moon Castle is said to have had a violent, mysterious past so Jack, Peggy, Mike and Nora are wildly excited when Prince Paul's family rent it for the holidays. When weird things begin to happen, the children are determined to know the strange secrets the castle hides . . .

Armada

is thick – that's your signal to open up into the soft-skinned vehicles. Have we still got ammunition for the mortar?'

'Yessir.'

'Set up the mortar team then to fire when they debouch. Catch them in the open. There's some nice stone walls down there, send some flints whizzing about. The other two tanks and the field guns will take out the other vehicles of the column.'

The other officers and sergeants had gathered round. Freddie pointed out the barns and orchards where he wanted them sited.

'I want them trapped on that road,' he commanded. 'Shoot them up from the front and the back. Tank commanders to take out any attempt to get off the road and down that slope to ford the river. My last report from the RAF was that they were about ten miles behind us, we should be able to expect them soon. Let's get into position.'

The village was a mass of moving men and vehicles, spreading out over its eastern edge. Freddie set up his command post in the Mairie, built of old stone, a metre and a half thick. On the wall of the room overlooking the meadow and fruit trees that led down to the river was a very old hand-tinted photograph of Louis XVIII. The room was musty; he opened the window and pushed back the shutter. He could see his men manoeuvring their tanks and guns, chopping branches, lifting hay, camouflaging their sites of attack.

'This is better,' he said, to nobody in particular.

The early morning mist had burned off, leaving a pale blue sky. As he watched from his window, he detected a faint darkening over the trees, a dirty smudging of the blue. He leaned out, cocking an ear. What he heard caused him to jog outside, and into the hay barn.

Hoskins had backed his Cruiser tank right inside, and had pulled the doors partly to. In the gloom he had created he had a perfect view down the road leading up into the village. He sat up in his turret, waiting.

'They're coming, Johnny,' said Freddie. 'I can hear them.'

The noise grew louder, soon they could all hear it. A grinding, a heavy roar of diesel engines, a rolling of numerous hard tyres, of rotating tracks.

Something poked its head out from the gap where the road cut through the trees, like a ferret sniffing the air. An armoured car: a powerful, fast-moving, eight-wheeled affair. Its turret and gun twitched to and fro. In the clear air Freddie could see its straight-sided black and white crosses. Wireless aerials on its hull whipped back and forth. With a plume of black smoke from its big exhaust, it moved forward. Behind it came dark panzer tanks, five of them, their black-uniformed commanders, in caps and earphones, head and shoulders out of their turrets. Half-tracks and lorries followed in a stream.

The armoured car rolled quickly over the bridge, followed by the tanks, black fumes staining the air.

'Cocky bastards,' Freddie muttered.

He heard the driver of the armoured car change gear, the powerful engine revving as it sent it up the hill into the village.

Hoskins' Cruiser tank fired, at almost point-blank range. The blast of the two-pounder gun blew the barn doors open; hay and fine dust billowed out into the air. The shell hit the armoured car with a huge clang, like a giant beating a saucepan. It smashed it sideways across the road, crashing into a stone wall, and it began to burn.

There was a fraction of a second's silence, just enough for his ears to sing, and then all the waiting weapons of his force burst into life. Through the sudden smoke he saw a young German commander smack back in his turret, lie across its top, half in, half out; saw a track suddenly spew out from under its cover, the heavy vehicle striking the wall of the bridge. A lorry burst into flames, men spilling out across the road in disorder, tumbling and falling under the heavy machine-gun-fire from the windows above him.

The dark panzer tank swayed in the gap it had made in the side of the bridge, propelled by its still-churning single track. One corner dipped and it tumbled over in the air, falling into the water with a huge white splash. In the orchard the two field guns were firing over open sights. Mortar shells burst down in the confusion, grey-uniformed soldiers fell like corn.

The small, deadly killing ground was wreathed in smoke. The short column of vehicles were burning.

'Pull out!' Freddie ordered. The tanks came wheeling from their hides, the lorries dragged the guns once more, the men came tumbling down from their shooting gallery.

'What now, sir?' Hoskins called, his face flushed with the excitement of the short battle.

'Good show, Johnny,' Freddie called. 'That should slow them up a bit.'

He felt a savage satisfaction. The Germans had had it all their own way ever since the shooting war had started, nine days earlier. It had been their turn.

'Where to, sir?'

'Dunkirk,' he said.

The small column, what was left of a regular battalion, hurried away along the empty road, heading for the coast, the sky behind them dirty with smoke.

'*There* you are,' Violet said. She stood on the quay, next to the big white sailing vessel. Behind her the bulk of the castle loomed dark against the fresh sky, in the green lawns the buttercups and speedwell shone yellow and blue. The banks of the water were alive with marsh marigolds and silver white ladies' smock.

'What are you doing? Dr Jennings called, wants to know why you aren't at the hospital.'

Fish paused in his assembly, large wooden-handled screwdriver in hand. He appeared to be fitting some kind of iron bracket to a hatch cover.

'P-putting in the m-mountings,' he said, not very helpfully.

'Mountings for what?' she asked patiently.

'The g-guns, of course. I had Githers the blacksmith make 'em up for me.'

'Where are you going in this vessel that you need guns?'

'Call's gone out,' he said succinctly. 'They want lots of small boats to go over to the French coast, fetch the soldiers back.'

'Is it that bad?' she asked, quietly.

'Complete m-muck up, apparently. The F-Frogs have folded like paper bags and we're going backwards as quick as poss. But not even the British Army can swim the channel.'

'Then I'd better get provisions on board,' she said equably. 'The chaps will be hungry, I expect.'

'Jolly good.'

'I suppose this means you're not going to the hospital for the operation.'

'No . . .'

'You missed it last time.'

'Bring some g-gaspers with you, darling, will you?'

'Dr Jennings said you weren't to smoke any more.'

Fish tightened a last screw and looked at his handiwork with satisfaction. He picked up a Lewis gun from the deck and put it in place.

'I always kn-knew it would come in useful. Yes, well, what did Alexander the Great say, eh? 'I am dying with the help of too many physicians.' You know that fearsome muzzle loader of Uncle's? I'm going to take it. I've always wanted to loose it off in anger. Shake some Jerry's fillings, that will, a quarter-pound of lead coming the other way.'

He reached inside his jacket and brought out a battered silver cigarette case.

'Found this old case you gave me. I've filled it up, but we'll need more. The chaps will be feeling like a gasper when they get on board.'

'You had that on the Somme,' she said quietly.

Fish helped himself to a cigarette and lit it with a gold Dunhill.

'You had that too.'

Fish coughed hideously as the smoke reached his lungs, bending almost double as the spasms racked him. After a few moments he straightened up and dragged in some air.

'That's better.'

'Dr Jennings—'

'Dr Jennings can g-get st-stuffed.'

'Fish,' she said suddenly. 'You're not to die, do you hear me? What am I supposed to do without you?'

The waxy pallor of his cheeks did not lift, but he smiled.

'I always do what you say, Vi, darling,' he said gently.

'Then you'll go in for this operation as soon as we get back?'

'The very minute.'

'All right, then. I'll go and organise the provisions.'

She walked across the lawns back to the castle. When she was out of sight, she took a handkerchief from her pocket and wiped her eyes.

'You're a good-looking woman,' the old man said appreciatively, turning from the window that overlooked the Thames, passing between the Houses of Parliament and the handsome Victorian buildings of Florence Nightingale's St Thomas's opposite.

'They gave me your name,' Lloyd George continued. 'I didn't know what you looked like.'

'Why, thank you, sir,' said Carlotta. She had been advised of the old statesman's continued interest in women, particularly good-looking ones, and had dressed appropriately in a bright spring frock.

'The Duke of Windsor sends his regards,' she said lightly.

'Does he now?' Lloyd George said indifferently. 'Civil of him, I suppose. You've come from him, I take it?'

'The Duke and Duchess have left Paris for the south, to avoid the fighting,' she explained.

He sat down on the chesterfield sofa of his office.

'Here, sit next to me,' he commanded. 'Not often I get the chance to be close to a girl like you these days. Different years ago, of course.'

Carlotta obligingly sat down next to him, and with long habit he put his hand on her knee.

'So what message do you have for me?'

'Chancellor Hitler also sends you his regards,' she said boldly. Lloyd George's eyes bulged slightly, he almost looked over his shoulder to see if anyone was listening.

'Does he, by God!' he said hoarsely. 'Seen him lately too, have you?'

'Both the Duke and I have contacts ...' she said carefully. 'We are able to receive and transmit messages from and to the German authorities.'

'You can, can you?'

'Yes. Chancellor Hitler wished it especially known to you how he still reciprocates your regard for him. He was much honoured when you referred to him after your visit to him – before this conflict – as the greatest living German.'

'I know when I saw him, damn you,' Lloyd George said abruptly, with an irritation born of nerves.

'He himself reveres you as the greatest living British statesman.'

Lloyd George's head, with its mane of white hair went back, his vanity massaged.

'So much wiser than Mr Churchill,' she said carefully.

'Winston is prime minister.'

'For how long?' she murmured, and let the question hang in the air for a few moments. Lloyd George sat staring out of the window in thought, but the hand upon her thigh began to move again.

'The Führer considers this war against Great Britain to be foolish and unnecessary.'

'Let him stop fighting us then!' the old man exclaimed.

'The British Expeditionary Force is in full retreat,' she pointed out. 'Once it is back across the Channel there need be no continued fighting.'

'You don't know Winston,' he said grimly.

'It is precisely because the Führer *does* understand the needlessly aggressive nature of Mr Churchill, his belligerence, his love of war and slaughter, that he is seeking ways to bring this unnecessary conflict to a close. Churchill is a practised liar, an inciter and agitator, a blood-covered dilettante aristocrat.'

Lloyd George's mouth twitched faintly.

'Chancellor Hitler wishes to send a message to the wise men of Britain,' she murmured. 'If Churchill remains in power, then the war will continue. The Führer asks anyone who doubts the power of Germany to look at what his forces have achieved in mere weeks. The destruction of all who oppose him! The occupation of all his enemies in Europe! With what will Churchill make the British people fight when the Expeditionary Force returns beddraggled and without its arms? Their bare hands? All it will lead to is the destruction of the great British Empire – a destruction which has never been the Führer's aim.

'A continuation of this struggle, which Churchill is bent upon, will end only in the complete annihilation of one of the two opponents. It will not be Germany. But by then Churchill will be drunk and in Canada, with the great British people slaughtered in their islands. So this is why the Führer seeks out the men of wisdom in Britain. To stop this stupidity on which Churchill is bent before it is too late.'

'And the Duke of Windsor,' Lloyd George murmured, 'our recent and abdicated King, where does he fit into all this?'

'His brother King George is a stupid man,' she said dismissively. 'He does not appreciate, as the Duke does, the deep similarities of blood and culture between the German and British peoples. He supports the warmonger Churchill.'

Lloyd George eyes widened a little.

'He wants to come back?' he murmured questioningly. 'As King?'

'Head of a government of true national unity,' she suggested, 'not of Churchill's bloodthirsty clique. All that is necessary is for the removal of Churchill and his cronies.'

'Winston has asked me to join his government,' he remarked. Carefully, and with a certain relish, he pulled up the hem of her dress until he could see the tops of her stockings, the milk-white of her thighs. She sat calmly back and let him. Men were pigs – you could lead them about as though they had rings in their noses.

He sighed, and pulled the material back down.

'I wish I was younger,' he said. 'I shall not be joining Winston. I shall wait upon events.'

She smiled pleasantly, got up.

'Please do,' she said cordially. 'For the British, events will only get worse. Hammer blows will soon fall upon the people of Britain and their cities. Then they will look for wise men, to lead them out of their difficulties.'

He showed her to the door courteously, closed it behind her. Then he went back to the window, where London lay smokily in her vastness, under a milky blue sky, and stood staring out once more.

*   *   *

'All right, Ned,' Fish called, from his seat at the wheel of the ship. 'Best take up stations.'

Furzegrove went forward to man the twin Lewis guns, and Violet took down the mainsail. They had come across the Channel under full sail; now they were amongst the darting shipping going into Dunkirk and coming out – destroyers and trawlers and sailing boats and pleasure craft, minelayers and tugs and even riverboats, all loaded to the gunwales with troops, like khaki bees. Fish navigated in on the inboard engine, the diesel thudding away beneath him. He peered through the drifting smoke towards the beaches where men stood patiently, lines of them, thigh deep in the water, for the small boats to come and take them home.

A destroyer came out of the main port entrance, the Gare Maritime, zig-zagging at full power to avoid the bombs of the Stukas queuing up above the town, circling like buzzards, dark and bent-winged, sirens howling as they dived. Smoke swirled over the water, the pom-poms of the ship were blazing away. The water was pock-marked with the splashes of shells falling from the German guns and tanks outside the perimeter.

The destroyer came out and past them at nigh-on thirty knots, its decks thickly covered with men, and they all cheered. They could hear the howling turbines, the roar as they sucked in air. Bombs from a diving Stuka exploded in front of it and steel fragments whined across the water. The ship vanished in the huge cloud of spray, and then they saw it reappear, still going.

Fish, Violet and Ned were all dirty. The smoke was sticky, oily; they had been going to and fro across the Channel for five days. *Parma's Pride* was no longer white, but streaked and stained. Fish peered through the smoke for the stone jetty where they had tied up before.

A fishing vessel, a small crabber, was just casting off, its engine hunting in neutral, decks crammed, and Fish slowed, putting his screw into reverse to allow it room. Its skipper, a small person in blue fisherman's trousers and hair tied up in a scarf suddenly waved furiously.

'Ahoy there!' she shouted. 'Hallo, Vi! Hallo, Fish, Ned!'

It was Felicity.

'I say!' she yelled, as she began to make way. 'What a lark! I haven't had so much fun in ages.'

An artillery shell burst in the water near by, and spray soaked them all. As it cleared they could see the crabber beginning to turn, water swirling white about its stern.

'Silly bastards can't shoot straight!' Felicity yelled.

'Flick, darling!' Violet screamed across the bedlam of noise. 'Come down to the castle when this is all over, we'll have a drink.'

'God, yes,' Felicity shouted. 'Let's get completely squiffy.'

She vanished in the smoke and spray, and Fish manoeuvred up to the narrow stone finger pointing out into the sea. A line of men were marching up. They were very dirty indeed. From their black berets they were tankers.

'I say,' their leader said, 'you don't know how glad we are to see you. Hoskins. Lieutenant Hoskins.'

'Hop aboard, Lieutenant Hoskins,' Violet said hospitably.

The young officer turned to the men. 'All aboard, chaps,' he said.

'Wh-where are your tanks?' Fish enquired, as the ship began to rock with the arrival of the men.

'Out there, sir, out there,' the officer said wearily. 'We were the rearguard.'

'Have a gasper,' Fish suggested. 'You don't know my brother-in-law, Colonel Freddie de Clare, do you?'

'My commanding officer, sir! He ... stayed back to command resistance in Calais. I haven't seen him since.'

The last men piled on board.

'Cast off!'

'Hold on, darling,' Vi said quickly. 'Somebody's coming.' Through the smoke she had seen a lone figure running along the narrow jetty. He came up alongside, panting, a red-cross armband about his sleeve.

'H-hop on.'

'Are you coming back?' the young doctor asked anxiously. 'I've got some wounded men up there. The Germans are beginning to push through the perimeter. If you're coming back I'll get them down here ready for you.'

'We'll b-be back,' Fish assured him. 'Have them here. If you're still here we'll take you off.'

'Wonderful,' he said in relief. 'I'll be here.'

Fish put the screw in gear, foam hissed at his stern. He manoeuvred out into the smoke, fumbling in his battered cigarette case, pulling one out with his lips. He lit it. From the bow the twin Lewis guns hammered at a diving Stuka. Fish coughed hideously as the smoke dragged at his lungs. Water boiled alongside as the bomb exploded, metal fragments whined through the air. On the packed deck, nobody moved. They were all asleep.

The engine thudded, he headed for the open sea.

'Sail up, darling!' he called. The stained white canvas bloomed in the breeze, they emerged into the clean fresh air, heading for home.

The tall, handsome man standing with Carlotta stared in a disgruntled manner down the beautifully mown lawn. From beyond the high wall in the distance came but the faintest hum of traffic going about Hyde Park Corner. A large wall of sandbags had been built across the lawn. In front of it stood, life-size and realistic, but painted upon cardboard, a German soldier in coal-scuttle helmet and rifle. Some small bullet-holes marred his snarl.

'My brother and Elizabeth come down here every morning and practise revolver shooting,' he said contemptuously.

'The King and Queen?'

'Yes. They say if the Germans invade they will stay here and start firing when they see the first one coming up the Mall. Ridiculous.'

'I heard that the Queen said the children were staying with her, she with the King and he wasn't going anywhere,' Carlotta said. 'It's a good line. But you know it means she and the King are for the war.'

'Fools, the pair of them,' Prince George, Duke of Kent and the King's brother said irritably. 'How many times does one have to say it, we have no quarrel with Hitler's Germany. What we need is a bit more of it over here.'

He glanced over his shoulder.

'Not that one's supposed to say that sort of thing just now. Not with that windbag Churchill making these provocative speeches and whipping everyone up.'

Carlotta pursed her lips. 'Things might change,' she suggested. 'The news is all bad, you know. They may sling Churchill out yet. I heard he got a very poor reception in the House of Commons the other day.'

'They don't trust him!' Prince George cried. 'He's done nothing but betray the Tory Party for years. And here he is, in charge!'

'As I say,' Carlotta said smoothly, 'things might change. You and I and your brother the Duke of Windsor aren't the only ones who see that this war is senseless. We should be partners with the Germans, not enemies. The Führer wants peace, you know, he's bending over backwards to be reasonable to the British. It's just that bloodthirsty swine Churchill who stands in the way. Get rid of him and . . .'

Prince George twisted the gold ring on his little finger, looking about the beautiful gardens of the palace.

'Who else?' he murmured.

'Lots,' Carlotta said quickly, eagerly. 'I've been sounding out a lot of people who matter. Of course we have the stalwarts like Mosley – all the fascists, of course – there's Admiral Domville, Captain Ramsay the MP, General Fuller . . .'

'Anyone else?'

'I think I've got Lloyd George,' she said quietly, significantly. 'The Führer wants men he respects in charge of the European countries – he wants Marshal Petain to be in charge of France, you know.'

'*Does* he?' the Prince said eagerly.

'Yes. He admires Lloyd George greatly, you know. He'd be very happy to have him lead Britain.'

The Prince looked up at the great bulk of the palace and his face became sour.

'*He* won't,' he said. 'Nor will she. Plodding John Bulls the pair of them.'

'Well yes,' she murmured, 'which is why your brother Edward is standing by. He wants your help, of course. The two of you, shoulder to shoulder. The King, your brother, he has no charisma, not like you two. You and he, and Lloyd George, on the balcony of the Palace, announcing peace with honour!'

His eyes glittered. 'What needs to be done?' he asked softly.

'A *coup*.' she said quickly. 'Churchill needs to be taken out. What happens to him isn't important. Shoot him, whatever. Mosley's fascists could do it. Like that. The country is in chaos as it is. Round up the old lot – Chamberlain, Halifax, Beaverbrook, all of them. Proclaim a government of national unity, headed by Lloyd George, to make peace with honour. The Führer will deliver his side of the bargain, I assure you.'

Prince George licked his lips, nervously.

'I can't come out publicly, you know that,' he said. 'But if it happened . . .'

'We can count on you?' she asked quickly. His eyes flickered about the garden, as though seeking out spies, and then he nodded.

'Now, look,' he said, quickly moving on. 'Want to see something special?'

'Sure,' she said amiably. They went towards the palace.

'A mutual friend is here,' he explained. 'Someone we both know. Godfrey de Clare.'

'Godfrey? I haven't seen him in ages.'

'I mentioned you were coming to see me. He said to bring you down.'

'Down?'

'He's one of our foremost art historians, you know. He's cataloguing the pictures in the vaults for the King. My brother is shipping them all out to some caves in Wales for safety,' he said disapprovingly. 'Keeping this war going, you see.'

As they went into the Palace he turned to her.

'Did you, ah . . .'

Out of sight, she opened her handbag and took out a package, slipping it into his hand. In a twinkling, it was gone.

'Thanks awfully,' he murmured. 'You've got no idea how difficult it's become . . . this wretched war has interrupted everything.'

'You can count on me,' she said. 'I know I can count on you.'

They came to a door where a liveried servant stood.

'This is the Yeoman of the Silver Plate,' Prince George explained. 'Take us down, please.'

The man produced a key from his waistcoat, opened the door and let them in. He locked it behind him and took them down some stairs. At the bottom was a metal grille. This too had to be opened, and then relocked behind them. On the other side was an ordinary industrial lift. They got in, and it took them further below ground. When it halted the Yeoman opened the trellis of the lift door.

'We'll ring when you're to let us out,' said Prince George. The lift hissed as it rose up again, and Prince George smiled mischievously at her.

'Here it is.'

She looked around her. A huge room was divided up by racks of shelving. Tarpaulins lumpily covered what was beneath. She lifted one.

A jewelled scabbard encased the blade of an ornamental sword, fully three feet long, chased with gold. A small zoo of Fabergé animals pinked diamond and ruby eyes at her in the light of the bare bulbs hanging down from the ceiling. Ivory decorated with jewels and gold lay in piles. He twitched the tarpaulin and it was covered.

'You have no idea how much of this stuff there is,' he said casually. He dropped his voice. 'Here. Can you get me more of that lovely powder?'

'Of course.'

'Have a look round while I have a word with Godfrey,' he murmured. 'Help yourself to a ring or something. There's loads about. Nothing too large. I'll take it out for you. You'll be searched, I won't.'

'All right,' she said, pleased.

'Back in a moment,' he said, moving quickly away. She saw his hand dip into his pocket for the packet she had given him and she smiled cruelly.

She found something she wanted quickly, lying with others on a shelf, rings and necklaces scattered haphazardly about. She took a beautiful ring, a huge diamond surrounded by fabulous emeralds, all set in gold, and slipped it in her pocket. She looked about her in awe: the place was simply stuffed with shelves, all of them piled high. The wealth was incalculable. She began to wander about over the floor of coarse carpet. Near a doorway, she heard the murmur of voices. Always curious, she peeked through by the hinges, where it was just ajar.

Prince George dipped a little spoon into the cocaine, and held it up to his nostril, snuffling it up eagerly. Godfrey stood watching him, an open catalogue on the table. He seemed slightly amused. The Prince's handsome face suddenly flushed pink, his eyes glistened and he smiled happily. He wrapped up the packet, putting it back into his pocket. He spoke quickly, his teeth flashing in a smile.

'Where is she?' murmured Godfrey.

'I let her have a trinket,' he said. 'Come on! Quickly, before it goes.'

She saw the front of his trousers bulging. He dropped to his knees, undoing Godfrey's fly buttons, taking him in his mouth. In only a few more seconds Godfrey pushed him face forward over the table, and she saw the Prince gasp with joy as he buggered him.

Moving quietly, she slipped away, stood casually admiring an entire row of golden chiming clocks standing silent under their sheeting by the wall. A minute or two later she heard the sound of voices. Godfrey and the Prince were threading their way through the maze of shelving towards her.

'Carlotta!' Godfrey cried cheerfully. 'How splendid to see you, George told me you were coming.'

'It's lovely to see you, Godfrey,' she agreed, smiling. 'This surely is an impressive place.'

'You won't find a greater accumulation of fine art and jewellery under one roof anywhere in the world,' he confirmed. He glanced at his watch.

'I think I've put in my eight hours,' he said. 'Do you want to come to a party with me? As soon as I heard you'd be here, I said, Carlotta *must* come to the party. Yes? Wonderful. Let's go upstairs and have a couple of scoops to get us in the mood.'

He smiled dazzlingly at her.

'There's somebody there who's dying to meet you,' he said.

The streets were very dark in the blackout; the hooded lamps of Godfrey's car hardly lit up anything beyond a dull yellow glow in front of them. She was quite lost, had no idea where she was. He stopped, wound down his window, talked briefly to somebody she could not see outside, drove on a short way and stopped.

'Here we are,' he said brightly. 'Let's go to the party, shall we?'

She got out. There seemed to be some kind of great building looming in the darkness. He took her arm, steered her, a door opened yellow in the gloom.

'Here we go,' he said. 'After you.'

She was in a windowless brick corridor, painted a dingy cream. Worn Victorian brown tiles were under her feet.

'What is this place, Godfrey?' she asked. 'Is it a college or something?'

'That's it,' he agreed. 'We're going to a sort of graduation party.'

'You'd think they'd have it somewhere nicer than this,' she complained. The place was making her nervous, for some reason.

'Oh, yes. I think they would,' he said enigmatically. They went up an equally gloomy stairway, smelling of ancient cabbage and potato. She turned, suddenly.

'Look, Godfrey, I don't think I've got time to—'

He urged her on, very much taller than she was.

'Oh, but you've been specially invited,' he said, smiling. 'You really can't leave, not now.'

He stopped outside a dark brown door. The varnish was bubbling.

'We're here,' he said, and opened it. He gave her a small push, she stumbled inside. It was a strange, horrid room. Stone flags, an unpleasant smell. A pit in the floor.

'Don't fall in the hole, will you?' he said from behind her. She turned to leave, to run from this place of danger, but he had her by the elbow. She was aware that he was very much stronger than she was.

'Stand here,' he ordered, and would not release his grip.

Feet suddenly crashed on the ceiling, she looked up in alarm. Bare wood rafters, the light shining through the gaps, people moving, roughly, quickly. A hoarse voice suddenly shouting out in terror. Brief, short hard words of command. A horrid gargling. Godfrey had her by both arms, forcing her to stand at the edge of the hole.

Suddenly, a terrible crash from above, and part of the ceiling fell in. A man fell through it. A rope was about his neck. She saw his face, contorted in terror, and then the rope snapped taut. He hung in front of her, stopping with a hideous jerk, a cracking of bone, the harsh hemp of the rope deep in his neck, his feet dangling in the pit, his hands lashed behind his back. A foul, dreadful stench of sudden death swamped her; his staring, open, terrified eyes stared into hers, inches away, and she screamed, and screamed.

Somebody slapped her. Smacked her viciously across one cheek, and then the other.

'Shut up, you bitch,' George de Clare said coldly. She cringed away from him in sudden fear, stumbled against the hanging man, whimpered in horror. A face appeared in the square gap of the trapdoor.

'You all right down there, Mr de Clare?' it enquired. 'If I let out the slack perhaps you'd lay 'is body flat.'

'Take his feet,' George ordered Carlotta, as Godfrey stood by the taut rope. She was frightened, very afraid indeed – she bent and did as she was bid. His feet were bare, the dead man's, bare and warm to the touch, but lifeless, unmoving. Above her the hangman let out slack, the man slowly folded along the flags.

'Up the stairs,' George snarled. He hustled her outside, almost at a run. She lost a shoe, started to protest, but he simply ignored her, dragged her upstairs like so much baggage. She found herself thrust into a room. The hangman was closing the trap, resetting the operating lever. He smiled.

'This the lady, Mr de Clare, sir?'

'This is the one,' George said.

The executioner stood looking at her for a moment, with almost cheerful eyes set in a ruddy face, clasping his capable square hands together. He looked like a village butcher accepting a side of beef from the supplier.

'About eight stones, I'd say,' he said. 'Here, Miss, step on the scales a moment for me, will you?'

In the corner of the room stood some broad butcher's scales, Victorian cast iron, red and green, with the maker's name on. She found herself standing on them as he expertly moved the weights in the bar.

'What's going on?' she shrieked hysterically.

'Length of rope, Miss. Varies with the weight,' he said knowledgeably. 'If we hang you with too much rope your head comes off. Makes a nasty mess down there. Too short and you strangles, see?'

'You can't do this!' she yelled. 'I'm an American citizen. I've done nothing.'

George jerked her off the scales, shoved her back against the wall so that her head banged on the brick. He was dressed in his old, unfashionable dinner suit. A black silk bow-tie was about his neck.

'You're a spy,' he said. 'A German spy. We can do anything we want to you, and we're going to hang you.'

He turned his head. The hangman was methodically measuring out a fresh length of hemp. At one end of it was the noose, already tied.

From the room below she could hear voices, rough men dragging the body out. One made a joke, they all laughed.

'Jolly good,' said George. 'When you're ready, then.'

He turned to Carlotta with indifferent eyes. Godfrey had come in, and was lounging against the wall as though attending a poor show in a gallery.

'Godfrey . . .' she wailed, entreatingly.

'Godfrey's taken on a second job,' George said. 'He's in intelligence, with me.'

Godfrey smiled at her, his eyes icy cold.

'We rounded them all up,' he said. 'Mosley and the others. All the fascist sympathisers. Domville, Captain Ramsay. All the ones you've been talking to.'

Her mind driven by desperate panic, as the hideous executioner carefully laid out his rope along the steelyard, she found what she was looking for.

'What about the Duke?' she blurted.

'Duke?' George enquired. 'Which Duke?'

The white cliffs stretched out into the distance, white in the late afternoon sun. The castle stood high above the crowded port, seething with troops, policemen, nurses finding and tending the wounded, NAAFI ladies serving tea and lemonade, with ambulances, with redcaps directing files of soldiers towards the station where the steam engines of the Southern Railway waited with their red carriages to haul them up through Kent. Fish brought *Parma's Pride* into the crowded quay under the directions of the naval sub-lieutenant waiting there, and they tied up.

Lieutenant Hoskins' soldiers stirred themselves, clambered off, formed up under the command of the small, tough sergeant-major, and shouted their thanks.

'That's it, sir,' the sub-lieutenant called. 'We're halting the evacuation; word from the others side is that the Germans are pushing into the town.'

'How many have come home?' Violet asked quickly.

'Over a quarter of a million of our own,' the young man said proudly. 'Plenty of French, too.'

'Just as well,' Fish said quietly. 'Or we'd have had no troops to fight with.'

'You don't know how well you did, sir, you chaps in the little boats.'

'Well, yes, but there's a ch-chap still waiting for us, over there,' Fish objected to the naval officer. 'With some wounded.'

'Sorry, sir. Orders are for it to be stopped today. Last boats went out three hours ago.'

'I s-see.' Fish turned to Violet. 'Darling, what about a c-cuppa, eh? Go and see if one of those nice NAAFI ladies will give us some. Ned, go and help her ladyship.'

Violet walked down the quay with Furzegrove. Her legs felt as though they were made from indiarubber.

'Are you tired, Ned? I am. I think I shall go home and sleep for a week.'

'The Earl, he looks none too well, Lady Violet.'

'He's got to go into hospital for this operation on his lung. Where he was bayoneted. He keeps putting it off.'

She paused, stopped in the middle of the crowded quay.

'Fish—' she said anxiously. She turned, began to push her way back, went towards the edge so that she could see.

In the harbour, the dirty, streaked shape of *Parma's Pride* was turning, making its way through the crowded waters towards the open sea, a streak of oily smoke coming from its exhaust, Fish bent over the wheel.

'*Fish*!' she screamed. 'Fish, you stubborn goat! Come back here this minute!'

Fish turned, straightened briefly as he waved – they saw him smile, then he moved forward. They saw the big main sail rise, fill with air, and pull the ship towards France.

They were waiting patiently, on stretchers, sitting on the jetty patched white and red with field dressings, when they saw the cutter pulling in through the oily smoke drifting from the burning town. They raised a ragged cheer. Fish laid up alongside, the engine hunting in neutral, and they began to limp, totter and drag themselves aboard.

'I didn't think you were coming,' the doctor said, in manifest relief. 'There's Germans up there in the town.'

'I th-think I'm about the last,' Fish admitted. 'I didn't see anyone else on the way over.'

'Where's your crew?'

Fish put the ship into gear, the jetty began to recede, and he turned the wheel.

'Making tea,' he said. 'They'll have tea waiting for us when we get back.'

The young battalion MO started to move among his patients, and Fish went forward to raise the sail. The pall of stinking smoke slipped behind them like a bank of evil fog, and they emerged into the fresh air. As they left the coast behind them the sail caught the wind, and they began to crash along through the waves at speed.

Fish was not the first to see it. A sharp-eyed corporal with a bound leg spotted the lean, dark shape knifing through the patchy cumulus, an aerial shark. It dipped a wing, turning.

'Ere!' he yelled in alarm. 'Jerry fighter up there, guv.'

Fish tied the wheel, and went as quickly as he could forward, where the twin Lewis guns hung on their mounting. On a pair of hooks by the coaming was the huge muzzle-loading elephant gun, still unused, but loaded.

He could hear the rising snarl of the twin engines, saw the sun flash on its wings as it left the clouds, straightening up on its run in. He put his shoulder to the wood butt, felt it warm from the sunlight, pulled the cocking lever back.

At about four hundred yards the hurtling bomber half-filled the ring sight, and he opened up, seeing scarlet tracer spitting away from him. The guns hammered, spilling golden cases into the sunlight. The aeroplane raced in, dark green; he could see the pilot inside the glass of his canopy, leaning forward.

Two black objects fell from beneath it, and it passed over the yacht with a ripping, tearing roar. The whole ocean suddenly boiled beneath the ship, white hot nails slashed Fish across the back.

He was on his hands and knees, looking down at the deck. Somewhere close by, a man was swearing, in short, Anglo-Saxon words. Blood was bubbling hot in his mouth. He looked up, half a mile away over the sea the German bomber was turning to come back. The boom swayed to and fro, slack, and then slammed forward under the wind, the sail filling again with air.

The elephant gun was in front of him. He pulled it from its bracket, resting the weight on his knees. He had the packet of percussion caps in his pocket. Quite casually, still watching the turning aircraft, he fitted the little shiny brass top, and pulled the hammer all the way back. Blood was filling his mouth, he spat it out in a gout of scarlet.

The bomber was returning on a second run. He propped an elbow against his knee and drew the weapon into his left shoulder. A vision came into his mind of pheasants, long ago, and he smiled to himself.

He could see the pilot clear: a young man, sitting crouched in his greenhouse, between his shining, whirling propeller blades.

He led the target, just a little, settling the foresight into the notch, and he squeezed the trigger. The huge rifle exploded with a massive roar, belching flame and smoke, and Fish's hunter eyes saw the glass shatter, the huge sudden blossom of blood as the pilot's chest was torn asunder. The bomber jerked, went overhead screaming like a dragon. He heard it crash into the sea in a crump and sizzle, and then it was quiet; just the rhythmic slap of the water running under the hull, and the same man nearby, cursing.

'You got him,' a voice said in disbelief. It was the doctor, feeling with quick fingers about his chest. 'You're hit.'

It was warm, in the sun.

'Wh-what about a gasper?' he suggested.

'I can't do anything on board. We must get you to a hospital.'

'G-got an app-pointment already booked, old man,' Fish said helpfully. 'Dr Jennings, what? You know how to sail?'

'No, no I don't.'

'Aim for the wh-white cliffs, dear chap. Run her up on the beach.'

'All right.'

Fish managed to bring his battered cigarette case out. It seemed very heavy to him. With difficulty, he put a cigarette in his mouth.

'Remind Gawaine that the buggers will come out of the sun,' he said clearly. 'And send my love.'

He lit the cigarette with bloody fingers.

He looked up at the young man with eyes as bright as a candle's last flame.

'I'm not to be buried at sea,' he ordered. 'I'm the Earl, I have to be with the rest.'

Very faintly, in the haze, he saw a glimmer of white where the sea met the land.

'Tell Vi that I love her,' he said. 'But she knows that already.'

48

New Jerusalem

London, July 1940

The door on the other side of the little office opened. She blinked, she had been far away. A portly figure wreathed in cigar smoke stood there.

'My dear Lady Windstone,' Churchill said, 'I have kept you waiting. I am so sorry. These are busy times, I have twice sent messages to the palace to say I shall be late to see the King, and now Lord Halifax has gone in my stead. Pray do come in.'

She found herself inside, clutching a glass of whisky. A small garden was visible through the window, the roses shining from the afternoon rain. The room seemed in some state of disorganisation, as though removal men were half-way through their work. A large Victorian map of the world with the Empire marked in pink hung on one wall.

'Mr Chamberlain and his wife have not long left,' he explained. 'I have moved from the Admiralty.'

He picked up a report from the desk, scowled at it, put it down.

'Edward, our former king,' he said. 'He is scuttling about southern Europe with that American woman of his. He is not behaving very sensibly, he keeps bad company.'

'He's a Nazi sympathiser,' Violet said frankly. 'Always was. We're much better off with his brother.'

Churchill winced.

'Let us say . . . he is misguided. He does not seem to realise what harm he can do us by his actions.'

'Perhaps he does,' Violet said levelly. 'Mrs Simpson certainly hates us.'

Churchill glanced sideways at her, then chewed his cigar ferociously.

'How do you find the people?' he demanded. 'Are they of good heart now that we are entirely alone?'

'I feel we are in some ways like a rather large and quarrelsome family, faced by a death in the house, and reunited by it.'

'Good, good,' he grunted.

'You've made my mother frightfully happy,' she said.

'I have?'

'Oh, yes. That appeal Mr Eden made for the Local Defence Volunteers on the radio.'

'I am thinking of naming them the Home Guard,' he said enthusiastically.

'Oh, yes. Very good. Well anyway, she and daddy had been niggling at each other as they do – she finds him a bit trying about the house all day – but when he heard Mr Eden he was off down to the police station to volunteer before he'd finished speaking! He's as pleased as a dog with two tails; they've made him a full lieutenant and given him a whole squad of other old boys. Now he's got plenty to do. Mother's delighted. If my brother Freddie will just get home everything will be perfect.'

'Where is your brother?'

'Well, he *was* in Calais, shooting at the Germans. He's a prisoner of war, but we don't expect him to remain one for long.'

'You are clearly a most enterprising family! How old is your father?'

'Eighty-two. He told them he was sixty-nine.'

'And what did he do, before he got on your mother's nerves?'

'Oh, he was a major-general in the Sappers.'

'Splendid! With such men on our side how can we do else than prevail! What is it, then, my dear Lady Windstone, that I can do for you?'

'We . . . have buried my husband, the Earl.' Again, she felt the tears prickle behind her eyes. She forced herself to keep her voice steady.

'He was a great patriot. We miss him. He spoke, many times in my support. In my darkest hour, you know, when I stood up in the House after Munich, I told them that it was no victory, that we had sustained a total and unmitigated defeat, that it was but the first sip of a bitter cup that would be proffered to us by Herr Hitler year by year. How they reviled me then, all my fellow members, so much so they began the process of removing me from the party, from my seat in Epping, and your husband the next day put on all his medals, which were very many, and included the cross of Queen Victoria, and went to the Lords and spoke in my defence, and none of them could say him nay, for he was who he was. I miss him dreadfully.'

'I . . . cannot go back to the castle, just yet. My son Gawaine has

just joined his squadron. My husband rests with his ancestors. I want
. . . I must have something to do. Something to help. Anything.'

Churchill took a pull at his large but weak whisky and soda.

'You are a de Clare,' he murmured. 'You come from a great
family of warriors and statesmen. I have commanded that a most
secret organisation be set up. Its task shall be to keep the flame of
resistance alive in Europe now that the evil forces of Nazism have
brought darkness to cover their lands. It shall bring hope to those
people, from we people here in our free islands, and one day it will
set Europe ablaze. Would this work interest you?'

'Yes,' she said. 'Very much.'

'I'll tell Colville,' he said. 'I can hear him creaking the floorboards
outside to let me know I must see Mr Cripps before he goes to
Moscow.'

A tall, handsome young man was outside.

'John,' Churchill grunted. 'Lady Windstone is going to help with
Special Operations. See to it.'

'Yes, sir.'

'My dear,' Churchill said warmly, 'you may ask to see me whenever
you wish.'

Then he was gone, and Colville smiled pleasantly and respectfully.

'If you're on board, you wouldn't help, would you?'

'Of course.'

'I have a de Clare waiting to see somebody. Perceval de Clare. No
relation?'

'My cousin. He calls himself Percy Clare and goes about pretending
to be one of the proletariat.'

'That's him,' Colville said in relief. 'You wouldn't see what he
wants, would you? Mr Attlee said he could come and talk to somebody about reconstruction but we're all rather busy fighting the
war.'

'Delighted,' she said. 'Show me to him.'

They found Perceval in a small room on the ground floor, clutching
a sheaf of papers.

'At last!' he cried, jumping up. 'Violet, what are you doing here?'

'I am helping the prime minister,' she said. 'He asked if I would
see you, as he is busy with other matters.'

'Well, few things matter as much as this,' he said enthusiastically.
'Let me tell you.'

Violet sat down at the oblong oak table that was against the wall
and lit a cigarette.

'Why don't you do that?' she suggested. Through the window she could see a little of the green of the park. She thought she might walk through it when she left.

'New Jerusalem!' he said, so fervently that she jerked her gaze away from the trees.

'What's that?'

'What we're fighting for,' he said intensely.

'I don't know about you, Perceval, but I'm fighting to avoid having Mr Hitler and his cronies marching down the street outside. What are *you* fighting for?'

'A world without want! A world free from prejudice of class, free of greed and exploitation, a world of Christian community, a world that cares for its citizens, shares equally, fairly between all—'

'You get that when you die, if you've been good,' she said drily. 'It's called Heaven.'

'We can have it here on earth. Here, in this Britain. In fact, we are starting to plan for it, now.'

'We are? Who is?'

'Me, and people like me.'

'You and people like you campaigned for world peace and disarmament, so successfully that Herr Hitler and the Nazis have gulped up all Europe and we are in the middle of a most desperate war,' she said acidly. 'Do we really want to trust you with plans for a new world once we have won it?'

He flushed red. 'I don't think that's a fair thing to say at all.'

'Get on with telling me what demented piffle you have come up with this time,' she said bitterly. 'If you must. I'm the only one here you've got who'll listen to you.'

'We shall make them all listen, before we are through,' he said determinedly. 'You see if we don't.'

'Who will?'

'We will. Those of us who believe in a New Jerusalem, a new society where there will be no poverty, full employment, where the citizen will feel the beneficent care of the state about him from cradle to grave, where men will work hard for the good of all, in new, garden city communities, where—'

'You're cracked, Perceval.'

'Am I?' he retorted furiously. 'Is Archbishop Temple cracked? Harold Laski? Mr Carr? Sir Richard Ackland? Dorothy Sayers? Yes, and Mr Attlee himself? Mr Butler? George Bernard Shaw? Kingsley Martin and Victor Gollancz?'

'The old gang,' she said. 'The stage army of the good. The ones who saw to it we couldn't stand up to Hitler before it was too late. The ones who grovel before a little stone god of Lenin. Listen, Perceval, if you want to do something useful in this war why don't you join the Home Guard, or become an air-raid warden?'

He stood up, and clutched his papers to him importantly.

'Nothing,' he said pompously, 'is more important than the reconstruction of our society. And please don't call me Perceval. The world to come is classless, and I am Percy Clare.'

Violet got up, stubbing her cigarette out.

'I am the Duchess of Windstone, and I have to go and fight,' she said. 'So each to his or her own.'

'You will see me again,' he warned. 'And next time I shall come at the head of a host, all demanding their natural rights.'

'You're full of wind, Perceval,' she said, and they went out. 'You always were.'

She changed her mind about walking through the park. It was disfigured with zig-zag trenches. They were all six inches deep in water, with crumbling edges. She went out into Downing Street and to Whitehall. In the middle of the great boulevard the Cenotaph stood, commemorating the dead of the Great War. As they passed, men quietly doffed their hats on their way, in respect.

Takes It With Him Wherever He Goes

Biggin Hill

Gawaine de Clare undid his harness and clambered out of the little cockpit, jumping down to the ground, clumsy and heavy in his flying boots and Sidcot. He took off his gloves, and for a moment ran his hand over the aluminium of the wing. Although the day was hot it was cold, smooth and cold. Up there, the air was chill.

'Happy?' asked a voice, pleasantly.

He turned; Hedges, the squadron commander was smiling at him.

'Smashing job, sir,' he said enthusiastically.

A Fordson tractor arrived at the concrete bay towing a petrol bowser. An airman climbed down and began to unreel his hose.

'This is Corporal Wilson,' said Hedges. 'He's bowser king around here. Wilson, this is Pilot Officer de Clare. He's just joined us.'

'Sir.'

A small engine on the tank began to thud and the air was suddenly fragrant with the 100-octane fuel gushing into the tank.

'Let's go over to the Mess and I'll buy you a beer,' suggested Hedges. His uniform was clean but old, and well-fitting, with a short medal bar that included the DFC on his shoulder. The award was bright, and new.

'Thank you, sir.'

Hedges glanced across at his new pilot. Gawaine had grown a moustache, a blond handle-bar. Hedges thought it made him look about twelve. He smiled ironically to himself and said nothing.

'We're front line,' he said pleasantly. 'You do your job here properly you call me boss, skipper or Harry. Save the "sir" bullshit.'

'All right, boss,' Gawaine agreed. 'What do I get called if I don't?'

'Dust to dust and ashes to ashes,' Hedges said, and the young man laughed. They walked across the grass, away from the line of cold, primed Spitfires sitting with their noses in the air.

'We took some losses over Dunkirk,' Hedges told him. 'They sent us north to refit, but now we're back. You're the first of our replacement pilots – we're still a little understrength. How did you find the Spitty?'

'Wizard. Absolutely wizard,' he said reverently.

'Yes, she's lovely, isn't she? Anything you found strange?'

'Not feeling the wind on my cheek.'

'Yes, I saw your log book. You're a glider man. Loads of glider hours.'

'My dad bought me one when I was ten.'

'Did he now? What flying club did you belong to?'

'Well, I – er – didn't really. My dad was the Earl of Windstone. We owned all the land about.'

'Oh . . . he was the Earl?'

'Yes. He was killed near Dunkirk. Got bombed in his boat, picking up soldiers.'

'Oh, I'm sorry. Who's the Earl now?'

'I am.'

Hedges looked amused. 'Do people call *you* sir?'

'No, boss,' Gawaine said determinedly. 'They call me Pilot Officer de Clare.'

'Fair enough,' Hedges agreed with a chuckle. 'All right. I liked your approach. You got a good report from Cranwell. Let's go up this afternoon and have a picnic somewhere over the trees.'

'Love to, boss.'

'They tell you anything about combat?'

From over at the butts there came a noise like some giant ripping a sheet of calico.

'We practised against each other.'

'Good. Remember, don't fly straight and level. Keep your head moving. use your mirror. If you see a spinner it's time to chuck it all over the shop. Frankly, to begin with I'll be happy to see you go up with us and come back safe. But if you see a sitter then blast away. Get close. Forget long-range marksmanship. Get bloody close, stuff your nose into his cockpit and let him have it.'

They came up to the Mess, a long wooden hut. Outside a group of young men dressed in eclectic style lounged about on chairs and old sofas dragged from inside the hut. They sat playing draughts, reading, looking up at the sky, smoking, throwing darts at an old board.

'This is Gawaine de Clare, chaps,' Hedges called. 'Our first replacement.'

They looked up at him with interest, called out their names, asked him about Cranwell. A lanky young man in flying boots and a dirty white cableknit sweater stuffed a battered paperback into his boot and got up, smiling welcomingly.

'Morton,' he said. 'Frank Morton. I'll buy you a beer.'

A head poked itself out of a window holding a telephone receiver. 'Group, boss,' it said.

Hedges took it. Gawaine was suddenly aware that all the pilots had stopped what they were doing, were frozen as they stood, listening. Hedges said a few words into the receiver and handed it back.

'Stand by,' he said. There was a shifting about, a gathering of gloves and helmets. Hedges fumbled in his pockets for a packet of cigarettes, produced a battered pack of Navy Cut.

'What's up, boss?' the lanky Morton asked.

'Big formation showing up on the plot over the Pas de Calais. Looks like this is it.'

He turned to Gawaine.

'Smoke?'

'No thanks, I don't.'

'We've been waiting for the next phase,' Hedges explained. 'They can't invade without air superiority. They can't have air superiority without getting rid of us.' He gestured at the group of waiting young men crouched about on the battered sofas and chairs.

'I'm sorry,' he said. 'Your picnic will have to be the real thing. Feel up to it?'

'Yes, sir – boss.'

'Good show. You can be my wing man. Stick to me like glue.'

Hedges lit his cigarette. Above his head the tannoy suddenly sounded.

'Scramble! Scramble!'

Cigarettes flew in the air. A short flight sergeant came out of the flight hut like a jack in the box.

'Start up!'

Men were running. Gawaine found himself among them, dashing over the grass. He could smell it, sweetly crushed by the pounding boots. The Spitfires were booming into life, one after the other.

Where was his? There. Yes, that was his. An erk was in the seat. As he ran up he could see him, as if in slow motion, pushing the cocks down, stick back, mags on, pressing the button. He came pounding up behind the wing; there was an LACW waiting, a young aircraftwoman wearing an overall held in by a length of string, she was smiling at him, waiting.

The erk had pressed the button, the big propeller turned, jerked, caught life with a noise like thunder and blurred. The exhausts vomited long blue flames enveloped in black smoke and the whole aircraft began to vibrate like a boiler under pressure.

As Gawaine scrambled up one side the aircraftsman was scrambling out the other. The LACW was strapping him in, he plugged in his helmet and voices were sounding in his ears. A smiling face, she grinned cheerfully at him.

'Good luck, sir!'

Machines from the flights were turning, bumping out of the flight line, rolling over the grass to their take off positions.

There. There was Hedges, passing him, he could see the big white numbers, 509. He waved the chocks away, the aircraftwoman jumped down and out of the way, he fed in some throttle, opened his radiator wide against overheating, and followed, in the huge din of the squadron moving out to fight.

Hedges was in his place at the head of the vic. Gawaine saw him glance round, checking they were ready; he gave the signal, opened the throttle. Behind him the other eleven were moving, rolling, tails lifting, the huge swelling bellow of the engines beating across the grass to hammer against the huts and hangars, wheels lifting from the grass, bumping, rising up, the legs tucking up into the mainplanes. The ground crews stood watching, hands on hips, eyes narrowed against the sun, their part done, dotted about by their bowsers and trolley-accs and the fighters having their fifty-hour inspections, ears deafened by the noise, which slowly died away and wings glinted in the light as they turned on course, vanishing into the blue.

Gawaine held formation in the tight vic as they climbed. They were all at full throttle.

The radio-telephone had been quiet for a minute or two. Now he heard the voice of the controller behind them, down on the ground at Group, watching his radar plot.

'*Hallo, Green Leader. Bandits angels fourteen crossing the coast over Dover. Vector one four five. Buster.*'

Hedges' voice crackled briefly in his ears. '*Green leader here. Vector one four five. Buster.*'

The formation altered to the new course, but kept their throttles wide open. Gawaine performed a quick check of his instruments: altimeter, rising steadily; artificial horizon, wings level; nose high; air-speed, pegged on one hundred and eighty knots; oil and cylinder-head temperature, pressure gauges, heading, warning lights. He checked his mirror, to reinforce the habit. He could see a lone Spitfire there: arse-end Charlie, guarding the rear.

There. There was the coast in the distance below. The sea shone gold. The ground was green and grey and wrinkled, unmoving.

'*Hallo, Green leader. Bandits coming up, one o'clock below.*'

He saw them. With a sudden rush of adrenalin into his stomach he saw them about four miles away, a big block of aircraft, bombers and fighters, punching its way inland, a swarm of insects.

Hedges held his course, crossing the sun, making it swing round to come behind them.

'*All right, chaps. Formation attack.*'

His wing tilted, the vic dived upon them. Gawaine released the safety catch with his thumb, switched on his sight and in its glow the enemy aircraft grew bigger.

He could see a few fighters peeling off from the bombers. With a sudden thrill he recognised Messerschmitt 109s and Dorniers, the one they called Flying Pencils. In front of him, at two hundred yards, Hedges opened fire, thin smoke and gold cases streaming from his wings.

'*Help yourselves.*'

Gawaine steep-turned with Hedges as he knifed into the formation. The green Dorniers were weaving and rearing like startled horses as the fighters cut into their even ranks.

There! There it was, right in front of him. He squeezed the trigger hard, jamming it into the stick and the eight guns roared, shaking the whole aircraft. The bomber was whizzing past him – he pulled the stick back into his stomach, through the grey it was still there, he fired again, inverted in his turn, bits flying off it. It was going down. Black smoke poured from one engine. He fired again, the guns hammering. Dark objects shot out of the bomber, tumbling black into the milky blue. Out of the corner of his eye he saw something white blossom, realised they were people. He fired again, and as it suddenly exploded, he pulled hard to get away from the tumbling rubbish.

A Spitfire shot by, seeming inches away, something hard on its tail. Two fish, streaking green and brown through the blue water. He felt the slipstream, saw the big straight-edged crosses, kicked hard left rudder, fired a sudden ripping burst, somehow felt no surprise as the Me 109 disintegrated, breaking up from just behind the cockpit.

'*Behind you Gawaine.*'

Where the hell was Hedges? He'd lost him. The sky was filled with swirling, tumbling aircraft, the clear air becoming stained with smoke.

'Break left! De Clare, break left. Behind you.'

God! That was him. Something smashed into his Spitfire behind him. There was a terrific crash as things started bouncing off him, he pulled the stick back so hard he passed out for a second.

The mirror was filled with a yellow spinner. Pieces of metal were streaming off his wing. He struggled like someone demented. twisting and turning all over the sky. His oxygen mask dragged down over his face, it skinned his nose, the blood streamed down into his mouth. He found he was cursing insanely, his head bouncing from side to side off the canopy. The sky was a hideous jumble of aeroplanes. Smoke was in his lungs from somewhere.

He thrust his nose down and dust and rubbish rose up the cockpit. He dived vertically for the ground. It was closer than he remembered.

The airspeed indicator went up and up – 410, 420 mph. Oil was smearing his windshield, streaming away like black rain droplets. He squinted over his shoulder, there was someone following him down. A black dot. It winked yellow flame from its centre, and the fuselage behind him screamed as a cannon shell howled off it.

The ground was very close. Roads and villages flashed under his wings. He came back on the stick, the air grunting from his lungs. The ground was no longer wrinkled, but alive and moving. Trees shot by, a church steeple. He saw tiles disintegrate, flying in the air as cannon shells ripped through it, doves scattering like snowflakes.

He managed to look behind him, and saw the Messerschmitt, black, a shark, three hundred yards distant.

He was at fifty feet, over the fields. Farm workers gathering hay into a wain ran for their lives as the two fighters shot over their heads. A hill, topped with a green copse, kept for the hunting, for the pigeons to flee into, rose up above him. He weaved to the right, and a line of explosions ripped up the hill, grass and dirt blowing high into the air.

He screamed round the side of the trees, his wingtip almost on the ground, the blast of his passage flattening the shrubs, the stick right back, and hauled the throttle closed, the Spitfire suddenly squashing in the air, cutting off speed. He shot round the back of the copse and then rolled it hard to the right, pushing the throttle wide. It caught with a huge bang, jerking the fighter forward, and the Messerschmitt shot by.

It all seemed slow motion. He fired and he could see the machine-gun bullets lash the enemy fighter from end to end. Pieces flew off, streaming away, smoke came out of the holes, followed by flames. The canopy blew away, tumbling glittering in the sun.

As he watched, the 109 rolled on its back, dense black smoke pouring from its engine. Flames gleamed yellow through the black. It went in inverted, hitting the ground at speed. Incandescent fragments sprayed in the air, as though from a firework, and it left a trail of blazing fuel along the ground. It ripped through a hedge, breaking up as it did so, and crashed into a bank in a blaze of sparks.

He began to climb away into the sky. A last glance below showed the skeleton of the Messerschmitt, burning fiercely, surrounded by a crown of blazing fuel.

At two thousand feet, something banged horribly in front of him. Hot oily smoke rushed all about him. He ripped back the canopy, undid his belts, his RT wires, oxygen. As he saw the first yellow flames in the smoke he rolled it on its back, and jumped.

The air was cold, blasted him, turned him upside down, filled his flying suit. He yanked at the ripcord and it came away in his hand.

For a long, hideous moment he thought it had broken. Then there was a huge bang, and a giant hand jerked him upright. He was floating peacefully through the air. Below there were green and yellow fields, a wood. A river glinted. It was very quiet. He wondered where the Spitfire had gone.

In the distance he saw a house, nestled amongst trees. The ground came up with a rush, thumped him hard. He scrambled to his feet in long grass, yanked at his parachute to spill the air, dragged it in, sat on it to stop it blowing away in the breeze.

He sat there for a few minutes, waiting for the feeling that he was going to be sick to go away. He had a sudden, intense desire for a cigarette, to get drunk, to lie in some girl's arms.

After a while, rather shakily, he got to his feet, and gathered up his parachute. It was RAF property – he had a feeling they wanted it back. He was hot; he unzipped his sheepskin jacket and took off his leather helmet.

He pushed his way over a hedge, and fell into a lane. he rather thought that the house he had seen was that way. He walked along. It was pleasantly cool and shady, a small brook babbled as it passed him.

He found a wicket gate, went in. A grey-haired lady was kneeling by the flower bed of a thatched cottage, a trug basket slowly filling with weeds at her side. She glanced up.

'Is that my parcel from Hatchards?' she asked.

'No,' he said, rather weakly. 'No, I don't think so.'

She slowly raised herself, and turned so that she could see him properly.

'No, of course it isn't. I thought you were Griggins, from the Post Office. Why are you carrying a bundle of washing about, young man?'

'It's a parachute,' he explained. 'I'm a pilot.'

'Pilot? Pilot? Where is your ship, then?'

'I fly aeroplanes.'

'Where is your aeroplane, then?' she demanded.

'It crashed,' he said clearly. 'I was fighting against Germans, and got hit. I had to jump out.'

'Fighting against the Germans?' she said. For the first time there was a note of hesitancy in her voice. 'You can't be old enough, surely?'

'I am nineteen!' he cried hotly. 'And I have just shot down three German aircraft.'

'Well!' she said. 'Good for you. You must come and tell Arthur.'

She swept around the corner of the cottage, and he followed in her wake. In the kitchen garden an old man was tending some canes.

'Arthur! This young man has just arrived from shooting down Germans.'

'Eh?'

He straightened up, peered at Gawaine through round glasses.

'Have you, by George? Quite right too. We don't want Mr Hitler and his nasty lot over here. What's your name, boy?'

'Gawaine, sir. Gawaine de Clare.'

The old man turned back to his canes, unfinished business on his mind.

'Know much about raspberries, Mr de Clare?'

'No, sir.'

'You know what the summer of 1940 will be memorable for?'

'No.'

'Raspberries!' he cried triumphantly. 'Best crop I've had since '28.'

'I need a drink!' Gawaine cried desperately. 'And a fag.'

'My dear chap,' the old man said reproaching himself. 'Of course you do. Thirsty work, shooting down Germans, no doubt. Come inside.'

The interior of the cottage was pleasingly cool and rather dark. Gawaine found himself with a whisky and water in his hand. The old man fumbled in a drawer.

'Smoke a pipe?' he enquired. 'Of course you do. Here. Let me fill this one for you.'

Somehow, he found himself wreathed in fragrant smoke.

'I must call my squadron,' he said, from around the unfamiliar stem. 'Have you a telephone?'

'Can't be doing with them,' said the large woman, whose name was Mabel. 'Such noisy things. What's wrong with a letter?'

'I have to tell them where I am,' he explained. 'So that they can pick me up.'

'To take you where?'

'Biggin Hill.'

'Biggin Hill? Arthur, doesn't cousin Lucy live over that way?'

'She does,' he said comfortably.

'Then go and fetch the car,' she ordered. 'We shall take this young man home and go and have tea.'

'You have a car, sir?'

'Oh yes,' said Mabel. 'We quite enjoy a run out from time to time. Now, you sit there and enjoy your drink while I lay the table. A cold collation is what we usually have at this time of the year. Have you finished that one? Let me give you another. Arthur! Young Mr de Clare would like to try some of your raspberries.'

The small black Austin Seven trundled slowly to a stop outside the main gate, and Gawaine clambered out. He was clutching his parachute, and a large bouquet of summer flowers wrapped up in a copy of last week's edition of the *District Advertiser*. Mabel put her head out of the window.

'Now don't forget to put those into water straight away, Mr de Clare, and cut the stems.'

'I will.' he said. 'And thank you again for—'

'Oh, don't thank us. Cousin Lucy will be ever so pleased. Arthur! Go down to the crossroads and turn left.'

He watched the little black car putter away down the road, and went through the main gate.

He trudged along the road towards the Mess. The sun was falling in the west, it was nearly early evening. From somewhere across the field an engine was running up, he could hear the note of it dropping and rising as someone checked the mag drop. A tractor was moving along the perimeter road. In a hangar he could hear the clink of tools, a clatter as a mechanic dropped a panel. Two Spitfires stood there with some of their clothes off. One of them was ripped and holed, two fitters were taking off its elevators.

He trudged up in the warm late sunshine, went into the Mess. By the bar a tall, lanky figure was just picking up a pint. He turned, beamed as he saw him.

'It's the brolly man! Look, chaps, de Clare's back.'

They crowded round him, slapped him on the back, thrust a pint pot into his hand. Morton held up his parachute, laughing.

'He's an umbrella man!' he cried. 'Look, takes it with him wherever he goes.'

Gawaine passed the wrapped flowers over the bar to the barman, clutched his new pipe between his teeth. Coming into the Mess, Hedges saw him, was pleased, thought he looked even younger than he had in the morning.

'You have to put them in water,' Gawaine said to the barman. 'And cut the stems.'

50

Some Suitably Ghastly Sinecure

Cascais, Portugal

Godfrey sat in the darkness. His car was parked at the end of the sandy track, where it meandered down and petered out at the beach itself. Behind him the Atlantic crashed rhythmically into a seething foam, faintly white in the starlight. Crickets creaked and shrilled in the pines. From time to time he rested a pair of large Zeiss binoculars on the surround of his door and focused on the brightly lit villa on the hill. The curtains of the great dining room were not drawn, and he could see inside. Facing him, with Wallis at his side, was Edward, the former king. He was dressed for the evening, as was she. When she turned to talk to one or other of the guests Godfrey could see her jewellery flash in the light of the great chandelier. The men were all in formal dress, and the women in silk frocks. The courses came and went, the air became tinged silver with cigarette and cigar smoke. Liqueurs circulated. He saw Carlotta, her head back, laughing.

Finally the powerful lamps of limousines lit up the grounds, splashing them with yellow as they made for the road. Godfrey sat silently, watching the great cars carrying their important passengers back into Lisbon.

Up on the hill, the lights winked out. He lit a cigarette of his own, shielding the flame with his cupped hand. He got out of the car, leaning against it as he smoked, watching the glowing phosphorescent foam of the waves.

Finally, he heard the crunching of feet coming down the sandy path.

'Godfrey!' a woman's voice hissed. 'Is that you?'

'Here,' he called softly, and she came towards him. It was Carlotta. She had changed out of her evening dress and was in jersey and slacks.

'God,' she said. 'Give me a fag. All this spying is killing on the nerves.'

He handed one over.

'Better than being hanged,' he observed. 'I don't think I've seen so many Nazis since I was at Nuremberg. What's happening?'

'Right,' she said, drawing in smoke and composing herself. 'You know that the Duke and Wallis are staying here with Santo e Silva. This is his house. He's a banker, and one of the chief local Nazi sympathisers. The Duke of Kent was here a few days ago, now he's gone and Edward's come.'

'So what are they up to? I saw von Hoyningen-Huene, the Nazi ambassador. Who was the man with him?'

'That's Schellenberg. He's Ribbentrop's man. He's head of the SD, the German Secret Intelligence. Wallis wanted him to be on hand.'

'So Wallis is still working actively with the Nazis?' Godfrey said quickly.

'She's been with them for a long time. She was fucking Ribbentrop when he was in London. You know that. Schellenberg is here because she sent orders for him to come.'

'She's more than an agent.'

'Of course. Look, she wants to give your country to the Nazis, that makes her fairly powerful, huh? What you might call a prime mover.'

'So what are they doing?'

'He's brought money, for a start. Fifty million francs in a Swiss account. Wallis always needs money. The Nazi authorities have guaranteed that Edward and Wallis's bank accounts in Paris won't be touched.'

'What has their lucre bought them?' Godfrey said, leaning back against the car and pulling on his cigarette, watching her closely in the gloom.

'Wallis and the Duke are working hard to destabilise the Churchill government. They think, and the Ambassador and Schellenberg seem to agree, that Churchill's political position is still very precarious.'

'It is.'

'The Duke has just sent a telegram to his brother the King demanding that he appoint a new pro-appeasement government in place of the Churchill coalition.'

'Who?'

'Lord Halifax, Sir John Simon, Sir Samuel Hoare. He proposes that Lloyd George be prime minister of a new fascist order in Britain which will become allied to Germany.'

'The King and Queen are both staunch patriots,' Godfrey observed. 'They will do no such thing.'

'Edward advises the Germans to commence heavy bombing of England, which he thinks will bring the people to their senses. They will demand the overthrow of Churchill. In the meantime, he and Wallis are going to go to America.'

'Oh?'

'Yes. You know how popular they are there. They plan to go from coast to coast on a peace platform, to stop the war with Germany.'

'Churchill and Roosevelt are planning for America to come into the war.'

'They know that. But this is election year. The Duke and Wallis will ally themselves with the isolationists. Roosevelt will have to come over to the peace platform or lose. If you Brits do badly in the air war that's starting Churchill will fall. The King and Queen will be kicked out with him and Edward and Wallis will return. Edward will take back his throne and Wallis will be queen.'

'It could just happen,' Godfrey said thoughtfully. 'All right. Is that it for the moment?'

'That's what I've got so far.'

'Good. There's something else I want you to do. Get in with Schellenberg. Point out your connections into English high society. You'll find that Wallis and Edward won't be going to America.'

'Where will they go?'

'They will go,' Godfrey said evenly, 'wherever we tell them to go. Some suitably ghastly sinecure will no doubt be arranged.'

'What if they don't want to?'

'The penalty for treason is death, as you yourself are aware,' he pointed out.

'Schellenberg is thinking of taking them to Germany.'

'Wallis does not have the mettle to gamble all on one throw of the dice. We'll see that she rots somewhere she'll hate.'

'Only if your fighter pilots win the battle,' she said acidly. 'If they lose she'll have *you* rotting in the Tower.'

'Yes,' he said languidly. 'Our brave boys in blue will have to do their stuff, won't they?'

Carlotta finished her cigarette, ground it out under her shoe.

'Why am I supposed to get in with Schellenberg?'

'You're going to be an agent for the Nazis in England,' he said smoothly.

'Oh, no . . .' she cried. 'I thought that doing this for you was it!'

'Oh, by no means,' he said smiling. 'Your life isn't yours any more. It's ours. For ever.'

When she had gone back up the hill he started his car, drove quietly away. When he got to the main road he switched on his lights, headed for Lisbon. The decaying capital was a place of bright lights, raffish and corrupt, a place of intrigue, secret police, refugees, spies and deserters.

Godfrey stopped his car at the side of the road, by a bar where people were still carousing despite the late hour. He sat down at a table outside, ordered whisky as he got his thoughts in order.

A chair scraped, somebody sat down beside him. He looked up, and into the grinning face of Freddie de Clare. He was thin, his battledress dirty and torn, he had not shaved.

'I'll have one of those,' he said. 'Hallo, Godfrey.'

'Good Lord, Freddie. You're supposed to be a prisoner of war.'

'Frightfully bad food, old man. I left the camp in a rubbish truck and I seem to have been walking ever since. Is this my drink? Bottoms up. I'm looking for suitable transport back home. Think you can arrange something?'

51

You Taste of the Air

Biggin Hill, 15 September

'*Up! Up! Up!*'

Gawaine stared uncomprehendingly at the flight sergeant. The cool air from his prop washed into his open cockpit, he ached, twisting and turning and fighting at thirty thousand feet, over seven miles high. He had landed, the flight sergeant was hopping up and down, his arms flailing in the air as though trying to pick the Spitfire up personally and fling it back up into the blue.

The tannoy was screeching something. Air punched his cheek. A gun. More guns. From somewhere nearby a Bofors was firing.

'*Scramble. Scramble. All Green aircraft scramble.*'

Jesus. They were scattered all over the grass, the ones that had come back. Hedges was dead, he had seen him go down on the first mission, a flamer. He had no idea who was leading the squadron.

He gunned the throttle, sent the Spitfire bouncing over the grass in a blast of dust. Jesus. The airfield was under bloody attack just when they had got down. He quickly checked his fuel state. About twenty gallons sloshing about. Still twenty seconds' worth of ammunition.

He scanned the field, gave it the fuel. On the perimeter the Bofors was firing steadily, red tracers streaming flatly over the land. They were low.

He got off quickly, light, tucked in his undercart. Full throttle.

There. There they were. There flashing up the valley, a shoal of them, green and grey, the fat bombers driving on, a swarm of fighters about them. They were so low he could see their shadows running dark over the ground.

He had no time to get altitude, to make a conventional attack. A hundred feet over the fields he banked steeply, and flew at them head on.

The reflector sight glowed brightly, he picked out the leading Heinkel and began firing in short bursts. Fire sparkled all over the canopy, armour glass shattered, glittered in the sun. Something exploded inside it and it reared sharply to the right. The bomber behind flew into the wreck. As he flashed through the formation Gawaine saw them tumble in locked embrace, felt the sudden huge buffeting of air as they exploded with full bomb load onto the ground below.

He pulled the Spitfire round in a savagely tight turn, right over the tree tops, screaming after the formation. Somebody else had got up; he saw another fighter diving into the shoal, saw yellow flame ripple along its wings. The German formation was streaming smoke. A Dornier was on fire, he could see its port engine belching flame. Bombs tumbled from it as the pilot desperately dumped his load, veering off from the formation, trying to put his stricken machine down before it burned.

Gawaine ignored him, he was gone. They were over the field. The bombers were attacking the buildings, the hangars. The flak was pouring in fire at enemy and friend alike. The first bombs went up, throwing huge gouts of brown earth and smoke high into the air.

He was in among them again. The buffetting of the slipstream was enormous, sending his wings flipping first one way then the other. The bomb blast beneath him lashed out at him like the kick of a mule. The Dornier in his sight had its bomb doors open. He squeezed the trigger hard against the stick, the whole fighter vibrating as he poured in fire. Pieces blew away into the air, the bomber suddenly dipped, dived, flew straight into the ground in a huge gout of orange and yellow flame.

A Messerschmitt came flashing across his path – he fired again, heard the scream of compressed air, the empty clanking of the breech blocks. He whirled away, back towards the field.

The air about him was suddenly empty. Smoke from the fires stained the clean morning air. He came over the airfield, saw the brown craters scarring the grass, saw some hangars burning, people running, fire tenders and ambulances racing. He dropped his gear, turned back towards the field, touched down past a big smoking crater, taxied in.

The flight line was still intact. He turned in at his bay, cut the throttle and switches, climbed out.

'Well done, sir!'

It was the flight sergeant again, beaming all over his face.

'That was lovely, that was. You give 'em hell, you did. Right where we could see it. Something to tell the missus, that is.'

Armourers were swarming about the aircraft. Corporal Wilson, the

bowser king, drew up on his tractor, Gawaine smelled the sudden cold
rush of 100-octane. Inside his gloves, his hands were shaking.

'My pleasure,' he said.

Violet opened the small door at the top of the narrow stairway and
she and Felicity stepped out onto the roof. They were high up, the
buildings of Mayfair were spread out about them, eerily unlit in the
moonlight like a ghost town. To the west the park stood darkly,
stretching to Kensington.

'Here we are,' she said cheerfully. 'Take a pew.'

The two women sat down on a small wall of sandbags. Behind
them was a small hut made out of sandbags, sitting on the wide, flat
lead roof.

'Is this where you spend your evenings?' said Felicity.

'Yes. I've appointed myself ARP warden at night, and Fergis the
porter does it in the day. It's jolly nice at the moment, sleeping up
here under the stars. Be a bit chilly later on, but we will have told
Hitler to push off by then, so it won't matter. Gasper?'

'Please.'

They sat smoking for a little while. Down on the streets they could
see buses crawling about with their dimly lit lamps on.

'You don't go down into the bomb shelters when there's a raid
on?'

'Goodness, no. The buggers are spraying the place with incendiaries,
you have to rush about chucking them off. Anyway, it's safer
up here.'

'It is?'

'Oh yes. My Uncle Harry told me that, when he was in the Navy,
got sent out to Japan – oh, turn of the century, it was – when we
were teaching the Nips how to have a navy of their own. They
decided to have a war with Russia and gave them a terrifically bad
time, so the Tsar sent a fleet all the way round the world to give
them a bloody nose for it. The Nips knew about it and were waiting
for them – the Russians were led by some chap called Resudsky, and
the others by Togo, and my Uncle Harry went out with Togo as an
observer. He sat out on the foredeck in a camp chair taking notes
all through the battle and only got up to change his uniform when
some chap got blown to bits all over him. They all thought he was
mad, but there was method in it, you see, as he said, because he
could only get killed by a direct hit, whereas inside the ship you
got all these splinters flying about chopping people up horribly. So

I consider I'm safer up here. Togo slaughtered Resudsky and his lot, of course.'

From somewhere in the depths of the city sirens began to groan and wail.

'Here we go.'

As the alert died away, they could very faintly here the sound of engines in the distance.

'But anyway, Flick darling, I haven't just asked you up here to talk about my Uncle Harry. How's your Frog? You do parlay, don't you?'

'Oh, yes. Marseille accent, I'm told.'

'Wonderful! Do you want something to do? I went to see Winston, you see, and he's given me a job. I need some people like you.'

'To do what?'

'Go over to France and do nasty things to the Germans.'

'Sounds my sort of thing,' Felicity said absently. 'Who do you work for?'

'SOE – Special Operations Executive. I'll take you in tomorrow.'

The noise of the bomber stream was becoming very loud. The darkness was suddenly lit up by flashes of yellow and scarlet towards Chelsea.

'Do you get frightened, Vi? I am, a bit.'

'Oh, God yes. I'm in a most fearful funk most of the time. I just can't stand the idea of cowering in some hole while those bastards fling bombs at me. I'd rather be up here doing something about it. What I usually do is retire into my hut and have a scotch while the swine come over. Then if we get any incendiaries I dash out and get rid of them. Scotch first, though.'

'Sounds all right to me.'

They went inside the little structure, and Violet lit a small storm lantern. They could hear the sound of bombs falling. The anti-aircraft guns were starting up, and light flickered in from outside as the shells hurtled up into the air. Violet poured them both large whiskies.

'Darling Fish swore by whisky when they were loosing off at you, and he was so right.'

'Lovely. How's Gawaine?'

'Down at Biggin Hill. I got a letter from him the other day. I think he's having a wonderful time, to me honest. Hurtling about up there.'

'You know, the whole war hinges on a few young chaps shooting these bastards down. The whole world, really. We're the only ones left fighting.'

'I know. I'm so proud of him, you know. I went down to Fortnums the other day to get some tea and the doorman there, he's an old friend, and he said 'Well, mum, we're in the Final. Just us and 'Itler, but it's going to be played on the 'ome ground.' I liked that.'

She gave Felicity an iron helmet. 'Here. I wear one of these. Fish brought some home from the war. Shrapnel helmet. Stops your hair catching fire.'

The lamp vibrated as bombs fell nearby. In a corner were some large shovels.

'Look, darling, if the incendiaries fall we have to rush out and chuck them off. I use a shovel and fling 'em over the parapet. Nobody's about down there. They're like rather large fireworks.'

'Give me another scotch before they arrive, darling.'

The two ladies sat quietly inside the little hut. A bomb went off not far away, everything rocked. There was a terrific clatter all about, smoke gushed into the shelter.

'That's it!' Violet cried. She tipped back her drink, thrust a shovel into Felicity's hand and they rushed outside. On the roof almost a dozen objects smoked and hissed scarlet flames, like brands from a bonfire. They ran through the smoke as the guns fired, scraping them up, throwing them into the void.

'*Green leader here.*'

It was Morton. There was nobody else left who could lead. He flew steadily at the head of the vic of five

'*Green leader here. Where are these bastards headed?*'

'*Looks like London again, Green leader,*' the controller down at Group replied.

'*They came visiting us at home this morning.*' Morton said laconically. '*We told them they weren't welcome.*'

The little formation continued to climb on its course. Somewhere out in the blue was another bomber force. London had been pounded by day and night for two weeks. In his place next to Morton, Gawaine glanced across at the others. He realised he didn't know who they were. The squadron had virtually been wiped out: they had lost eighteen pilots in three weeks, the CO that morning. On his tunic, under his sheepskin jacket was a small fresh ribbon. His DFC had come through the day before.

The morning was bright, the sky a shiny, polished blue. Below the land was just beginning to take on the faintest yellow and red tint of autumn. They went into a great bank of haze, and the woods and fields below disappeared into the blur.

They emerged a few minutes later, the visibility suddenly becoming crystal clear. Below, the Thames estuary lay spread out in front of them. Gawaine recognised Sheppey, and glancing to port he saw the winding signature of the great river going into London. The docks were crammed with shipping, a thin layer of blue smoke covered the mighty city.

The haze curved away over to sea, they were flying along its edge.

'*Jesus bloody Christ!*'

Out of the haze came an armada, a towering tidal wave of black aircraft, stacked layer upon layer, rank upon rank, climbing up into the sky. They darkened the sky, like some hideous migration of primeval insect life.

'*Help yourselves, chaps,*' Morton said laconically. They sat forward in their armoured seats, switched on their sights, turned up the oxygen, took off the safeties from their guns and flew at them, full throttle.

The air around him was suddenly full of whirling aircraft. A 109 flashed past, white plumes spuming from its wingtips. he fired a short burst, and missed.

A bomber. Dark green, yellow flashes winking at him from its gunner. He pushed in left rudder, hard, stitching bullets all along its body; it lit up, from within, began to roll. Another 109, streaming golden cases as it fired.

Head on. A 109, filling the windshield, at less than 100 yards. Its big red spinner and apparently slowly turning prop filled his vision. The wings and spinner lit up all over as it flung itself at him. As he fired there was a huge bang and his windshield splintered into an opaque wall. For a second he was frozen. Something huge ripped over his head in a blast of air and noise. Oil poured over his canopy as if from a hose.

For a fraction of a second all went black through the scarred, filthy hood. He could see nothing. He hit something with a crash that sent him smacking forward in his seat. His face, in mask and goggles, cracked into the instrument panel. In front of him there was a hideous scream as the propeller splintered to nothing and the engine exploded. Something tore at him, twisting the aircraft over and over as though cracked by a whip, and his head smacked off the sides of the canopy. He pulled frantically at his harness.

There was a tremendous bang. Air blasted all over him. He had a fleeting a glimpse of his ruined Spitfire in a deathly embrace with a Dornier. Two bodies spilled out of the wreck. he tumbled over and over, clawing at his ripcord.

The parachute opened with a booming jerk, snapping him upright. The sky was somehow clear of aeroplanes, though marked by dark, smoky trails where they had died. The bombers and the battle was above him. He was over London. He could see the river below. The docks were on fire, shipping was burning.

The breeze was pushing him from the suburbs into town. Like a huge white dandelion seed, he floated down, at the wind's mercy. He could see the green of the parks. Bombs were hitting the West End, he saw smoke and dust rising into the air, saw a building fall in on itself, rubble gushing into the street.

The roofs were coming up at him, grey slate, sloping down towards the street, chimneys poking up at him, wires crossing high over the pavements below.

He hit with a crash, bounced off the roof in a shower of breaking slate. He grabbed at a heavy pantile, missed, slid along the roof, still dragged by his parachute. It pulled him off the edge and he fell onto a small dormer window poking out. A hundred feet below people were running in the street. He clawed frantically at the old black guttering with his gloved hands. For a moment he hung there, dangling over the drop, and then the rotten metal broke, flinging him into the void.

He fell, and then was pulled up with a jerk, slapping him hard against the side of the building. Rough brick ground against his face as he swung from his harness. He could see the cords taut above him, vanishing over the roof. The parachute had caught on something.

He felt it rip. He fell a few feet, scrabbling futilely at the bricks, trying to gain purchase. His feet felt a break in the wall below. As he fell further he was grabbed, small furious, hard hands, seizing him, pulling at him. He was half over a windowsill, a young woman had hold of him. She was yelling something he couldn't understand and had a foot up on the sill, heaving as hard as she could. he grabbed at the windowframe and heaved, and fell inside.

They clasped to each other. From somewhere there was a rising shriek, a great explosion. The floor underneath them vibrated, bounced as though it was an earthquake. She pulled at him, mouthing something in the din. He yanked at his release harness, they scrabbled across the floorboards, she dragged him under the bed, a big, brass-framed bed. Another bomb howled down nearby, exploding with a shriek and a roar of shattering masonry. They clung together in frantic embrace. The third bomb in the stick went off further way; he could hear the steady rise and fall of the siren, the clanging of firebells and ambulances, the shouting of voices.

They lay together, gasping. The raid seemed to have moved on, like a thunderstorm. They could hear the droning of aeroplanes becoming distant. She sat up on one elbow, her dress torn. He could see her breasts, smooth and pink and round. She smiled at him with white teeth and green eyes.

'I say,' she said. 'We haven't been introduced. Molly Francis.'

She held out a small hand, and he shook it, quite formally.

'Gawaine de Clare,' he said. 'It's very nice to meet you.'

'I think we can probably crawl out now,' she said, and they emerged. His parachute was still dangling half out of the window, and he went and pulled it in. The street below was covered in shattered glass.

She stood in front of him. She had done up the buttons of her dress.

'Do you make a habit of dropping in on girls like this?' she asked.

'I . . . was up there,' he said. 'I hit a Dornier, had to come down on my 'chute.'

'Do you make a habit of that?'

'Just recently,' he said, standing in front of her so that he could watch her. She was overwhelmingly beautiful to him.

'This makes the fourth time,' he said. 'In the squadron, they call me Brolly. I'm the umbrella man.'

'Brolly,' she said, repeating the word, as though it tasted very pleasant. 'Brolly. I shall call you Brolly too. Do you shoot down a lot of German aircraft in exchange?'

'Fourteen, at the moment,' he said.

'Well, it's a fair exchange. We seem to be doing better on the bargain.'

'Yes.'

She was so lovely all he wanted to do was stand looking at her.

'I must go to the hospital,' she said. 'They will be bringing in the casualties.'

'I have to go back to the station,' he said. 'Biggin Hill. The Germans will be coming back, the chaps will expect me to go up with them. We're very short of pilots, you see.'

'Then we must get together,' she said gravely. 'When we are not otherwise occupied.'

'Yes.' He thought for a moment, his face brightened. 'Come down and stay at the pub. I get off in the evening.'

'You don't fight at night?'

'No. Can't see.'

'Good show,' she said. 'I have some days off next week. What pub is it?'

'The King's Arms. They have nice rooms around the garden.'

'I'll find it,' she said. 'Come and get me on Wednesday.'

'I will.'

She moved, took a nurse's blue uniform out of a cupboard, laid it out on the bed with a belt with an ornate silver buckle.

'I must get changed,' she said. 'They'll be bringing them in.'

'Yes. I must get back.'

He folded up his parachute into a bundle, wadded it up under his arm, went to the door with her.

'Molly?'

'Yes?'

'I think I'm already in love with you.'

'Yes,' she said seriously. 'I know. Now go back to your aerodrome, Gawaine de Clare, and we shall find out all about each other on Wednesday.'

He bent, and they kissed.

'You taste of strawberries,' he said.

'You taste of the air,' she said. 'So high up.'

'Wednesday.'

'Yes.'

He went down a winding stair, found the hallway, went out into the street. It was covered in a yellow dust, and broken glass. A lugubrious man in a brown dustcoat was sweeping it into piles with a stiff broom. His shopfront was open to the air.

'If this 'Itler feller keeps on like this, 'e will get hisself much disliked,' he said disapprovingly.

He looked Gawaine up and down.

'You in the Raff?'

'Yes.'

'Give 'em what for then.'

'I will.'

Gawaine began to trudge down the street, his boots crunching on the broken glass. As he emerged into the main road a passing taxicab sputtered to a halt.

'British?' the driver enquired, staring narrowly at him.

'Of course.'

The man beamed under a flat hat.

'Where you going, then, guv?'

'Biggin Hill.'

''Ow come you're 'ere?'

Gawaine held up his parachute.

'Collided with one of theirs.'

''Op in then. You'll be needing a new aircraft.'

He got in the back, and they jerked away down the street. As they did so a man came hurrying down some steps from a house. He was smartly dressed, in a striped blue suit, His hair was oddly long, he pushed it off his forehead, and seeing the taxi coming he raised a peremptory hand.

'It's 'Arris.'

'It is?'

'The loony doctor,' the cabbie explained. 'Mind if I drop 'im off? 'E goes to 'is clinic.'

He slowed and stopped, and the doctor got in.

'Takin' the pilot 'ere to Biggin 'Ill.'

Doctor Harris peered closely at Gawaine, brushing his long hair out of his eyes.

'You're contused,' he said.

'I baled out.'

'You're a fighter pilot?' he asked keenly.

'Yes. I hit a Dornier, I had to jump out.'

'How is your mind? I see the bruises on your face, but what of those on your mind? I'm a psychiatrist, tell me about your pain.'

Gawaine looked sideways at him and said nothing.

'You see, you're typical!' the doctor exclaimed irritably. 'This sickening British stiff-upper-lip attitude. Look at you! You've almost been killed! In the name of God let your trauma out!'

'I'd rather have a pint, if you don't mind.'

'Bah!' Harris said in disgust. 'Recourse to alcohol merely masks the symptoms. We are all sick! Look! Look out there!'

They were passing a police station. It had been damaged in a raid, wooden shuttering blocked out its windows. On it a constable had painted: Be Good. We Are Still Open.

'Not bad, eh?' said Gawaine. He found his pipe and began to fill it from the tobacco pouch he had brought.

'More denial,' Harris muttered, throwing himself back in his seat. He looked at the pipe.

'Oral substitutiary comfort again, like your need for alcohol,' he said sharply. 'Did your mother breast-feed you?'

'I wouldn't know,' Gawaine said austerely. 'It is not a subject we have ever discussed.'

'Precisely!' he cried in triumph. 'All your problems are ones of repression! You are unable to talk frankly to your mother about your needs.'

The taxi drew up outside a drab building in the middle of an area that had clearly taken considerable damage from the bombers.

''Ere we are Doc.'

Doctor Harris peered out expectantly, and then his face crumpled with disappointment.

'Where are they?' he cried. 'The council has hired me, at great expense to the taxpayer, to provide psychiatric counselling for the trauma the citizens of this borough have suffered, and *nobody comes.*'

'They're prob'ly down the boozer, having a bit of a sing-song,' said the taxi driver.

'Our society is sick!' the doctor said bitterly. 'This denial of trauma, this perverse "we can take it" attitude. We should all be healthy, admit it, say, "I am in pain, I can take no more, help me." That's what I am here for, to help people, to say, "talk to me, I feel your hurt." But no. They are all, apparently, down the boozer, singing sentimental folk songs.'

'But we *can* take it,' said Gawaine.

The psychiatrist got out, paid the driver some money, and went angrily across the road, to his empty clinic. The taxi sputtered away.

'See what I mean?' the driver said, grinning in his mirror. ''E's the loony. The loony doctor.'

Gawaine filled his pipe and lit it, silvery smoke drifting out through the window. He sat back in the seat, thinking of Molly Francis. Soon it would be Wednesday.

He realised he was leaning against a kind of parcel, all rolled up in a blanket.

'I say,' he called, 'I think somebody's left something in the back here.'

'Eh? What's that, guv?'

The cabbie glanced over his shoulder.

'No, that's mine, guv.' he said. 'That's what I sleep in. Kip in the cab, I does, since we was bombed out. Come back home last week and found Jerry been there before me.'

'I'm sorry,' said Gawaine. He could still see her breasts, through the rumpled dress. 'Nobody hurt, I hope?'

'Just me Aunt Flo,' he said. 'Found her feet in our house and her head in the neighbours.'

He paused at the crossroads, headed south.

'Died 'appy, I reckon,' he said ruminatively. 'She was always inquisitive.'

52

You've Just Been Scorched

Banks of cloud hung over the land like gigantic ramparts. Clusters of flak appeared out of nowhere and hung black along their flanks. From the battlements fighters and bombers swarmed towards the climbing Spitfires like the defenders of a castle.

The first contact, the aircraft formations breaking up into a confused mêlée. A Heinkel exploding like an enormous flak shell, a dark expanding mushroom spreading out across the sky, incandescent debris spraying out across the white cloud. A Spitfire going down, belly up. Three parachutes suddenly smacking into view.

Gawaine twisted and turned in the swarm. The fighters swirled and snapped like demented predatory fish. Nothing but huge scarlet spinners, yellow bellies, black crosses and clipped wings, roundels and ellipses. Multi-coloured tracer striped the air, dazzlingly bright.

The red filaments of his gunsight encircled a grey and green Messerschmitt. They were turning tightly across the sky, he grunted as the air forced itself out of his lungs. His oxygen mask was loose, dragging itself off his nose and down over his mouth. He fired in short deadly bursts, pieces of debris flying off the German fighter.

There was a thunderclap of noise, a burning slap of fire across his face, a shriek that pierced his eardrums. A cannon shell smashed through the windshield. Hammer blows rocked the Spitfire, beating into its body, metal screaming off metal.

The cockpit exploded into flame, he was sitting in a furnace. He howled with the sudden agony. The huge 300-mph gale blew the fire into his face like a vast blowtorch.

He did as he had been trained, did it without thinking. He pulled the split pin out of his sub-harness with his blazing gloves, disentangled his oxygen and radio-telephone wires, yanked back the canopy and rolled the doomed fighter on to its back.

He was falling through the sky. His hands were somehow up near his face. Smoke streamed off the charred gloves. They hurt, fearfully. His face hurt. All of him hurt. He managed to pull the ripcord. The harness whipped him upright with red-hot straps, and he screamed in the sky.

He hit the ground without knowing it. He could hear voices, people running, somebody shouting to call an ambulance.

Somebody was talking to him. No, not talking, issuing orders. He focused on her. A severe woman with iron-grey hair drawn back under her nurse's hat. She was looking at him in disapproval.

'Sit up, young man,' she said. 'Mr Green is coming on his round.'

'Who might you be?' he asked. It hurt his mouth to talk.

'I am the sister in charge of this ward and you do as I say.'

'I'll have my pipe. Where is it?'

'Smoking is not permitted. When Mr Green talks to you you will lie to attention.'

'Who is he? Does he fly?'

'Certainly not. He is the consultant surgeon.'

'Doesn't fly? Balls to him then.'

The sister's mouth tightened grimly.

'He holds the rank of colonel in the RAMC. You will address him as "sir".'

'I am the bloody Earl of Windstone. He can fucking call me "sir".'

He felt unconsciousness welling up inside him again. He closed his eyes to shut the woman out, and as he went under he felt only slight surprise to realise that nothing came over his eyes.

'Hallo, darling.'

'Hallo, Mummy.'

Violet bent to kiss him. He smelled sweetish, like underdone pork and crackling. She smiled, and not for an instant revealed that she could not recognise her son. His name was at the end of the iron-framed bed.

'Pretty poky hole this, darling,' she said.

'Look, Mummy, there's a couple of things need fixing up. Firstly, the old cow who runs the ward won't give me my pipe. And I can't close my eyes. My eyelids have got stuck to my eyebrows or something.'

His eyelids were burned away.

'That's what I've come for, darling. I've found this frightfully good chap, specialises in unsticking eyelids, that sort of thing. Name of

McIndoe. He's over in East Grinstead. Nice place, much better than this.'

'Plenty of pubs?'

'Five for every church, apparently.'

'I just need the old eyelids fixing, and then I can get back to the squadron, you see.'

'That's it,' she agreed. 'Does it hurt?'

'It does a bit.'

'I ought to have brought some butter with me,' she smiled. 'We could have buttered you all over.'

She reached in her bag, took out a brand new Dunhill pipe and tobacco pouch.

'I forgot the butter, but I brought this. I think you must have lost your old one, so I've got you a new one.'

He stuck it into his mouth triumphantly with his reddened, weeping hands. Violet reached into her bag again and took out a hunting flask. She took off the top and filled it.

'Your father swore by a tot of whisky,' she remarked, handing it to him. 'It was his cure for everything.'

It went down like liquid fire as the sister of the ward pounded up in outrage.

'Alcohol is forbidden on—'

'I am Lady de Clare, the Countess of Windstone,' Violet said, cutting her off effortlessly. 'I have come for my son.'

They had covered half his face with some kind of gauze. It had solidified into a kind of armour, stuck to him in rigid sheets. He had seen only a town through the windows of the ambulance, red-bricked buildings and trees, hospital grounds, a group of temporary huts. The white Morris ambulance with its red crosses had pulled up outside the biggest of these. He had managed to get to his feet and walk in.

It was called Ward Three, he found out. Almost the very first thing they had done to him was lie him on a bed and begin to soak off the gauze bandages. Two young nurses did it for him; pretty girls, very pretty girls.

It hurt, it stopped him from trying to see what was going on. He somehow liked the noise about him, it was like being back in the mess. The bandages stuck to his face, and however careful the young nurses were they pulled and tore at his lacerated, burned flesh. Once he cried out, and he heard a voice by his ear.

'Oh, dear,' it said. 'You'll have me sobbing on the floor in a minute if you go on like that. Let me take a peer at you.'

Gawaine swivelled his eyes and found something looking at him. It had no ears, its lips were burned. A kind of sausage made its way from its forehead to where its nose had been. Looking further, he saw that it was mounted in a wheelchair, that its hands and feet were both burned as well.

'Oh,' it said dismissively, 'you've just been scorched.'

The burned man turned his wheelchair, as the girls finished their task and took away the pile of sodden gauze. He propelled himself with his burned hands over to the wall. A wooden chair stood there. He leaned forward and picked it up with his teeth, resting the legs on his wheelchair. He turned, and came back, slinging it alongside.

'Have a seat, old boy,' he said.

Gawaine climbed off the bed. He hurt almost all over, but with the torched man in the wheelchair watching him, he simply made himself smile.

'Gawaine de Clare,' he said, and held out his own burned hand. 'Though they call me Brolly. I keep jumping out of my Spit.'

'Bill Perkins,' said the wheelchair man. At the end of the ward stood a large barrel of beer. Not far away was a grand piano. Two men, with one pair of hands between them were thumping out a show tune.

'What is this place?'

'This is the Guinea Pig Club,' Perkins said proudly. 'I am the secretary.' He held up his hands gleefully. 'I can't write! Pete over there is the Treasurer.'

Gawaine looked to where a legless man was playing table tennis from his chair. Perkins watched him intently.

'He can't abscond with the funds?' said Gawaine. He thought that he was beginning to understand how this place worked.

'You'll do, laddie, you'll do,' Perkins said approvingly. 'Trot down to the barrel and get me a pint.'

'I think I'm going to like it here.'

'Wheels down, chaps,' said Perkins.

The old car came round the corner on two wheels, and Gawaine closed his eyes, partly for the sheer pleasure of doing so. He had eyelids. They lacked lashes, had previously been on the inside of his wrist and were too large, but it did not matter. They would shrink to size, and they went up and down at will. It was wonderful.

When he opened them, Perkins had pulled up with a screech outside the pub and the collection of men with Hurricane burns and an uneven number of hands, fingers and feet, with faces like patchwork quilts, were clambering out in a cacophony of rattling plaster casts, crutches, sticks and wheelchairs.

They piled into the pub.

'Just time for a couple, chaps,' said Perkins. 'I want to be in the theatre after lunch, the boss is putting Harry on the slab to do his hand and I want to watch. My turn next week.'

'I'll come too,' said Gawaine. He had got used to the fact that in Ward Three, the normal hospital regulations did not apply. If you wanted to get up in the night, you got up. If you wanted to have a drink, you helped yourself. If you wanted to see how the boss, McIndoe, was going to carve you, you put on a theatre gown and went in and watched him doing it to one of the others. A Hampden navigator with no fingers but two working thumbs cut out of his hands began playing darts with a Hurricane pilot who was blind, calling out directions. They both laughed uproariously.

Perkins took a small box from his pocket and opened it.

'Look at this, old man. The boss got them for me.'

He took a pair of remarkably lifelike ears out of the box and secured them over the puckered, scarred flesh where his own had been.

'Wax,' he said proudly. 'Until the boss can make me some proper ones.'

Gawaine sank the first quarter of his pint, and reached for his letters. The postman had arrived just as they were leaving.

'Oh, I say,' he said, pleased. 'My uncle's back.'

'He's been away?'

'Cook's tour, old boy. Calais, Stalag Luft something, Spain. He's a tank colonel.'

'We must drink to him,' Perkins said solemnly.

'We must, we must. Fred! Tee up two more of the same, my uncle's escaped from the Jerries.'

Gawaine peered at his mother's letter.

'He's going to Combined Ops, whatever that is. Good show.'

Perkins cleared his throat.

'I say, old man, there is a terrifically good-looking piece of knitting looking at us. Me, probably. I'm more handsome than you are. It's my new ears.'

Gawaine glanced up. His skin went ice cold, then hot, his heart began to pound. She was standing by the door.

She smiled, beamed at him, came forward, tripping over the carpet

light as a feather. She put one slim and strong arm round his neck and
kissed him. She tasted of strawberries.

'I say . . .' Perkins breathed in awe.

'Hallo, darling,' Molly said. She stood by him, took his hand in
hers. 'It's taken me ages to find you.'

'But . . . what, how—'

'You stood me up, you rotter,' she said cheerfully. 'I turned up at
the pub that Wednesday with my hair in a braid and you weren't
there. I'll have that drink, now.'

'Fred!' he called hoarsely. 'G and T over here, please.'

Perkins goggled at him. 'Introduce me, old boy,' he urged.

'Molly, this is Bill Perkins. Don't have anything to do with him.
He's a reprobate and can't even fly straight. Bill, this is my girlfriend,
Molly Francis.'

'How do you do?' Perkins said, holding out his mutilated paw,
and she shook it without a qualm.

'Very well, thank you.'

The light from the window became dim. They looked up to see a
very large policeman standing there.

'There is a car parked outside causing an obstruction to the traffic,'
he announced pompously.

'Mine, officer,' said Perkins.

'Why have you left your car outside, sir?'

Perkins removed his ears and stuck them to his forehead. He peered
at himself in the mirror before turning back to the policeman, standing
imperturbably waiting.

'Well, the bally car doesn't drink.' He hobbled to the door to move
it, and Gawaine was left alone with her.

'How long can you stay?' he said. It was vitally important, every
second with her was important.

'Oh, quite a while,' she said, smiling. 'I've transferred here. I'm on
Ward Three.'

'Oh . . .' he said, and choked. Tears spilled up over his new eyelids,
ran down over his patched face.

'Oh,' he said. 'Everything's all right now.'

53

The Master of Disaster

Plymouth, August 1942

'Oh, it's you, Freddie,' said the man with vice-admiral's rings on his sleeve. He was sitting at a table with Perceval de Clare. Through the immense window of his office the crowded port was clearly visible, packed with vessels of war.

'Hallo, Lord Louis. Perceval. What are you doing here?'

'Playing my part in the war, Freddie,' Perceval said, sounding pleased. 'I'm bringing Lord Louis up to date with the forthcoming Beveridge Plan.'

'All that New Jerusalem stuff? Pie in the sky. Don't you think we'd better win the war first?'

'We *are* winning the war,' Mountbatten asserted forcefully. 'Percy's right, we have to win the peace too. The people are going to win freedom from want, freedom from the giant evils of the past.' He picked up a printed sheaf of paper. 'It's all in here.'

'New Britain!' Perceval cried. 'Freedom of Want, of Disease, of Ignorance, of Squalor and Idleness.'

'Well I'll drink to that. But I'll believe it when I see it.'

'It's here, Freddie!' Louis Mountbatten said cheerfully. 'Don't be so hidebound. There'll be a new socialist order in Britain after the war, believe me. A new world.'

'I didn't know you were a socialist.'

'Oh, my wife Edwina's opened my eyes to a lot of things. I'm for the new order, all right.'

'I thought your wife was frightfully rich,' Freddie said drily.

'It doesn't mean she can't hold progressive views,' he expostulated.

'Insulates her from the pain of it all, what?' Freddie said genially. 'Well, if you've finished, Perceval, I'm supposed to be seeing Lord Louis about eliminating the giant evil of Nazism.'

'Oh, yes. Are you Brigadier Reynold's replacement?' Mountbatten enquired.

'That's it. Slipped off a Churchill tank and broke his leg, so you've got me.'

'I'll keep you up to date, Dickie,' said Perceval, leaving.

'Please do,' Mountbatten said sincerely.

'Back to the war,' said Freddie.

'Oh, yes. In fact, talking of the war, have you heard about this marvellous film Noël's made about me? I've been helping him, of course. He plays *me*. On the *Kelly*. When we were sunk and dive-bombed. *In Which We Serve*.' Mountbatten paused, savouring the title. '*In Which We Serve*. It's terribly good, you'll love it. I've already seen it a few times. You mustn't miss it when it comes out.'

'I won't. I believe I'm to be an observer.'

'Eh? Are you going to review it?'

'No. There's some operation you're planning. I'm to observe for the Tank Corps, see how the tanks get on.'

'Oh, yes.' Mountbatten lowered his voice, became serious.

'Operation "Jubilee",' he said quietly. 'We're going to smash the Germans in Dieppe.'

He made a fist, punched the air savagely.

'Bam. We're going to crash through them at dawn from the sea. An amphibious assault from two hundred and fifty craft. Five thousand soldiers, an entire division with tank and artillery support, smashing straight through the town. You'll witness a feat of arms the like of which you'll never have seen before. That's what we've been planning and preparing for here at Combined Ops. The latest in modern warfare.'

'It sounds impressive.'

'It is. It's the curtain-raiser for the invasion, you know.'

He tapped his brand new golden rings, and grinned boyishly.

'I'm allowed to wear a lieutenant-general's uniform and an air marshal's as well!' he crowed happily. 'I've been to the tailor's for them. The word is that the American general marshall is to be supreme commander and I'll be his chief of staff.'

'Wonderful,' Freddie said politely.

'Monty will be frightfully miffed.'

'What's the opposition?'

'Well, Monty, of course.'

'No, in Dieppe. The Germans.'

'Oh, we've got them fooled. Maury's run a first class intelligence operation – he's my head of intelligence – and the place is only garrisoned by a pretty battered battalion of infantry from the Russian front. Our boys are crack Canadians and they'll go through them like a knife through butter.'

He chuckled charmingly.

'Our only problem will be stopping them from driving on Paris! We've practised it until we could run it on Broadway, let me tell you.'

He looked musingly out of the window at the immense array of warships in the harbour.

'You know, with all the experience I've amassed here, I wouldn't be surprised if they make *me* supreme commander,' he said thoughtfully. 'Anyway, listen up, Freddie. Don't go too far. We're on our way soon. Can't tell you just when, all hush-hush, you know. Just don't stray too far away!'

'I won't. This should be something.'

'It will, dear chap. Look, I'll try to get hold of a copy of the *Kelly* film for you. You'll love it. I'm thinking of showing it to the troops here, before they go, put them in the right spirit.'

'Freddie!'

A black Rover that was moving off pulled up; somebody wound down a window, called to him. It was George. He grinned, went over to him.

'Good Lord, are all the de Clares here today? I've just seen Perceval giving Mountbatten a lot of bull about the glorious new order we shall all enjoy after the war's won. I personally think we'll all be too exhausted to do anything except order another round.'

George glanced alertly at him.

'You've been seeing Mountbatten? I've been giving a report to his intelligence chief, if you can call him that.'

'What do you mean?'

'Hop in. I'll buy you a drink.'

Freddie got in and they went away through the streets of the port.

'There's a decent pub down on the coast. Mountbatten's head of intelligence is a failed Cuban racing-driver-cum-playboy called Maury. One of his cronies.'

George turned onto the esplanade, headed out of the town.

'Mountbatten doesn't employ professionals,' he said savagely. 'He prefers his "Dickie Birds". They all tell him how wonderful he is. What are you doing here, Freddie?'

'I'm to be an observer. For an operation he's mounting,' Freddie said carefully.

'"Jubilee",' George said instantly. 'That half-baked idea to invade Dieppe.'

'Yes,' Freddie said, puzzled. 'I'm on stand-by for it.'

'Balls,' George said contemptuously. He turned into the forecourt of a pleasant hotel on the sea front. '"Jubilee" has been cancelled. Monty saw the fuck-up Mountbatten made of the rehearsals – absolutely everything that could go wrong *did* go wrong – and he's put a stop to it.'

'I don't think so,' Freddie said with a frown. 'Dickie told me it was ready to go ahead.'

'Sit over here, I'll get a couple of pints.'

He emerged from the hotel a minute later and joined Freddie at a white-painted metal table looking out to sea. White roses were climbing up the walls, and pink hydrangeas foamed about them.

'No, take it from me, it's off,' George continued. 'The planning's a joke and if you ask me there's serious opposition there. Casa Maury thinks there's a worn-out battalion in Dieppe. I don't. Maury trusts his French agents. I don't.'

'What do you mean?'

'This crap about the brave French resisting the Germans is fine for the BBC propaganda,' George said savagely, 'but crap is all it is. The bastards are collaborating to a man over there. I wouldn't trust any of them to tell me the time, let alone the truth. Dial in planning by Dickie Mountbatten and you've got the makings of a real mess.'

'He talks a good war. That pansy Coward is making a film about him.'

'God!' George cried. 'What a country ... only here could an incompetent like him get two ships sunk and be turned into a hero! You know what his comrades in the Navy call him? "The Master of Disaster"! The one thing Dickie's really good at – apart from promoting his own career – is killing people. The only problem is they're always on our side.'

'So how is he in charge?' Freddie asked, puzzled.

'As far as I can see, people promote him to get him out of their particular hair. This process has gone on so long that instead of doing what he is fit for, which is sending Aldiss signals with a lamp, he is running a truly enormous show like Combined Ops. I only hope they will promote him to some stratospheric post where he has no real command of anything before he manages to do some genuine harm.'

'I'm glad it's off, then. I'll hang about until the end of the week and claim business back at Aldershot. I'm going to young Gawaine's wedding then anyway. You be there?'

'If I can. Nice girl?'

'Lovely. Molly, her name is. The right sort, too. He's a lucky chap.'

'How's his face?'

'Patched up.'

'Still in the Raff?'

'Going to fly for SOE. Dropping agents, Vi told me.'

'Waste of bloody time,' George said viciously. 'Let the bloody French rot.'

Out on the sea a big boxy landing craft was going by, its powerful engines pushing it through the water at speed. They could see the American sailors of the crew, all in white, with their upturned caps, the stars and stripes flying from the short mast.

'God, it makes me sick to see them here, polluting our water,' George commented. Freddie frowned.

'At least they're here,' he said. 'We're winning the war, with their help. They're not bad chaps, the ones I've met.'

'I hate the lot of them, their filthy ways, their stinking culture.'

'You hate a lot of things, old man,' Freddie observed quietly.

'Yes, well, we're fighting a war,' George snarled, turning on him. 'A bit of hate comes in useful.'

'You started hating things a long time before the war,' he said.

George drained his mug. 'Life . . . oh, never mind. I'll give you a lift back. Come on.'

They got back into the Rover, drove along the sea front.

'I told you I saw Perceval. Filling Dickie up with his socialist guff, he was.'

'Can't have been difficult. He gets a diet of it from his wife.'

'So he said. What's she like?'

'She's a useless cow,' George said frankly. 'Rich beyond avarice, spent the last twenty years screwing as many chaps and girls as she could. Now she's thrown herself into progressive politics, good works and campaigning against the system that's made her rich. Hard to know in which guise she's more repellent. She and Dickie are made for each other, really. Here. This do you?'

'Fine. Thanks for the beer. See you at the wedding.'

'Brigadier de Clare!' a voice called. Freddie turned at the dockside. The destroyer he was about to board hummed with life. Out in the harbour the night was filled with whistles and clankings, with the sounds of command coming over loudhailers, the squeal of steam-powered derricks, all the noise of vessels preparing for sail.

'Yes?'

A messenger came hurrying down the quay.

'Important call for you, sir. You can take it down here.'

Freddie followed him down, was shown into a room with a green telephone. He picked it up.

'Brigadier de Clare here.'

'Freddie, it's George. Does your telephone have a scrambler button?'

'Yes.'

'Press it. Done? All right. Is it true, is "Jubilee" on?'

'Yes.'

'Jesus Christ. It's not even authorised. Look, the bloody Germans will know you're coming. You're going to sail smack into the middle of one of their convoys. I know. I can read . . . signals. I've been on to Mountbatten's HQ, but they aren't listening to me.'

'I don't see what I can do about it.'

'Dear God, man, just don't go! Stay on the bloody dock side.'

'I don't think I can do that, old man. Not on, really, is it? But thank you for telling me.'

Freddie put the telephone down, and went back out into the dark. Landing craft banged against their attack transports, chain cable rattled up through hawsepipes, warship bugles sounded. Out on the water, the first craft were beginning to move out to sea.

Freddie could smell burning. It came from a nearby destroyer that had been damaged in the firefight. They had run into the German convoy exactly on schedule. The sea was glossy with starlight, over at its far rim the coming dawn brushed it with the palest grey. The armada of over two hundred and fifty ships hung poised to attack. He could hear the young Canadians clinking as they climbed into their assault boats, heavy-laden with their weapons and ammunition.

Almost as one, the great wave of landing craft surged forward, and the air was filled with the roar of their engines. As they made their run into the silent, dark port their phosphorescent wake stood out behind like shining diamonds laid on blackest velvet.

Bells rang inside the destroyer, and it moved forward. The dawn was coming quickly. Freddie could see the narrow shingle beach of the town and its esplanade hiding behind its high sea wall, the brooding buildings of the sea front.

'For God's sake!' he suddenly cried out loud. 'Is there no bombardment? Where is the barrage?'

The assault craft swept in towards the shore. The leading vessels grounded on the shingle, the ramps went down. The soldiers pushed forward and the entire sea front erupted with fire, with machine-guns, with rifles and grenade launchers, with mortars and anti-tank guns pouring in shell over open sights. On the ramps of the landing craft the young men danced briefly, bloodily like puppets as the bullets and shrapnel tore them apart. They fell into heaps. The survivors had to crawl over the piles to reach the beach, where they were massacred in their own turn.

The big LSTs grounded, and the Churchill tanks ground down the ramps under the fearsome fire. One or two made their way towards the esplanade, others lay helpless, their tracks grinding futilely in the shingle. One after the other, they exploded in shards of flying armour, and began to burn.

Overhead, the sky was suddenly filled with the roar of aero-engines, the scream of the dive-bombers. The sea erupted into seething foam, the sky was striped with tracer and shell, acrid black smoke drifted through the air. On the flat water ships were exploding, burning and drifting without command. The beach was edged with brown and red where the young men in their battle dress lay dead and dying.

'It was a bad show,' said Mountbatten, in his vice-admiral's uniform. He shook his head regretfully, pursed his lips in censure. 'A bad show indeed. General Roberts was hardly the commanding officer I had been led to believe.'

Freddie suddenly felt a savage flame of anger ignite inside him, sitting among the staff as they reviewed the raid.

'I don't quite follow you,' he said, standing up. '*You* were in command.'

'I provided General Roberts with all the facilities at my disposal,' Mountbatten said smoothly. 'But of course, on the day, the force commander takes responsibility. He insisted on making a frontal assault.' He shook his head again. 'Very bad. And the Canadian troops were hardly of the highest quality, although he insisted upon using them.'

'I assume General Roberts was following the plan drawn up by your staff,' Freddie said. He had remained standing. He was very angry indeed. 'His troops were an élite force. They were massacred before they could even get out of the assault craft.'

'Freddie, Freddie,' Mountbatten said gently. 'I understand how upset you are. You were there, you witnessed it all. Such a combination of bad luck . . .'

'They knew you were coming, you incompetent bastard!'

Mountbatten looked left and right at his beautifully turned-out staff officers, seated each side of him, raised his eyebrows.

'I do hope you're not blaming *me*,' he said.

'There was no bombardment. There was no heavy bombing. Jesus Christ, man, the last time we let troops walk into sustained enemy fire like that, unsupported by anything, was the first day on the Somme. I know, I was there.'

'My dear chap! If you have criticisms of the ground and air forces please address them to the generals and the air marshals. I'm just a sailor who tried to help them with their plans.'

'They gave you a general's uniform, and an air marshal's one too,' Freddie said quietly. 'The boys who are dead and maimed today trusted you knew what you were doing.'

He pushed past the staff officers, went to the door.

'Poor chap,' Mountbatten murmured behind him. 'Taken prisoner, you know. Affected his mind.'

Freddie turned.

'The only one insane here is you,' he said levelly. 'Insane with ambition. You murdered those boys yesterday as sure as if you shot them yourself.'

'We have learned invaluable lessons. Lives, in the long term, will have been saved. When this little bit of bother is over people will see that I was right all along. Now, gentlemen, shall we get to work? We have already identified some of the causes of the failure on the ground. General Roberts and his men obviously take principal responsibility. Monty cannot be absolved, he attended the principal planning meetings. Bad luck, of course, attended the convoy, running into the Germans. MI6 must take its share of responsibility for misinforming us of the troop levels in Dieppe itself . . .'

Freddie went out and into the street. He stood breathing in the fresh air, until the sweat on him cooled and dried. He walked away, leaving the port behind him.

54

Personal Recommendation

London, April 1944

The King stood looking out of the window. His view of the skyline had been altered by a German bomber the night before and he watched, in the uniform of an admiral of the fleet, as people scurried over the ruins of a mansion block, cutting and extracting its wood, carrying it off for fuel. Godfrey came across the vast room, still chill from the freezing winter, and paused respectfully on a worn runner carpet, the gift of a Rajah to Queen Victoria. Geometric Asian pattern, changed course under his feet. King George looked round.

'Ah,' he said. 'De Clare. Th-there you are.'

'You asked to see me, sir,' Godfrey said smoothly, his hands clasped behind his back.

'I did. Yes.' The King picked up a half-drunk glass of whisky. 'Want a Scotch?' he asked. 'They s-send it down for us from Balmoral, you know. Help yourself.'

Godfrey glanced around. They were entirely alone in the giant room, filled with its ancient artefacts of empire. There were no servants at all – the door had been quietly closed behind him, leaving him secluded with the King. His interest quickened, he helped himself to whisky, and topped it up with soda from a glass siphon. They sat together on an enormous sofa stuffed with horse hair. The King took a quick pull at his glass.

'Got a special request to make of you,' he said. 'Damned useful, having you here in the Palace. R-resident art surveyor and MI5 man. Couldn't be better.'

'MI6 now, sir. I transferred. How can I help, sir?' Godfrey asked quietly.

'MI6, yes. That's it, see? You're in intelligence. And you're an art historian. Well known. Could be good c-cover, eh?'

'I'm sure it could sir,' Godfrey said patiently. 'What did you have in mind?'

'Invasion's coming. Oh yes it is. I know. See Ch-Churchill, y'see. Yes, invasion's on its way. Wouldn't be surprised if you aren't involved somewhere.'

'I have . . . certain duties,' Godfrey said cautiously.

'Good man. Don't want to know what they are. Must keep security.'

'Oh, yes.'

'It's afterwards. Once the great armies are advancing into G-Germany.'

'Yes, sir?'

King George cleared his throat. He succeeded in looking tremendously embarrassed and worried at the same time. Making a great effort, he began to speak.

'My b-brother David. Who was king.'

'King Edward,' Godfrey murmured.

'King Edward, yes. God knows, de Clare, I didn't ask to have this job, but I have d-done it to the best of my ability.'

'You are a great monarch, sir.'

'No, no. I'm not really. No good at speaking to people. But with the Queen's help . . . anyhow, that's by the by. I am k-king, and I do my best.'

The King got up, and kicked both feet hard a few times against the monolithic construction of the sofa.

'Damned cold gets in your b-bones, don't you find? Can't f-feel my feet sometimes.' He sat back down. 'Yes. David. King Edward that w-was. He . . . wasn't always sensible. Let that damned woman lead him on, I'll be b-bound.'

The King appeared to come to a halt. He snuffled up some whisky.

'In what way was he not sensible, sir?' Godfrey asked helpfully. The King turned to look at Godfrey and suddenly a hunted expression filled his face.

'The Nazis, man!' he said desperately. 'My brother collaborated with them, he was working for the overthrow of this country. He betrayed military secrets to them, he connived at our defeat . . .'

'I know,' Godfrey said quietly, firmly. 'I do know, sir.'

'Yes, I kn-know you do . . . you were involved in finding out.'

The King took a grip on his tumbler with both hands.

'What I most fear, de Clare, is that the German r-records of all this – and they do exist, believe me, they exist – will come to light. They will be uncovered by those who follow the advancing Allied armies. The whole terrible business will be exposed to public view. What my brother did was treat with the king's enemy in the hour of our most m-mortal peril, and th-that is High Treason. The penalty is death. In this hideous . . . in this nefarious affair he was aided and abetted by my other brother, Prince George. He is dead now, of course, killed in the aeroplane. But David is not. Even while shut up as g-governor in the Bahamas he c-continued his plotting with the N-Nazis. I f-fear for the very existence of the House of Windsor should such secrets ever become public knowledge.'

'Yes,' Godfrey agreed thoughtfully.

'I want you to find them, de Clare. All the relevant documents. Bring them to me here, they shall be shut up with the Royal Archives in Windsor. I h-have a cover for you. Yes. You shall be my personal emissary to recover the great correspondence conducted by my illustrious ancestor, Queen Victoria, with her many German relations, to bring them back to this country for safe-keeping. You shall be armed with whatever warrants you require, that will enable you to go anywhere, see whatever you wish. I shall see to it.'

'You will supply me with your own personal letter, as the King, describing me as your trusted emissary, acting upon your own orders?'

'I will.'

'Then I shall do as you ask, sir,' said Godfrey solemnly. 'Your secrets will be safe in my hands.'

'That's good!' the King cried in enormous relief. He went to the salver and splashed whisky vigorously into his glass.

'Another?'

'No, thank you, sir. I have to go to a meeting.'

'MI5, eh?'

'Yes, sir.'

'The invasion, I'll be b-bound. Well, I mustn't keep you. I'll get those letters to you.'

Godfrey bowed as he took his leave.

'Thank you, sir,' he said, in deep sincerity. 'You don't know how much it means to me to have earned your trust.'

'Well, well,' Godfrey said cheerfully. 'This is a family gathering, isn't it? Good morning Violet, Felicity.'

'You're late,' George grunted sourly.

'Taking whisky with the King.' Godfrey said airily. '*Droit du roi*, that kind of thing.'

'Well, let's get on with it. D-day itself. Finally, the invasion of Europe.'

It appeared that Violet and Felicity had only just arrived as well. Violet produced a solid gold cigarette case and offered them round.

'God but it's good to have real tobacco again,' she said. 'The poor French are smoking hay.'

'I like your fag case,' said Godfrey.

'We get given them. Solid gold, in case you need funds in a hurry.'

'Can we get down to business?' George asked testily. 'The Diamond Network.'

'Is ready and waiting,' Felicity said calmly. 'Violet and I have been in France for the past seven months seeing to just that. We were picked up last night from a field outside Caen. We are in place, we await instruction.'

'Good. Good. Now you must listen to me closely, just as the agents of the network must listen to you. There must be no, repeat no acts of aggression against the Germans before the word comes. The word is in fact a message, a line of poetry. You'll hear it on the radio. You know when. It will say: The chestnut casts his flambeaux.'

'Housman,' said Felicity.

'Yes. It's easy to remember. This is your signal to begin Plan "Violet" – not actually named after you, Vi, so don't look smug – which will disrupt German telecommunications.'

'We have the trunk cables, overhead wires, repeater stations all marked,' said Violet.

'Good. After that you move on to Plan "Vert", sabotage of rail communications, and "Tortue", the disruption of German road travel. I can't tell you how much it all matters. The Allied armies will have a tough job getting ashore from the beaches, the more we can slow up the arrival of the Germans the more help we'll be giving the troops to get established on French soil. There is something I want to say. Although your *resistants* have been armed by us with good quantities of Sten guns, grenades and so forth, you are to avoid actual fighting as much as possible. Your task is sabotage and disruption.'

He cleared his throat.

'There is, however, a possibility you may have to fight. If things get hard for the troops we may have to throw everything in to slow the advance of the German troops. If you hear the second line of the poem transmitted at your listening hour by the BBC, it is the signal for insurrection.'

'Our *resistants* aren't trained soldiers,' Felicity commented.

'I know. As I say, it will be in part a measure of last resort to help the invasion force. An effective one, if costly. Let's hope it doesn't have to happen. All right. I just wanted a quick briefing once you got back. Let's meet for a full session before you return to France. How long have you got off?'

'Two weeks leave,' said Violet. 'We're going down to the castle.'

'I'm going to go fishing,' said Felicity. 'Apparently the Water's seething.'

'Lovely. All right, Thursday fortnight then? Same time?'

The two women went out.

'When's Garotte due?' said Godfrey.

George glanced at his watch. 'Half an hour.' He glanced out of the window at the river, watched a procession of huge black barges being towed by. 'I had lunch with one of the Americans. OSS chap, seconded to Six. Name of Angleton.'

'I know him.'

'Hmm. Clever fellow, I have to admit. Seems to think that counter-intelligence can be turned into a science. Looking into the future, he sees the next contest as being against the Soviet Union.'

'Oh?'

'Yes. If I understood him correctly, which I think I did, even through a glass of the most hideous Algerian wine which was all the club could offer, the central axiom of his theory is that you must penetrate the enemy's counter-intelligence service. This is essential. You are then able to manipulate him into an unreal world where he in effect does as you wish.'

'Rather as we are doing to the Abwehr at the moment.'

'Quite. Garotte, for example. They believe her to be theirs, whereas she is ours, and tells them what we wish them to know. Looking into the future, Angleton proposes a similar penetration of the Soviet NKVD.'

'Well, well. We shall have to keep in touch with Mr Angleton, won't we?'

'I thought you would want to know. Being an astute man, he also raised the possibility of us being penetrated by them.'

'The Soviets,' Godfrey said, without expression.

'Yes.'

'What did you say?'

'I told him that it was quite impossible for the British secret services to be penetrated by a foreign power. I pointed out that the wrong sort of fellow would never be allowed in the door. That we only recruited from people with the right background. Chaps we knew personally.

Had been to school and university with. Knew socially. Met at the club. That we relied on personal recommendation from people of sound judgement, who had close acquaintance with the candidate.'

Godfrey looked blandly out of the window.

'Chaps like us, in fact,' he said.

'Isn't is grand to be back?' said Violet. 'What do you say we treat ourselves to lunch at the Connaught and then on down to the castle? We'll be in time for an hour's fishing before dusk.'

'Why not? Why don't we cut up through the park? I've missed seeing the English blossom so much.'

They paused at the side of the road to let an old red double-decker bus pass. It went by in an acrid cloud of smoke, filled with passengers. As they crossed Felicity suddenly grabbed at Violet's elbow.

'Vi. Look. Isn't that Carlotta?'

On the other side of the street a woman in a smart grey suit was walking, moving quickly, going the way they had come.

'Lord, so it is.'

'Should we say hallo, do you think?'

'Not personally,' Violet saud drily. 'Carlotta is nothing but very bad news.'

'Where is she going, in such a hurry?' Felicity asked, watching her. 'Let's follow and see.'

'Honestly, Flick! Spying's got into your blood.'

'Come on. Look, she's going down to the river.'

At a distance, they followed her. Suddenly, with the Thames in sight, she turned into a tall, drab, red-brick office building.

'Vi,' Felicity said quietly, 'we just left there. That's where George is. MI5.'

55

We'll Go Home Now

France, June 1944

The air rushed cold through the yard-wide hole cut in the bottom of the Halifax bomber's fuselage. Through it, looking down through the black night, they saw a steady flashing from the ground, long and short, Morse code.

'That's it,' the dispatcher shouted above the racket of the four engines and the roaring gale. He began to flash back the reply letter as the pilot wheeled gently round in the sky. Violet and Felicity pushed themselves up from the hard bench where they had been waiting, their parachutes, Sten guns and grenades weighing them down.

Violet sat down, made the awkward sideways shuffle, swivelled at the edge of the hole, dangled her feet out as she had been trained. Through the hole she could see the L-shape of bicycle lamps below, indicating the drop zone and the prevailing breeze. The pilot was bringing them back on to the field. They would drop in quick succession, the bomber would fly on to Caen a few kilometres further on, where the dispatcher would fling out a load of propaganda leaflets from the Political Warfare Executive, thus explaining the mission of the low-flying bomber. By then, Violet and Felicity, F-Section's two agents would be back in the heart of the Diamond Network.

'Coming up,' the dispatcher yelled.

The red light turned to green, the dispatcher's arm swept down.

'Go!' he cried, and she pushed gently forward, springing to attention as she did so. Like a guardsman, she fell straight down through the hole. The air whipped at her, the great bomber's dark belly rushed above her. With a snap and a jerk, her parachute opened and she floated down in the cool night air. She could see the lights of the drop zone, she steered towards them. The pilot had dropped her in the perfect place; the light breeze was blowing her directly at the field. Glancing back and up, she saw something dark drifting against the moonlit sky, and knew that Felicity had dropped successfully as

well. The night was quiet, with just the grumble of the departing
Halifax fading in the distance. Down near the lights she saw figures
moving, it would be the reception committee, Gaspard, Arnaud and
the others.

As she came down the breeze died, close to the ground. She was
dropping short. The river ran between the fields there, with trees that
poked their roots into the water. She did not dare risk getting caught
up in their branches, accepted the logic of the wind and settled for
landing on the other side of the river, and getting her feet wet when
she waded across.

She landed with a thump in the long grass of the meadow, got to
her feet to collapse the canopy, drew it in. Against the sky she saw
Felicity landing by the lights, heard the soft exclamations in French.

She unbuckled her harness in the darkness. Suddenly, the night was
filled with the clamour of automatic weapons. The hedgerow beyond
lit up with the muzzle flashes of Schmeisser machine-guns, yellow and
orange.

The burst of fire lasted but a few seconds. Then she heard harsh,
shouted commands in German, the sound of somebody in the field
beyond screaming hideously.

She saw the troops, dark figures pushing through the hedge, further
commands, knew that they were coming for her. Desperately, she
shrugged off the harness, dumped her sack of grenades. The water
gurgled dark and swift by her side. She crawled frantically through the
long grass, rolled into its current, and the river tumbled her away.

In the small attic room, Carlotta put her attaché case down on the
table, set herself on a chair in front of it and opened it. Through the
window she could see the sprawl of Victoria, going down to the river.
Buses and military lorries were crossing Vauxhall Bridge, dirty smoke
was drifting from the old factories south of the bridge. She reached
out and tugged the curtains shut – you didn't need any nosy parkers
peering across at her from some other garret.

Quietly and efficiently, she brought out her Morse key and plugged
the radio set inside the attaché case into the mains with its round-
pronged Bakelite plug. She switched on, and the little dial jumped to
life. She took out a sheet of typed notepaper, and began to transmit.

'Have just returned from ports of east coast and south-eastern
England,' she tapped. 'Saw with my own eyes the Army Group Patton
preparing to embark. Came close to General Patton himself, heard
him remark that now the diversion in Normandy was going so well,

the time had come to commence operations around Calais. The King, Churchill, Eisenhower and Field-Marshal Brooke have all visited First US Army Group command post at Dover Castle. General Marshall of the American Army arrives here from Washington on the 9th or 10th of June to see Patton and the troops off. These assault troops comprise at least five airborne divisions, a sea force of ten divisions, and FUSAG itself will have over fifty divisions, most of which are here already.

'In the light of this must warn that Normandy invasion currently under way, known as D-day is a feint. The real invasion will take place on the Pas de Calais in a few days time. I transmit this in the conviction that the D-day assault is a trap set with the purpose of making us move all our reserves in a rushed strategic redisposition that will lead to our defeat when Patton and FUSAG invade unopposed at the Pas de Calais. Ends.'

She lifted her hand from the transmitter key, and flexed her stiff fingers. Silently, she switched off.

Godfrey got up from the chair where he had been listening and watching, and took the typed sheet of paper.

'Well done, Garotte,' he said. 'We'll send them more of the same tomorrow. Patton will have had a hold-up. The invasion will be delayed another day. They'll sit waiting there in front of empty beaches, waiting for a force that never comes.'

The message was coming through: F-Section had put in a new wireless operator to replace Felicity – Tony, who had worked in Vichy France in '43. Violet waited in the little farmhouse, while he wrote down the groups that came through from London, and watched out of the window. Somebody was coming up the dusty red lane through the vines. She sighted on him with the sniper rifle that had arrived in the big C-type canisters, packed in with Sten guns, cyclonite landmines that looked like cow droppings, soup plates, tobacco and chocolate. It was Gilbert, her *maquisard*. She put down the long rifle with its big telescope, and Tony came in, handed her a sheet of pencilled letter groups. She sat down, began to decode them.

She heard voices. Gilbert came in in his collarless blue shirt, baggy chambray trousers and beret. Tony poured *rosé* wine, sharp and acid, into chipped glass tumblers as Violet finished writing out the translation of the message. She looked up.

'I have some news,' said Gilbert.

'So do I,' she said. 'But tell me yours first.'

'Felicity is alive,' he said.

Sudden hope burst inside her, she bit on a knuckle to control the emotion.

'Injured,' he said.

'Of course. She was gunned down. Quickly, where is she?'

'The Gestapo have her,' he said grimly. 'She is in the prison in Caen. Tell me now, does she have knowledge of this place?'

'No. Nor did I. When we were ambushed I then assumed that all previous plans were unsound.'

'Good. Good.'

'We shall have to break into the prison and release her.'

'How?'

'We have a force of thirty *maquisards* under arms. We are well supplied with weaponry, with explosives. We *must* get her out.'

His mouth tightened, he stayed silent for a few moments.

'Do you know how we were betrayed?' she asked. He shrugged, his mind still on the fearsome prospect of having to attack a heavily defended German building.

'There are traitors,' he said. 'We shall find the one, and then – *zut.*' He ran a finger across his stubbly throat. 'But you have news,' he reminded her.

'Yes . . . yes. Our forces are still held up in the *bocage* country. They have yet to take Caen. The Germans are moving units towards them. One is the 2nd SS Panzer Division, *Das Reich.* It has had to come from Montauban. *Das Reich* is considered of the most formidable fighting units anywhere. Twenty thousand SS troops, seventy-five self-propelled assault guns, sixty medium tanks, one hundred heavy tanks, including Tigers.'

'General Montgomery will not welcome the arrival of this force on his battlefield,' Gilbert observed. 'Why is London sending us messages about it?'

'The division has been harassed by *maquisards,* Jeds and F-Section all its way. The railways have been made useless, it is travelling under its own power by road.'

'*Oui?*'

'It's coming through here,' she said quietly. 'They have asked us to assist.'

Gilbert smiled mirthlessly.

'Truly a tale to tell our grandchildren, should we have them. But I regret, there you have your answer. We cannot attempt to free Felicity.'

'No,' she whispered.

'*Violet,*' he said urgently, pronouncing it in the French way. 'Violet, the only news I have is that she was alive when taken into the prison. The Gestapo . . . and on a wounded woman . . .'

'They will have tortured her.'

'For sure. That is what these swine do.'

'Yes,' she said grimly. 'Then we must see what we can do to these other swine, the men of *Das Reich*.'

She hesitated.

'There is something I did not tell you. In revenge for the atacks made on them on their journey they have murdered six hundred people in a village they passed through. Oradour-sur-Glane. They are all dead.'

'Then why do we wait?' he asked. 'Let us kill some of them.'

Noises came through the dark. The moon had sunk, a white sickle, towards the far horizon, the sun had not yet painted the west. The hoarse grinding of huge diesel engines, the squeaking of tracks, the steady tramp of boots, the clink of equipment, it formed a whole, the sound of men and tanks on the march; it filtered out through the trees and over the hedges, it reached Violet on the steep hillside. The narrow, winding road below began to be lit by hooded yellow lamps, moving towards them.

'Now,' she said, and Tony spoke into his radio set.

'*Maintenant. Le feu.*'

There was a pause, then a short bang in the night, and flickering yellow flames that grew, until a blaze lit up the area below. A lorry, wedged across the road, was burning furiously. In its light a column of SP guns, tanks and infantry stood, the men deploying off the narrow, walled road. The shouting of orders was drowned by the rising bellow of the lead tank's engine. It pushed forward, black in the yellow light, ready to ram the truck from its way.

There was a second explosion, a burst of light under its tracks, it slewed sideways, slammed into the wall. On the road, in the flames, they could see a double line of circular objects.

Tanks were beginning to force their way off the road, but it was narrow, bounded by walls and ancient, deep ditches covered with primeval trees, bound together, hundreds of years old.

'Open fire,' said Violet, and the hillside erupted with guns.

Dawn sunlight coloured the stinking smoke that drifted through the valley. Violet could taste it as she lay in the bracken, high up on the steep hillside. A tank was burning, part of the scrub and trees on the far side was on fire. The rocks echoed to the sounds of machine-guns and grenades. She could see dim figures trying to push up the scree. The ambush had been well sited. The column was still out in the open, and not safe in laager.

She had the radio with her. Tony was dead. Blood ran down into her eye from her forehead, sliced open by flying shards of rock. Hidden in the bracken she switched it on, tuned to the frequency she had been given.

'Yellow leader, this is Team Oliver,' she said clearly. 'Team Oliver calling Yellow leader.'

'Yellow leader here, Team Oliver,' a voice replied immediately. 'Yellow section airborne, awaiting instructions.'

She spread out her map in front of her, and carefully read out the map reference.

'Leading elements of the *Das Reich* division are on the valley floor,' she said. 'Team Oliver holds the high ground.'

'Stand by,' the unseen voice said unemotionally.

She rolled on her back, peering through the drifting smoke at the polished sky above the valley. A few seconds later something flashed over the ridge, a fighter, a fighter-bomber. Its wings erupted in flame, rockets streaked through the air, screeching, ejecting fire, exploding with short vicious crumps. Through the stems she saw the turret of a Mk IV tank rip off, turning over and over, lazily, to crash into the hedgerow. The huge-nosed Typhoon leaped back out of the dim valley light into the dawn sunshine, climbing almost vertically, its huge engine howling, rays of sun glinting from the pilot's clear canopy, its black and white invasion stripes glowing.

'Thank you, Yellow leader,' she said.

They came through one after the other, a whole section, and the valley floor boiled with filthy, belching black smoke, lit from within by flickering yellow flames. The Typhoons cannonaded the survivors. Violet saw the troops running, falling. She crawled up through the bracken, and over the ridge, slipping away through the pine trees on the other side.

Caen

She had seen the great air fleet fly over from the fields outside, had heard the roar of an earthquake as the bombs fell, had seen the immense column of dust and smoke blackening the sky, rising up to the very clouds above.

Now she picked her way through the ruins, just one more refugee woman with a filthy, bloodied bandage about her head. The German troops pushing through the rubble towards the front line they had fortified from the wreckage paid her no attention. The roads were choked with rubble, pocked by great craters from the bombs the Lancasters and Halifaxes had carried. Great cubes of rock like enormous stone sugar lumps lay scattered everywhere, and all was covered in dust.

Here. It was here. The wreckage of the prison. It had taken a direct hit, maybe more than one. The upper storeys were entirely gone, ragged walls and empty window-frames stood up like stone hedges. She went into the ruins, calling.

'Flick! Flick!'

Something moved in the mess of wood and iron and stone. A dog, foraging for dead meat.

'Flick! Flick!'

Parts were entirely destroyed. A great crater marked where the bomb had struck, she could see the bare earth beneath the ruins.

'Flick, *cherie*! *C'est Violet*!'

What was that? A small, weak cry. It came again. She heaved at a wooden beam, moved it. Stone rubble slid down the man-made scree. There was a hole in there.

'Flick?' she called softly.

In the darkness, something whimpered. Very carefully, she climbed down. A stone wall, a bundle of rags in the corner.

'Flick, darling, it's me.'

She held her, she was hot with fever, her eyes were glassy and bright. She was huddled up, clutching herself. Through the torn prison uniform Violet saw hideous wounds. Burns, livid cigarette burns marking the white skin. No fingernails. Purple, bloody, pulped toes. Old injuries.

For a second, she seemed to know Violet.

'I didn't tell them!' she cried out, and her voice broke. Violet held her tight in the wreckage, and in the street, a column of troops tramped by.

'It's all right, now, darling,' she said softly.

In the darkness she heard a tank engine start up, heard the squeak of its tracks. She thought it was a Sherman. In the ditch she picked Felicity up again, staggered on along the road. She glanced up at the stars, she was still moving north-west. Suddenly the darkness was ripped open by a harsh voice.

'Who goes there?'

'Friend,' she croaked. The voice had been English. 'Friend. Please help me.'

She tottered forward, felt friendly hands on her, a light flashing in her face. The soldiers went to take Felicity from her arms, and she screamed, piercingly, clutching onto Violet.

'I'll take her,' she said, walking on. 'She was tortured by the Gestapo, she fears men. Find me a doctor, please.'

She passed through the front line.

'We'll go home now, darling,' she whispered, but Felicity made no reply.

56

Fast, Fast, Fast!

Kandy, Ceylon, August 1945

Major-General Freddie de Clare climbed down from the Dakota and walked across the tarmac to the airport building. It was very hot, the flight from Burma had taken a long time. He went underneath an immense white sign that proclaimed it to be Supreme Command Allied Forces South East Asia. A smartly turned-out military clerk was behind the desk when he went in, large wooden paddle-bladed fans turned on the ceiling. Outside, he suddenly heard the sound of sirens and engines, saw a vast white Cadillac limousine driving away from the airfield building through the palms and bougainvillea, surrounded by a flotilla of motorcycle outriders, their whirling lights flashing blue on the shimmering white uniforms of the riders.

'Who the hell is that?' he enquired. 'Has President Truman arrived, or is it Mae West?'

'Neither, sir,' the man said proudly. 'That's the Supreme Commander himself, Lord Mountbatten.'

'Does he always go about like that?'

'Always. He's come for someone important.'

'President Truman?'

'No, sir. Big-wig politician from London, sir. Man from the Colonial Office, Mr Clare.'

'Perceval?' Freddie said disbelievingly. 'I am General de Clare, are you sure he didn't come for me?'

The man consulted a list.

'No, sir.'

'How am I meant to get to headquarters?'

'I'll see if I can find you a jeep, sir.'

They were playing golf when he got there. He climbed out of his jeep outside the King's Pavilion and somebody shouted 'fore' over the music of a full orchestra playing. He went in, hot and sweating, and found himself in the middle of a reception. Pushing through, he came across his cousin.

'Freddie!' Perceval said absently. 'What *are* you doing here?'

'Having a conference with Dickie, I hope,' he said shortly. 'But first, a bath.'

'Join us for dinner.'

He was in time to find Perceval as drinks were being served before dinner. He took a whisky and soda from a uniformed, white-gloved steward and went up to his cousin as he moved through the crowd.

'Hallo, Perceval. Have I caught you between bores?'

An expression of great displeasure went over the other's face.

'For God's sake, Freddie!' he hissed. 'The name is Percy. Perce for short.'

'Oh, sorry. I've been too busy fighting a war to remember the fine detail.'

'Now we're in, we'll have a society without class. I'm leading the way.'

'If you're leading the way old man, we can be sure it'll be without class,' Freddie said jovially. 'Well, you did get in, though. They dumped Winston. There's gratitude for you, I suppose. I hear that this new welfare state is going to happen.'

'As I always said!' Perceval cried smugly.

'You were ahead of us all there. A beneficent state will look after us all from cradle to grave.'

'Exactly!'

'Yes. How are you going to pay for it, old boy? We're broke, and the Americans have just told us there's no more money.'

He stared keenly at Perceval over his whisky.

'Must cost a lot, this sort of thing,' he said encouragingly.

'It does,' the other said proudly.

'So?'

'Simple. During this long war we have been through, the countries of the Empire all operated their finances through the Sterling Bloc. They had to bank with us, in other words. We set the exchange rates to suit ourselves. Plenty left over to pay for the new welfare state.'

'I rather have a feeling that if you do that sort of thing with other people's finances in real life you land up in the Old Bailey. It's called fraud.'

'The people of Great Britain fought for a better tomorrow! We promised it to them and they have elected us, the Labour Party, to give it to them! We shall not betray that trust!'

'You'd rather betray the people of the Empire.'

'Really, Freddie, you have a terribly simplistic approach to life,' Perceval said loftily. 'You'd do better to stick to tanks.'

'All right, what will you do when this . . . heist, as the Americans say, this heist of other people's money runs out?'

'Well, don't forget that Great Britain is in a very advantageous situation. Our manufacturing industry is intact, Europe's is destroyed. We shall sell machinery to the Empire.'

'At our prices.'

'Of course.'

'What if they don't want it? If I recall rightly our machines were pretty rickety even before the war.'

'They have no choice. It's us or nothing,' Perceval snapped.

'I personally back the Germans to be back in the race in five years. What if they sell better machinery cheaper?'

'They can't to the Empire,' Perceval said sullenly. 'We shan't let them.'

'And there I was thinking that we British invented the doctrine of free trade,' Freddie said mockingly. 'All this seems to presuppose that you'll be raising money through tax, of one sort or another.'

'Well of course,' Perceval said seriously. 'The society of the future will of course have high taxes. High taxes, high benefits.'

'Give your money to the government, who decides how much to give back? I'm more used to the old system of deciding how to spend my money myself.'

'Oh, no. A system run by the state is far more efficient. More wise, more beneficent. You'll see.'

'I think that's what I'm afraid of,' Freddie said drily.

'Ah, there you are, Percy!' a loud female voice cried. 'Shall I rescue you from the clutches of the military? It's time to go in.'

Perceval brightened. A thin woman of faded beauty in a beautifully cut silk frock bore down on them.

'Certainly, Edwina! Do you know my cousin, General Freddie de Clare? Freddie, this is Lady Edwina, Dickie's wife.'

Freddie and Lady Edwina exchanged one brief glance of instant and mutual loathing.

'Right, I must have you, Percy. I want you to tell me all about the brave new tomorrow we are creating in Britain. So nice to see you, General.'

They went into a fabulously decorated dining room, white and gold, with glorious blooms lush in shining cut-glass bowls and vases. A long table was set with silver upon damask, a string quartet played lightly in a corner, and uniformed native servants were on hand. Freddie found himself somewhere in the middle order. At the head of the table Lord Louis Mountbatten presided, smiling and laughing, in full white dress uniform, with decorations and *aiguillettes*. Lady Edwina dominated the other end. Delicately smoked fish of some sort was served, beautifully chill on a bed of salad, and a clear crisp hock poured into tall, green-tinged flutes of cut glass. After his long flight Freddie began to feel slightly disoriented. The war was over, the Japanese had been atom-bombed into surrender. There was a fearful mess to be cleared up.

Washing down some of the fish with his wine he caught Mountbatten looking at him.

'Ah, General de Clare. I didn't know we had the pleasure of your company today.'

'Well, yes,' said Freddie. 'You and I are to meet in conference in the morning.'

'But didn't you get my message? I have had to cancel our meeting. I am to show the Minister here around in the morning and then I am flying to Singapore.'

'I got no message,' Freddie said grimly. 'I shall have to accompany you to Singapore.'

'Sorry,' Mountbatten said charmingly. 'Our three aircraft are all full with my staff.'

'Then we had better sort the details out now.'

'I really don't think—'

'I am in Burma,' Freddie said, ignoring him. 'We are at the moment the authority in charge.'

'I know. I won the war there.'

'If you say so then I am sure you are right,' Freddie said stonily.

Mountbatten suddenly flushed red.

'Don't you insult me, General,' he said in a low voice. 'I have a long memory.'

'Freddie's always outspoken,' Perceval butted in. 'Don't mind him, Dickie.'

'I want you to mind me a lot,' Freddie said hotly. 'I am attempting to restore order and your representatives are thwarting me at every turn.'

'Good Lord, Dickie!' Edwina cried from the other end of the table. 'What is going on?'

'I don't know, darling,' Mountbatten called charmingly down the table. 'The general here is having trouble with his soldiers, wants me to sort it out.'

'I am having *no* trouble with my men at all, who are without exception performing a wonderful job in difficult circumstances,' Freddie said loudly. The other guests were listening with interest, sensing a first-class entertaining row.

'I am having trouble with the representatives of the Supreme Commander here, who are providing succour and support to U Aung San, leader of the Burmese National Army.'

'So they should!' Edwina cried. 'What a wonderful young man. He is an inspiration to us all.'

'The Japanese certainly found him an inspiration. He was on their side. He fought for them. Our enemies.'

'Oh, I don't think you should be too hard on him,' Mountbatten said childingly. 'Don't you think that any young Burmese of spirit could have been expected to accept the Japanese offer of independence?'

'You're just an old hidebound imperialist,' Edwina cried. 'You can't understand people in Asia wanting to be free of our rule.'

'Japan was not offering independence,' Freddie said savagely. 'No more than Hitler gave freedom to any of the countries under his rule. Like him, the Japanese offered satrapies to those turncoats prepared to exploit and oppress their own people. U Aung San was one such. A Burmese quisling. Now those who remained true in their hearts to us in the war, loyal Burmese, are shocked to find that we, the British are consorting with our former enemy. They cannot understand how we accept them, those who exploited them in the war, who took their food, money and women. They expected U Aung San to be shot, they did not expect us to negotiate away the country to him.'

'Typical!' Edwina called scornfully. 'Can't you see that it is those ridiculous people who accepted the rule of the British who are the real quislings? The real traitors to their people? U Aung San is their future, young, vibrant and virile, he is the sort of leader they need.'

'Then let him prove it. Burma has to be led slowly and carefully towards self-government. Democratic institutions have to be set up and put into motion. There must be an independent civil service, functioning independent political parties.'

'Slow? Always slow, slow, slow!' Mountbatten said derisively. 'I say fast, fast, fast! Let us do it all at maximum speed!'

'Democracies are not good at doing things quickly.'

'All the more reason for giving power to young nationalists like U Aung San. They are the future, not an outmoded past,' said Edwina.

'Then you will end up with a one-party state as in Soviet Russia.'

'What better model for a young country?'

'I am old-fashioned enough to believe that democracy is the worst form of government except for all those other forms which have been tried from time to time.'

'You are just an old-fashioned imperialist Tory, General.'

'No, madam. I vote for the Whig party, on the rare occasions it fields candidates.'

He turned to Mountbatten.

'I want to lock up U Aung San and his cronies and put them on trial for war crimes as they are to do with the Nazis back in Europe. I have your permission?'

'Of course not!' Mountbatten said, shocked. 'We are trying to create good will, not ill will.'

Freddie pushed back his seat, placed his white linen napkin next to his plate.

'Then I must get back,' he said. 'There is still a lot to do. I thank you for a most pleasant meal.'

He went out, and an excited buzz of conversation resumed.

'Dickie, darling,' Edwina drawled. 'Don't you feel we ought to find General de Clare something else to do?'

Mountbatten's face brightened. He always enjoyed sacking people who got in his way.

'Good idea, darling.'

He speared a piece of fish, chewed on it happily.

'I'll see to it right away,' he said.

57

We Just Didn't Lose

Windstone Castle, December 1946

'I say, Vi,' Freddie called, from the great doors, as he came in. 'Are you milking the cows or something?'

Violet put down the two galvanised buckets she had been carrying across the marble-floored hall. She was wearing about four cardigans and had her head in a commando's balaclava.

'I am not!' she said with spirit. 'I am gathering up the rain as it comes through the roof. The Fourth Army when it lived here did not make any repairs to the damage it caused. The place is as water-tight as a sieve.'

'It's about as cold inside as it is out,' Freddie admitted. 'Shall I light some fires?'

'Oh, do, that would be such a help. The de Clares have held Christmas here ever since 1067, and I'll be damned if we are going to break the tradition now. I do want to get the temperature above freezing before Gawaine and Molly bring the baby.'

Freddie parked his suitcase and went off. After a while he reappeared, pushing a wheelbarrow he had laden with logs and kindling. He set to building a big fire in the mighty grate and soon the big circular hall flickered with the light of the flames. He worked steadily, bringing in wood, and lighting fires, and imperceptibly, the temperature began to climb.

'I recall that Uncle had a team of servants to do all this,' he remarked cheerfully, as he passed Violet, who was wheeling in a large pine tree in an ornately decorated pot.

'There's just you and me,' she said. 'Are you hungry? I've got a rabbit pie in the oven, I went out yesterday and shot a few. They're overrunning the place. Tell you what, let's have a drink, I've been at this since dawn.'

'You have grog?' he enquired.

'I walled up the cellar before I let the Fourth Army in,' she said triumphantly. 'And plastered and painted the wall. I broke back in last week, they never found it. There's a decent bottle of claret warming in the kitchen by the range. Pink gin or Scotch?'

'Gin,' he said.

They went through to the kitchen where the black Victorian range radiated a welcome warmth. The scent of the cooking pie was in the air. Violet splashed gin into tumblers, added angostura bitters. They sat down on wooden chairs round the scrubbed table.

'God . . .' she said thankfully. 'I don't know what I'd do without booze.'

'That reminds me, I've got treacle tart, apple pies, Christmas cake and mince pies in the car. Clarissa's been baking like anything. There's an entire general's allowance of sugar in there.'

'Marvellous. We're going to go out to the lake later. A flock of geese has thankfully taken up residence. You'd better shoot straight or there'll be no Christmas lunch.'

'I shall do my best,' he said solemnly. He drank some gin, and allowed the heat of the stove to penetrate his chilled flesh.

'Is everyone coming?' he asked. 'I'm picking Clarissa and the children up from the station later.'

'Molly and Gawaine will be here with young Bertram tomorrow. It's open house for the de Clares; all the others know they can come if they want, even Perceval, rot his socialist hide, if he can bear to show his face.'

'What's income tax now? I heard a rumour out there it was coming down.'

'No such luck. Ten bob in the pound for the ordinary folk, nineteen and a Rick surtax for aristos like us, living in our unimaginable luxury in our fabulous piles. It makes you sick.'

'Think it'll go down? The war's over.'

'What's that got to do with anything? That little swine Perceval is proud of this ghastly taxation. He told me so. Taxation, he boasted, is just as effective as violence or outright confiscation, and at the same time lacks all their disadvantages.'

'I can't see that anybody is any better off for it. This welfare state seems to translate into simply everybody being destitute instead of some.'

'Fish would turn in his grave. He thought income tax was immoral, something only turned to as a last resort for the survival of the country.'

'Different times, different mores.'

'Meanwhile, we have to decide how to keep the fabric of the castle in sufficient repair to actually stop the roof falling in on us. A lot of us, our kind, are simply giving up, you know. The big houses were used for government purposes during the war, they're all damaged, they all need a fortune spending on them and just about none of us have got the money, certainly not while we're paying to buy the coal mines, railways and all the other nonsense Perceval and his lot have their hearts set on. There are patrician families who are simply ceasing to exist, just being . . . blotted up in the amorphous mass of the middle classes. A couple of bouts of death duties – it's up to seventy-five per cent, Freddie! I hope to God Gawaine doesn't trip going down the stairs – then you've nothing left to sell, and land is only fetching now what it did eighty years ago. Somebody sings a song and you hand over fifty acres.'

She took a pull at her drink.

'Well, it isn't going to happen to us,' she said. 'We're the de Clares.'

'What do you have in mind?'

'I think,' she said slowly, and thoughtfully, 'that we're going to have to open the doors. Let the masses in. There's almost nine hundred years worth of history here, and we still have fabulous amounts of artefacts. Armour, portraits, guns, crossbows – all kinds of weapons – hordes of clothes, medals and honours, carriages, cars, even Fish's aeroplanes! The boats, come to that. The great library, the very castle itself! The Keep, this part we're in now, the battlements, the Traitor's Tower, the moat. All our history, Freddie! We're a microcosm of English history itself. I'm sure we could run coach tours through here. Charge 'em half a crown and a cream tea for sixpence. Windstone ale if they're thirsty in the Yeoman's Inn. What do you think?'

'It's a novel idea,' he admitted.

'You can come and help run it. We need a military mind. You're good at organising the chaps. You must be getting ready to retire from the army anyway.'

'They're talking of sending me out to India for a last posting. We're going to pull out, that's for certain. They'll need a lot of troops to maintain order – there's this latent hostility between the different groups, the Hindus, the Muslims, the Sikhs. There's no reason why anything should go wrong. Viceroy Wavell's very capable, but it needs to be handled with care. I'll do that if they ask me. But yes, I'd like to come and help. I've always loved it here.'

'We can put a wing aside for us to live in. Luckily Gawaine and Molly think like us. If we all pull together we can do it.'

'Here's to coach tours!'

From above there was a clattering of feet.

'Hallo, hallo!'

'Isn't that George? Down here!'

The feet came down the stairs and George came in bringing a breath of cold air about his worn blue Crombie coat.

'I say! A warm kitchen and gin too!'

'Help yourself, George. It's good to see you. What were the roads like?'

'Bloody awful. It's snowing.'

He sat down with a tumbler of gin and bitters.

'I've brought lots of chocolate,' he said.

'Chocolate! Where on earth did you get chocolate?'

'America,' he said evenly. 'I've been over there with a few others. We had some Americans with us in X-2 . . . They're setting up a new intelligence agency. Central Intelligence. CIA. I was there, that's where I got the chocolate. They have lots of it . . .'

He stared unseeingly ahead of him, his voice trailed away.

'You all right, old man?'

'Eh? Oh, yes. I was just thinking . . . I buried my son while I was there, you see. I'm still not quite used to the notion. Him not being there, that is.'

'Oh, George . . .'

'He took pills, you see,' George said, his voice suddenly savage.

'Pills? Was he ill?' Violet said, puzzled.

'No. That's what they do, over there. In America. In Hollywood. They take pills to give themselves pleasure. My son, he became an American. He took pills like they did and he was sick in his sleep, he breathed it in and he is dead. In America they drive enormous vulgar cars, they spend money on things they don't need and they take drugs. That's what their filthy society is made of.'

'I'm so sorry,' Freddie said sincerely.

George drank some gin.

'Better watch out,' he said. 'You've got children. That's what'll happen to them.'

'Not here,' he said. 'This is Britain.'

'Yes, here!' George shouted. 'Don't you understand? We British didn't win the war, we just didn't lose. The Americans and the Russians, they won the war. The Russians have their bit – Poland, Czechoslovakia and all that – and the Americans have the rest. See if I'm not right. Their filthy diseased culture will be here before you know it. Films and drugs and buying things you don't need. There will be no decent people left . . .'

'Honestly, George, I haven't the faintest idea what you're talking about,' said Violet.'

'I'd better get my stuff out of the car,' said Freddie, getting up. 'There's rabbit pie for lunch, George.'

'Eh? Oh, good.'

'I'm so sorry about your son, George,' Violet said sympathetically.

'Oh, thank you. I knew he was doomed, you know. America kills anything good. But look, I won't go on about it. I've come down for Christmas.'

'Can I ask you something? Now the war's over?'

'Yes . . .' he said, cautiously.

She got up, put a pot of peeled carrots on to the range to boil.

'Before we – Felicity and I – went out to France again before D-Day, for F-Section, we had a conference with you at MI6.'

'Yes.'

'When we left, we accidentally saw Carlotta on the street. We followed her. She went into your building.'

He was silent for a few moments.

'And you want to know why?' he said, looking up.

'I'm curious.'

'I'm not supposed to talk about anything like that. But I will, because I know you won't say anything. It's very simple. We at SIS had something called the XX Committee. XX – Double Cross. It ran turned German agents. After the war had been on for a bit we realised we had all their agents. We ran them as double-agents, we told the Germans what *we* wanted them to know. Carlotta was an agent. We called her Garotte. We picked her up through that awful little creep the Duke of Windsor, when he was busy trying to sell us down the river. That's what she was doing with me. A lot of things went on to make D-Day a success that people don't know about.'

'I see. Thank you. I won't let it go any further.'

'Please don't. How is poor Felicity?'

'The same. When we got her back to England she was treated by a foremost nerve specialist – Dr Roberts, a Harley Street man. She's still in the clinic. He says she may never recover. She says nothing. She is in some kind of withdrawn state, catatonic he calls it. When we have the castle inhabitable again I'm going to bring her back here. Being here may bring her back to normal, slowly. I can't bear to think of her just caged up in the clinic, anyway. She ought to be with us.'

The carrots began to boil, the lid rattling over the steam, and she shifted the pot towards the edge. She went and collected some plates, putting them over the range to warm.

'I wish I knew who betrayed us,' she said. 'They were waiting for us as we came down.'

'I know,' he said sympathetically. 'You won't find out now. The extent of French collaboration with the Germans was quite beyond belief. They ran the whole place with a handful of Gestapo men. Once we'd invaded suddenly there were forty-five million people all claiming to be *resistants* but the reality was the other way about. About forty-five million *collaborateurs*.'

'I know,' she said sadly. 'There were damned few you could trust. Are you sticking with MI6 now it's all over?'

'Oh, yes,' he said with a disarming laugh. 'I'm not qualified to do anything else.'

'What about Godfrey?'

'Ah, well Godfrey *is* qualified to do other things. He's leaving. Surveyor of the King's pictures, of course, but also he's got the job as Director of the Portsman Institute of Art. Part of London University. Post-grad college.'

'Oh, he'll like that.'

'Mind you, I may make use of him from time to time. He had a very good intelligence brain, did Godfrey.'

'I'm going into the museum business, myself. We're opening up the castle to the public. Freddie's going to help, too.'

'How very enterprising of you.'

'I put all the stuff into storage before the Fourth Army came. You wouldn't believe some of the stuff I found.'

Freddie came down carrying a large box, and began to unpack pies and cake.

'Vi says you're going to open up the castle with her, Freddie.'

'Eh? Oh, yes. Should be great fun. I've got to go to India first, help Wavell grant independence, of course.'

'Wavell?' George said, looking thoughtfully at his cousin. 'No, you wouldn't have heard.'

'Heard what?'

'Our new government doesn't like Wavell. They feel he lacks charisma.'

'Charisma?' Freddie choked, drinking the last of his gin.

'Yes.' George appeared to be getting some sort of grim amusement from what he was saying. 'They feel that the granting of independence should not be perceived by people as weakness, as a decline in British power and resolution. They want someone who will carry it off with grandeur and panache, the celebration of Britain's mission of trusteeship.'

'I've never heard such rubbish in my life,' Violet said sharply.

'How do you know this, George?' asked Freddie.

'We're the secret service,' George said blandly. 'We like to know what's going on.'

'So who *is* going to do this charismatic job?'

'Mountbatten.'

'God help us all,' said Freddie.

'God will help *us*, Freddie, because as is well known, He is an Englishman. Will he help the poor benighted Indians? That is the question.'

Violet put knives, forks and napkins on the table, brought a golden-crusted pie from the oven, drained the carrots.

She pierced the lid pf pastry, and fragrant steam came out.

'Will you do the wine, George? The damned rabbits did well out of the war, if nobody else did, I'll tell you. There's thousands of them out there.'

She lifted pastry and rabbit and bacon and onions and gravy on to their plates, and they ate.

58

The Bastard Offspring of a Court Chamberlain

The Punjab, India, July 1948

The stench hit them as the jeep came around the rocky corner of the road and into the valley. Sitting next to Freddie, the young lieutenant jammed on the brakes. Dust rolled forward and coated the edge of the dead. Huge, multi-coloured flies buzzed furiously about them, some vultures flapped clumsily into the air. Sensing no threat, they circled about, landing back where they had started from, and continued their feeding.

The narrow valley that led north to safety was jammed with the swollen, stinking bodies of women, men and children. They had been killed with machine-guns, rifles, machetes. Limbs, breasts, genitals lay scattered among the rags, carts, prams and rags on the filthy ground where they had been hacked away.

'Muslims, Charlie,' said Freddie.

The young man was holding a handkerchief to his face against the smell.

'We can't get through this way, sir,' he said in a muffled voice.

'Detour through the village then,' Fredie ordered. 'How many do you think are there?'

'Two thousand?' the young officer, hazarded.

'Nearer three, I'd say. Quickly, then, Charlie. The sooner I can get down to Delhi the sooner we can get troops up here and stop all this.'

The jeep turned on the hot, dusty road where nothing moved, and went back the way they had come. They turned off to cut through the village they could see in the distance on their way to the airfield, racing under the shade of the trees, and alongside a pretty river.

A man was standing at the edge of the village.

'Slow down, Charlie.'

The man was standing in front of a telephone pole. He wore darkly stained baggy trousers, a loose shirt. As they came closer they could see that he was strapped tightly to it with rope. A great pool of blood was all about, it ran across the road in front of them and hordes of insects were feeding on it. Then they saw that none of the man's limbs were connected, they had all been sawn through as he stood there. Freddie felt the bile rise up in his throat, and forced himself to swallow.

'Keep going. We can't do anything for him.'

He glanced up at the telephone pole. The wires hung loose, moving a little in the hot breeze.

They came into the single street of the village. It was blocked by a band of men in khaki uniforms, all wearing turbans. They were heavily armed with rifles, tommy guns and grenades. A wireless van with whip aerials and some trucks stood parked at the side of the road.

'Sikh *jatha*, sir,' the young man said nervously. He pulled up, keeping the engine running. The circle of men opened, and a man in an officer's uniform came through. Behind him, within the circle Freddie, could see a group of naked women, their clothing torn off them and lying on the ground. They wailed in abject fear. He got out of the jeep.

'I am General de Clare,' he said loudly. 'I command this area. I order you to disperse.'

The Sikh smiled.

'Where is your army, General? I am a humble captain, but I command more men than you.'

'Are you responsible for that massacre back there?'

'I regret not. We are on our way to attack another column of filth. We came across these women and are going to treat them as they should be treated.'

He gestured contemptuously behind him.

'They are Muslims,' he explained.

'I order you to let them go. I shall be returning with many troops. I shall hunt you down if you harm them.'

'You are not returning at all, sahib!' the Sikh commander cried delightedly. 'We may do what we wish.'

He turned, and issued a rattle of sudden orders. The watching men all grinned and laughed, they moved back.

'Go! Go!' the Sikh shouted at the women, and they ran through the ranks, screaming.

'Perhaps we shall have fun, hunting them,' he said, turning back to Freddie.

'I shall return also with aeroplanes,' Freddie said stonily. 'If you are still in these parts preying upon the refugees we shall machine-gun and bomb you from the air.'

A wary expression came over the man's face. He stepped back, waved at the jeep to continue.

'Then we must waste no time, General,' he said.

The Viceroy's palace stood white and massive, symbol of a mighty empire. Freddie jumped out of the jeep that had brought him from the airport. No car had been waiting for him, he had commandeered one.

'Thank you, Corporal,' he said, and the man drove away. Freddie went inside. It all seemed strangely deserted. A Hindu servant stood impassively in the marbled hall.

'Yes, sahib?'

'I am General de Clare. I need to see the Viceroy urgently. Mountbatten, man.'

The man bowed.

'Mountbatten, sahib. Please follow me.'

He led Freddie along white and gilt corridors and up richly carpeted stairways. Finally they paused outside a panelled door.

'Through there, sahib.'

Freddie stepped forward, jerked the door smartly open and stepped inside. He stopped short. He was in the wrong place. This was a bedroom. A man, an Indian, lay back in a huge rumpled bed, goggling at him in shock.

'Who the hell are you?' he demanded.

'I could say the same thing,' Freddie said furiously. 'People are wasting my bloody time and every minute I waste, people are dying.'

The man leaned forward from his pillows.

'Which people?' he asked urgently. 'Tell me.'

'Muslims. Trying to escape from the Punjab.'

The man smiled, lay back again.

'Oh, Muslims. That is not very important.'

The bedclothes about him were moving, and Freddie saw that somebody else was down there. A sheet was pulled back, and Edwina Mountbatten's naked form came into view.

'God!' she said angrily. 'It's that ghastly man de Clare. Why on earth have you brought him in here, darling?'

Freddie suddenly realised he was looking at Nehru, the leader of Congress in India.

'I didn't,' Nehru said mildly. 'He came in.'

'I am looking,' Freddie said icily, 'for your husband.'

'He's downstairs,' Edwina said contemptuously. 'Playing with his flags. Now just bugger off, de Clare.'

She vanished back under the sheets, which started to move once again. Nehru smiled at Freddie.

'Goodbye, General,' he said.

Freddie went out. The Hindu servant was still standing there.

'So sorry,' he said, with transparent insincerity. 'This way, sahib.'

Eventually, he found Mountbatten. The Viceroy was cross.

'Have you brought them?' he snapped, sitting behind his very large desk. He was working on a huge piece of thick ivory paper with ruler and pen, forming the skeleton of what appeared to be an extensive family tree.

'Brought what?' Freddie snarled. Mountbatten looked up.

'Oh, it's you, de Clare,' he said disappointedly. 'I thought it was the man with the flags.'

'What bloody flags?'

'*My* flag. As governor-general after independence. We've been deciding the design. Pandit!'

A young Indian boy, standing patiently at the side of the room jumped forward.

'Bring me those brassards.'

The handsome youth brought forward some brassards on a tray.

'Just look at it!' Mountbatten cried petulantly. 'The lion's whiskers are much too big. I shall seem quite foolish. I've ordered them changed.'

'I want troops,' Freddie said loudly. 'A lot of troops. Also some squadrons of fighters.'

'Troops?' the commander said nervously. 'Whatever for?'

'The situation in the Punjab is deteriorating into civil war. Murder, rape, arson, mutilation, torture and desecration of temples has become rife. Innocent women and children are being slaughtered. The Sikhs have started it, but the Muslims are retaliating. I can restore order if I am allowed the ruthless use of force. I require troops and air power. I can get the Gurkhas in—'

'Don't be ridiculous! Nehru would never stand for the use of Gurkhas. He can't stand them. No, no, look, everything is going to work itself out. I'm in charge. I've set up a proper war room, maps, the lot. It's a very exciting time, very exciting. I can see that you're a bit upset, but I assure you, I see the big picture, and it will all be fine.'

'It is *not* going to be fine!' Freddie said angrily. 'It has all the makings of a really giant man-made disaster. *Your* disaster.'

'My dear fellow,' Mountbatten said, smiling reproachfully at him. 'You're always seeking to blame me. Don't you think that perhaps you should take a long hard look in the mirror, and work out who's really responsible for this refugee problem?'

'I need, at the very least, some squadrons of Typhoon fighters to bomb and cannonade the armed bands. The message will very quickly get through.'

'Good God! Can you imagine the effect that would have in the press? Never. I think a policy of benign neglect is best. You'll see. In twenty years' time you'll look back at it all and see that I was right all along.'

'I see.'

Freddie tried to swallow the fury that was boiling inside him. Mountbatten peered keenly down at his great sheet of paper, absently running his hand over the young boy standing next to him.

'What are you working on here?' Freddie enquired.

'This? Oh, fascinating. It's a relationship table of all the European royal families. All the family connections. Each person has a proper label to identify them. I invented it myself.'

'Did you? My uncle used to use it for stock breeding of his cattle. Are you there?'

'Of course!' he said proudly. 'Look.'

Freddie traced the connections with his finger.

'This is your grandfather?'

'It is. Prince Alexander of Hesse.'

'As I recall, it is pretty common knowledge that your grandfather was the bastard offspring of a court chamberlain and so not a prince at all.'

Mountbatten's face went a sudden, dangerous brick red.

'The massacres I have outlined are but the start,' Freddie said coldly. 'What pitiful efforts there are to establish refugee camps will shortly be totally overwhelmed. Supplies of medicine, food and safe water will run out. I expect epidemics of cholera, smallpox and typhoid within weeks. The death toll is going to be beyond belief – hundreds upon hundreds of thousands. Now do I get my troops and fighters or not?'

'No!' Mountbatten cried. 'I can't become governor-general with that kind of blood on my hands.'

'Dear God,' Freddie said quietly. 'Three and a half centuries of Empire here and it ends like this? Your wife is upstairs, performing fellatio on Nehru. You are down here, giving the country away to him.'

Mountbatten got up, went over to the wall, peering keenly at the huge map of the Continent.

'Which little part have you come from? Hmm. You know, de Clare, I think your tiny force has outlived its usefulness. Yes. As from now, you're disbanded. Catch a plane. Yes. You can go home. Pandit! Let's go and see if those flags are ready.'

He put his hand about the boy's shoulders, and they went out.

59

Garotte Told Them So

Windstone Castle, April 1962

Godfrey sat on the lichened stone seat hidden in the arbour cut and clipped in the yew hedge. He looked out over the glittering Windstone Water, its banks gold and starred with marsh marigolds, primroses and cowslips. The slopes of the hills beyond were pink and white with the blossom of cherry trees, crab apple and rich yellow gorse. He wore grey flannels and a tweed hacking jacket. His long fingers cradled a tall glass of whisky and soda, and he sipped on it from time to time.

He heard a faint creaking sound coming from the castle behind him, the murmur of a woman's voice. He saw Violet, pushing a wheelchair towards the edge of the Water, where a seat had been placed by a small copse of maples. A white-haired woman sat, very folded up, immobile in the chair. Violet parked it carefully and sat down on the seat next to her companion. Godfrey got up, and padded over to them, his feet silent on the turf.

'Oh, look, darling!' Violet cried, pointing in the air. 'A Peacock butterfly! I do declare it's the first I've seen this year. It's bound to be a good summer. Just see that blackthorn and gorse over there. Just mounds of white like snowdrifts! I believe we should make gorse wine again.'

Out on the Water a big fish splashed.

'What do you think, darling? Too early for Mayfly. They get the big chaps up from the depths, don't they? I saw Gawaine and Bertram getting their rods in order. Once the Mayflies start I shan't see them from morning 'til dusk.'

'Hallo, Vi!' Godfrey said cheerfully. He came and sat next to her. 'Hallo, Flick.'

The figure in the chair, as thin and bent and folded as an old doll said nothing, simply stared lifelessly over the Water.

'Hallo, Godfrey. They said you were coming down.'

'I do love to get out of London after the winter,' he said. 'It's become an annual rite, to see the castle in the spring. I spend so much of my time closeted in galleries and lecture rooms. Lovely to get out in the fresh air. Are you getting ready to open up?'

'Next month. They'll all come flooding in up the drive. And flying in. Since we opened the Stuart wing as the hotel we get Americans flying into Gawaine's airstrip direct from Heathrow, especially for the shooting and fishing. We keep the two sides pretty separate.'

'Wonderful. How's Flick?'

'You're pretty much the same, aren't you darling?'

'Does she talk?'

'No, you don't talk, darling,' Violet said softly. 'But I know you know what's going on.'

She turned to Godfrey.

'I like her to come out in the fresh air, see the blossom and flowers. It may be that the specialist is right, and she'll never be herself again, but I don't believe that.'

'It's been a long time,' Godfrey commented.

'We've been here a long time, but we're still here,' she said sharply. The breeze pushed a lock of her silver hair onto her face, she pushed it back.

'You'll be coming to Bertram's wedding?' she asked.

'Of course. Who's the lucky bride?'

'Oh, Fenella. Such a lovely girl. They met at Oxford, you know.' She glanced over her shoulder at the castle. 'I'm waiting for the committee.'

'What committee?' he asked, and drank some of his whisky.

'The committee to save Windstone Halt. That little squirt Perceval wants to knock it down.'

'Really?' he said languidly.

'Well yes, really. Have you seen what his lot have done to Windstone town? Some of the Nash crescents and square were damaged in the great Baedecker raid and, as MP, Perceval used it as an excuse to have them demolished. They've been bomb-sites for over ten years, and now he's sponsoring this hideous rebuilding programme. One-way traffic systems! Car parks! Shopping centres! When I tell you that the Elizabethan town hall has been razed you will know what I mean.'

'They don't need a town hall?' he said curiously.

'You're missing the point. It isn't big enough.'

'Why not? The council meets every other Thursday, if my memory serves me right, in Queen Bess's chamber.'

'Exactly. The chaps sort out whatever needs doing on their way back from work and Mr Prentiss the town clerk puts it in motion. Perceval says it's anachronistic, that Windstone needs a proper bureaucracy. They're building one. A revolting affair of concrete slabs where the Corn Hall used to be. You can see it from the Keep. The glass glares most hideously in the sun.'

'And he wants to level the Halt?'

'He does,' she said grimly. 'It is a grand example of Great Western Railway architecture. It has cantilevered awnings each side of the waiting room and the booking hall was designed by Brunel. He intends to have it demolished and replace it with yet more concrete. It is as though anything to do with our heritage is abhorrent to him.'

'He wants to take us into Europe,' he said mischievously. 'You know, this Common Market thing.'

'Of course! Yet more bureaucracy. We need less government, not more. Do you know, Godfrey, when I was a young girl in this country you could live your whole life without coming into more contact with the government than the post office or the local policeman. If you were able to look after yourself, they left you alone. Now there appears no area of one's life in which they do not wish you to fill out forms and pay them taxes for.'

'I had a drink with Perceval the other day. He says that before the end of the century there will be no old nations in Europe. Just a United States of Europe.'

'Now I know he's off his head. You do comfort me, Godfrey. Perhaps we can have him certified.'

They heard a voice calling from the castle, saw somebody waving.

'Oh Lord. There's Gawaine. They must be here. We're going to demonstrate outside the Halt with one of the castle cannon, get the press along to take photographs.'

'How exciting! Will it be charged with powder and shot?'

'Of course. We're the de Clares, we never bluff. Godfrey, you wouldn't sit with Flick until Molly comes, would you?'

'Of course.'

'How's your drink? Do you want it freshened?'

'No, that's fine. I'll sit here.'

He watched Violet walk purposefully away over the lawn, turned back to Felicity, sitting broken and still in her wheelchair.

'I drink more than I did,' he said to her.

She did not respond.

'I suppose it is the pursuit of this strange life of mine. I didn't notice it before, but I do now. That and not being able to talk to anyone.'

He drank a little from his glass, then waved a hand in front of her eyes. She did not blink.

'I suppose I could talk to you,' he said. 'I mean, it would be nice to talk to somebody, even a vegetable like you. Do you mind? No? I didn't think you would. I think it's just that I would hate to be exposed, after all these years.'

He looked out over the Water. The breeze was making the waves chop, they glittered in the sunshine. A pair of white geese took off, climbing over the hill.

'I mean, I have a grand position. Director of the most prestigious art foundation in the land. Adviser, courtier to the Royal Family. Respected by all. And I'm a spy!'

He looked closely into her eyes.

'Anything going on in there?' he enquired. 'No? I'll tell you about it anyway. I spied for the Soviet Union for years. You wouldn't believe the number of secrets I gave them. The number of influential people I suborned. Why, *I* gave them the entire MI6 network in Eastern Europe in 1945! Yes! Me. Every single blessed agent. They rolled the lot up, shot 'em and put them in the Gulag. Serve 'em right. Best place for spies!'

Godfrey put his head back and laughed uproariously.

'I'd hate to be unmasked, you see,' he said, when he had calmed down. 'That's probably why I drink a bit more than I did. Don't want to be betrayed. You know about that, of course. You were betrayed to the Gestapo, weren't you? That's why you sit there like a vegetable. Of course, it wasn't really you as much as Violet. It was supposed to be Violet. I've always hated her, haven't you? Well, no, you didn't of course. All you de Clare bitches stick together. You and bloody Fish and Gawaine and Freddie, so festeringly brave and honourable. God, how I hate you all. Why can't you be like me?'

He took a long pull at his glass, finished it.

'I could get really drunk,' he said. 'But I won't. Mustn't give myself away. Where was I? Oh yes, betrayal. I think I'm safe. They discovered Burgess and Philby and the others. Not me, though. It's tricky, isn't it? Must be such a surprise. Did you get a surprise, when they started shooting at you, those horrid Germans? It was no accident. They knew you were coming, Garotte told them so.'

He grinned, savagely.

'You see,' he said. 'I told her to.'

He glanced up, looked across the lawn.

'Well, thank goodness. Here comes Molly. One more de Clare

bitch. It would be lovely, wouldn't it, to roll all the de Clare bitches up in a big pile and set fire to them. Such fun.'

He stood up.

'Molly, darling,' he said, beaming at her. 'I've been having such an interesting chat with Flick, I've been giving her all my news.'

'Violet!'

It was dark, black. Violet sat up in bed, her heart pounding, fumbled for the light. Outside in the corridor, someone was shouting her name, banging. She threw back the bedclothes, hurried to the door. It was Molly.

'It's Flick!' she said urgently. 'Come quickly, she's having some sort of fit.'

Violet ran as quickly as she could down the corridor. In the bedroom where Felicity lived, Gawaine was bent over the bed. Felicity lay rigid, her limbs twisted into strange shapes. Her face was a terrible purple, her eyes started out from the stretched skin. A hoarse gargling came from her throat.

'She's trying to say something,' Gawaine said. He listened desperately to the hideous bubbling. Felicity's body arched, as rigid as a bow, then with a gasp, she fell back on the sweat-soaked sheets, and was still.

'What did she say?' Molly cried. 'What was she saying?'

'She said "Garotte",' Violet said quietly, her face very set. 'I heard her say "Garotte".'

60

Two Hundred and Seventy Feet Above the Water

'What the hell is this place?' Carlotta snarled. She hung back at the top of the winding stair, but it was of no avail. They took her by the arms and sat her in the awful stone Traitor's Chair which faced the dark, yawning hole in the floor. They locked the iron belt about her waist, they fastened it to the length of heavy, thick-linked chain that wound about the vertical chute, and she could not move.

'This is the Traitor's Tower,' said Violet, stepping forward out of the shadows, and the others drew back. 'This is where those who betray the de Clares meet their end. We stand two hundred and seventy feet above the water below. The chain you see before you begins very small, it slowly gets larger and heavier. Once the first links are thrown over the edge of the pit they will pull all the others after them, until finally the heaviest section of all hurls the traitor down to their doom.'

Carlotta sat in the stone seat, staring at the ancient stone shaft. Outside, it was dark, the hole itself was impenetrable.

'You're going to kill me,' she said in disbelief.

Violet stooped at the edge of the circular pit and tossed the end of the chain in. It began to fall, dragging the other links behind it with a pretty tinkling. The yellow stone of the edge was grooved and scarred where the chains of the past had worn it away.

'Nothing stops it now,' Violet said. 'Except this.'

She held up a length of cord that ran to a thick pin in the heaviest section of chain.

'That can be pulled out, but it very rarely is.'

'You can't do this to me!' Carlotta screamed, staring in horror at the vanishing chain. It was beginning to take on a harsher note as it speeded up. 'This is murder!'

'You murdered Felicity,' Violet said coldly. 'You were Garotte, you told the Germans we were coming.'

Carlotta looked up at her rival with a flash of pure hatred.

'I wanted you dead,' she said venomously. 'I enjoyed it.'

Violet stepped back into the gloom.

'Die then,' she said.

The chain was roaring and as it swept round and round. Yellow stone dust streamed up into the air, drifting bright in the dim light of the oil lamp.

'It wasn't me!' Carlotta screamed. 'It was Godfrey! He told me to do it!'

Nothing moved in the gloom.

'You want traitors?' she yelled, as the fall of the chain became a booming clamour, and the air was tinged with burning from its passage. 'Godfrey and George work for the Russians!'

The last lengths were swirling round the edge of the pit, blurred into nothing by their speed. The cord suddenly jerked, the pin came loose. The last giant length caromed off the edge and fell the full length of the shaft. They heard the roar die away, smoke rose up from the pit.

Very slowly, Carlotta got up from the seat. She was drenched in sweat, she tottered forward, trembling. Her smile, however, was triumphant as she faced Violet.

'Yes, your precious de Clares are traitors,' she said viciously. 'They've betrayed you all.'

'How do you know?' Freddie demanded, stepping out from the wall.

'I followed them. I followed them both, one at a time,' Carlotta said, turning first this way and then that. 'In the war. When they left. I didn't trust them, I knew they had something to hide. They went from their offices in the evening, they went out carrying briefcases, they met men in pubs. They handed things over. I followed the men, they went to the Soviet Embassy.'

The chamber was silent.

'They never thought anyone would follow them,' Carlotta sneered. 'George was in charge, see? A gentleman. English gentlemen don't betray their own, isn't that right? Well these ones did.'

'Why didn't you tell the authorities?' Gawaine demanded.

An expression of sudden terror went over Carlotta's face. She backed away from him.

'You don't understand,' she muttered fearfully. 'Godfrey, he would have killed me. You don't know Godfrey, he—'

Her foot backed into thin air, she swayed, her arms whirled, she vanished into the waiting pit. They heard her scream as she fell, all the way to the bottom.

61

1 Traitor

Violet heard the footsteps coming up the narrow, dark, winding stone stair. She stood by the open window, looking out over the Windstone Downs stretching to the horizon, and smoked her cigarette. Finally, the climbing feet came to the top, and George pulled himself into the room.

'I say, Vi!' he gasped, out of breath. 'I haven't been up here in years. What a climb!'

'Have a drink,' she offered.

An old lichened wooden table stood by one wall, and on it was a bottle of whisky and a jug of water, with two tumblers.

'What hospitality!' he said cheerfully. 'Shall I pour you one?'

'Please do,' she said, without turning round.

'Are you thinking of having a bar up here? That would be an attraction for the visitors. Climb two hundred and seventy feet and claim your reward, what?'

He poured two drinks and gave one to her. He looked around the room.

'My God,' he said in alarm. 'The Traitor's exit's not covered up.'

He went near to the awful stone chute falling vertically to the waters of the moat below. He picked up a small fragment of stone and tossed it in. It seemed a long time before they heard it hit the bottom. He shuddered, looking at the graded coils of iron chain piled up nearby.

'Terrifying!' he exclaimed. 'Is this what you asked me up here to see? Your new attraction for the visitors?'

'No,' she said. 'It's a working part of the castle.'

'Working part?' he asked, puzzled. 'The whole place is a museum, Vi.'

'No, it isn't, George,' she said evenly. 'It's a microcosm of England. We're a great people, George. More good than bad, fortunately, and great. The world's the way it is because of us. I don't think we did a bad job, do you?'

'You know I don't,' he said stoutly.

'No . . .' she said, quietly. He drank some of his whisky, rather nervously.

'What is it exactly that you do, George?' she enquired.

'Counter-intelligence is my field,' he said carefully.

'That means the destruction of enemy stratagems, the defeat of those who would enslave us.'

'Yes.'

'You're very important, George. Didn't we learn that in the war? The XX Committee proved that if you could penetrate your enemy's foreign intelligence service sufficiently, you could eventually control your enemy's ability to conduct its own defence. That's what we did to Germany.'

'A stupendous triumph,' he agreed. He peered out of the gap in the stone tower.

'My, God, it gives you vertigo,' he said.

'What if our enemies do it to us?'

'That's what we're here for,' he pointed out. 'MI5. That's what we do. We make sure that can't happen.'

'Our enemy at the moment is communist Russia,' she said. 'In the past it might have been Spain, or France, or Germany, or Japan. Now it's Russia. Next century, who knows? We have been allies with all the people who have also been our enemies. The important thing is that we defend ourselves.'

'Of course.'

He peered into the darkness of the chute.

'Terrifying . . .' he murmured. 'How many people went down there to their deaths, I wonder?'

'Hard to say. It was only built for traitors. We're the de Clares. We dispense justice ourselves.'

'Who was the last person to go, I wonder?' he mused. 'The one who murdered those girls, I suppose. They threw him down there.'

'They did,' she agreed. 'But he wasn't the last.'

'No? You surprise me.'

'Carlotta's down there.'

'What?' he said, startled. 'Carlotta? Are you sure?'

'Of course,' she said calmly. 'I was here at the time.'

George tipped back his whisky.

'That's terrible . . .' he muttered. He went to the table and refilled his glass.

'She was a traitor,' Violet pointed out with icy precision. 'She worked for our destruction. We kill those who do that.'

'Vi, you shouldn't be telling me this . . . there was no trial . . .'

'She was guilty.'

George looked up at her from the table.

'I say, old girl. You aren't drinking.'

'No,' she agreed. 'I won't drink with you, George. In fact, this is the very last conversation we shall ever have.'

He seemed quite bewildered.

'I don't follow you, old thing. What do you mean?'

'You're a spy, George.'

'Well, of course I am . . . you know that. That's what I do.'

'It is what you do,' she agreed. 'You spy for the Russians.'

He half-laughed, astonished.

'I catch Russian spies, you mean.'

'You are a traitor. You and Philby. You and Maclean. You and Burgess. You and Godfrey. All traitors. All working for the Russians.'

'I think that you have finally gone off your head,' he said angrily. He had gone quite pale.

'Have I? You can see, if you like. I've written an article for the papers about it. It'll be published in *The Times* in a couple of weeks. How you betrayed us to the Russians in the war, when we were fighting for our lives, how you haven't ever stopped since. You and Godfrey, you must be the Fourth and Fifth Men. The ones who organised it all. The traitors.'

'Stop it!' he suddenly shrieked, and his voice echoed in the stone chamber.

'At the end of my article, I invite you to sue me, if I haven't got my facts straight.'

She lit a fresh cigarette and peered coldly at him through the smoke.

'Shall I see you in court?' she asked. 'They will want to know, you see.'

'Who will?' he blurted.

'Everybody you know,' she said brutally. 'Everyone whose opinion matters to you. The members of your club. The chaps at your shoot. Your old school chums. The old girls at your bowling club. Your gardener. The man who runs the wine shop in your village.'

She paused, but he did not say anything.

'The congregation of your church,' she said mercilessly. 'The readers of your local paper. The manager of the little bookshop where you go and browse. The landlord of your pub. The man who services your old Bentley.'

'Don't, Vi . . .' he whispered.

'Don't snivel,' she said, very quietly. 'You're a de Clare.'

He remained silent, as white as chalk.

'When they know you don't deny it, when they know that you've been a traitor all these years, then nobody will talk to you, George. Your name will be a hissing and a byword. You will be cut by all. We the aristocracy will cast you out. The middle classes will despise you. The working classes will spit on you in the street. You will, should you want company, be forced upon whatever cads and bounders will tolerate you. You will end your days in poverty and misery. You will probably have to go to your masters in Russia. There like Burgess and Maclean you can drink yourself to death in some squalid concrete box in the Moscow suburbs, wearing your old school tie as you weep into your glass.'

There was silence in the cold ancient tower for several moments.

'What is it you want of me?' he whispered at last.

She opened her bag and took out a sheet of paper and a pen.

'The names,' she said. 'The names of all the traitors. All the ones you infiltrated. You injected them into us like a disease, filthy bacteria destroying us. I want to know who they are, where they fester.'

'All right,' he muttered. He bent over the desk, and began to scrawl names of people, institutions, agencies. When one side was full, he turned over the page. When he was finished, he handed it to her. She took it as though it were infected.

'Dear God . . .' she whispered angrily. 'You got them in everywhere! MI5, MI6, the Foreign Office, the Admiralty . . . Why, I know this little bastard, he made policy at the Colonial Office.'

She looked at George with icy eyes.

'We abandoned our empire because of people like him, scuttled and ran. How you must have laughed . . .'

'I didn't have control over them, Vi,' he said pleadingly.

'You knew what you were doing,' she said mercilessly. 'Here, I know this swine too, he's at the Treasury. And this one, wasn't he first secretary at the Washington Embassy? Him, he's a physicist, worked on the bomb. My word, George, I'm surprised you had time for work, providing access and clearances for all these.'

'It wasn't just—'

'It wasn't just you? No, I can see his name here. Godfrey. I've always known Godfrey's a wrong 'un. I didn't know he was this bad, not for certain.'

She folded the paper, put it in her bag.

'Come on,' she said. 'Let's go down. They'll want to debrief you. It'll take a while.'

'It would never have happened, all of it,' he said, as they clattered slowly down the cold, winding stone stair, lit only by the arrow slits in its sides. 'If only I'd done it.'

'It wouldn't have happened at all if you'd not been a traitor,' she said sharply.

'No, in the war, I tried to kill myself. Fish stopped me, he cut the firing pin from my revolver and I didn't have the guts to try it again.'

They walked across the grass.

'Rob was going to make his cricket pitch here,' he said. 'Clare Rules . . . you got twelve if you made the battlements . . .'

'Sit down,' she said, inside the great hall. 'I'll call Freddie, tell him we're coming.'

'I'll get a drink,' he said, as she dialled.

'Freddie? Yes, he's confessed. I have a list. I'll bring him over. You'll have them waiting? Good.'

Violet put the telephone down, turned, looked for him.

'George?' she called.

In the quiet of the castle she heard footsteps hurrying away down the corridor. Moving as quickly as she could, she went after them. The gun room was at the end. As she came up, she heard a sudden, flat bang, a thud and clatter.

He was lying on the floor, a twelve-bore by him. Blood and brains were all over the ceiling, spattering down onto the table.

'Damn!' she said bitterly. 'Damn, damn, damn.'

The game book lay open on the table. There was one entry on the page. George's pen lay there next to it.

1 Traitor.

62

A Highly Developed Sense of Justice

Godfrey leaned back in his chair behind the wide cherrywood desk, inlaid with green leather. Behind him, through the clear glass of the Robert Adam windows, Violet and Freddie could see the fresh green leaves of the elegant square. Beneath them the exclusive art foundation hummed quietly with life.

'So nice to see you,' he said pleasantly. 'I have to go off to see the Queen shortly, but I can spare a few minutes. We're having an exhibition at the Academy this winter, she's letting us hang some absolute treasures. But what can I do for you? Is it about the wedding? Only a week or two off, isn't it? You must be so thrilled.'

'We are,' Vioet said evenly. 'But we haven't come about that.'

Godfrey looked grave.

'Then of course, it must be poor George. Such a tragedy. To kill himself like that – and at the castle, too. I can't think what made him do it. Such a distinguished career.'

Freddie nodded grimly.

'Exactly,' he said. 'He was a Soviet spy. We unmasked him, and he was unable to take the shame. I don't believe that he shared any commitment to them in the end, but of course, that wasn't good enough. They would insist he kept working for them.'

'Oh, absolutely,' Godfrey agreed. He got up, opened the window a little. A pleasant soft breeze came in, bringing the faint noise of the Oxford Street traffic with it.

'They never let someone go, once they have a grip on them,' he said, and sat back down.

'Before he committed suicide he named you as another agent,' Violet said clearly. Godfrey raised impassive eyebrows at her.

'Did he really?' he said indifferently. 'How pointless of him.'

'Not pointless at all,' said Freddie. 'You will soon be on trial and charged with treason at the Old Bailey.'

'No, I won't,' Godfrey said confidently. 'I shall be arranging the Queen's Winter Exhibition at the Royal Academy.'

'You seem very sure of this,' said Violet.

'Oh, I am. I am,' he said, quite certainly. 'Do you want to know why? The English establishment looks after its own. Treason? When your beloved Winston Churchill took power in 1940 he could have had half the Cabinet shot for treason and Lloyd George too, had he a mind to. He didn't of course, he couldn't. He had a war to fight. What about when the war was won? Shall we charge Lord Mountbatten with treason? Come on, Freddie, you've talked about it often enough. Didn't you say when you came back that he should have been shot for what he did in India? Yes? Didn't he betray all those people in the Empire who believed in the British? How many died out there? A million? At least. He was the Imperial Undertaker who never wore black. Scuttle and run, that was his model; now it's going on in Africa. Scuttle and run and let the most ruthless fight it out for themselves.'

He looked left and right at his two relations with savage, contemptuous glances.

'Didn't he destroy all the British ever built in India?' he demanded. 'But was he shot? Was he hell. Lord Mountbatten is currently Chief of the Defence Staff. You see, the establishment always looks after its own.'

'You aren't powerful enough for them to bother about you,' Violet pointed out.

'You're right,' Godfrey agreed. 'I'm not. But they still won't lay a finger on me, and I'll tell you why.'

He leaned back in his chair again, clasping his hands behind his head, and admired the Poussin oil painting on the wall.

'At the end of the war, I undertook a mission of special importance for the late King George the Sixth. He needed an experienced intelligence officer he could trust, and I did not let him down. I retrieved for him the documents of the German foreign office and SD, the secret intelligence service. These files, intelligence reports, telegrams and so forth concerned the treasonable activities of the Duke of Windsor, the former King Edward and his wife, who actively collaborated with the Nazi authorities to bring down the government of this country and install a fascist regime.'

Godfrey sat forward.

'So I spied for the Soviets? So what? In comparison with what *he* did, a mere peccadillo.'

He smiled contemptuously at them.

'Put me in the dock, and I shall tell all. Every single, stinking little betrayal he made.'

There was silence in the room.

'They won't let you,' Godfrey said certainly. 'They won't let you lay a finger on me. The establishment always looks after its own. Now, if you'll excuse me, I must prepare myself to advise the Queen about her pictures.'

Violet and Freddie went downstairs. They left the Institute and found Freddie's Jaguar at the meter. They drove away in silence. Finally, Violet spoke.

'We'll have to kill him,' she said.

Godfrey sat silent and brooding at his desk, all traces of his contemptuous self-confidence wiped away. He looked deep in thought, and worried. Finally he got up, went searching through his bookshelves. He found what he was looking for. It was the official history of Windstone Castle. Leafing through it he came to the part he wanted. There was the Traitor's Tower. Underneath the historian had written about its significance. 'The de Clares,' he said, 'early on possessed a highly developed sense of justice and loyalty. Those who betrayed them they executed in this tower, without mercy.'

Godfrey glanced at his watch, pushed the book back onto the shelf. He went out into the street. If he took a taxi he would be in plenty of time. He went to a red telephone box, fed in coins and dialled. A foreign voice answered.

'This is me, Igor,' Godfrey said. 'I need to see you.'

63

It's the Future

Windstone Castle

The towers of the castle were bright with flags and pennants. A pleasing breeze had arisen mid-morning, while all the guests were seated in the chapel, and the bride had come down the aisle on her father's arm to join the groom. She was beautiful in Victorian cream silk. The Bishop of Windstone had officiated and Bertram, Viscount Windstone, became married to Fenella. When they emerged a light breeze was blowing in the sunshine, and they sipped champagne on the lawn. The sides of the marquee were rolled up, the tables set were resplendent with the Windstone silver and plate – gold chased, bearing the ancient arms. On the tower above, the battle standard of the de Clares stood out, scarlet and blue with white and gold, waving lazily, occasionally snapping its mighty tail. The dragon bared its teeth in defiance and the family motto was writ for all to see. *Death Before Dishonour.*

'What a delightful occasion, Vi.'

She turned, elegant in a lemon-yellow suit, and woven straw hat, splashes of gold and jewels shining and glittering at her throat, on her wrist.

'This is a surprise to see you here, Godfrey,' she said calmly. He smiled, faultlessly dressed in his morning suit, his silk top-hat gleaming in the sun. He bore a small parcel under his arm.

'But I was invited,' he said. 'It would have been churlish to refuse.'

He held his little parcel in both hands.

'I wanted to ask where the presents for the bride and groom are being displayed.'

'In the Crecy room.'

'I'll leave it there, then. It's a Poussin. A fragment from the *Adoration of the Golden Calf.* I've authenticated it myself. I'm the world's leading authority on Poussin, you know.'

'I heard,' she said. 'Also this century's leading traitor.'

A pained expression came over his face.

'Now, now, Vi. I thought we'd come to terms on all that once we'd had our little chat. You really mustn't chide me every time we meet. And anyway, I'm sure Philby would be most upset to think I outranked him.'

'Philby at least scuttled off to Moscow to drink himself to death. Are you sure you won't be joining him?'

'Why no!' Godfrey said, horrified. 'It's frightfully barbaric out there. I have my position to consider. Director of the Institute, you know, and the Queen, she does depend upon my advice.'

'Godfrey, do you have no problems reconciling these opposing positions?'

'No,' he said honestly. 'None at all. Well, I'll get myself off to the Crecy room. By the way, where are Bertram and Fenella – such a lovely girl, isn't she? Where are they going for their honeymoon?'

'*Parma's Pride*'s waiting for them at Brindisi. They're going to cruise among the Greek islands. Gawaine's flying them up to Heathrow in the Bonanza after lunch.'

'Lovely . . . Bertram must have inherited his grandfather's love of the sea. Fish liked a sail, didn't he?'

'Just go, Godfrey, before I have someone put you in the moat.'

Godfrey smiled waspishly at her, and went towards the castle. Her eyes followed him, thoughtfully.

Inside, he deposited his present with the others on the Knight's Table, forty feet of oak in the Crecy room. When he came out into the corridor he saw a portly figure talking animatedly on the telephone. It was Perceval. He put the receiver down crossly.

'Hallo, big brother,' Godfrey said languidly.

'Oh, it's you, Godfrey. It's ridiculous. I have a most important meeting in Brussels tomorrow to discuss our entry into the EEC and I can't make my connection on the train. The stationmaster down at the Halt is being most unhelpful.'

'You're trying to raze his station and put him out of a job,' Godfrey pointed out.

'Progress!' Perceval shouted. 'He should be thankful for our advances instead of mulching his blasted raspberries! That's what he told me. "Oi can't be helping you just now, oi've got to mulch my raspberries." Damn his bloody insolence!'

'Spoken like a true de Clare. Why don't you catch a lift with Gawaine in his aeroplane? He's taking the happy couple to Heathrow this afternoon.'

'*Is* he? Well yes, I could have dinner at *Le Cochon Rose* . . . Yes, I'll track him down.'

He spotted Freddie in the great hall.

'Freddie, where's Gawaine? I need to catch a ride to Heathrow.'

'I think we have room,' he said. 'There's me and Gawaine, and the two young people. I'm going out to crew.'

'Good. Is it time for lunch?'

'The trough awaits,' Freddie assured him. 'Salmon from the Water itself – I caught two of 'em. Strawberries and cream.'

'I'm starving.'

'You're always starving.'

They went out into the sunshine, where the marquee stood shining white on the lawn, and Godfrey strolled after them.

Windstone was below the port wing. They could see what was left of the ancient town, imprisoned by the harsh scars of the outer and inner ring roads, the radial feeder routes, the sprawl of car parks and high-rise housing.

'Look at that!' said Gawaine. 'I've a good mind to drop you into it like a blasted bomb, Perceval. It took centuries to make Windstone, and you and your lot have wrecked it in a decade.'

'It's the future!' Perceval protested. 'We must move forward, not stultify.'

The Bonanza continued to climb into the clear sky, heading north-east, and the town slid behind them. In the back, Bertram and Fenella kissed each other happily.

The explosion, when it came, was not very loud.

'What the hell—' Freddie exclaimed. The controls were suddenly slack in Gawaine's hand. The nose fell, the noise of the air rushing over the fuselage began to rise. His hands moving very quickly, he throttled back, tried the trim. He reached forward, pulled down a lever on the panel. The noise increased, there was a strong buffeting, they could hear the electric motor protesting as it lowered the undercarriage into the gale.

'What's happened, old man?' Freddie asked calmly.

'The elevators have gone,' Gawaine said. 'There's no trim either.'

He glanced at the panel in front of him.

'Eight hundred feet a minute,' he said. 'It seems to have stabilised on that. One hundred and seventy knots. I'll put the flaps down and try and bleed off some speed.'

He turned round to address the others.

'I'm afraid something has happened to the controls,' he said clearly. 'There's going to be an accident. I'm going to try to make it as slow as possible. Fenella, darling, if you climb over the back seat you should just be able to get into the luggage compartment. Get behind the suitcases. Lie with your back to them.'

'I'll help her, Dad,' Bertram said, and the young woman clambered over the back of the seat. There was just room for her to squeeze in.

'I love you,' she said.

'See you in a minute,' he assured her.

The ground grew closer. Gawaine lowered the flaps, a notch at a time, the roaring air buffeting against the metal.

'You aren't meant to do that,' he commented. 'But I don't suppose it matters now.'

The ground was very close.

'Looks like we should prang in that meadow,' he said, his voice very steady. 'All right, chaps. Here we go.'

They had been harvesting the hay, it lay in neat rows on the ground. Just for a moment, before they hit, they could smell it, sweet and fragrant in the air.